The Purrfect Pet Sitter

The Purrfect Pet Sitter

Carol Thomas

Stories that inspire emotions
www.rubyfiction.com

Published 2019 by Ruby Fiction
Penrose House, Crawley Drive, Camberley, Surrey GU15 2AB, UK
www.rubyfiction.com

A CIP catalogue record for this book is available
from the British Library

ISBN: 978-1-91255-011-1

Printed and bound in Great Britain by Clays Ltd, Elcograf S.p.A.

For Mum and Dad, with lots of love xxx

In memory of Milo – my gorgeous, slightly cross-eyed boy!

Acknowledgements

It has been fun doing the research for this book. I have
learnt a lot and met some very helpful people along
the way. Special thanks must go to the following:

Kirsti Lelliott, for pet sitting advice and anecdotes,
though I have to point out Kirsti is a much
better pet sitter than Lisa Blake and has never
had an animal go missing on her watch!

Greg Dowswell and Adam Wood of Shore in East
Wittering, who offered wetsuit advice, answered my many
questions and allowed me to wander around the shop with
my notebook, what seems like a very long time ago now.

Paramedics Nicky Nicol and Cat Wyn, who kindly
answered my questions, offered insight and helped
me ensure Fred got the right treatment.

Madison Thomas, Alfie Boyle, Holly Hotston and
MacKenzie Hotston, who had the funniest conversations
after a year two sex education lesson and kindly leant
their words to Felicity's children. Thank you also to
Natalie and Fiona for not finding it too odd that I still
had your children's words written down two years later.

My followers on Facebook who helped with Christmas
present ideas – your suggestions were all very helpful
in sourcing appropriate presents for the characters
in this book. Thank you also to those who helped

with my request for prom memories, especially
Beverley Palmer and Ann Reilly (and family).

Clementine Slater Amplis, my lovely French teacher, for
correcting and triple checking my French and for not
telling me off (too much) when I missed lessons and
didn't do my homework to concentrate on this book.

My lovely husband Mason, who needed no coercing
to take me to France to play in the snow, and my sister
Angela who looked after our children while we went
off on this *research* trip. Thank you also to Amelia,
Madison and Edward for being good for Auntie and for
always giving me lots of support and encouragement.

On the technical front, a big thank you must also go to:
Kirsti Lelliott and Angela MacAskill for reading drafts
and offering plot suggestions. Fellow Chindi Author,
Jane Cable for the loving kick in the right direction.
Choc Lit, for the wonderful opportunity to be published
by Ruby Fiction. The amazing Tasting panel (Melissa C,
Dimi E, Jennifer S, Sally B, Jo O, Gill L, Isobel J, Ruth N,
Luise P, Hilary B and Gurnam S) who enjoyed my story
– I am hugely grateful to you all. My editor for her
insightful and encouraging editing. My cover designer.
And, finally, all of the authors in my new Choc Lit/
Ruby Fiction family for being so lovely and welcoming. xx

Prologue

Lisa looked up into Nathan's deep blue eyes; their mouths were just inches apart.

'You look stunning … really stunning,' he whispered.

'Thank you; you look pretty amazing yourself.' She smiled.

They had been together since the third year of secondary school; in that time they had grown up together, become best friends, and – as boyfriend and girlfriend – shared many intimate moments. But, after the excitement and desire-fuelled intensity of the limousine journey, an evening of dancing with Nathan Baker, while he was wearing a charcoal grey, Moss Bros hire suit, was causing Lisa to have all kinds of thoughts and feelings she had never experienced before.

She had been looking forward to the prom for months, not only because it marked the end of her A-levels but also because she and her best friend, Felicity, had spent hours looking round shops, discussing what to wear and how to do their hair, nails and make-up. Now Lisa's long blonde hair had been teased into shaggy curls and pinned at the sides around a tiara, and she was wearing the spaghetti-strapped, taffeta-skirted dress of her dreams, she felt more grown up and less like herself than she ever had.

Lisa looked at the familiar faces all around her, united in their celebration of the people they had become and their anticipation of the different futures they each had yet to embark upon. Her mum was right when she had said the night was significant; everything was changing and, in the balloon arch and crepe paper festooned school gym, that change was palpable. The head teacher was posing for photographs with those he had spent the last seven years reprimanding, teachers were laughing and chatting with ex-pupils and even the Goths, who had spent their entire school career avoiding social situations, had made an appearance. Lisa caught Felicity's eye as she took a swig from a Pepsi bottle Lisa knew she had Malibu and Coke in and smiled. Felicity winked causing Lisa to laugh. *Some things will always remain the same*, she thought.

Nathan leaned in to ask if Lisa was OK.

She hadn't realised she had stopped dancing. 'Yes, it's just ...'

Nathan lifted her chin. 'What is it, Lisa?'

The song changed tempo, enabling her to move in close enough to speak and to begin to move in unison with him once more.

'I was just thinking. As I left the house I asked my mum and dad if they had any last minute words of wisdom.'

'Risky.' Nathan laughed.

'Ha, well, my dad said I should work in the prom business because I'd make a fortune between the months of June and July. But my mum got all deep and meaningful. She said tonight's not about what's ending but what's beginning.'

'She did?' Nathan seemed surprised.

'Yes, and I guess she's right.' Lisa thought about her mum's parting words. 'There's a whole world waiting for you, Lisa Blake.' And she knew it was true; she was on the cusp of a new beginning. The thought was exciting, scary, and a little overwhelming.

Nathan slipped his hand further round the sequin-encrusted bodice of Lisa's lilac dress bringing her closer to him. She felt the race of his pulse as he held her and the last song of the evening, Kelly Clarkson's 'A Moment Like This', started to play.

Nathan swallowed before taking a step back. 'Here's to new beginnings.' He breathed.

Chapter One

'Jack! Jack! Come back, Jack!' Lisa thudded through the undergrowth, trying not to stumble on the tree roots amongst the ferns and moss of the damp forest floor. Walking, she had felt cool under the canopy of the trees, but now that she was running there seemed to be a lack of air; she couldn't fill her lungs fast enough and she could taste the pungent, earthy smell that hung in the atmosphere. *I am so not cut out for this!* Her chest felt tight and her shins burnt.

Her life in London, sitting in an office, had not prepared her for this. She had only been pet sitting for two months and this was her second runaway! How could working with dogs have turned out to be so very different to writing about them? Blazing a trail through Houghton Forest – well, attempting to run through it anyway – she missed the comfort of her desk and the security of her old job. Writing for *Paws about Town* magazine didn't seem so bad now, did it? Lisa thought about her desk tucked in the corner of the office, the unpredictable air conditioning that blew hot and cold on her and her colleagues who did the same as deadlines drew near. Absence really was making her heart grow fonder. She looked at the blue poo bag in her hand, swinging back and forth as she ran; this was all so desperately unglamorous in comparison.

'Jack! Jack!' The name was becoming more of a pant than a shout as she tried to co-ordinate the difficult act of breathing with bellowing. Perhaps she should conserve her energy; she hadn't actually seen Jack for a while. He could even be out of earshot. Leaning against a lichen-covered tree, she paused in an attempt to catch her breath. Trying to listen over the sound of her own breathing, Lisa hoped to hear Jack making a kerfuffle somewhere. But there was not a single, giveaway sound.

An image of Winnie's face slipped into Lisa's mind and she knew returning without Jack was not an option. That dog meant everything to that dear, sweet, old lady. Winnie had been Lisa's first client when she started her business, the first person to put their faith in her. The weight of that faith pressed firmly on Lisa's shoulders now. She had to think what to do.

Maybe he had headed back to the van without her. Lisa imagined Jack wagging his happy tail, waiting for her to return, looking at her as if she had been the one who had gone missing all along. And if he wasn't there, though she didn't want to think too much about that, at least heading back to the van meant she could catch her breath. Then she could come up with a plan and beg the people in the tea kiosk to ask everybody they served if they had seen a cross-eyed, black Labrador with a grey beard and the deceptive speed of a Whippet. Maybe they would even announce it on their tannoy – well, not the part about the cross eyes and the speed, but the fact Jack was missing. Then everybody would know to look out for him.

That seeming the best, perhaps even her only, option, Lisa pulled the laces on her hiking boots a little tighter in readiness to set off again and winced at the blisters she could feel forming. Like her, the boots weren't made for running.

Glancing at the trees surrounding her, Lisa began to panic. In her desperation to follow Jack she had left the path and was unsure which direction to head off in. It all looked so similar now. As her eyes flicked from tree to tree, searching for something familiar, the branches seemed to move in a little closer; suddenly, the notion she was lost and alone sent a cold shiver down her sweaty spine. Not wanting to loiter on the spot any longer, Lisa took a punt on the direction and set off again. Loneliness was something she was used to from her life in London, but actually being alone, occupying a space entirely by herself, that hardly ever happened. Thudding along again, her pace was now more of a slow jog, while her arms and face did all the actions of a speed runner.

Finally glimpsing a path, she burst through the line of trees, stumbling onto the ground before a pair of middle-aged walkers, complete with all the gear. They stopped abruptly at her sudden appearance.

Attempting to catch her breath, Lisa stood and panted, 'Ha- ha- have ...' *Oh God!* She sounded crazy. Swallowing in an attempt to encourage saliva into her mouth, she noticed their stunned faces. As she tried to compose herself so she could actually speak, it occurred to her that she must look like some wild woman of the forest. She had rosy cheeks, mad hair, sweat beading across her forehead, wide eyes from the exertion, slashed legs from the brambles, and clothes covered in lichen and fuzzy burs that clung like Velcro. Lisa brushed herself off and adjusted her hair in an attempt to look saner than she felt. 'Have ... Have you seen a black Labrador ... anywhere, please?' she finally implored.

The woman looked at her, reading the words 'Lisa Blake, the purrfect pet sitter!' emblazoned on her T-shirt.

'He slipped his collar!' Lisa provided, registering the look of disdain in the woman's eyes, as she waved her hand to reveal the dog-less collar and lead she still held there.

The woman gave a judgmental 'Hmmm,' before softening slightly. 'Black Lab, you say?'

'YES!' Lisa burst with relief.

'Grey beard? Wonky eyes?'

'YES! YES! Oh, that's him!'

'Lovely dog.'

'Yes! Where is he?' Lisa felt ready to shake the information out of the woman if she didn't answer soon.

The couple looked at their watches before the man added, 'Must have been five or so minutes ago now.'

'Moving on more for ten, I'd say.'

Lisa looked between the man and the woman in disbelief, trying hard to ignore her growing temptation to grab their walking poles and use them to extricate the information from them; she tucked her hands behind her back.

'He's just over there at the kiosk.'

'What? Where? Where's the kiosk from here?' Lisa realised she was now jogging on the spot ready to go as soon as she knew where.

'Just round that bend,' they finally offered, pointing in unison along the path they had just walked along.

'Thank you! Thank you!' The burn in her legs having dissipated with the thought of getting Jack back, Lisa gave both of the walkers an unexpected kiss on the cheek and sprinted in the direction they had pointed.

Finally, seeing the grassy picnic area and car park, Lisa fixed her eyes on the little tea kiosk. 'Jack! Jack! Come back, Jack!' Tears stung at her eyes when she couldn't see him. She really didn't want to return to Winnie without Jack, as it would almost certainly finish her off to lose him. He had to still be there. As she cornered the wooden hut relief flooded through her. He was there! Wagging his tail and looking thoroughly cheeky, just as she imagined and hoped he would be! But he wasn't looking out expectantly for her; in fact, he barely noticed her approaching. He was too busy being fed a bacon butty by one of the bikers who used the picnic area and tea kiosk as a regular stop off.

Suddenly hit by the emotion of finding Jack, Lisa's voice cracked and sounded weak, 'Jack, Jack.'

As she reached out for the dog the leather-clad man stood up. 'All right, Rose, calm yourself.'

Confused, Lisa met his gaze. 'What?'

'You were calling Jack so desperately there I thought you must be Rose.'

Lisa glared. She didn't know what he was referring to.

'Jack, Rose ... *Titanic* ... the film. You must have seen it.'

Finally the penny dropped. *Cheeky sod.* This was no time to make jokes. Though Lisa conceded her lungs felt so constricted from the run she might as well have been drowning on the bloody *Titanic*.

'You've got my dog.' She blurted the words more curtly than she intended.

The man raised his eyebrows and placed a protective hand on Jack. 'Funny that, he seems to want to be with me and he has no collar. Are you sure he's yours?'

Lisa looked at the smirk tugging at his lips and his way-too-cheeky-for-the-situation eyes. She was in no mood for games, she had left her patience somewhere back in the forest. 'Look, this is his collar. He's called Jack. Now, please, can I just have him?'

Jack wiggled back between the man's legs. *Judas!* Lisa looked at his little cross-eyed face, *the picture of innocence*, and let out an exasperated squeal.

'Here ...' The man's expression softened as he smiled, and gestured to take the collar and lead. Lisa reluctantly handed it over, watching as he slipped the collar round

Jack's neck and pulled it a little tighter to ensure it stayed in place. As the man checked the clip on the lead he paused to read Jack's identity tag before unleashing a full-on smile at Lisa and standing up. 'Then you must be Winifred Adams. Nice to meet you, Winifred.'

Lisa looked at his outstretched hand. *Oh for goodness' sake!* 'No … I'm—'

With a puzzled expression he withdrew his hand. 'But you said—'

'I'm … I'm Jack's pet sitter,' Lisa muttered, embarrassed at how unprofessional she appeared.

'His what?' The man shot back, not bothering to stifle his giggle.

'Pet sitter, dog walker, you know.' Lisa pointed at the words across her T-shirt and blushed even more at the fact she was pointing at her still heaving chest. Moving her hand she added, 'I'm Lisa Blake.'

'"The purrfect pet sitter" indeed,' he said with a laugh as he passed over Jack's lead.

Lisa wanted the ground to open up and swallow her into oblivion. 'Honestly, I don't normally lose my clients' pets. I really am generally *very* vigilant,' she assured, blinking away an image of the back end of Rusty the snappy little Jack Russell disappearing down the beach the previous week. *Thank goodness he didn't want to cross that patch of seaweed!* Without that she knew she never would have caught him.

'I'm sure you are,' the man offered, his voice a little too teasing. 'I bet plenty of dogs slip their collars every day!'

'Not on my watch,' Lisa shot back and cringed, regretting her hasty response on at least four counts that instantly sprung to mind:

1) All evidence pointed to the contrary.

2) His words had actually absolved her of all blame in the situation – now it seemed she protested too much.

3) It just wasn't true.

4) And, perhaps the point she regretted most, she had pointed to her eyes, then at him and winked for added emphasis as she spoke.

'I'm sure.' He chuckled, apparently finding her predicament as the worst pet sitter in the south amusing. Tapping his nose in mock similarity to her gesture, he added, 'This had better be our little secret then, hadn't it?'

Lisa giggled despite her best efforts not to.

No longer the centre of attention, Jack barked, reminding them of his presence. Lisa jumped, realising any moment now might be a good time to look like a pet sitter who actually gave her charges her full attention. She bent down offering Jack lots of fuss, tickling him around his ears and under his soft, wobbly jowls. Only then did she notice she was still holding the blue poo bag, now a mushy mess from her run. And worse, she was actually flapping it around in Jack's face. *Fail!* Quickly tucking the bag behind her back, her cheeks reddened and she suddenly felt the need to be gone; away from the awkward situation, away from the leather-clad dog-napper and away from further scrutiny. 'OK ... so, thank you.' Lisa turned to leave, dragging a reluctant Jack with her.

'But wait, I ... don't go ... I didn't even introduce myself. I'm D—'

But it was no use, Lisa was striding back to her van, reminding herself that returning Jack to Winnie, maybe even on time if she drove quickly enough, was her only priority.

Realising she had no intention of turning back, the leather-clad man shouted, 'It was a pleasure ... see you around, Rose!'

Lisa groaned and picked up her pace.

Chapter Two

Felicity pressed the button to take the picture of her plate of ham, egg and chips, and sent it straight to Facebook, tagging herself as feeling happy at the beach. Then she put the phone down and sighed flatly. She didn't want to eat it. It was too greasy, but the options at the soft play adjacent to the beach were limited and the chicken burger had given her a dodgy stomach the last time she had ordered it. She wouldn't have bothered with a hot lunch, but she knew Pete would be home this evening as he was not doing a shift at Cin Cin, where he had been earning a bit of extra cash at his mate's bar after work, and the idea of getting everybody's main meal out of the way was too appealing; especially as getting the children to bed early was integral to what she had planned for Pete later. As the waitress popped two plates of over-fried curly fries and pizza fingers onto the table, Felicity rolled her eyes. *Sorry Jamie Oliver!*

Searching for her children, Felicity scanned each floor of the soft play. She could hear them but she couldn't see them. She looked at Fred's little face. She could hardly abandon him in the highchair to go and search for the others. She had told them dinner wouldn't be long and yet they had disappeared. *Why don't they ever listen?* Hiding her purse under the 'essential' paraphernalia she carried on the bottom of the pushchair, Felicity lifted Fred out of his highchair and hoisted him onto her hip. Fred let out a grizzle; getting a look at the food and then being dragged away from it was a horrible tease, *poor love!* Slipping her shoes off Felicity threw back the oversized gate latch and entered the over-threes' zone.

'Mummy, Mummy, Callum's stuck!' Alice's sweaty face met her mum's exasperated look on the spongy stairs.

'I told you to look after him. Where is he?' Felicity sighed.

'In the squishy rollers.' Alice lifted her hands in a gesture of innocence, accepting no responsibility for her brother's predicament.

'What? Where?'

'Up there.' Alice motioned her pointy finger upwards.

Felicity looked at the next floor, accessible via tunnels and twists she wasn't sure her bottom would fit through. 'Oh, crikey! Here, you watch Fred for a mo and I'll fetch Callum, OK?' Felicity deposited Fred and Alice in the baby area and began the chubby-hip-bruising ascent to extricate her son.

'Mummy!' Callum beamed at the sight of Felicity hauling herself out of the tunnel. He held out his arms and wiggled his chubby little fingers. Felicity's thudding-a-little-too-much-after-a-teeny-weeny-bit-of-exercise heart melted at the sight of him.

'Are you stuck, Pumpkin?'

'Um ... no!'

'But Alice said you were stuck.'

'No, I tease her.' He grinned, showing all of his shiny, white milk teeth, looking very pleased with himself.

'Oh, Callum, Mummy just came all the way up here and dinner's ready.'

'Goody! Let's do the slide!' Callum wiggled effortlessly out of the squishy rollers and grabbed Felicity's hand. 'Come on, Mummy.'

How could she resist that little, freckly face? He was her only child to inherit Pete's red hair and all of his cheek too. Not sure that any minute now she wouldn't be bellowing for the waitress to call the fire brigade to report her bottom being stuck on the slide, Felicity scooped Callum on to her lap. She pushed off and was surprised to find that she actually moved and, as it happened, gathered quite a speed. 'Wheeeeeeee!' She sounded more enthusiastic than Callum, but she couldn't help herself. It was the most fun she'd had for a long time. As they reached the bottom a multitude of rainbow coloured balls erupted into the air as the force of Felicity's feet hit them and Callum burst into giggles.

Through the net that separated the baby-n-toddler and over-threes' area Alice cheered. 'Do it with me now, Mummy!'

Unsure why, but not wanting to miss out on the fun, Fred clapped his hands. Felicity felt like she had won the lottery having achieved the admiration of three out of her four children in one fell swoop. Looking at their beaming faces she felt overwhelmed with love for them! Of course, there were times when they overwhelmed her with a whole lot of other feelings, but, at that moment, with all of them happy, she knew she could have eaten them up!

Remembering the food congealing at their table, Felicity rounded her children up and settled them into their seats. Once she had sorted everybody's drinks, asked for the second time for a spare plate for Fred, chopped up everything that needed chopping and squirted out more packets of sauce than was probably necessary she looked again at her own dinner. *Ewwww!* It hadn't improved with the delay. She picked at it, leaving the plastic-looking ham and dipping a few chips in the egg until she ran out of runny yolk. Pushing her plate to one side she rummaged in her bag for three boxes of dried apricots and raisins. She needed to do something to redress the bad food balance of her children's lunch. Feeling like a thoroughly bad mother she pondered how much salad she had in the fridge to offer them with sandwiches or crackers for tea.

Picking up a signal her phone beeped with the five 'likes' her Facebook status had achieved. Raising her eyebrows, Felicity pressed to see who had left them, but as she noticed the time she realised she ought to hurry the children along. Her mother-in-law was due to drop Megan back soon, and Felicity couldn't be entirely sure how much mess she had left the house in as they'd finally shut the front door that morning.

Pete's mum never actually said she disapproved of Felicity's housekeeping skills, but, nonetheless, Felicity could feel her disapproval whenever she caught her off guard with a drop-in visit. And it wasn't that Felicity was particularly tardy when it came to housework; every evening by about nine o'clock the place looked fabulous. But during the day she just couldn't see the point.

When Megan was little clearing up after her had been manageable, then when Alice came along it was a little harder but she could enlist Megan's help and achieve tidy moments in the day. However, once the two boys came along, and Fred learnt to commando crawl and then walk, clearing up became futile: a challenge to see who was fastest – her tidying up or her boys on a destruction mission. They won almost all of the time! Once she stopped trying to clear up, she could actually keep an eye on them more fully and stopped having to replace the crockery they regularly pulled out of the cupboards.

Wiping the children's sauce covered faces and greasy fingers, Felicity agreed to just ten minutes more in the soft play, deciding that would be just enough time to let Alice and Callum run off their food high without letting Fred get too tired before his afternoon nap. If she was lucky, he wouldn't fall asleep in the car and she could get him down at home, put *CBeebies* on for the other two and tidy up ready for her mother-in-law's inspection. Then, she might just be able to give Megan a bit of attention and hear how her show rehearsal went before teatime.

Ideally, Felicity had been hinting at her mother-in-law having the little ones while she took Megan to her ballet rehearsal, but she apparently misheard that and steadfastly fixed on the rehearsal details before Felicity could repeat the request. Felicity sometimes wondered what her mother-in-law thought she was going to get up to if she had a moment to herself. She always seemed to view any request she put in for help with an air of suspicion. It was madness. The only things she ever wanted to sneak off and do were to drink a warm cup of tea and have a wee without an audience! *Let it go, Flick*, she breathed. Maybe she was being unfair, comparing her mother-in-law's manner to the easy way her own mum had always offered to help.

Felicity sat in the baby area of the soft play, keeping one eye on the pushchair while Fred clambered over big, spongy, coloured blocks practically half his size – his big, nappied bottom sticking disproportionately into the air. She could hear Callum giggling with Alice on the floor above. *What would you have made of my boys, Mum? Would you have melted at their cheeky faces, and kept up with their boundless energy?*

Tears welled in her eyes as Felicity felt how keenly she still missed her mum and the close relationship they'd come to share, all too late. She thought about all the time she had wasted being angry with her as a child – not a day passed now where she didn't think of something she wished she could share with her; silly things, as well as important things.

As a child Felicity had spent too long feeling she had somehow ruined her mum's life, mistaking her mum's eagerness for her to have more, do more and be more as her spurning what her own life as a single parent had become. On reflection she had spent too long rebelling against guilt her mum never intended her to feel. *Funny how things that can seem so important at the time can be obliterated into insignificance by something else!*

Much to Fred's disgust, Felicity picked him up for a cuddle she needed more than he wanted to give. Blowing a raspberry on his belly she got him to sag into her arms. Relaxing his rigid body as he laughed, Fred grabbed a handful of her hair and yanked it. As Felicity squealed in pain Alice shouted from the floor above.

'Mummy! Mummy. Callum's stuck!'

Putting Fred down, Felicity rolled her watering eyes and decided it was time to go.

Chapter Three

Winnie wheezed her way back to the G-plan teak table precariously holding the cup, saucer and teapot-laden tray. Lisa had learned not to offer to help, as the gesture seemed to insult Winnie, who always insisted there was 'plenty of life left in the old girl yet'. Taking her seat opposite Lisa, Winnie smiled with self-satisfaction, before leaning forwards to stir the teapot. As she looked at the tray, she began rocking in her chair in readiness to get up again.

'Look at that now, I've forgotten the biscuits and I got those ones you like too.'

'Oh, let me, please,' Lisa insisted, holding Winnie's hand before she could lift it from the edge of the table.

'No. There's plenty …' Winnie swung her slippered feet twice more into the air, but having still not achieved a standing position she relented. 'Oh bugger it, all right then!'

Lisa chuckled. She had never known Winnie concede to accepting help and she had never heard her swear, but she was pleased to be able to do something to help.

'Just there in the barrel, my lovely.' Winnie pointed at the biscuit barrel that Lisa thought you might describe as retro if it wasn't for the fact it had been in use since the 1970s. It had an orange, floral pattern all round it; a worn, gold knob on top; and some kind of beads that you could hear moving in the lid as you pulled it off. Perhaps they were there to aid freshness. Lisa decided not to ask in case the noise was the result of a four-decade crumb build-up trapped in the lid.

Returning to the table, Lisa looked inside at the custard creams Winnie had replenished for her. *Bless her, such a kind gesture.* Lisa thought she had probably eaten more custard creams since beginning to walk Jack than she had in her entire twenty-nine years before; she was even getting used to the taste of them being tainted with the ginger nuts ever present in the bottom of the barrel. She ate them because Winnie got them for her and that made her feel like she mattered. To this dear, old lady – maybe even to Jack, though he didn't always show it – she mattered. She had earned a place in Winnie's heart, well, her biscuit barrel anyway, and she liked that.

Lisa had thought that moving back to Littlehampton, the seaside town she had grown up in, would feel like coming home. But the reality felt very different. Everybody had moved on with their lives. They weren't holding their breath for Lisa Blake to return. She had lost contact with even the closest of her old friends and felt she could hardly front up with a 'Remember me?' on their doorsteps. Not after so much time had passed. She knew they would have every right to think she had ignored them for too long. Lisa feared she had not only burned her bridges, as her Granny Blake would have said, but it had been so long that she may well have positively cremated them.

Lisa looked at her watch.

'You in a hurry today, my lovely?'

'No.' Lisa knew she really should be more focused on slotting in the next client and building her business, the way her dad had told her. But it would be rude to rush off when Winnie had always put the kettle on and warmed the teapot. 'You know I've always got time for my favourite client.' Lisa smiled.

Winnie dipped her ginger nut into her tea, as Jack settled down under her chair. 'So, my lovely, what's been happening with you? No more bites this week, I hope.'

'No.' Lisa laughed. 'I'm not feeding Dexter this week.'

Just thinking about the pesky parrot made her still-sore fingers ache.

'Oh, good. So I don't need to worry about you on that score then.' Winnie smiled. 'And how about getting out and about? Been anywhere? Met anybody new?'

'No, not out anywhere special but ...' About to reveal she'd had an encounter with a mysterious man in leather, Lisa realised she couldn't mention that without relating the whole tale. Having paused too long she had to think of something to say to the now eagerly waiting Winnie. 'Well, there's Toby; he's tall, dark and handsome,' she finally offered.

'Ooh, yes.' Winnie's eyes lit up at the idea that Lisa had found a man. She was always telling her she should get out more and find someone new. That 'life's too short'.

'Quite a looker really, for a Newfoundland!' Lisa added, biting on her custard cream, rather pleased with her quick thinking.

'What?' Winnie took a moment to process the information. 'A Newfoundland? A dog ... you've met a dog?'

Lisa nodded.

'I thought you'd met a man.' Winnie batted a hand at her. 'You're a rotter, Lisa Blake.'

'I'll be seeing a lot of him. He needs a lift to his swimming class twice a week,' Lisa continued teasingly.

Winnie laughed so hard she began to wheeze again, as she started to catch her breath she said, 'Who ever heard of a dog having a swimming class?' Brushing away some of the crumbs she had sprayed on the table, she added, 'In my day we used to take 'em to the beach. Let 'em loose in the sea! Dearie me, what's the world coming to? A swimming class for dogs! Who'd have thought it?'

'I know, but at least it means I can't lose him at the beach.' Lisa stopped herself. She had to remind herself that Winnie was a client. Being so familiar, so at ease in her company, sometimes made her forget. 'Anyway, I just have to take him, throw his toy, supervise, dry him and return him home.'

'Good for you. Sounds like money for jam,' Winnie put in decisively, recovering from her wheezing fit of laughter.

About to defend the honour of her job, Lisa stopped, aware there was no point. Winnie was of the age where she felt her experience meant she knew best and her age meant she didn't have time to waste with subtlety. In many ways it was refreshing compared to the falsity of those she had known in London. And, besides, if anybody had told her, even as little as six months ago, that she would be earning money by taking a Newfoundland to his swimming lesson twice a week, Lisa would have scoffed herself.

Winnie dunked another ginger nut and nibbled at its edges. Lisa noticed the curve and stiffness in her fingers, her body showing its age while her mind remained agile. *Age, such a sneaky bastard to us all!* Lisa tried to push the thought away. She couldn't let her mind linger on that subject.

'No word from *that* Ben, I suppose.'

Thankfully, Winnie's words broke her thoughts and Lisa laughed. Winnie always referred to Ben as *that* Ben, her opinion of him clear in that one phrase. Lisa wondered what Winnie would think of him if she told her the real reason they had broken up. Not that she ever would. She knew the words wouldn't come if she tried.

'No, not a word.'

Winnie sipped her tea. 'Well I can't say I'm disappointed to hear it.'

Lisa didn't want to think about the fact Ben hadn't even cared enough to check she was OK, and decided to change the subject. 'So how about you? How was your weekend?'

Winnie sat back. 'The usual, my lovely. That boy of mine had his wife phone me again. He's too busy she said; too busy indeed! He'll be busy arranging my funeral before he picks up the phone. After what happened with his father you'd think he'd want to speak to his own mum while she's still on the right side of the grass!'

'Oh, Winnie, I'm sure he really is busy and just wants to chat properly when he can.' Lisa bit her custard cream before she accidentally told Winnie what she really thought of her son. 'How about your grandson?' Lisa deflected, hoping to lighten the mood.

Winnie's eyes sparkled as her expression softened. 'Ah, my Nicky! He's a good boy. He came to see me just the other day. Brought his old Nan a bunch of flowers, he did. He's split up with that last girlfriend of his. Good riddance, I say. I told you rotten eggs have a way of making their smell known in the end.'

Lisa giggled, knowing that it was unlikely Winnie would deem anybody good enough for her grandson.

Chapter Four

Felicity ran a steaming, hot bath, adding plenty of her Tropical Transfusion Radox Smoothie to the flow under the running tap. The smell made her think of sun-kissed holidays. Not that she had actually been on any, but coconut, with its association with Malibu and suntan lotion, had a way of teasing her mind; she could almost feel warm sand between her toes! She longed to be one of those people for whom the sun meant luxurious holidays spent lazing by the sea, as opposed to putting out three loads of washing on a rotary line made wonky by the children swinging off it. She stripped bare and wondered about venturing onto the scales, but decided after leaning her big toe on the edge not to bother.

Having four babies had made her round in all the right places, but some of the wrong ones too. She loved her boobs, and knew Pete did too. She was grateful having children hadn't sent them too far south. Maybe the fact that they had always been big meant the pregnancy effect was less dramatic. She knew she should lose a few pounds, but she didn't want to be skinny. Voluptuous was her thing. It always had been. She didn't understand the desire to be Victoria Beckham thin. How she had managed to have four babies and remain so pencil-like was beyond Felicity's comprehension. Her own belly, hips and thighs had been well and truly rounded out by her babies.

Scooping her hair into a messy bun, Felicity stepped into the water, standing for a while until her legs grew used to the heat. As she lay down she slid into the bubbles, pushing them away from her neck and hair as she rested her head back against the edge of the bath. She didn't often get time to indulge in a bath, but she was determined to have some time to herself this evening. She wanted to get 'in the mood', ready for Pete's return. She hadn't been that great when it came to the bedroom lately. It wasn't that she didn't fancy Pete or that she didn't *want* him, she quite often fancied him in the morning or as he came in from work – all ruffled and mucky from his day spent landscaping his latest client's garden. But they were hardly practical times of the day with a house full of children. Fred especially had an I'm-going-to-holler radar whenever she and Pete shared a cheeky moment in the day. But in the evenings, even when Pete wasn't working at Cin Cin and they could make time for each other, the truth was she quite often felt too tired to make an effort. Either she found herself wanting a moment of peace, to be left alone to read or catch up with Facebook, or to curl up and fall asleep. Sometimes she spent her day being pulled in so many different directions she felt like everybody wanted a piece of her and if she didn't have time to recuperate, find a moment to herself at some point, she might just shatter into all those pieces.

She knew she had been slipping into bed in her scruffy, old, comfy knickers and baggy T-shirts a little too often lately, even fibbing to say her period had come early or stayed a day or two later than it actually had to remove the expectation at times. Poor Pete, he didn't really deserve that. She really did love him and, despite it frequently being her fault they hadn't touched base in the bedroom, even she missed the physical spark they used to share.

Well, not tonight! Tonight she was going to go for it. She had rummaged in her wardrobe and found something positively silky hiding in the back. She vaguely remembered buying it in the La Senza closing-down sale en route to Tesco Express one day, after it had called to her from the window. As she had rediscovered it in the back of her wardrobe she had touched the silk to her cheek. It felt cool, smooth and sexy. *Perfect!* The thought of surprising Pete with it inspired her to run a bath instead of going downstairs to catch up on her ironing and soaps – Australian, never British, she couldn't be doing with the dark moods and violence when there was silliness in the sun to watch.

Enjoying her soak Felicity closed her eyes and pushed away thoughts of all the things she had to do the next day. With her head almost clear of shopping and the zombie costume she had to make for Megan's Halloween ballet performance, she finally relaxed and had to remind herself not to fall asleep in the bath; it was a habit she enjoyed but one her mum always berated her for. But, then again, it was so very cosy, propping her feet at the end of the bath, relaxing her head back, laying cocooned in warm, bubbly water. It wasn't her fault it always got the better of her. Besides, with her eyes closed she couldn't see the pile of washing at the open-just-in-case-the-children-needed-her door, or the dust on the bottles of long-forgotten cleansers, aftersun and goodness knows what else on the spice rack pretending to be a bathroom tidy in the corner. She could just be anywhere. Maybe even in a luxury hotel – waiting for Pete to come and wash her all over.

Jumping suddenly, Felicity realised she had succumbed to the hot-water-and-bubbles comfort blanket. Sitting up, wide eyed, she listened, unsure if one of the children had actually called her or if she had dreamt it. Her heart was racing, but, thankfully, all was silent. Splashing water onto her face she reminded herself she had to stay awake and she had to stay focused. She had a sex-kitten mission to fulfil. Grabbing what she thought was her sponge, but actually turned out to be a glittery, Disney-princess sponge that chafed from the sparkles, she washed herself over and stood up. *Bugger!* The heat from the water meant she looked like a rhubarb and custard, bright red where the water had touched and pasty white where it had not. She hoped the lines would disappear by the time Pete got back. It really wasn't the look she was going for!

Rubbing herself dry with a line-dried towel with the harshness to exfoliate whether she wanted to or not, she applied a concoction of oils and lotions she hadn't had the time or inclination to use before. Her body welcomed the attention, especially her knees that were dry from kneeling to pick up toys, changing nappies and playing trains, little Fred's latest favourite. All of the smellies were birthday or Christmas presents from Pete's mum. She always bought her such gifts as if she thought Felicity had time before getting the children dressed to apply Dove in six different varieties to various body parts on a daily basis. Felicity had been saving them up to put in the Christmas raffle at school, but as the collection fell out as she had rummaged in the back of her wardrobe she had thought, *well, why not?* Smelling them all together mixed with the Tropical Transfusion bath smoothie, she felt she knew why not. Nevertheless, she decided it was probably better to smell like an overly sweet fruit salad than of the fried food and sweaty children odour that lingered on her from soft play.

Taking out the silky number, Felicity smiled. It was funny how the thought of getting dressed up and making a bit of an effort was an aphrodisiac in itself. Pete would be shocked for sure. She panicked at the thought that he might have a heart attack, but pushed the notion away, attempting to focus on enjoying the surprise she imagined on his face and the stirrings she hoped to evoke elsewhere. She wondered how she would look to him. She was aiming for gorgeous, but feared bloody stupid might be what she achieved. She hadn't seen a lot of porn, but she had seen enough to know she looked more 'readers' wives' than 'professional temptress' these days.

Slipping the deep-purple chemise over her bust with a bit of a heave, she wiggled it down into place. *Hmmm*, it was tighter than she remembered and flattened her bust a bit. It was no good, she would have to do the old scoop and lift to get the desired effect. Spillage from the top had to be better than flattening below the bust line. She didn't care if it made her look more voluptuous than was intended; they were her assets and she intended to use them.

Looking in the mirror she remembered having the matching undies somewhere. She looked in her knicker drawer, but they weren't at the front. That was reserved for her black collection of maxi-briefs. Searching in the back, she found a long-discarded pair of 'Merry Christmas' boxers, complete with cheeky robin, from her ooh-get-me-I-still-have-it phase, and an overstretched pair of Mothercare maternity briefs. Judging by how stretched they looked Felicity decided that Mothercare maternity too-brief briefs might have been a better name. She launched the knickers into the bin. 'I won't be needing you again!' She said it with confidence. Not the unfounded confidence she'd had before Fred came along – the result of a moment of madness while Pete was on the waiting list for the snip – but the confidence of a woman who was content in the knowledge that she'd had her last baby. At last she knew her sleepless nights were numbered.

Ah ha! Pulling out the crumpled bundle of purple from the drawer, Felicity looked at the knickers. They were pretty and trimmed in black lace, perhaps a bit creased and a little small, but they would complete the look perfectly. With a little chuckle to herself she slipped them on. *Hellooo, Felicity, you still have it!* She was relieved to see she looked good enough in them to know Pete wouldn't be disappointed. All that was left to do was to prop herself up on the sofa with a glass of wine and wait for Pete's return.

Chapter Five

Lisa stared at her iPad, waiting for her mum to answer. FaceTiming her parents had become a twice-weekly ritual, though with her in the family home and them away in France, where they spent at least six months of the year since taking early retirement, she felt more like the parent than the child in the situation. Finally her mum picked up.

'Hi, darling, we can't chat long tonight; there's a festival in town.'

'Really, you're going to a festival?'

'It's a bit of a do to mark the end of the summer hols, *la rentrée* as the French say. There's a parade through the village to welcome the autumn and then a party at the lake.'

'Really! And you're going, just the two of you?' Lisa knew she sounded dismayed and stopped herself. Just because she was facing another Saturday night alone in front of the television didn't mean she should resent her parents having a good time.

Lisa's mum laughed. 'It's about the community and fitting in. For the village, you know.'

Lisa sighed; it seemed everybody was living life more fully than her and she felt like she had forgotten how.

'By the way, talking of festivities, did you know Luke's joining us for Christmas?'

Lisa felt a bubble of joy swell in her chest. Having her brother home for Christmas would be great. She hadn't relished the thought of being home alone with her parents. Not in a bad way, it's just after leaving home and having Christmases in London with Ben – with the lights and amazing window displays in Oxford Street, enjoying the rides and bars at the Hyde Park Winter Wonderland, partying until late before returning in the early hours to the flat they had shared – returning for turkey, cracker charades and the Queen's speech with her mum and dad wearing coloured paper crowns at jaunty angles felt like a step backwards.

'That's great, when's his flight?' Lisa thought she might meet him at the airport to make up for missing waving him off when he left for Australia.

'I'm not sure exactly. He's planning to be here early December, in plenty of time to help us pick a tree.'

'Pick a tree! Mum, what happened to Bing?' Lisa felt shocked. Bing was the ugliest artificial tree she had ever seen, but he came out every year like an aged member of the family. She had decorated him in red and gold to the deep, rumbling tones of 'White Christmas' every year as a child.

'Bing! Don't get me started on that old thing.' Lisa's mum rolled her eyes; the tree was a gift from her mother-in-law soon after she was married, displaying it was an annual obligation she had begrudged. 'It's safe to say Bing is *not* coming here, oh no. You can't do artificial in a pine chalet in the snow, my darling. A real tree, roaring fire, an after dinner ski and a soak in the hot tub with a view of the Alps, that's Christmas for me this year!' Lisa's mum punched the air, as if she had won some long-awaited victory.

'What? Won't you be ... coming home for Christmas?'

'We'll be here, Lisa. I told you that when you said you were moving back ... don't you remember?'

Lisa thought about it, *no*, she didn't remember that at all. But, then again, she had only really been focused on getting away from London when she had called her mum. Tears welled in her eyes. She hadn't realised quite how much she needed the reassurance of all those silly rituals she had thought she was dreading until they were suddenly being taken away from her too. The thought of no Ben caused an ache in her chest – even if he had been a git – adding the fact that now there would be no Bing, cracker charades or paper hats suddenly made her feel bereft.

'But you can come too, Lisa. We want you to join us. Come on, darling … don't sulk.'

'I'm not sulking, Mum.' Lisa unfolded her arms.

'Luke might bring his girlfriend. You can meet her.'

Lisa's bubble felt well and truly deflated. Staying in England would mean she would be Benless, flatless and familyless for Christmas, and going to France meant she would be the only one without a partner – the only one well and truly *célibataire*! She felt the last of her Christmas spirit fizzle away like the alcohol on a well-lit Christmas pudding. She imagined the empty chair next to her at the table and sighed. *Almost thirty, single and Christmas in France! Really!* 'I just thought we'd all … be together … at home this year, Mum.'

'Oh, Lisa, you haven't been home for Christmas for so long. And with you gone and Luke in Australia, it just wasn't the same. We only stayed in England these past years for your Granny Blake. But since she's passed now, your dad and me, well, we just thought it was our time to do something … something different. You know.' Lisa's mum gestured to her husband for reinforcement, who it seemed had been listening just out of vision of the screen.

'For us, Lisa, you understand.' Her dad placed his hand on her mum's shoulder.

'Come on, darling, come and join us. We'd love to see you, and you never know you might enjoy it here; everyone's so friendly and there's a view you'll never tire of.'

Clearly spending Christmas at home wasn't up for

discussion. As her parents waved their goodbyes with reassurances that it would all work out fine, the room fell silent. Lisa dropped her iPad onto the sofa, thankful that Christmas was still three months away. Maybe things would be different by then. Maybe she wouldn't be alone, maybe Ben would ... *Do what?* Lisa wasn't sure what Ben could do to make things right now.

Shaking all thoughts of Ben away, Lisa reached for the remote control. Browsing her viewing options she wasn't sure she had enough energy to face the *Strictly* and *X Factor* marathon without at least a glass, or maybe a bottle, of wine. Checking her watch, she decided she had time to head to the supermarket for a few essentials before she settled in for the evening.

Grabbing a basket Lisa glanced at her list and wondered where she might find the items she was after. 'Wine, Maltesers, headache stuff, coffee, hmm.' She had spent most of the past three months consuming the contents of her mum's cupboards, freezer and wine rack, only shopping for a few bits here and there as she needed them. She had also befriended Mr Chung, the elderly gentleman serving in the Chinese takeaway en route from Winnie's to home. Lisa wasn't sure if he actually spoke much English beyond what was written on the menu, but he always smiled politely and nodded while she spoke about her day as she waited for her order. After waffling to Winnie and a chat to Mr Chung, she often went home feeling free of the baggage of the day. Even if reflecting on that fact frequently made her feel like she desperately needed to find some friends her own age!

Despite it being several weeks away, Halloween had hit the front of the shop big style. Lisa thought it was funny; when she was little she could barely remember marking it. Now there were costumes galore on sale for all ages and more plastic-pumpkin-and-ghost-type tat than she could ever have imagined. Even little jam-filled teacakes had become vampire bites! Reminding herself she didn't have time to get distracted looking at it all if she was still going to fit in her Saturday night viewing marathon on catch-up, she attempted to walk away. But as she passed the adult costumes the baby section caught her eye. There was an array of cute sleep suits, T-shirts and bibs with apt Halloween slogans written across them. Stroking her hand across the 'Mummy's little pumpkin', 'I'm a screamer' and 'Halloween scares the poop out of me' bodysuits, Lisa gave a small smile. Rubbing away the ache in her chest, she decided to head for the wine aisle at the far end of the shop.

Glancing up at the large signs hanging above each aisle, she spotted the medicine section. Having already decided she was going to need something for the post-wine headache she was anticipating in the morning, she took a detour down it. She knew she would be unable to sleep it off. Especially as she had to be up and looking human by eight o'clock in the morning to feed three cats and a rabbit, whose lucky owners were having a 'naughty weekend' in Bath – a detail she could have done without as she took the booking.

Sidestepping along the aisle, reading each label in search of whatever would be cheap and effective, Lisa could smell something odd. It was unpleasant. It was ... *oh hell*, it was sick. The woman standing next to her smelt of sick, or at least sick mixed with a sweet, fruit cocktail of other scents. If she had attempted to spray something to mask the smell it hadn't worked. She smelt awful and though she didn't like to look too closely, Lisa was sure she could see a few pieces of carrot stuck in her hair. Trying to grab her tablets and move away as quickly as possible without heaving, Lisa knocked down an entire display of paracetamol. 'Bugger!' She couldn't just leave the packets scattered across the floor, so she began picking them up. Attempting not to inhale while scooping them she could only achieve something akin to the dexterity of a clown wearing boxing gloves.

'Here, let me help.' Joining Lisa on the floor, the woman moved closer and so did the smell.

Lifting her head slightly as she scampered about on her knees, Lisa couldn't help but notice the woman's huge cleavage as her coat gaped open revealing ample flesh bulging over a too small chemise. *Bloody hell!* Noting the fact the woman had come out with regurgitated food in her hair, smelling of sick and wearing some kind of purple-and-black silk number under a duffle coat, Lisa decided it would be best to keep her distance. She wanted to get away from the woman as quickly and politely as possible. Attempting to not inhale, Lisa stood. Cradling the packets she had gathered awkwardly, she looked at the woman's face for the first time. About to thank her Lisa gasped, dropping all the packets back to the floor.

'F- F- Felicity!' was all Lisa could manage. She couldn't believe it. It was definitely her, Felicity Forster! Older, slightly rounder, dressed very strangely, definitely emitting an awful smell and standing right there, larger than life, before her in the medicines' aisle of Tesco. In all the years she had imagined seeing Felicity again she never dreamt it would happen like this.

Chapter Six

By the time Lisa was back on her sofa she had replayed the scene with Flick over in her head many times. She and Felicity had never shared an awkward moment before, but the meeting in the supermarket had been cringeworthy. As Lisa pictured herself standing speechless opposite Flick, who couldn't wait to get away, she could still feel the palpable shift in their relationship. Reimagining the situation she thought of all the things she could have said and – given that Felicity looked in the middle of a personal crisis – the things she should have said, as a friend. But that was it, despite the fact they had once shared everything and known each other's most intimate secrets, they had become ... *strangers*.

Lisa pushed the idea away. How could she and Felicity ever truly be strangers? Strangers would have reacted differently; they could have passed each other by anonymously. The encounter in the supermarket would have been a casual, momentary meeting of two people, easily put to the back of the mind and forgotten. No, Lisa knew she and Flick could never be strangers, but that meeting in the supermarket had left her in no doubt – they were no longer friends. Lisa's heart and head hurt at the thought.

Searching for a distraction, she turned the television on. But it was no use, *The X Factor* still had too many contestants to hold her interest, and even the usual comedy crowd-pleasers weren't doing it for her. And the participants on *Strictly* were so smiley she could barely look at them. Nothing could stop the nagging at the back of her mind: *Flick Forster*, *Felicity Forster*. Thinking about the years that had passed since they had last spoken, Lisa realised their friendship had met with such a slow demise she had barely noticed it slipping away until now, and now, well, it seemed it was too late.

Lisa looked round the living room. She was sure being back in her parents' house, the place where she and Felicity had shared so much, was making her feel sentimental. She knew she needed to get a place of her own. Once she had finalised things in London with Ben – not that she intended to address that situation any time soon – a place of her own would be her next priority.

Sitting on her parents' bedroom floor, rooting through a box of old photographs on a Saturday night felt like a new all-time low. Lisa had hoped it would make her feel better, that there would be some comfort in the pictures, but the reality was it all looked a lifetime ago. She and Flick were pretty much inseparable back then, together in almost every photograph. From missing teeth and their Cabbage Patch Kid phase to sharing the same hairstyles – *oh Lord, those fringes* – the same make-up and even the same terrible taste in clothes – *surely leggings with that much pattern on were never fashionable?* They had gone through it all together.

Lisa stared at their first school photograph, with thirty-two children attempting to look like an orderly class, as they grew used to wearing their new uniforms and abiding by the words of Mrs Marsh, their ever-enthusiastic teacher. Lisa noticed how both she and Felicity were grinning at each other. Not looking at the camera at all. It was typical of their relationship. Theirs was a friendship formed on collusion from the start. Since Lisa had wet herself on the first day at infant school and Flick doused her from the water tray and accepted a telling off to save her embarrassment and hide the evidence, it had been them against the world. It was supposed to stay that way; *it should have stayed that way!* Lisa riffled through the box, flicking through the years they had shared until an idea struck and she went downstairs.

Lisa wanted to know what Flick was up to now. She wanted to see what her life had become. She generally disliked Facebook. Ben had a profile, but she had only created one recently because her dad suggested it might be wise to have a business page – not that she had got round to that yet. But now she wanted to check out Flick's life, firing up her laptop and heading to Facebook seemed her only option. What else was a woman to do when she wanted to spy on someone without actually making contact with them?

Lisa's own page might as well have had tumbleweed blowing across it; no action since she had last logged on. No new friend requests – well, she hadn't really expected Winnie or Mr Chung to be on Facebook – but nothing … *really … nothing?*

Typing in 'Flick Forster' Lisa leaned forward and waited for her face to appear in the search results. *Nothing!* She tried 'Felicity Forster', but still nothing appeared. The thought that Flick might have got married had never occurred to Lisa before. *She can't have! I'd know … wouldn't I? Didn't we promise to be each other's bridesmaids?* The years they hadn't made contact stretched out in Lisa's mind.

It had been eleven years since she left Littlehampton. When she had first gone away she and Felicity had chatted on the phone regularly, over time, contact slipped to monthly calls and sending the odd letter or postcard. Eventually, distance, and the fact they were both living different lives meant even months slipped by and turned into years. Lisa tried to remember the last time she had contacted Felicity and cringed at the memory of a hurried phone call on Flick's twenty-first birthday. *Really? Was that it? Eight years ago.*

Lisa realised there was so much Flick didn't know about her own life in that time; there was no reason the converse wouldn't also be true. *But married? Could she be?* Thinking back, Lisa remembered Flick mentioning a boyfriend. *Pete ... Pete somebody!* But without his last name she couldn't get any further and she just couldn't remember it. Holding her phone in her hand, she wondered if her mum would know. But, then again, she knew her parents spent so much time in France they barely kept up with the details of her life, let alone those of the people she had gone to school with.

About to give up, Lisa pondered searching other, or at least one other, old school friend. It was something she had promised herself she wouldn't do when she left home, but now, having seen Felicity and being in her parents' house, she just had the urge to see what had become of him. She knew it was probably a bad idea. Would searching for Nathan Baker be too much of a wallow into the depths of the past? He was her first crush, her first love, her closest friend after Felicity and the reason she moved away.

Before she could convince herself otherwise she typed in 'Nathan Baker'. A list of Nathan Bakers appeared, but none were *her* Nathan, not unless the years had been very unkind to him. Not yet ready to give up on her trudge through time now she had started, she typed in the name of Nathan's best friend. Brett Austin's obviously still-cheeky face appeared as the first in the list. *Ah ha!* Lisa leaned into the screen. Clicking on his name she was intrigued to see how he had aged. It was weird seeing people from school after a big leap of time. His face, minus a few wrinkles, was still the face she knew, but his tummy was rounder and his hair much thinner. He still didn't look very tall, she noticed.

Sure that he and Nathan must still be friends Lisa started scrolling through his pictures. *Blimey!* He had visited some places, that was for sure. Brett Austin had obviously got some money from somewhere. Then she saw it, Nathan's face beaming out from the screen. Her heart jumped and she pushed aside the thought that perhaps heading off to Europe hadn't quite been the leave him behind and move on from him cure she had thought. *Damn!* He still looked good, too good as always next to Brett who had always been his sidekick, never quite growing out of the shadow of his taller, better-looking friend.

She saw the tag, Nate Baker, *so it's Nate now, is it?* She tested it out, saying it aloud. She didn't like it. Nathan suited him better. Her finger hovering over her laptop, she looked at the link. Hesitating momentarily, she bit her lip, clicked on it and went directly to his page. His pictures weren't giving away many clues, apart from the fact that he had either become a fireman or a male stripper in a fireman's outfit, *hmmm!* Either way, he looked pretty impressive in the uniform. There were some pictures of formal-looking functions in which Nathan looked every bit as good in a suit as he had at their, or rather *that*, prom and some of him doing some adventure-style sports: skiing, kite surfing, mountain biking. *Crikey!* If the pictures were anything to go by, he had turned into quite the adventurer. Clearly, Nathan hadn't embarked on the settled-down life he once wanted. With an ache in her chest and feeling slightly depressed that both Brett Austin and Nathan Baker were living life to the max in one way or another, Lisa decided not to search any further.

About to cross it all off, she decided a little peek at Ben's page might not hurt. She had avoided it so far, aware there was nothing truly to be gained from looking, unless he was updating his status with messages relating to how sorry he was, and the abject misery he was feeling since she left. She typed in his name. Glancing over his page, the words 'Ben Hurst is single' smacked her in the face. *Oh, Ben! So that's it, you really didn't care!* She recoiled from the screen. *Could this night actually get any worse?*

* * *

When Lisa finally woke on the sofa, having drowned her evening sorrows with too much sherry – the only alcohol she could find in the kitchen – and a slab of Dr. Oetker cooking chocolate she hoped was still in date, her head hurt and her stomach groaned. She wished she hadn't deserted her shopping in Tesco after the shock of seeing Flick. Her choice of comfort food had not provided the lasting coma of ignorance she had hoped to achieve and she had no paracetamol. Flick's face in the supermarket and Ben's declaration all thudded back into her mind. Feeling a sudden surge from the stomach up, she ran to the toilet. Pretty unpleasant going in, the sherry and cooking chocolate mix was hellish coming out. Wiping her mouth and leaning back against the wall to take a breath, Lisa was pleased she felt better for the clear out, but she needed a shower. As it was already twenty to eight, she also knew it had to be a quick one. Flushing the toilet and checking her mum's precious white pedestal was unscathed, Lisa began to strip off.

Finally refreshed, dressed and heading out the door, with five minutes to go before she was due at her first client's house, Lisa checked her diary; 'Kitty-Kat, Sheldon, Mr Mistoffelees and Powder Puff' were written in for eight o'clock. Lisa couldn't help but think how very different her diary looked compared to the old days, when appointments with her editor, professionals in the pet care and pet food industries, and luxurious lunches with Ben were the order of the day. Seeing 'Jack' typed in for one o'clock at least made her smile. Knowing she was assured a cup of tea with Winnie by the end of the day was always a welcome thought. About to put her phone away, it buzzed: it was a Facebook notification. Glancing down at the words 'Nate Baker accepted your friend request' made her stomach lurch; *Oh no! What have I done?*

Chapter Seven

Felicity couldn't believe it; poor little Fred had been up nearly all night being sick. It was the last thing she needed, her children getting ill. There wasn't time for it, what with Megan's ballet rehearsals for her Halloween performance, and Fred's birthday party looming. One of them was bound to be down with something at a crucial time, especially as they never just got these things all at once. With four of them in the house, one of them being poorly always threatened a month of illness as the germs worked their way through each of them individually. She knew she had taught them to share, but sharing germs she could most certainly do without.

'Could it be something he ate?'

Pete's words sent a vision of pizza fingers and curly fries through Felicity's mind. *Yes!* 'Maybe,' *almost certainly*, 'but in some ways it might be better if it is,' she added, thinking on her feet while trying to appease her own guilt.

Pete guffawed. 'Yes, let's hope our son has food poisoning.'

Felicity hit him. 'You know what I mean. If it's a bug, well, we're buggered! Pardon the pun. If it's something he ate, it will be over within a matter of days. Fewer sleepless nights and days occupying poorly children all round.'

'I love my wife's logic.' Pete pulled Felicity into a cuddle.

She snuggled in, loving the feel of his arms around her. *Perfect!* 'And I love you!'

'Good, because you owe me some attention later,' Pete joked with a squeeze.

Felicity's momentary warm fuzzy feeling fizzled as she

pushed Pete's arms away. She had been up almost all night with Fred, her attempt at seduction had gone well and truly wrong, she hadn't had time to begin to process seeing Lisa in the supermarket, and, really, she wanted to curl up in Pete's arms, have a good cry and fall asleep for possibly one hundred years.

'Have you ever thought that telling someone who looks after four children all day and who has been up nearly all night that you want them to give you a little attention later is not such a great turn on?' Felicity realised the words came out more caustically than she intended, but she couldn't help it.

Pete looked at her, eyes wide, like a spurned puppy. 'Flick, I was trying to be nice, you know ... sexy!'

'Sexy? Well, what you achieved was demanding. Along with everybody else in this house, you want me to take care of you.' She knew she sounded like a cow, but she was tired, verging on well and truly knackered, and she had been enjoying that hug.

'But, last night, you wanted it. If Fred hadn't turned into something from *The Exorcist*, you were the one being all Miss Whiplash.'

'That was then ... and I really wasn't aiming for Miss Bloody Whiplash. Honestly, Pete, I've been covered in sick, gone to Tesco practically in my underwear, been up all night since then ... and ... to top it all ... I bumped into Lisa.'

'Lisa who?'

'Lisa. My Lisa. *The* Lisa.'

Pete looked confused.

'For God's sake Pete, Lisa Blake! My frie— ex-friend; you can't have forgotten her.'

Finally registering whom Felicity was referring to, Pete

sighed. 'Really? Here? In Littlehampton? What does she want?'

Annoyed that Pete would think Lisa was back because she wanted something, Felicity took a breath before she could speak. 'I don't know.' *I couldn't speak to her. I didn't know what to say; really, I just wanted to … to hug her!* And she knew Pete wouldn't begin to understand that.

'Please don't tell me you are going to let her hurt you again, after all these years.'

Felicity sighed in exasperation, *after all these years!* She wasn't sure she had ever stopped being hurt over losing Lisa. And she didn't need Pete to remind her how many years it had been. Felicity remembered all too well Lisa's phone call on her twenty-first birthday, when she was so pleased to hear her voice, delighted she had remembered and devastated when Lisa hung up so quickly – before Felicity could say how much she needed a friend and how scared she was that she was pregnant. When Lisa stopped writing back and getting in contact, Felicity had thought she was gone forever. She tried to tell Pete how she had felt at the time, but she knew he didn't really understand. Grieving for the loss of someone who wasn't dead didn't register in Pete's world.

'When did you see her? What did you say? What did you say?' Pete's arms were back round Felicity, his voice softer.

'She didn't say anything and I didn't say anything sensible. It was in Tesco last night, while you and Fred were in the bath.'

'Really? So you hadn't actually seen her, what … well, since before you met me, and then you saw her covered in sick, wearing my coat over your you-hoo undies. Oh Christ!' Pete ventured a giggle. Hugs and humour were his usual tools for winning Felicity round.

'Is that supposed to make me feel better?' Felicity thrust her head into his shoulder. 'Because, I've got to tell you, it's not bloody working!' Despite her protestations she welcomed his hug and the kisses he placed on the top of her head. *I can't believe she's back!*

Collecting up all the washing festering from the night before, Felicity found herself drawn to the box she had secreted away under her bed. Her mum would have understood the significance of her seeing Lisa again. She would have told her what she ought to do. Sliding out the memory box, which she kept for herself as much as the children, Felicity ran her hand over the top, removing the thin layer of dust that had settled there since the last time she had opened it. She loved the box – a wooden chest she had rubbed down and varnished as part of her self-induced therapy after losing her mum – but whenever she opened it she had to brace herself. Even now she was still struck by the smallness of it all. The bits and pieces, the randomness of the remnants of a life. Most of it only significant to her and her children through the stories she had shared with them, but all of it precious. Pictures, jewellery, little keepsakes, even a postcard her mum had sent from her trip to Cornwall the month before her car accident. The fact it was addressed to her 'Gorgeous grandbabies' and included the message 'never forget how much Nana loves you' made it special, as if it included the boys she had never got the chance to meet.

Felicity pulled out a picture of her mum with Megan draped around her shoulders and Alice tiny in her arms. Life had marched on so much since it was taken. Alice was a newborn and Megan, not looking at the camera, was divided between being excited at being a big sister and

42

concerned that this new, little interloper might usurp her nana's attention. But her mum's expression, beaming with pride, was perfect; Felicity loved it. She loved knowing that her mum had been proud of the person she had become and the family she had created.

Felicity wished her mum could have met Callum and Fred – her adorable boys – seen their cheeky little faces, known their boundless energy, held them and shared in the joy of them as she had too briefly with the girls. And she wished she were there now, to confide in about seeing Lisa again.

Chapter Eight

Thick, grey clouds gathered overhead threatening a drenching Lisa hadn't come equipped for. Hurrying Jack along, her eyes frequently turned to the sky. If they were lucky, they could be back in the van before the first drop fell.

'Come on, Jack, nearly there!' Lisa encouraged the black Labrador along as he looked at her excitedly. 'There's biscuits, water and a cosy rug with your name on it in the van; well, technically, it's my name on it, but I'm happy to share with you.'

Jack trotted along, wonky eyes wide, oblivious to what Lisa was waffling on about but well aware that whatever it was must be something good.

Reaching the van, Lisa gave him a stroke, a large bowl of water and a well-earned biscuit before removing his new harness – *ha ha, you couldn't escape from that, could you?* – and securing him in his crate with the promised blanket. He snuggled down, content from his walk. As she shut the van door, Lisa looked up at the sky. It was that time of year where the weather couldn't quite make up its mind from one moment to the next and it seemed getting sodden was another of those occupational hazards she had underestimated when she had embarked on her new career.

'Looks like we beat the rain today!' she announced cheerily, her smile fading as her stomach flipped on a huge rumble. *Oh God!* She thought she had got rid of the sherry-and-cooking-chocolate cocktail from the night before, but her stomach had other ideas.

Glancing across the green to the toilets she held her

tummy as it began to feel warm. Too warm. *Oh, not now, please!* She hated public toilets, especially when they were cold, metal, had no seat and homed too many spiders for her liking. She hopped from foot to foot, not quite believing she felt rough again. She had been OK for most of the day – admittedly she had wrapped a tea towel round her nose and mouth while she fed the cats and emptied their litter trays – and she had avoided eating anything, but now she was wondering if perhaps she should have had something. Some nice toast or crackers, as her Granny Blake would have prescribed for an upset stomach. *Bugger it!* It was too late now. As her stomach began to bubble, she realised she would never make it back to Winnie's. 'Oh blimey! Won't be more than a few minutes, Jack,' she promised.

Unperturbed, Jack rolled his wonky eyes, not even lifting his head from his blanket.

Locking the van, Lisa made a dash for the toilets. They were every bit as grim as she remembered from the one and only time she had ever ventured into them before. Only now, the light wasn't working. *Great!* With no window, the only way to let light into the cubicle was to leave the outside door open. Not knowing what noises the eruption of her stomach might make, she didn't particularly want to do that. So darkness and expedience it was. When she was finally done and opened the toilet door she sighed.

In the time it had taken her to use the rather-lacking facilities the clouds had decided to burst. She could hear the raindrops coming thick and fast, hitting the outside door. Washing her hands she rolled her eyes; she was stranded in the horrid and now less-than-fragrant toilet unless she wanted to get soaked. She didn't relish the thought, but she didn't particularly want to stay put either. Taking a peek outside, she could see the sloping path had become a mini-

45

river in a matter of minutes. An inch of water continuously rushed passed. *How could so much rain fall in so little time?* Even a dash round to the kiosk would see her drenched.

Sticking her head out of the door, she had an idea. Running straight for the kiosk wouldn't work, but making a dash for the next toilets along might – she could seek shelter en route. Was it the men's or the disabled? She wasn't too sure. But if she could shimmy her way along to the kiosk via the other toilets she wouldn't get so wet. Standing under the shelter and getting a takeaway tea while waiting for the rain to pass was certainly more appealing than staying in the ladies'. The clouds were heavy, but the sky off to the right was blue. The rain couldn't stay for too long. It seemed like a plan.

Swinging from the sides of the doorframe as if she was about to launch herself into a sprint, Lisa leapt from the door. Splosh, splosh, dive. She burst through the next door, smacking herself into the firm chest of the man who was attempting to exit at the same time.

'Oh, sorry!' Lisa flushed crimson. Even before she looked up at his face, she knew it was him. Staring at the leather-clad chest she had just bounded into, she wished she had taken her chances and stayed in the dark with the spiders.

The man stepped back and rubbed his chest, exhaling. 'Rose?'

She had winded him, she had actually smacked into him so hard she had knocked the breath right out of him. Their last encounter had been humiliating, but this ... this was excruciating. Lisa felt like a complete klutz.

'It's you ... Rose ... isn't it?'

'Yes, I mean, no.'

He let out a giggle, regaining his composure.

Blathering on, Lisa tried to correct herself, wondering

why she had bothered as soon as she had started. 'Well, I am me … but I'm not … not who you … not Rose, it's Lisa.' Feeling a fool she held out her hand.

'Nice to meet you, Lisa, I'm Dom.' He took Lisa's hand and shook it, smiling cheekily. 'And where's Jack today, not drowning in this, I hope?'

Removing her hand from his, Lisa answered earnestly, 'No, no, quite safe. In my van.' Realising it was a joke as Dom raised an eyebrow at her, she felt like an idiot. *Great.*

'So do you always use the men's?'

To add to her mortification Lisa remembered where they were. 'Umm, no. I was actually en route to the kiosk.'

'Via the men's?'

'Sheltering before I was brave enough to make the final dash.'

'OK, I'll join you then. Come on, let's be brave together and go get a coffee.'

Lisa felt Dom's hand on her arm and her cheeks redden; deciding she had embarrassed herself enough for one day she made her excuses. 'Oh no, I can't. I have to get back. Jack's waiting and all that.'

'OK, another time then. Give me a date and I'll be here. Well, you know, not here,' he motioned drawing attention once more to the fact they were standing in the doorway of the men's toilets.

Lisa rolled her eyes at the sign on the door.

'Give me a date, and I'll see you at the kiosk,' Dom repeated with a grin.

A date? Lisa wasn't sure about the word date. *Was that as in a 'date' date?* She wasn't ready for that. *What if Ben …? Ben what? Apologised? Actually regretted being an utter bastard?*

'Next week, same time,' she said, before she had engaged

her brain to think it through. *What have you done?* Suddenly flustered, she looked out the door across the green. The rain had slowed. 'I have to go. Sorry about …' And now she was patting his chest, his rather firm and lovely leather-clad chest. *Oh God!* Not wanting to embarrass herself further, she removed her hand and ran.

Bemused, Dom called after her. 'Next week then, Rose. I'll be here.'

Pete looked warily at Felicity. 'Are you sure that's a good idea?'

'No, but it's got to be better than nothing. I can't just ignore the fact she's back.'

Pete sighed. 'But you don't even know where she's staying.'

'I'll start at her parents' house, see what I can find out. Go from there.'

Pete conceded. 'Look, if this is something you need to do, then do it. Just … you know … be careful.'

'Careful? Pete, I'm only going to *talk* to her.' Felicity knew she sounded more confident than she actually felt; *if only it were that easy.*

'I know, but—'

'I know you're looking out for me, you always do,' she said, smiling, 'but this is just something I have to do. She's back, Pete. I have to speak to her.'

Pete walked away shaking his head.

Felicity watched him leaving the kitchen. She loved the sight of his broad shoulders in his green work T-shirt. It was funny how something like that could just make her feel how attracted she was to him, to really want him. 'Pete!' she called after him, hoping for a hug at least; she wanted to feel his firm body next to hers.

'It's fine, honestly. Talk to Lisa if it's what you need to do.'

Felicity threw her head back and groaned.

Chapter Nine

'I love the harness, Winnie! How fab is that?' Lisa was feeling more human than she had felt all day, even if her mind couldn't decide whether to continue to obsess over her encounter with Flick or to panic about the fact she had agreed to meet a complete stranger for a ... *well*, not *a date*. *A cup of coffee. On the edge of a forest. Alone. Next week. Oh God!* The more she thought about it the more it felt like a scenario she might see on a *Crimewatch* re-enactment – if she was ever brave enough to actually watch a full episode.

'Well, I don't know if it's any good. Nicky gave it to me – said he got it from a friend who used to own a big dog. He thought it might help me with Jack being such a strong lad.'

Lisa looked up. As much as she was sure Winnie would love getting out and about by herself with Jack, she would really miss her if she were to cancel Jack's walks. 'I'm not that easy to get rid of you know. You start walking this handsome boy yourself and I might have to come along just to keep you company anyway!'

'If only!' Winnie chortled. 'He's too strong for me, the blighter. If he saw a cat, he'd have me over before you could say, "Bob's your uncle."' Stroking Jack's head, Winnie's voice gave a little wobble. 'No, my days of walking this fine lad are over, I'm afraid, despite what Nicky might think his old nan is capable of.'

Recognising the sorrow in her tone, Lisa patted Winnie's hand, noticing her papery thin skin. She was such a formidable character in spirit; Lisa often had to remind herself that Winnie's feisty nature belied her aging body. 'Anyway, you don't need to. You've got me,' Lisa reminded her.

Jack tilted his head as if listening to their conversation, his wonky eyes peering inquisitively at them both.

'Too right, my lovely, too right. But don't worry if you don't want to use the new-fangled harness thingamajig.'

'Oh no! Honestly, it's great. Jack couldn't wiggle out of it if he tried. Not that he would, of course,' Lisa hastily added, realising the implication of what she had said.

Jack tilted his head at her. *Thank goodness you can't speak*, Lisa thought as she gave him a wink.

'And since you're so good with Jack, I wanted to ask you. Well, I don't want you to think I'm taking advantage.'

Lisa couldn't imagine Winnie ever taking advantage; she owed her more than she knew for all the kindness she had shown her. 'Anything, what is it?'

'Will you come to church with me and Jack a week Sunday?'

Lisa did a double take; had she heard that right? 'You and *Jack*? To church?'

'Yes, there's a pet blessing. You know, my lovely, the service in honour of St Francis of Assisi.'

Lisa really didn't know. 'St Francis of who?'

'Assisi – the patron saint of animals,' Winnie tutted. 'Don't they teach anything in schools nowadays? His feast day's October 4th, mine and Stan's – God rest his soul – anniversary.'

Lisa couldn't help but think her life was getting slightly more obscure by the day, but she certainly wasn't about to let Winnie down. 'Of course, it'll be fun.' *Or possibly a nightmare*, Lisa thought. She wasn't much of a churchgoer. She and Flick had been a couple of times when they were Girl Guides, a venture that was short-lived, as they were asked to leave after Flick smuggled cigarettes in her bedroll and they were found smoking out the back of their tent on camp. Other than that she had attended the odd wedding, a christening and, more recently, her Granny Blake's funeral. She couldn't imagine taking a dog into the quiet confines of a church. Not with a host of other pets around them. 'We'll use the harness; it'll be fine,' Lisa stated, attempting to convince herself as much as Winnie.

'Ah, lovely. I asked my Nicky, but he's busy, and I so wanted to take Jack for a blessing and to show him his dear, old dad's grave. Makes me feel closer to Stan just being there.'

As Winnie wiped a tear from her eye, Lisa swallowed – pleased she had said yes and feeling like this trip to church was going to be even harder than she imagined.

As they changed the subject and embarked on tea and biscuits, Lisa found herself tempted to tell Winnie about her forthcoming date; *not a date, just a cup of coffee! Urghh!* No, she couldn't talk about that. Winnie would get all excited and make more of it than necessary. She wanted to tell her about seeing Flick in Tesco. She needed to tell someone, it was making her head ache holding it all in. But, as she sat there, she wasn't sure how to begin.

She had been pondering it all day, wondering why she hadn't seized her opportunity there and then to tell Felicity how sorry she was. She'd had every opportunity to as they had stood staring at each other, but she hadn't. She didn't like to admit it, but Lisa was beginning to wonder if not facing the issues that were right in front of her was her thing. She had written enough articles about animal behaviour to know that in any given situation your options came down to fight or flight. It seemed her natural instinct was flight. *When the going gets tough, Lisa Blake gets going!* She tried not to pursue the thought, even as visions of her leaving Nathan after the prom, leaving her parents' home, leaving behind her friendship with Flick, leaving Ben, leaving her job and leaving her life in London trailed through her head. How different might her life have been if she ever stopped running?

Not wanting to raise specifics with Winnie, whom she was pretty sure would give an honest opinion, Lisa decided to go for a more general question. 'Winnie, do you have many regrets? In life, I mean ... you know, things you wished you'd done differently.'

'I try not to. Life's too short for all that business.' Noticing the sorrow that flicked across Lisa's face, Winnie continued, 'You know, you can only really have regrets when you die. We make our own peace, my lovely.'

'I guess,' Lisa pondered, processing Winnie's words, 'but what if it's too late to change something? What if you left it too long?'

'Well, you know, you can't take back the passing of time, but until you meet your maker, well, my lovely, there's always time to change.' Winnie spoke slowly, seeming old and wise before she added, 'Unless you're talking about *that* Ben and then you should leave well enough alone. Some things shouldn't be regretted; they are just good fortunes we haven't yet recognised. Lucky escapes we don't yet know we had!'

Lisa almost choked on her custard cream. Yes, she could rely on Winnie for an honest answer. Perhaps she should have told her about her encounter in the men's toilets instead!

On her way home, Lisa drove past the house that Flick had lived in when they were children. It looked so different. There was a people carrier parked out the front and what had been Flick's mum's rose garden had been made into a driveway. Lisa was surprised to find herself saddened that the Forsters no longer appeared to live there. Not that she was going to be brave enough to knock on the door, not today, anyway, but it was just another symbol of the void that had grown between her and her once best friend. Life had moved on. They had all moved on.

Chapter Ten

Felicity sat in her car trying to decide if she was brave enough to go and knock on the Blakes' front door. There had been no sign of Lisa's parents or anybody else for that matter since she had pulled up. There was a van on the driveway, but with the glasses she was in denial about needing tucked in the drawer at home, she couldn't make out what it said on the side. She didn't fancy going over if it meant explaining herself to a workman or causing a scene in front of a stranger. Looking round the car she had an idea and reached into the back to grab Alice's *Dora the Explorer* binoculars. Holding them up to her eyes, Felicity fiddled with the focus until the writing on the van became clear. Even when Swiper popped up, slightly obscuring her view with his annoyingly cheeky face and thumbs up, Felicity could see the words clearly; she swallowed before reading them aloud, 'Lisa Blake – the purrfect pet sitter'. As she stared, motionless, she tried to decide if her pulse was racing with excitement at finally pinning Lisa down, or fear at the prospect of going over and talking to her.

A knock on the car window broke her thoughts and caused Felicity to jump. 'Bugger!' She threw the binoculars into the air and over her shoulder. Attempting to look casual she smiled, but the disgruntled face at the window was not going away. Reluctantly, she pressed to open the window just a couple of inches.

'Harold Martin, neighbourhood watch.' The man's nose was in the gap, as she was sure it was in everybody's business within moments.

Felicity looked into his eyes. His fingers were laced behind his back. Though bent over, he had the poise of an old sergeant major and, worst of all, no intention of leaving without an explanation.

'Felicity Willis, um ...' *Think, Flick, think*. '... twit ... twitch ... TWITCHER!' she lied, hoping desperately that it was the right word for a birdwatcher. *Why the hell didn't I just say 'birdwatcher'?*

'Reeeaaally?' The man elongated the word and glanced into Flick's car.

The car seats, toys and crumbs galore didn't suggest 'twitcher'; Flick was grateful the sun blinds on the back windows obscured his view and hid her binoculars of choice. He was clearly an old busybody. She knew she just had to sound convincing. After all, she hardly looked like she was a burglar casing the scene of her next crime. She was innocently in her car minding her own business, unless you took into account that she was spying on Lisa. But he didn't know that. What could he possibly accuse her of? *Nothing* ... She could blag her way out of this, she was sure.

'So you're a fellow twitcher?'

Felicity sighed. She might have guessed he'd be a twitcher, a man this nosy had to have a fascination with binoculars, telescopes and long-lens cameras.

'And what are you in pursuit of Miss ...?'

'Mrs Willis,' she started confidently, before realising her knowledge of birds was pretty damn limited. *Oh hell!* What was she in pursuit of? *An ex-best friend who had gone AWOL until reappearing in Tesco!* 'The Lesser ...' she began, unsure where the sentence might end, until her mind clicked into gear. 'No, no ...' There was definitely something there, something she had heard on the news at some point. '... I mean the Greater ...'

'Hmmm?' Harold leaned a little closer squinting his accusing eyes.

'I mean ... the Greater Spotted Cuckoo!' Felicity finally blurted, surprised and impressed at her own response.

It appeared Harold was a bit impressed himself. 'In these parts?' He stood up glancing around at the trees before returning his nose to Felicity's window. 'In our little neighbourhood?'

Thank God! 'Yes! It was right there in that tree.' Felicity couldn't believe she had actually managed to convince him she had seen a Greater Spotted Cuckoo; she didn't even know what one looked like. Spurred by his reaction, she found herself eagerly pointing to a tree in Lisa's neighbour's garden. As he swung round to look at it, she instantly wished she had chosen one in the opposite direction.

Harold stood tall. 'Well, the BBC will be here, for sure! It really is quite a find. Great recon there, Mrs Willis; I can't believe he slipped my radar.'

'Oh, the BBC, really?' Felicity shrunk in her seat. It had taken all her courage to drive to Lisa's. She had pondered actually getting out of the car for about fifteen minutes before she had fathomed out what the writing said on the van and confirmed Lisa was there, and now, now there was Harold and his hopes of the BBC to deal with. Her visit was feeling increasingly doomed. Perhaps it was a stupid idea. What good did revisiting the past do? Except, if she was honest, Felicity knew a small part of her had always remained in the past. Not wanting to move on without Lisa.

Trying to decide if she was brave enough to move Harold on and still go over to Lisa's door, Flick groaned and looked up. But, as she glanced at Lisa's house, she saw her getting into the van and heading out of the driveway. Aware Harold was still talking about the non-existent cuckoo and had even moved on to sharing his hopes of meeting Bill Oddie, Felicity groaned. She couldn't believe she had missed her opportunity again. Angry at herself and the meddling man still at her window, she gave him a sharp look. 'Too late, the cuckoo has flown!' she scolded. With that she closed her window and started her car. As Harold banged his hand on the roof, Felicity sped off, leaving him gesticulating in the road behind her. Though she was unsure what she was going to do when she caught up with Lisa, Felicity suddenly felt full of determination not to let the opportunity to speak to her slip by again. The time had come. Lisa was going to have to face her. The years of wondering were over. 'Lisa Blake, you will bloody well talk to me.' Felicity had a vision of herself looking like Cruella de Vil in *101 Dalmatians*, driving like a mad woman, screeching round corners, foot pressed firmly to the floor. Had she known she would be stopping sharply outside the Chinese takeaway just two roads away, Felicity wouldn't have followed in quite such hot pursuit. As it was, the screechingly abrupt halt she came to directly behind Lisa's van meant she missed piling into it by barely an inch.

Thankfully, Lisa didn't notice. As much as Flick wanted to talk to Lisa, she didn't think the Chinese takeaway was the place to do it. If Lisa were getting food, then surely she would be taking it back home. Slinking down so as not to be seen, Flick waited, shifting restlessly in her seat. She'd never known anyone take so long to collect a takeaway before. This was turning into quite the stake out. As her phone beeped, signalling a message, Felicity jumped. Deciding she wasn't cut out to be a detective – her nerves would never allow it – she leaned across, took out her phone and read her message. It was from Pete: We love you, Flick.

Glad he couldn't see what she was doing, Felicity smiled

and sent him a message back saying she loved him. She knew he was worried about her. Since he saw her fall apart over her mum's death, he hated anything upsetting her. She could understand his concern, but some things just had to be done and she really wasn't as fragile as he thought. Besides, she wouldn't forgive herself if she had it within her grasp to speak to Lisa and she let it slip. When Lisa finally came out clutching a white, plastic takeaway bag, Felicity took a breath, watched her drive away, counted slowly to five and started her engine. *OK, this is going to happen!*

Lisa went inside the house and put her takeaway on the side. It probably wasn't the wisest thing to eat after an upset stomach, but she was now feeling so hungry she didn't care. Besides, it had been good to have a chat with – or rather at – Mr Chung, especially as she felt she could divulge details to him she wouldn't want to worry Winnie with. The last twenty-four hours had been so bizarre: seeing Felicity in the supermarket, Ben's public declaration that he was single, becoming 'friends' with Nathan on Facebook, meeting her leather-clad man in the men's toilets, arranging a date – *Oh God*, she'd almost forgotten that horror – and Flick's house looking so different. All she really wanted to do now was eat her Chinese and hibernate under a duvet until life became less complicated.

A ring on the doorbell halted her midway through peeling back the lid of her chicken chow mein. Lisa groaned and went to take a peek out of the lounge window in the hope it would be someone she could ignore. Even before moving the bright, white, floral net curtain, she could see an Espace parked on the driveway; *the cheek!* Attempting to get a better look at who was not only intent on disturbing her peace but also taking liberties with her driveway, she pulled the curtain back a little further and looked towards the door. She couldn't believe her eyes. It was Felicity. Right there. Parked on her driveway and ringing her bell!

Lisa ran to the kitchen. Not knowing what to do with herself she stood at the sink, sat at the table and stood up again. Her heart was pounding. She pushed her fingers through her long blonde hair and remembered that it still had the caught-in-the-storm look of earlier. *Why is fate so cruel?* The doorbell rang again, making her jump even though she had been anticipating it. Lisa wondered what to do. She really wanted to speak to Felicity; she wanted to make things right with her. She knew that now. But she wanted to do it properly, not in a caught-off-guard, muddled mess. She wasn't ready. She had no sensible reasons to give for why she had lost contact with her and no words to convey how much she really missed her.

'Lisa, I know you're in there. Please, let me in.' Felicity's voice echoed through the empty hallway as she called through the letterbox.

Lisa swallowed. *Oh God!* 'Hang on,' her pitch sounded too high and forced. She didn't know if Felicity could hear her, but she knew she had no choice but to answer. If she didn't open the door now, she might never get the opportunity to speak to Felicity again. Her knees felt weak and her legs uncooperative as she walked along the hallway to the door. Preparing to open it, she attempted a smile, but the anxiety she felt welling inside made her mouth too taut. At the sight of Felicity dressed normally and looking so much more like the Flick she remembered, Lisa let out a breath and desperately wanted to hug her. Convinced it wouldn't be welcome she held back. She had so much she wanted to say, but she didn't know where to begin. She knew it should have been her turning up at Flick's house.

She owed her an explanation and an apology that probably would never be enough for losing contact as the years had slipped by. With Winnie's words churning in her mind – *'you can't take back the passing of time, but until you meet your maker... there's always time to change'* – she knew she had to seize this opportunity.

Nerves getting the better of her, she went into an obscurely formal mode, in which she noticed she sounded too much like her own mother, and found herself inviting Flick into the kitchen.

Felicity had been to Lisa's house so many times in the past. She had stayed over so often it was like her second home when they were younger. As she followed Lisa slowly down the hallway, she was overwhelmed by how weird it felt to be back inside the Blakes' house and how odd it was that it had barely changed. Even the hint of the smell of the takeaway couldn't mask the distinctive vanilla-scented potpourri she remembered so well. The paintwork remained pristine and the floor was as highly polished as ever. How could it be that the Blakes' world had remained so unscathed by time and life? It was very different to the chaos of her own coat-strewn and shoe-scattered hallway, and she was pretty sure if her mum were still alive, she wouldn't want to see her old house any other way.

The kitchen door drawing closer, Felicity thought of Pete and her children; they were her life now. Why did the past matter so much? She had moved on. She had a whole life beyond Lisa Blake now. She knew Pete couldn't understand why she couldn't just let it go. Entering the kitchen, she was beginning to question that point herself. *Why didn't I just listen to him?*

'Can I get you something: tea, coffee, water?' Lisa asked.

Felicity could hear the tension in Lisa's voice and swallowed, hoping her own words would come out more evenly. 'Water will be fine, thanks.' She walked over and pulled out a chair from the table, which scraped too loudly against the floor. The formality felt obscure in a place where she had once helped herself to drinks and Club biscuits from the fridge, and snuck whisky from the bottle Lisa's dad kept at the back of the tea cupboard.

Lisa ran the tap and placed two glasses of water on the table before sitting down. Felicity let out a breath and felt a calm resolve come over her. Finally, she was going to speak to Lisa. Finally, there would be closure. And then she knew. That was it. That was what she needed. Felicity had always envied Nathan Baker for getting his proper goodbye. People had understood why it was that he was devastated when Lisa left. Everybody had spoken about how hard it was for him, while Flick had been told not to worry, that she and Lisa would always be the best of friends. As time went by, hardly anybody had noticed Lisa slipping from her life; hardly anybody realised Flick had lost a part of herself. Felicity needed her goodbye, the one she deserved, and she needed closure. Straightening her back, she finally knew she would get it. In fact, she wasn't going to leave until she did.

As Lisa joined her at the table, Flick decided to just lay her feelings out. She had nothing to lose by telling Lisa how she felt. She wanted her to know how hurt she had been at all of those ignored calls and unanswered messages, how much she had needed her over the years, and how unfair it was that she never got her goodbye. She knew Lisa probably wouldn't care, it was all a long time ago now, but she just wanted – needed even – to say it. Taking a deep breath she began, 'Lisa, I—'

'Flick, I am so sorry I lost contact with you. I'm so, so

sorry.' Lisa's words burst out in a flood of emotion followed by a torrent of tears that Felicity joined in with.

Before either of them had time to process the enormity of the situation, or what should have been said, their arms were round each other and the years they had spent apart slipped away.

Chapter Eleven

They each welcomed the hit of caffeine as the two once-best friends sat with steaming mugs of coffee in hand, both a little shocked to find themselves red eyed, sitting together in Lisa's mum's kitchen. Lisa wished there was something stronger in the house, even the cooking sherry she had downed the previous night would have been welcome. There was so much to catch up on and so much to be explained, they hardly knew where to begin. At first they reminisced; it was safe ground, sticking to the past they had shared. They laughed together, understanding jokes from the past only they knew and, probably, that only they would have ever found funny.

As Lisa poured them a second coffee, she decided she felt brave enough to broach their first reunion. More than anything she wanted to apologise for running from Tesco the way she had, leaving Flick when she seemed to be in some kind of trouble.

Felicity giggled. 'Oh, Lisa, I wasn't, and I'm not, in any sort of trouble. I just have a toddler.'

Lisa looked at her discombobulated, trying to fathom the connection and to take in the fact Felicity had a child.

'Seriously, getting to the supermarket at all is a miracle sometimes, going covered in sick when I really wanted to be at home snuggled up with Pete is—'

'Pete Willis!' Lisa gestured for Flick to continue, not wanting to reveal she had spent too long trying to remember Pete's surname during her Facebook snooping session.

'Yes, you remember. I told you about him. I met him the second summer after you left. He was an apprentice, working with his dad, landscaping Mum's garden.'

Lisa nodded silently without actually remembering the details.

'Anyway, going to the supermarket covered in sick, it's not something I normally do, but when needs must, well … well, it's just an occupational hazard.'

Lisa smiled, overwhelmed by the knowledge Felicity was married and still processing the fact she had a child. 'So tell me … tell me about your toddler.'

'Oh, there's not just Fred, though he's a handful enough. There's four of them.'

'Four!' Lisa couldn't take it in. *Four! Married with four children!* If everything else wasn't enough to show how long it had been since they were last together, the thought of Flick with four children was. Felicity had a whole life. *A whole Lisaless life.* Lisa wondered how her own life would have differed if she had never gone away. Would she and Nathan Baker have a whole little tribe to call their own? Lisa didn't want to feel any ill will towards Flick and attempted to rub away the pang of jealousy she could feel forming at the pit of her stomach. *Married with four children.*

'Megan's just turned eight – she's my feisty one in lots of ways, but she can be sensitive too. Alice is six and my little helper – she wants to be a doctor. Callum is my little pumpkin – with his daddy's red hair and good looks, and he's just started school; and Fred, well, he's my baby – he'll be two next week.'

'Wow!' Lisa didn't know what else to say.

'You'll have to meet them. I really want you to meet them.'

'Of course.' Lisa felt terrified at the thought of meeting them and terrible for not having met them before. After all the promises she and Flick had made to each other as they had grown up, she hadn't been there. Her phone calls had become fewer and fewer over the years, and her trips home had become so fleeting that visiting Felicity didn't feature – no time to stop when she had Ben and her life in London to get back to.

Lisa sipped her coffee before continuing. 'And your mum, how has she taken to you having four? Does she love being a granny?' Lisa was trying to collate things in her head. She knew Flick's mum hadn't wanted Felicity to have children young. A single parent at the age of eighteen herself, she had always made it clear to Flick and Lisa, when she could, that she expected girls of their generation to do more, to want more. This stance being one of the few things they had in common, they were words Lisa's own mum had often echoed too.

'Oh, Lisa, you don't know, do you?'

Lisa sat silently, listening, struggling to take in Felicity's words as she told her about her mum's accident. When she finished Lisa put her arms around her and they sobbed together for the second time that evening until their tears ran dry.

'Flick, if I had known—'

'It's OK, really, I didn't try to tell you.'

'Oh—'

'I mean it was about four years after I'd last heard from you. I needed you, really needed you, you were the closest thing I had to a sister, but …'

Lisa swallowed.

'But Alice was a baby, Megan was heartbroken and I, well, I fell apart.' Felicity wiped her eyes.

'Of course you did.' Lisa looked at the box of tissues they had already emptied, stood and returned to the table with the kitchen roll. She was in shock, trying to come to terms with the news herself. Flick falling apart was completely understandable. It had been years since Lisa had seen Mrs F and yet the thought that she would never see her again saddened her.

'Mum loved my girls, you know.' Flick smiled, 'Of course, she was shocked and cross to start with, when she found out I was pregnant – you know how she never wanted that for me, she didn't want me to struggle the way she had – but, once she saw I was happy and Pete wasn't going anywhere, things changed. In some ways it was like Megan coming gave us something in common. At my scan ...' Felicity wiped a tear that trailed down her face.

Lisa passed her a wad of kitchen roll.

'When Megan appeared on the screen, my mum reached out and squeezed my hand. She didn't say anything; she didn't have to. I could feel it, you know.'

Lisa didn't know. All she had seen at her own scan, barely six months ago, was a dark void where the flicker of a little life had once been, but she nodded silently.

'It was then ... then I knew everything would be OK. My baby was strong and wiggly, and Mum and Pete were by my side. It was like it made us a family, more than we had ever been.'

'Oh, Flick, I'm so glad they were there for you.' Lisa blinked, attempting to push away the tears she could feel forming and the painful memory of sitting in the scanning room alone.

'And they adored each other, Megan and Mum.' Felicity told Lisa how she knew and took comfort in the fact her mum had loved being a nana. 'Funny, isn't it? If I hadn't had Megan when I did, Mum might never have been a grandparent. My life would have taken a different path.'

'Sometimes things happen for a reason.' The words slipped out automatically, it wasn't a sentiment Lisa held much faith in, but it felt like something Winnie might say and she always seemed to know the right thing to say. Lisa couldn't believe how much Felicity's life had moved on – how much she had coped with in her absence.

'I guess.' Felicity took a breath and smiled. 'Sorry, I've been talking for so long. What about you? What have you been up to these past years, Lisa Blake?'

Lisa thought about her life, searching for something to say. She attempted to smile.

'Travelling. Backpacking. Europe at first. Then, as you know, I met Ben who was going to India, and I joined him. It was a bit of a culture shock; the heat, the number of people, the noise and the intensity.' Lisa remembered that her call to Felicity on her twenty-first birthday had been from Delhi, Ben was rushing her as he wanted to explore Paharganj, the main bazaar next to the railway station. 'Eventually, we returned to Europe. We took seasonal work and travelled together for a couple of years, until just before my twenty-third birthday when we moved to London, rented a flat, got jobs. After that—'

A ring at the doorbell interrupted her. As much as Lisa was relieved not to have to go into any more depth about her life in London, she didn't entirely want the moment to end. It was as if moving would shatter it all. She and Flick were talking. Actually talking. As the doorbell rang again, Flick and Lisa sat staring at each other. There was still so much to say, a lot yet to be explained, but it was a start. The two of them together again, sitting back at Lisa's mum's kitchen table like they had so many times before. The doorbell rang once more. Reluctantly, Lisa stood.

As she walked down the hallway, she wondered who it might be and began to panic at the thought it might be Nathan Baker. Looking at her door as if it had become a portal to the past she held her breath. *Surely not!* Everybody knew Facebook friend requests weren't actual, real-life friend requests, didn't they? He wouldn't just turn up at her parents' home the way Flick had, *would he?* Preparing herself, Lisa opened the door, but as she took in the sight before her she did a double take.

'What the …' It seemed her day, and life in general, could indeed get more surreal!

Felicity heard the shock in Lisa's voice and a commotion beyond the door.

'Flick! Flick!'

Alarmed by the urgency in Lisa's voice, Felicity hurried to the door, stopping in her tracks and swallowing hard when she saw Lisa standing open mouthed in front of Harold Martin, Chris Packham and a cameraman who, judging by the large van parked across the driveway beyond them, was from the BBC.

Felicity's cheeks turned crimson as all eyes turned to her. She wrung her hands and offered a small smile before clearing her throat. 'So, not Bill Oddie after all then.'

Chapter Twelve

Lisa stood, dripping wet, while Toby the Newfoundland settled into a steady swimming pace. He had made such a splash as he thundered in after his canvas training dummy that Lisa was surprised there was any water left in the pool. She needed to get some sensible waterproof gear or at least wear shorts so she could dry off with a towel. As it was, her wet jeans clung to her legs, and she was getting increasingly cold as the minutes passed. It was fun watching Toby swim though; he loved it. His huge, webbed feet and thick rudder of a tail made him appear to power effortlessly through the water. For a big boy he was pretty speedy too. He had more strength and stamina than Lisa, whose arm ached just from throwing the sodden dummy each time he returned with the soggy offering, dropping it expectantly at her feet ready to be thrown again.

Watching Lisa, the pool owner stepped from behind her counter. 'You can go in with him if you like.'

Lisa turned to look at the overly optimistic woman now standing beside her and then glanced back down at the water. Despite the brush she had given Toby before they set off – extricating enough fur to make Toby a mini-me – the water was thick with floating, black hair. Lisa imagined it sticking to her and brushing past her legs like seaweed. 'I'm not really dressed for it today,' she stated, relieved that she had worn her jeans.

'Ah, next time then. They love it you know, swimming with you. Such gentle giants these Newfs.'

Lisa couldn't argue with that; despite the moulting that

always meant a complete hoover out of her van, the drool, which, admittedly, wasn't as bad as she had expected, and his sheer size, Toby was a sweetie – all 135lbs of him. 'Yes, I'll have to get a swimsuit … or something.' *Something that will cover me from head to foot*, Lisa thought.

'Babs will be here soon. She loves a swim with hers. She's an expert, been training Newfs for years. You should ask her what's best.'

As if on cue the door opened and a woman flanked by two Newfoundlands strode in.

'Babs, look, we have a Newf newbie. I was just telling …' The woman paused and looked at Lisa's T-shirt. '… Lisa, here, that you love a swim with your boys. Lisa wants to get in with Toby, but isn't dressed for it today.'

Lisa couldn't help but feel that 'Lisa wants to get in with Toby' was a bit of an over statement, but she smiled nevertheless and played along, greeting Babs and muttering about how silly she felt for wearing jeans.

Taking in the sight of Babs as she berated and mocked her for the error of her wardrobe choice, Lisa imagined she was the type of person who spent half her life outside and the other half knocking back red wine in front of a roaring fire built from logs she had split herself. She had dishevelled, curly, black hair, ruddy cheeks, a rotund figure and what could only be described as a hearty laugh. She was the epitome of the saying that owners look like their dogs.

Continuing her façade of enthusiasm, Lisa bent to give Toby a pat before tossing his toy back into the water. 'Next time, Toby, next time.'

'There's nothing better you know. Hold on, I'll show you.' Babs paused while she released her dogs and started to wiggle out of her jeans and flannelette shirt.

Unsure where to look, Lisa turned her full attention to the water.

'You need one of these,' Babs finally announced, patting her sides and stomach as she revealed a shorty wetsuit.

Glancing round, Lisa couldn't help but wonder how Babs had poured herself into it. The neoprene was doing its best to keep everything in place, but what couldn't be contained was bursting out wherever possible. Lisa wasn't sure how to respond.

'Short enough that you can move easily,' Babs said, doing a few stretches to illustrate the point, 'super-flex seams to keep everything in,' she continued, pulling at a seam that was almost certainly already flexing further than the manufacturer intended, 'and titanium lining over neoprene to keep body heat in and the chill out. Bloody marvellous invention!'

Lisa smiled, trying not to imagine Babs as a character from a *French and Saunders* sketch. 'It looks great; I'll have to get one.'

'Well, I'm sure I've got an old one at home. Too small for me now. I'll bring it along next week. You can give it a whirl.'

'Oh no, honestly, it's fine …' Lisa still wasn't entirely sure she wanted to get in the murky, hair-ridden water with Toby, let alone doing it in Babs' cast-off shorty wetsuit. It was a generous offer, but some things, especially those that clung in all the wrong places, shouldn't be shared.

'But you must!'

'No, really—'

'But you must!'

'No—'

'But—'

'Honestly.' Lisa put her hand up before Babs could speak again. 'You'll see; I'll have my own by next week.'

'Oh, great, we can get in together.'
Oh bugger!

Hours later, Lisa sat waiting for Dom while pondering how she might get herself out of buying a wetsuit without borrowing one from Babs. She had walked Jack and settled him into the van. Taking him with her made meeting Dom feel more casual, like the other times they had met, and meant she had the perfect excuse to leave should she need it. Lisa watched several motorbikes come and go, but couldn't see Dom's. She wondered if he drove a car too and realised she actually knew nothing about him. Not for the first time, the title music to *Crimewatch* began to play in her head. Before she terrified herself by letting her imagination get the better of her, she decided to go and get a hot drink, the plan being that if Dom hadn't appeared by the time she had finished it she would go. A thought that, she was surprised to note, made her feel a bit disappointed. Despite all her misgivings about the date – *it's not a date* – she knew her ego needed the boost.

As she wandered towards the kiosk she stopped. She could hear an announcement being made over the tannoy – and not just the normal 'number eight, your order is ready' or 'thirteen, bacon and egg roll' type announcement. They were calling a name. At first she couldn't catch it, but then she realised it was her name! She listened more intently and crossed her fleece over her name emblazoned T-shirt, worn as another ploy to help her nerves and remove the date pressure. She couldn't believe it; they were definitely saying her name. Feeling heat rise in her cheeks, she reached the counter of the kiosk. The man serving looked at her expectantly.

Lisa kept her voice hushed and attempted to be discreet. 'I'm Lisa Blake.'

'Pardon?' The man frowned, tipping his head, trying to hear her the way Jack sometimes did.

'I'm Lisa Blake.'

'Eggs and bacon?' the man asked.

'I'm Lisa Blake,' she repeated more firmly.

'What, luv?'

'I'M LISA BLAKE!' Lisa shouted in exasperation opening her fleece in a flasher fashion to reveal the name on her T-shirt.

The man's eyes goggled. 'Whey hey, so you are,' he said laughing, before regaining his composure and noticing Lisa's stern expression. 'Oh, of course. Right. Hold on.' He walked over to the phone and returned with a notepad. 'It's a message from Dom,' he began. '"Sorry, I can't make it. I've been called away on an emergency. I never meant to leave you stranded and will be in touch soon. So don't say your goodbyes and hold on to that, Rose."' The man looked up from the pad and passed her the piece of paper that also had a number on it. With a confused expression, he added, 'Whatever that means.'

Lisa felt completely humiliated. Not only had she been stood up, the fact she had shouted her name meant she had drawn attention to herself; all eyes were on her. And to top it all, Dom had left a stupid cryptic message that she suspected had something to do with the film *Titanic*, if her memory served her correctly. She felt like a fool. She thanked the man, spun on the heels of her walking boots and tried desperately not to make eye contact with any of the onlookers as she began to stride back to her van. *Called away on an emergency, indeed; motorbike needs a polish, does it?*

'But wait, there's more,' the man called after her.

'It's OK,' Lisa called back, having no intention of

returning to the kiosk. She couldn't believe it; she wasn't sure she had ever felt so embarrassed – stood up and publicly humiliated in one. She started ranting to herself, 'Honestly, why make the date if he wasn't going to keep it? Not that it probably ever was a date – oh, Lisa Blake, you are such a fool!' But as she reached her van she heard the man's voice over the tannoy once more.

'This is for you, Lisa Blake.'

Lisa stood glued to the spot dreading what on earth was coming next. But as Celine Dion's voice burst out over the tannoy with the theme to *Titanic*, she couldn't help but smile.

Chapter Thirteen

On the journey to return Jack, Lisa decided not to mention Dom to Winnie. There was nothing to report really and she didn't want Winnie to get her hopes up – should she think she was moving on from Ben – or to worry about her should she fear Dom's intentions; *dum, dum de dum, da de dum, bloody Crimewatch!* No, until she knew more about him or if they would meet again – she wasn't sure she would ever use the number he had left her – there was no point making more of it than there really was.

She could, she thought, mention Nathan Baker. She had received a couple of messages from him that she hadn't yet decided how to answer. He had obviously been looking through her Facebook pictures too – not that she had many – as she had received notifications to tell her he liked them. She found it very odd, until she reminded herself that she had also snooped through his pictures, albeit with the decency not to alert him to the fact by liking them. She knew she would have to speak to him at some point. She was the one who had instigated the contact with her drunken friend request after all and delaying just meant that thoughts of Nathan were occupying her mind, more than she had allowed in a very long time. But she just didn't know what to say. She wondered if Winnie would help her with that. *What do you say to the man who was your teenage crush, your first kiss, your first love and the one you let get away, even though you were still in love with him? Ugh, why talk about what ifs?* Lisa decided to focus on reality, things that had actually happened; her rekindled friendship with Felicity, now that was progress. That was moving on with life more than dates that didn't happen and uncensored thoughts of Nathan Baker.

After the BBC debacle, and offering Chris Packham warmed up Chinese takeaway – an offer he vehemently declined – and a drink to ease his disappointment over the non-existent Greater Spotted Cuckoo, Lisa and Felicity had swapped numbers, and parted over a long hug and the agreement to meet again before too long. Since then, they had shared texts and even the odd phone call in which Felicity had again said how nice it would be to introduce Lisa to Pete and her children.

Lisa couldn't deny she was more than a little intrigued to see Pete – the man Flick had made a life with. Growing up, they had both raided *Smash Hits* magazine for posters of the cast of *Friends*. Lisa loved Ross, but Flick was a staunch Joey fan. Nathan pretended not to be interested in the show, but readily took posters of Rachel off their hands. Lisa wondered if Pete would look like Matt LeBlanc. But she was nervous about meeting Flick's family too. Flick being happily married with four children – *four* – was a huge concept to comprehend. For the moment, Lisa was enjoying having Felicity back. She didn't want to move too fast, and push herself or their fragile 'friendship' too far, too soon.

Winnie was on her second cup of tea and third ginger nut biscuit by the time Lisa had finished relating everything; unable to stop while in the full flow of sharing it all, Lisa had told Winnie how she and Felicity had been the best of friends, and how over the years, and once she met Ben, they had lost contact. She spoke about seeing Flick at the supermarket and her evening spent looking through old photographs – minus the drunken Facebooking. Finally she spoke about Flick turning up at her house and the two of them talking for hours, and her hopes for the future of their friendship – omitting the unexpected visit from the BBC.

'So, you see, we are talking again and if you hadn't told me that until we die there's always time to change – or whatever the nice way you said it was – I might never have been brave enough.'

As she stopped talking, Lisa took a breath and noticed how silent the room seemed. She had become louder and more animated as she had gone on while Winnie sat, taking it all in, offering nothing more than the occasional nod. It was only now it was all out that Lisa realised how much she had gone on. 'Winnie, I'm sorry, I—'

'Well, now …'

Lisa stopped, wondering what Winnie was going to say. She felt like she had well and truly overstepped the client-pet-sitter boundary of their relationship – even if Winnie was a client with custard cream benefits.

'Well …'

Lisa couldn't decipher the look on Winnie's face; she seemed at a loss for words, a state Lisa wasn't sure she had ever seen her in before. 'Oh, Winnie, I—'

'Well, I think we are going to need more tea.'

Lisa released her anxiety in a giggle, and lifted the knitted tea cosy, automatically placing her hand on the side of the lukewarm pot, the way Winnie often did. 'Sorry, I really did go on, didn't I? I'll make us a fresh one.'

To Lisa's surprise, Winnie didn't protest. Instead, she gave directions to where Lisa could find everything, as if she hadn't seen Winnie make the tea many times before. With a new pot brewed and two fresh cups poured, Winnie wiggled herself to the back of her seat, sitting up more fully. Lisa felt her tummy twist.

'Well, my lovely, I have to say, that explains a lot.'

Lisa frowned. She didn't know what she had expected Winnie to say, but she knew it wasn't that. She wasn't sure what she was referring to; she certainly didn't feel like she had 'explained' a great deal. She had gone on a lot, blurted it all out, but what it 'explained' she really didn't know. 'Does it?'

'Yes. Don't you see?'

'See what?'

'That you, my lovely, forgot about the things that were important to you. You lost yourself in your relationship with *that* Ben and you lost contact with those who loved you most.' With that Winnie sat back decisively.

'But ...' Lisa thought about her fleeting visits to her parents, the fact that she hadn't made it to her brother's going-away party, that she never saw her Granny Blake in her final year, and how she had let Flick slip from her life. 'But I had a life with Ben; I didn't lose myself. I mean it wasn't just about him, I ...'

Winnie raised her eyebrows. 'So you've got other friends from London, built new friendships since you've been with him?'

Lisa pictured her work colleagues from London and those she considered friends from Ben's circle; she and Ben had been out with them, had a laugh and shared drinks. But now she thought about it, the realisation hit that not one of them had called or texted her to check she was OK, not when she was off sick and not since she had returned home. She didn't know what saddened her most, that thought or the fact she hadn't missed them. 'Well, not exactly.' *There's you, Mr Chung ...*

Winnie raised her eyebrows.

A moment passed in silence while they each sipped their tea and took a biscuit from the barrel, more out of habit than the desire to eat them. Lisa nibbled at her custard cream.

'But you, my lovely, are a lucky one; you have a second chance. Some people don't realise until it's too late. Heaven knows I made Stan my world, and now he's gone and my own son doesn't want a bar of me. Thinks I took his dad's side over his, you see. Robert needed money for his business, and his dad said no; Stan wasn't one for throwing good money after bad. All I could do was stand by and watch. I had nothing of my own to give. And by God, they battled over it. Broke my heart it did and now ... well, now, I've lost both of them.'

'Oh, Winnie, you have me, Nicky ... and Jack.' Lisa hoped she was saying the right things; she had always thought of Winnie as someone who had life sorted, who had all the answers.

'Ah well—'

Remembering Winnie's own words, Lisa interrupted, 'But you said ... you said Winnie, until you die, there is always time to change ... Stan has gone ...' Lisa paused to gauge Winnie's expression as she didn't want to upset her. '... but you are here; you're still alive. It's not too late for you to sort things out with your son.'

Winnie chortled. 'When I first met you, you wouldn't say boo to a goose, and now look at you all feisty.'

Lisa laughed. 'I've had a good teacher.'

Chapter Fourteen

While its name made it sound like a magazine you would find in the fetish section on a top shelf in the corner shop, Wild, Wet and Windy's website insisted it was 'the best one-stop wetsuit shop on the south coast'. As much as Lisa didn't relish the thought of wetsuit shopping, she was in no doubt that purchasing one before her next swimming session with Toby was preferable to slipping on the previously used offering from Babs. Passing a row of shops she took the right turn dictated by her phone and pulled over in front of Wild, Wet and Windy, next to a pale-blue-and-cream, split-screen Volkswagen camper van, *of course*. Lisa took a breath. She tried to remember if she had learnt any surfer language that would stand her in good stead from her years of watching *Neighbours* with Flick. *Why didn't they surf more? They lived in Australia, for goodness' sake!*

The black sun awnings that hung over the large shop windows had the words 'Quick Silver, Rip Curl and Reef' written across them. *Oh Lord!* Lisa already felt out of her depth, and even the words had more energy implicit within them than she did. To her right there was a large display of canoes and kayaks – elaborately decorated with flashes of bright colours and flames – and the seats outside the shop windows were a trendy arrangement of wire cubes filled with beach pebbles, topped with driftwood benches. Lisa bit her lip and wondered if slipping into Babs' used wetsuit might be the easier option after all. She didn't want to be laughed out of the shop if she confessed all she wanted was a wetsuit for swimming in a heated pool, with a slightly slobbery Newfoundland who erred on the lazy side of life.

Her memories of *Neighbours* being no use, she tried to remember what Babs had said she should go for. Engaging in an in-depth conversation with someone whom she assumed would be a surfer-type sales assistant wasn't something she particularly wanted to do anyway. Maybe if she got the facts straight in her head she would be able to just pick one up off the rail – it had to be that simple, didn't it? *They need never know I'm a complete wetsuit novice.*

Deciding that walking in and looking like she knew what she was doing was the way forward, Lisa got out of her van and slammed the door. Reminding herself that going through with this meant she wouldn't have to face borrowing a wetsuit from Babs, she took a breath and reached for the door handle. Noticing the word 'Animal' written on the blind she smiled; *ha*, maybe she wasn't going to feel so out of place after all!

As she walked in Lisa did a double take. The shop was much larger on the inside than the outside had led her to believe and, on first glance, there wasn't a wetsuit in sight. *Bugger!* She began to wander around, attempting to look as if she knew exactly what she was after and where to find it. The shop was much more stylish than she had imagined too. Not in the way of the shops she frequented in London, of course, the ones where you were paying for the floor space as much as the garments, and where they tried so hard to impress that everything about them – from the highly polished floor to the thoroughly tailored serving staff – shone. But, nevertheless, Wild, Wet and Windy had style. It was evident in the hard wooden floors, inlayed with checker-plate metal; brown leather sofas placed to allow comfort while pondering which of the many trainers, hiking boots or sandals – despite the season – suited your sporting or leisure needs; and the carefully arranged displays in front of scenes of the great outdoors. This was a shop that took itself and its sports seriously.

Lisa was fascinated. The array of equipment for almost every outdoor sporting eventuality was quite something. She looked at the skateboards and helmets; the idea had always appealed but she and Flick had skipped the skateboarding phase in favour of rollerblades. An image of them giggling and attempting to glide, while mostly falling over, through the high street with a Sony Discman each clipped to their hips sprung to mind and made her smile.

'You OK there?'

Lisa jumped and turned to see the young male sales assistant standing beside her. He smiled as her cheeks inexplicably turned red.

'No!'

'You're not OK?' He raised his eyebrows.

'I mean, yes. Sorry, I thought you asked if I wanted anything.' Lisa grimaced.

'And do you?'

'Do I?'

'Want anything? Something I can help you with, maybe?'

The man, in his early twenties, was perfectly nice, friendly and helpful, not intimidating at all, but somehow the words 'I am after a wetsuit for swimming with a dog' didn't want to pass her lips. 'I just need ...' Lisa gazed round the shop. 'Um, one of these,' she stated, striding towards a display of woolly hats.

'Ah, well we have plenty of choice here. Did you want a beanie, headband, bobble beanie?'

'Bobble beanie?' Lisa laughed.

'They're very popular.' The man smiled, passing Lisa a hat that was striped in colours reminding her of Neapolitan ice cream, topped with a large, pink bobble. She slipped it on.

Oh wow! Lisa was surprised by how soft and warm it felt. A quick glance in the mirror confirmed it didn't look too bad either; not compared to the pom-pom hats her Granny Blake had knitted her when she was younger. The autumn was off to a mild, damp start, but she could imagine that having such a warm, cosy hat when the weather turned would actually be a good idea with her new profession.

Fifteen minutes later Lisa was standing by the till paying for the bobble beanie, a scarf and a pair of mittens, all in matching colours. Matt, as she had learnt the sales assistant's name was, certainly knew how to up sell. If it wasn't for her bank balance, and the fact she still had a wetsuit to find and purchase, she would easily have been adding a pair of waterproof boots and thermal socks too. Pleased with her stash she took her bag and smiled.

'Thanks, Matt.'

'No problem, I hope they keep you warm.'

'I'm sure they'll be a godsend. I'm a dog walker, out in all weathers,' Lisa responded easily.

'A dog walker. How funny! You don't swim with them too, do you? We had one in last week after a wetsuit.'

Lisa stopped. 'It's funny you should say that, Matt.'

As Matt led Lisa up a flight of metal, checker-plate stairs, she couldn't help but notice the intense smell of rubber and the large display of Sex Wax that lined the wall. Recalling her earlier fetish thoughts relating to Wild, Wet and Windy she attempted to stifle a giggle and coughed.

'It's strong, isn't it, but you get used to it. I'm pretty immune to the smell myself.'

'Oh, yes,' Lisa responded, before doing a double take as they reached the top of the stairs and a room with a large array of wetsuits in a variety of styles and sizes.

'Shall I leave you to have a look around?' Matt asked.

'Oh, sure.'

Lisa tried hard to remember what it was Babs had said she needed. Matt busied himself behind a desk adjacent to the large changing room, which looked somewhat like an après-ski lodge, with a sixty-inch LED television on the wall showing extreme action shots, and two more brown, leather sofas for those waiting for cubicles. Through an archway beyond, Lisa could see a display of bodyboards and surfboards. Grateful she didn't need one of those, because she wouldn't know where to start, she turned her attention back to the wetsuit room.

She walked between the displays and noticed a whole section dedicated to dry gear for kayaking. She knew she needed some for dog walking in the wet weather and picked up a jacket.

'That's not a wetsuit,' Matt called across.

Lisa laughed, realising he was teasing her. 'Thanks, Matt, even I, a wetsuit novice, know that.'

'Ah, so you are a novice.' He grinned. 'Would you like some help then?'

With Matt's guidance – wetsuits seemed to be his mastermind subject – Lisa was soon in a section of 'smooth skin' wetsuits, apparently so the dog's claws didn't snag the material so easily, looking for the suit that would allow the 'greatest flexibility' for swimming. Lisa felt Matt was being over optimistic about the extent of actual swimming she intended to do with Toby, but happily played along, taking three wetsuits to the changing room.

Wondering how on earth Babs managed, Lisa heaved and wiggled her size twelve figure into the first, her favourite because it had a purple trim – wetsuits were not Lisa's mastermind subject. She wanted to get a better view of what she looked like. It wasn't that Toby would particularly care how she looked, it was just that personal pride wouldn't allow her to look like a hippopotamus in public. The only way to obtain a better view was to open the curtain of the cubicle and stand further back from the surfboard shaped mirror. Deciding it was better to embarrass herself now in front of Matt, who she would never see again, than everybody at Toby's swimming class, who she would have to see on a regular basis, she pushed back the curtain.

Taking in the now clearer view of herself, she screwed up her face and squinted. *Hmmm.* Well, it wasn't exactly unflattering, it did a bit of squashing here and there and she might have to stay off the Dr Oetker, but otherwise it wasn't too bad.

'So this is where you've been hiding!'

'Bloody hell!' Nathan Baker was the last person Lisa expected to see when she had stepped out of the cubicle. 'I mean ... Nathan ... you're ... you're here.' Her heart was pounding too fast through the 'smooth skin' of her wetsuit and her cheeks were firing up to beacon heat. She attempted to rein her reaction in as she took in the sight of him, despite the fact he looked even better in the flesh than he had when she had been snooping on his Facebook photos.

With fine stubble across his chin and ruffled hair, he looked every bit the rugged outdoor man. He was wearing a T-shirt with a surfboard on it and light-blue Levi 501 jeans, the way he used to, though his muscular legs clearly filled them out better than Lisa remembered. His jeans had a lived-in look that probably belied their real age. Even as a teenager, Nathan had liked dressing well. Lisa had spent many Saturday afternoons taking the train to Brighton with him and wandering round the clothes shops, trips that always seemed to involve him coming home with more bags than her.

'So, why have you been hiding from me, Lisa?' He smiled as he walked towards her with the clear intention of giving her a hug.

The fact she was wearing a wetsuit meant the contact was more intimate than she was prepared for. She hoped he couldn't feel how rapidly her heart was beating. 'Oh, I haven't been hiding,' she offered with an overly light laugh.

'Well, clearly you are not hiding now.' Nathan raised an eyebrow, stepped back and looked Lisa up and down in her wetsuit. 'But you have been ignoring my messages.'

Lisa couldn't quite believe it. The thing about pivotal moments in your life, especially ones involving a rejected declaration of love and a heart-wrenching farewell, was that they were never meant to be followed up over a decade later by meeting in a surf shop while inappropriately dressed in a wetsuit. Lisa had seen enough films to know that disappearing into the sunset meant the credits rolled. And yet here they were.

'I haven't been ignoring you,' Lisa protested. 'I've ...' *Been thinking about you a lot recently, got no idea what to say to you.* '... I've just, you know, been busy.' She hoped that would be enough to excuse the fact she hadn't answered, not even when he had invited her out for a drink.

Nathan grinned at her.

Oh Lord! If only he hadn't grown quite so very well into his looks.

'Too busy for me?'

Lisa smiled, hoping her cheeks weren't turning purple. 'Just busy.' She felt as if her nerve endings were all tingling as her body reacted to the shock of being back in the proximity of Nathan Baker. It reminded her of being back at school when just glimpsing him across the dinner hall could send every cell of her being into a frenzy. She found she could barely speak; the wetsuit was constricting her chest, her body felt too hot inside the rubber and more than anything she needed to make an emergency call to Felicity, just like she had the first time Nathan Baker had asked her out.

'You know, I get busy too, working shifts; I'm a fireman.'

Lisa nodded and congratulated herself on not letting slip she thought he was a male stripper, and attempted to push away the – unhelpful in her already over-heated state – image she still had of him in his uniform in her head from her evening of snooping on Facebook.

'But I'd make time for you,' he added, unleashing a very lovely smile.

'Oh!' was all she could manage to utter, wishing she wasn't feeling quite so weak at the knees, and caught off guard by her feelings and the situation.

Realising Lisa wasn't going to say any more, Nathan changed the subject. 'So what brings you here?'

Lisa looked down; seeing as she was standing in a shop called Wild, Wet and Windy in a wetsuit it seemed a bit of a stupid question. She laughed, welcoming the release from the tension she could feel inside. 'I needed to get some groceries.'

'Ha ha! But I think you know exactly what I meant.'

She didn't.

'What sport are you into? Your shorty wetsuit, while mighty fine on you, could be used in ... many ways.'

Trying not to over think the meaning of Nathan's pause, she took a breath. 'Well, this is simply going to be used to swim with my good friend Toby.' She was aware she was using Toby as her Bunbury once more, but she didn't want Nathan to think she had presumptuously contacted him in the hope they could pick up where they had left off, or that she was a desperado in the love department.

As Lisa wondered if that was a hint of disappointment she saw flick across Nathan's expression, Matt stepped through to the changing room area. He greeted Nathan like an old friend before directing his attention back to Lisa.

'Sorry. This is Nate Baker. He teaches our surf school during the summer, for the local primary kids.'

Words failing her, Lisa nodded.

Matt continued, 'What do you think, Nate? Lisa here's a pet-sitter, she needs the shorty for swimming with a client. I think it'll be just the job, don't you?'

'It's perfect!' Nathan smiled a knowing smile at Lisa, leaving her in no doubt he knew she had intended him to think otherwise.

Uh oh, double desperado!

'Actually, Lisa and I go way back—'

'Oh cool, you know each other,' Matt responded cheerily.

Nathan smiled. 'Sure, we do. We were good friends once.'

Good friends! Lisa felt a sting of disappointment at the words and couldn't help but think how she and Nathan had been oh-so much more than good friends.

Chapter Fifteen

Where are you? I neeeeeeed you! Lisa fired off the text as soon as she had managed to pull over two roads from Wild, Wet and Windy. She hoped calling on Felicity for advice didn't fall into the category of pushing her friendship too far, too soon, but she was still in a fluster after seeing Nathan again and needed to speak to Felicity. She had been there throughout their relationship as teenagers, from the weak at the knees sightings at school – or, more shockingly, out of school – the stomach-knotting waiting for phone calls, dizzy first dates and the lost-in-love-head-over-heels phase, to the prom where it had all come to its final and regrettably so-very-public conclusion. Lisa had to speak to Felicity or she might burst, especially as she had agreed to go out for a drink with Nathan and had no idea what that might mean.

Jiggle and Sing in the church hall, here 'til half eleven; hope all's OK. Come and meet Fred.

Lisa read the message twice. She didn't like the sound of 'Jiggle and Sing', but then again it was in the church hall, a place known for over-70s aerobics, the West Sussex watercolour group and town Christmas bazaar. How intimidating could it be?

OK, see you there.

Half an hour later, Lisa was pulling her van into the car park amongst cars ranging from people carriers to a white mini convertible, all of which contained car seats and three of which had very hectic-looking sticker families on their rear windows. Pushing away the thought of the lone stick-lady sticker she could have on her own back window, Lisa went to find her way in.

She could hear singing beyond the double doors and decided mid 'Five Little Speckled Frogs' might be a good time to slip in unnoticed. Had she known that, as she opened the doors, eleven women, one man and fifteen children – a mixture of babies and toddlers – would abruptly stop singing and turn to face her from their circle of chairs, she probably would have waited. As it was, her cheeks turned crimson for the second time that day. She introduced herself to the entire group and scurried across the hall towards Flick who was waving to get her attention and laughing at the same time. As 'Five Little Speckled Frogs' began again, Lisa watched Felicity singing along in unison with the other adults, each with their little ones on their laps or leaning against them.

With his messy, blond hair, blue eyes and freckles, Fred looked a cutie. While Lisa thought he must have got the strongest of his features from his dad, she could see Felicity in him too. He was a little person, created and loved by her once-best friend and yet she had never met him before. Ignoring the song Lisa leaned across and stroked the dimples on the back of his hand. 'Hello, I'm Lisa.' She smiled.

Fred turned his head in towards Felicity's arm and hid himself.

'He's a bit shy of new people,' Flick explained mid-song.

Lisa sat back. It was funny to think of herself as a new person in connection to anything to do with Flick's life. But it was true, she was a new person to Fred, and this whole world of babies and groups of people coming together and singing nursery rhymes in the middle of the week was new to her. She didn't belong. She looked across the circle at a woman who was heavily pregnant. *What was I thinking?* Realising a baby group was the last place she should be, Lisa decided she should just go and catch up with Felicity later. She felt foolish for flustering over Nathan Baker; she wasn't a teenager any more! There were bigger issues in life than Nathan Baker and his unnerving good looks. About to make her excuses and leave Lisa was stopped by the lady next to her.

'We'll be stopping in a mo, but I'm bursting. You wouldn't hold her while I pop to the loo, would you? Fred's not up for sharing Flick today,' she whispered over the sound of 'Polly Put the Kettle On'.

Lisa looked at the sleeping baby girl, a slight sense of panic growing in her chest. But before she could say anything, the soft, pink bundle was passed over. Her little, warm head, with a downy covering of dark hair, was placed into the crook of Lisa's arm. She could see the baby's eyes wiggle under her closed eyelids and her mouth move almost into a 'coo' shape as the outline of her lips whitened. She was gorgeous and smelt perfect. With a reassuring check that her baby was OK and a double check with Flick that she would keep an eye on her, the baby's mum disappeared off to the toilet.

Lisa sat mesmerised by the baby, and paralysed with fear that she might do something wrong and wake her. More than anything she had to focus on holding back the tears; she could not cry, if she started crying holding the precious little girl, she might not stop, and if she thought too hard about how right she felt in her arms, she might never let her go.

Flick smiled reassuringly, unaware of Lisa's inner turmoil. With the singing drawing to a close, the group leader asked if there were any birthday boys or girls in the room. Fred, still with his head slightly buried, raised his hand. Felicity smiled and confirmed Fred's birthday was approaching. It was a welcome distraction. Lisa knew she had to be seen to be singing along to this one, smiling and joining in, belying her true feelings. Felicity was smiling proudly and Fred was daring a little peek out from behind his mummy's arm.

As the baby's mum finally returned from the toilet, looking much relieved, she thanked Lisa and took her little girl back. Lisa's arms felt cold and bereft of her weight in them. Everyone clapped to mark the end of Fred's birthday song, and the leader announced it was time for drinks and biscuits. Lisa guessed she didn't mean of the alcoholic variety and thought she might have a strong coffee. Fred clambered down from Felicity's lap and headed for the bags of toys that were being put out. Excitedly he rummaged through, displacing many a random pre-loved toy on his mission.

'He's looking for Thomas. It's a favourite,' Flick stated, before turning her attention more fully to Lisa. 'So what brings you here neeeeeeeding me?' she mocked.

Lisa felt silly. It all felt insignificant after holding the baby and completely out of place at Jiggle and Sing. 'Oh nothing, it was just about … a man.'

The lady with the baby who had retaken her place next to Lisa leaned in. 'Oh please tell us; living vicariously is all we can do these days.' She laughed, before realising she had completely butted in on the conversation. 'Oh and I'm Melissa, by the way, married for fourteen months, mother to Bella here, she's nocturnal,' she added as if this explained everything.

Unsure how to respond, Lisa smiled and looked at Flick.

'How about I get the coffees and you can tell us all about it.' Flick grinned.

'I'll help.' Lisa stood, not sure she wanted to be left alone with Melissa and Bella. If the conversation turned to baby talk she didn't know what she would say.

As they stood in the queue at the serving counter, awaiting the hot drinks being made by the group leader, who wore all the hats, Fred came speedily past, trailing a pull-along Thomas the Tank Engine behind him. His hand was up at the counter and into the biscuit tub before anyone could question his queue jumping. Sauntering back past all those who had been foolish enough to wait their turn, he gave a smug little grin and bit into his chocolate digestive. At almost two, he clearly had this baby-group business sussed.

'Melissa's great – sit down with your biscuit, Fred – we met in the supermarket, when I found her staring at the frozen peas.'

'What?' Lisa wondered if she had misheard.

'It's a new-mum thing,' Flick explained.

'Staring at frozen peas?'

'No, forgetting what the hell you were actually doing.' Flick laughed. 'Anyway, I took her to the café for a drink. We've been friends since. She's a teacher, hubby's a rugby player, fit as—'

'Lucky her; so why the vicarious living?'

'Bella's nocturnal.'

Lisa wondered why everyone thought this explained things and then she realised what they were referring to. 'Oh, I see. I haven't got that type of man trouble.'

'Lucky you!'

'No, I mean, I do, but … but I don't have a man not to have sex with.'

'Ahem!'

Lisa turned to see she had reached the front of the queue and she was being glared at as if that was a highly inappropriate thing to say in such surroundings. Both Lisa and Felicity looked at each other and laughed. 'Sorry,' they announced in unison, causing them to laugh harder. Lisa couldn't help but think that something about being back together was making them behave like the teenagers they had once been!

After very briefly filling Melissa in about her past with Nathan, Lisa confessed to her and Felicity about her drunken Facebooking, the subsequent messages she had received from him and seeing Nathan unexpectedly that morning, cringing when she got to the part where she told them she had agreed to go out for a drink to 'catch up'. They hung on every word as she described how he looked and how it felt to be hugged by him while she was inappropriately dressed in a wetsuit.

'So, you see, Flick, I had to find you, so you could talk some sense into me.'

'Oh my God, yes; why haven't you – Fred give that back – gone out with him already?'

'But … wait, what?' Lisa wasn't expecting that. 'It makes no sense.'

'You said he wants to catch up—'

'But—'

'But nothing, it's – Fred, Mummy said, "No".'

Lisa watched as Felicity went to sort out an altercation between Fred and another boy, wondering if her friend ever actually finished a sentence in the presence of her children.

'Perfect!' Felicity finally offered, returning to her seat.

'I'm not sure you could describe what happened between Nathan and I as perfect, Flick, you were there.' Lisa pushed away an image of Nathan's shocked and hurt face at their prom.

'But that was all so long ago. It will be different now.'

Lisa thought about seeing Nathan at Wild, Wet and Windy, his arms around her; it did feel different. But perhaps not in the way Felicity meant.

'You two used to get on so well. A catch up might be … fun.' Felicity wiggled her eyebrows.

Melissa paused mid sip of her coffee. 'Hmm, a grown up "catch up". It sounds good to me. That's what Adam and I need.'

Flick leaned round to watch Fred as he set off to get his second biscuit. 'Seriously, Lisa, you used to be great together. Nathan was your closest friend – after me, of course. But I concede, I never carried your schoolbag for you. I never pinned Wayne Tully up against the wall for swearing at you. I didn't fill your locker with flowers on Valentine's Day. And – my personal favourite from the Nathan Baker years – I never got a train to London just to stand in line to get Robbie Williams' autograph for you when your parents wouldn't let you go.' Felicity paused to lift Fred on to her lap before continuing.

'Look, Lisa, I didn't see Nathan much after you left. I guess you were what we shared in common and we were both too raw about you going.'

Lisa swallowed down the feeling of guilt she felt as a lump in her throat.

'But I know he was miserable without you, and despite other girls from school offering to console him, in one way or another, I know he didn't accept. At worse the way you ended is too much to put aside, but if not, then you could be friends, or more. What have you got to lose?'

My dignity.

'What's stopping you?'

How hard it was to get over him the first time and the fear that I never have. The fact being around him might remind me what I once had and all that I let go.

'What other plans have you got?' Melissa asked.

'None!' Weighing up a night out with Nathan opposed to another evening in with Simon Cowell and co in her mind, Lisa realised there was no contest, even with all of her misgivings. 'OK, I'll go, but, seriously, if he does a Dom on me, I'm blaming you!'

'A what?' Both Felicity and Melissa's eyes boggled.

Chapter Sixteen

Lisa couldn't believe she was getting up at such an ungodly hour to go to church. Let alone that she was going to church with a dog. She had FaceTimed her parents the night before and, after her dad had stopped laughing about it, he had reminded her to take along business cards and to wear her logo-emblazoned work T-shirt. It felt a bit odd fronting up at church with business in mind, but as they pulled up outside there was no doubting it looked like an opportunity to tout for business. Even with just a glance across the green in front of the church, Lisa could see eleven dogs, three rabbits and a lamb! Add to that whatever was skulking in the many pet carriers she could see, and it all made for a captive audience of potential clients.

'All set then?' Lisa grinned at Winnie.

'Thank you for this, my lovely. Me and my Stan used to bring him as a pup. We haven't been for a few years now. Thought I might never get to bring him again.'

Lisa swallowed. Coming along was such a small gesture on her part and yet it meant so much to Winnie; it appeared to stir up warm memories for her. Lisa wished for Winnie's sake that her grandson had made it too. She wondered if she was disappointed he wasn't there.

'Of course, when we brought Jack before, he tiddled on the lectern. We'd best keep the blighter close.'

Lisa giggled. 'OK, good to know!'

Inside the church was warm, bustling and noisy. It was bizarre to see so many animals gathered together in such an unusual setting. It made for a welcoming atmosphere, though, and a very colourful congregation. Unable to sit still, the animals all wiggled and fidgeted. Everybody turned as a yap from the back was followed by a growl and audible gasps, and a hasty reshuffle of seats.

Winnie knew many of those assembled. Lisa was pleased to see her in a communal setting. She didn't like to think of her alone with a grumpy son who rarely called her and a grandson who was too busy to accompany her to such an important event.

'You remember Jack … yes, such a big lad now. And this is my friend, Lisa,' Winnie kept saying as another person she knew passed their pew. Lisa felt bad for wearing her 'pet sitter' T-shirt and attempted to cross her arms over her chest, making her hold on Jack's lead rather awkward. She liked being introduced as Winnie's friend. Touting for business no longer felt a priority.

As the vicar took to his lectern in readiness to give the service, he tested his microphone. An almighty whistle screeched through the church. All the dogs began to bark and every owner began to work on hushing their precious pet. A good five minutes later order was restored – as much as it was going to be under the circumstances.

'Welcome, everyone, to this rather special service in which we welcome those with two, four or, as in the case of dear, old Tripod there, three legs into our church.'

Lisa held back a giggle as she caught site of the aged, three-legged cat on the front pew. He seemed to sigh and roll his eyes as if he'd heard the vicar's attempt at a joke many times before.

'And no legs!' came a voice from the back.

Everybody swung round to see a small boy swoosh his goldfish into the air, slopping water from what appeared to be a rinsed out mayonnaise jar. His mum turned red as she smiled apologetically and encouraged her son to lower the fish before it sploshed out of the top.

Wriggling from his mum's grasp he continued, 'But you should have said no legs too. You can't forget Fluffy!'

The boy's mum looked like she might combust with the entire attention of the congregation on her. 'Fluffy's the fish. He, umm ... well, he wanted a guinea pig.'

The vicar chuckled, good-humouredly, despite the interruptions. 'Sorry, young man, you are right. I should also have said all those with no legs, like good, old Fluffy the goldfish there, who is also very welcome to this special service of thanks today.'

Winnie looked at Lisa. 'There's always one!' she blurted in an attempted whisper that was loud enough for everybody to hear.

Lisa looked back and smiled apologetically at the boy's mum who was still cringing from the whole episode, as the vicar went on.

'As Saint Francis of Assisi taught us, we are all creatures of one family ...'

Jack settled at Lisa's feet and she relaxed into listening to the service. It was quite humbling. The vicar spoke of the love between an owner and a pet, and about how losing a pet is often the first loss felt by a child. Lisa looked around at the owners gazing fondly at their furry, and in the case of Fluffy, not-so-furry pets – it was an emotional experience. She thought of Jack and how she had become so fond of him over their time together. Looking down to give him a loving smile, her eyes went wide. He was standing proudly before her, with a thoroughly pleased, cross-eyed expression on his face, but in his mouth he was holding Tubby the Yorkshire Terrier, the beloved pet of Winnie's friend from the pew in front. It was clear that Tubby was coming to no harm in Jack's soft, retriever jowls, but, nevertheless, it wasn't acceptable behaviour at any time, let alone at a service blessing all animals, big and small.

Not wanting to draw attention to the situation Lisa coughed and pointed at Jack – his sign to 'leave it'. Jack ignored the command and tilted his head, causing Tubby to squirm and let out a loud echoing yap. Before Lisa could respond the little boy she had found so sweet with Fluffy the goldfish screamed and pointed in their direction. Giving up on trying to be discreet Lisa shouted the command, 'Leave it!' At which point the woman in the pew in front turned and saw her beloved Tubby being released from Jack's hold in a pool of drool.

'Oh, you cheeky boy, now's not the time to play,' Lisa bluffed, patting Jack and scooping an extremely soggy Tubby off the floor. As she lifted him to pass to his horrified owner a blob of Jack's slobber slipped from his back to the floor with a squelch. Lisa attempted a smile and motioned for the vicar to continue in the hope to distract the congregation, who were staring aghast at the whole scene. Even the animals who had spent most of the service being thoroughly animated seemed to stop and stare. 'Nothing to see here,' she continued with mock nonchalance, waving her arms round more animatedly, revealing her pet sitter T-shirt, and deciding never to take her dad's business advice ever again.

'My poor Tubbywubby!' The woman in the pew in front cooed at her violated, precious pooch.

'No harm done, Maureen, my lovely. Here, take this.' Winnie shook out a laundered handkerchief and passed it to Tubby's owner. 'Tubby will be right as rain when he dries off.'

In an attempt to restore order the vicar continued,

reminding everybody of his central theme of love to all – no matter what their size or species.

Winnie leaned across to Lisa, gestured to Tubby and whispered, 'He's like a rat that one!'

'Shhhh,' Lisa urged.

'Snappy little wot-not!'

But with Winnie's whisper clearly audible to all, Tubby's owner swung around.

'What did you say, Winifred Adams?'

Deciding that the time had come to draw the service to a close before either the animals or humans got carried away with their snapping, the vicar called everybody to order, and invited them to take drinks and nibbles, strictly of the food variety, on the lawned area outside. Everybody welcomed the chance to stop restraining their now beyond-restless pets and headed for the door.

After being outside for a while and getting some rich fruit cake inside them, everybody calmed down. Even Winnie managed to offer Maureen an apology of sorts for insulting Tubby, who graciously accepted before adding that a 'boisterous' dog like Jack needed careful watching.

Feeling the sudden urge to put Maureen in her place – Jack was playful and sometimes a little cheeky, but he certainly wasn't 'boisterous' – Lisa decided it was time for a change of subject and a move away from Maureen, her precious pooch and unwelcome opinions. 'Now, how about I get those flowers for Stan?' she offered, stepping between Winnie and Maureen.

Winnie sucked in a breath through her teeth. 'That would be lovely.'

Lisa told Jack to stay, ran to the car and fetched the bunch of lilac asters Winnie had picked from her garden in readiness to visit Stan's grave. As she returned to Winnie,

Lisa swapped the flowers for Jack's lead. Silently, Lisa held Winnie's arm and the three of them made their way into the small churchyard adjacent. It was noticeably calmer than the chaotic lawn they had left just a few feet away, though the shadow cast across it by the church made it seem colder. Lisa looked at the headstones; some were so ancient they had sunk into the ground – their weather-worn lettering no longer visible and visiting family members long gone. Winding their way down the narrow, uneven path Lisa noticed the headstone of 'Stanley Nicholas Adams' before they reached it. It was a white marble open book, embellished with an ornate tassel carved into the centre between the pages. He had been eighty-four when he had died. Lisa didn't know how old Winnie was, but she guessed Stan had been several years older. The words 'Greatly missed husband, beloved father and grandfather' made Lisa think of her Granny Blake. She hadn't been to visit the crematorium since the day of her funeral. She hadn't seen the plaque her parents had chosen to display for her in the garden of remembrance. She made a mental note to visit it soon. It was one of the many things that had been neglected while she lived away.

While Winnie stood looking down with a sigh, Jack lay on the grave, his head resting between his paws, all signs of the normally playful glint gone from his eyes. As he let out a whine, Winnie bent to pat him reassuringly and bit her own trembling lip. It was such a sad scene – the two of them, united in their grief for the man who once meant so much to both of them. Lisa felt tears well in her eyes. Still holding Jack's lead she stood to one side to give them their moment.

But as she moved, her attention was drawn once more to the headstone. At first she had been looking at Stan's name and the loving epitaph written for him, but now all she could see was the other side, the blank page; an untouched page of highly polished, white marble. Clearly it was left, waiting for Winnie to join her husband. Lisa felt goosebumps prick uneasily at her skin, and wondered how it made Winnie feel to see that empty page each time she visited. Was it a comfort to know that one day she and Stan would be reunited? Or did she fear the day her name would be etched into the marble? Lisa wasn't religious, but events of the past year had made her question life and death more than she ever had before. She placed her arm round Winnie's shoulder.

'Ah, he was a good 'un, my Stan.' Winnie sighed.

They stood silently for a few moments, their feet sinking into the grass that was still sodden underfoot from the rain that had fallen over previous days. Lisa could feel the first hint of the bright, autumn sun touching her back as it began to rise high enough into the sky to appear above the church. Though it wasn't warm enough to remove the early-October chill from the air, she welcomed the sensation.

'A good 'un indeed,' Winnie finally continued.

'Yes, I'm sure—' about to add that she would have liked to have met him, Lisa was interrupted by Winnie.

'And a passionate one too.'

Lisa closed her mouth, unsure what to say to that.

'My Stan, you know, by God he knew how to treat a lady! The things we got up to when we took our bikes out of a Sunday afternoon. You should've seen us. Going alfresco, Stan would call it.'

A giggle burst past the lump that had been forming in Lisa's throat. 'Winnie!' Lisa was shocked and somewhat pleased she hadn't seen them.

'The daft beggar! Ah, I miss him. I miss every bit of that man, I can tell you—'

'No, honestly, no need,' Lisa interjected.

Realising how positively pink Lisa's cheeks had turned Winnie chuckled with a wheeze. 'Oh you youngsters! You're a funny lot. Well, I can tell you this, it's a bloody shame he's gone. You give your whole life to another person – you know, your heart, mind, body and soul – but before you know it they've gone, just like that. When you thought you had forever, that they'd never leave you, suddenly it's over and your whole world shifts. Everything you knew is different; he was my north star, you see. What I wouldn't give for another day in the arms of that man.'

'Oh, Winnie, I'm so sorry!' was all Lisa could manage; she knew she'd cry if she attempted to say more.

'Ah, we're learning, aren't we, Jack.' Winnie stroked Jack's head. 'Learning to live without him. But it's a wound – a wound so deep that it'll never completely heal, my lovely. There'll always be a scar. A part of me marked by the fact he's gone.'

Lisa stroked Winnie's arm, not really knowing what to say.

Winnie took a breath and lowered her voice. 'I was selfish, you know. Even though I knew it was coming. I'd been there, seen the results – I knew nothing could be done – but I just wasn't ready to let him go.' Winnie bit her lip as it trembled once more.

Lisa felt that this was something Winnie had, perhaps, not shared before. It was a very intimate moment, just the three of them standing at Stan's grave. 'I think that's understandable, Winnie. How could you be ready for that?'

'He was. He needed to go – the pain was too much. But I wanted him to stay, I needed him to still be there. But you can't stop time; it marches on if you're ready or not.'

Lisa knew that all too well.

Chapter Seventeen

'Tell me again, why is Lisa coming to this?' Pete asked as he selected the next animal cutter from the tub. With a plate of ham sandwiches shaped as monkeys and Marmite sandwiches shaped as elephants already done, he decided to go with the lion cutter for the cream cheese.

'Because, Pete, I thought it would be a way of you all meeting her without putting too much pressure on the occasion. You know there'll be a lot going on. I think she has been delaying it, coming to meet you.' Flick plopped another foam crocodile into the turquoise jelly she had already smashed up to form the base of her swamp.

'Of course, and there's never any pressure at a birthday party, is there?' Pete guffawed.

'I'm ignoring you now.' Flick bit the head off the next crocodile from the packet and popped her finished jungle-swamp jelly into the fridge.

'But are you sure about this? I—'

Feeling saved by the avalanche of plastic tubs and lids that fell from the cupboard Pete had opened, Felicity bent to help him pick them up.

'The thing is, Pete, I think you'll like her once you actually get to know her.' Felicity paused to blow a hair off one of the lids, before she thrust it onto a precarious pile she was building on the side. 'She's back now and we've got a chance to move on. It would be great to have the two of you getting along.' She stood up and began trying to match lids to tubs.

'I know and I do get it. And I will try. It's just, I might not have met her but I know she was important to you and she let you down. Whether she meant to or not, she hurt you. I just want you to be happy.' He slid his arms round Felicity's waist.

'I know you do. But I am fine. She's not my only friend now, is she? And, besides, I've got you,' Flick added with conviction, 'and why do none of these sodding lids fit?'

Lisa checked her watch and ran into the sports centre; she didn't mean to be late, but the woman in the shop had insisted the lion costume was incomplete without the mane and she didn't want Felicity's children to think she hadn't made an effort. The woman at the reception desk looked at her quizzically.

'Fred's party?' Lisa twitched the black face paint tickling her nose.

'Oh, the jungle party.' The woman giggled and then coughed. 'It's in the gym!' She motioned down the corridor.

Lisa gave her an exasperated glare and turned with a swish of her tail. Finally reaching the gym, she paused and took a breath. Nerves gnawed at the pit of her stomach. It was a daunting prospect meeting the rest of Felicity's children and Pete all at once, but she knew, as much as part of her wanted to run away, she was lucky to be invited. Felicity wanted her there and she was grateful to have the opportunity to be there. Her own fears about the situation weren't important. *It's just a party; you managed Jiggle and Sing, how different can this be?*

Lisa pushed open the double doors and promptly discovered two things. Firstly, children's parties had moved on a great deal since the days of pass the parcel and musical statues in her mum's lounge. And, secondly, the words 'We're having a jungle party' written on an invitation referred to the theme, not the dress code!

Lisa Blake, you are a fool!

'Lisa Blake, you are amazing!' Felicity beamed walking towards her from across the room, as all the adults turned to stare.

'I am stupid!' Lisa said into Flick's hair as she embraced her.

'Not at all. I should have said you didn't need to dress up, I'm sorry. I just assumed.'

Lisa felt Flick's apology would have been more convincing had she not been laughing while saying it.

'Come on, come and meet Pete.'

But, before they could reach Pete, the children had caught sight of the lion in the room and, with the exception of a few delicate souls who ran to hide amongst the adults, decided the entertainment had arrived. Lisa, or Lisa Lion as she quickly became known, was dragged towards the ball pit, aptly named crocodile creek, and soon had more children and toddlers hanging off her than she had seen in all her years in London. Their energy was boundless, their demands and noise intense, but she was actually enjoying it – laughing out loud and enjoying it! *Look at me now, Ben Hurst!* Her tail was pulled off and her mane had gone beyond wild. She had no idea who the children were; which, apart from Fred, of course, were Felicity's; or if the way she was playing – or doing as she was told – was right, but it was fun. Lisa could barely remember the last time she had laughed so much.

By the time food was announced she was exhausted, and remembered why it was she had come to the party. At least with the children being called to the table she could rest for a moment, try to straighten herself out a bit and salvage some decorum in preparation for meeting Pete. Spotting Melissa and Bella she went to say hello to them first; it seemed an easier option.

'Well, I'll certainly know who to call when it comes to Bella's party,' Melissa said, with a beaming smile.

'This isn't funny, I had no idea people wouldn't be in costume and that the children would have so much energy!'

'It looked like you had it all under control from here. Bella and I were super impressed.'

Both Lisa and Melissa looked down at Bella who was fast asleep.

'Well, OK, I was impressed; honestly, you're a natural!'

Lisa swallowed. It was kind of Melissa to say it but she knew she wasn't a natural when it came to children. Not *mummy material*, Ben had said, and even her own body had agreed. Explaining that she had to go and introduce herself to Pete, Lisa thanked Melissa and attempted to straighten her mane. Assuming Pete was the only man hovering round the food preparation area, she decided offering to help, while Felicity was still attempting to find seats for all those who wanted to be with particular friends, would be a good way to break the ice. As she approached, Pete smiled a warm, but, Lisa thought, slightly wary smile.

'Hello, I'm Lisa.' She held out her hand and realised she was still wearing her paw mittens. Pulling them off, she presented her hand again. 'It's great to meet you after all this time.' As soon as she'd said it, she wished she hadn't drawn attention to quite how much time it had been.

'Pete. I've heard lots about you.'

As he shook her hand Lisa wished hers wasn't quite so sweaty.

'Some of it good, I hope.' Lisa ventured a smile.

Pete hesitated.

Scared about what he might say, Lisa threw her paw mittens under the table. 'Here, let me help you.'

She held out her hands and Pete passed her the tray of

sandwiches he had been attempting to remove the cling film from.

'Thanks.'

As their focus turned to passing out the food, the awkward moment passed.

'Oh, thanks so much.' Flick flashed Lisa a smile as she busied past her and set about offering a tray of sliced veg to the children.

'Sandwich?' Lisa asked each child as she walked along with the tray of impressively animal shaped sandwiches.

'Oh, not for Milly,' a woman called, 'she's gluten free.'

Lisa apologised and moved on; by the time she had gone round the whole table she had learnt that toddlers these days have more dietary needs than she had ever imagined possible – she wasn't sure she had even known a vegetarian when she was at school, let alone a coeliac, a vegan and someone with a nut allergy. Feeding toddlers seemed a bit of a minefield.

As the food from the plastic tubs and serving platters was gradually devoured, and increasingly smeared around the children's faces, Lisa noticed how the noise increased, until it was time to sing 'Happy Birthday'. Everybody hushed as the lights were dimmed. Pete carried the cake, while Felicity started the singing and stood ready with the camera opposite Fred. His little eyes lit up as he beamed excitedly at the cake. It was quite something. Lisa couldn't imagine that Felicity had made it, not unless she had developed quite a sugar-craft talent in their years apart.

It was an amazing, two-tier tower, one layer covered in zebra stripes and the other with leopard spots. Standing between the tiers were sugar-crafted jungle animals. It looked delicious. As the singing stopped, Fred took an almighty breath and huffed out his number-two candle.

Everybody clapped before the children took the cake being done as their signal to leave the table, and ran to the corner towards a man who appeared in readiness to create and give them jungle-animal-inspired balloons. The giraffe was particularly popular as it was the biggest.

'Give us a hand, Lisa,' Felicity called.

Lisa turned to see a red-faced Felicity chopping into the cake like a woman possessed.

'From now to getting out the door is the worst part. Grab the napkins, would you?'

Lisa picked up the cheeky-monkey napkins and began wrapping cubes of cake.

'Chuck them in those bags,' Felicity said as she gestured along the food preparation table.

Lisa looked in the direction she had pointed. Leaning against the back wall was a row of party bags. She opened one and looked inside. 'Wow! Whose birthday is this?' she said it automatically and then wished she hadn't. She didn't want Felicity to think she was being rude, but the bag contained a balloon, sweets, stickers, a bendy monkey, a bag of chocolate animal biscuits, a lion notepad and a pencil with a zebra topper.

'Madness, isn't it?' Felicity affirmed, without further explanation.

Lisa didn't question it and continued to play her part in the party bag production line. As the last slice of cake, that it turned out Pete's mum had made, entered the bag, Felicity called for Fred. He came over and listened intently as Flick gave him the very important role of passing out his party bags. Turning apparently too slowly and not looking focused enough for Flick's liking he was promptly called back.

'Megan, Alice, help him, will you.' Felicity beckoned

to the two older girls at the party, who Lisa recognised as Flick's even though she had never met them before. They had their mum's blue eyes and unruly curls.

'No, Lisa Lion!' Fred insisted, turning from his sisters.

Lisa could have burst she felt so happy. Fred wanted her to help. She had made an impression and it was a good one. Fred put out his hand and Lisa took it.

Smiling, Felicity watched them walk away as tears welled in her eyes.

'Ten minutes and the next party's in.'

Looking at the teenage sports leader standing before her, bin bag, dustpan and brush in hand, Felicity jumped into action.

'Oh Christ! Quick, Pete, stop eating and help clear the table will you. Alice, Megan, follow them. Lisa doesn't know who those party bags are for any more than Fred does.'

Chapter Eighteen

Lisa didn't have the heart to tell Felicity and Melissa that they had picked the wrong person to live vicariously through. The truth was she still didn't know what to say to Nathan. That and the fact the feel of the hug they had shared had kept her awake, causing her to question her feelings towards him, made her think it was best to avoid seeing him in the flesh again. To mark this decision, she sent Nathan a message cancelling their drink, saying she had a client meeting to arrange looking after three cats for a week – a financial opportunity she couldn't miss. It wasn't true, but she thought it sounded convincing. A chat with Mr Chung, and chicken chow mein in the company of *The X Factor* and *Strictly*, wasn't the same as the prospect of a night out with Nathan Baker but it was the easier option.

Having parked behind a Ford Fiesta, Lisa wandered over to the restaurant door, but as she glanced back to press her key and check her van had locked she saw a car pull up behind it. *Oh God! Oh no, it can't be!* Lisa couldn't believe it. He was there. At the Chinese restaurant. Nathan Baker had pulled up behind her van. She didn't know what to do. She was only a few steps away from the door. Going back to the van would mean she would definitely be seen, but, perhaps, she thought, if she was lucky he wouldn't be going into the takeaway. Her name wasn't on the back of her van, he could go wherever it was he was going and the panic would be over! With that in mind, Lisa darted into the Chinese. It felt like a safe haven. In there, she could pretend Nathan just wasn't there. *Ignore him, he might go away!* It was a childish tactic, but one she hoped might work.

She didn't dare look out of the window in case he was still there. With every fibre of her mind, she was willing him to disappear.

Lisa no longer felt hungry. Unsure what to do with herself once she was in the confines of the small takeaway, she grabbed a newspaper from the counter and sat in the corner. Opening it wide she obscured herself from view of the window and attempted to steady her nerves. Aware that Nathan hadn't followed her and the door hadn't opened since she entered, Lisa breathed a sigh of relief. After what felt like several minutes had passed she decided to venture a peek from behind the paper, only to see Mr Chung staring at her with a raised eyebrow. She attempted to smile. Feeling foolish she hurriedly closed the paper and stood up. 'I ... I ... um ...'

'Ah, Miss Lisa, you want usual, no?' His eyes flicked expectantly from Lisa to the small pad in front of him as he scribbled down numbers, grinning widely.

As Lisa went to speak she was aware the door had opened. 'Yes ... please,' she responded on autopilot. Without even looking she knew Nathan was standing just a few feet behind her.

'Prawn crackers?' Mr Chung nodded.

Lisa didn't actually want anything, not the chicken chow mein, not the special fried rice and certainly not the prawn crackers. 'No, thanks,' she replied too sharply. She felt terrible as Mr Chung's generally ever present smile faded, but, really, unless he had a *Mission Impossible* zip wire form of exit on the menu, or maybe even a time machine, there was nothing she actually wanted. Her van was trapped outside the takeaway restaurant, and now she felt well and truly trapped inside. Having received confirmation of Lisa's order Mr Chung disappeared.

'Hello, Lisa.'

Lisa could hear the grin in Nathan's voice and took a breath. A couple sat in the chairs next to the fruit machine, while another man read a newspaper at the end of the counter. A large ominous-looking fish stared from an enormous tank in the wall, while a colourful, grinning cat, sitting next to a can of Coke and a can of Fanta, waved from a shelf above the counter. Slowly, Lisa turned to face Nathan. The woman in the chair nearest the fruit machine nudged her husband and coughed dipping her head in their direction. Oblivious, the man looked up blankly. 'What?' Still attempting to be subtle the woman gave him a death stare, her glaring eyes urging him to look at the two people standing in front of them. Lisa wondered if she could feel the tension between them, the attraction she could feel, or was she imagining it based on their past?

Finally, Lisa spoke. 'Nathan, I didn't ... I mean ... how very unexpected ... to see you, here. The client, with the dogs—'

'Dogs?'

'Cats, I mean cats. They cancelled.'

'I see. So you thought ...' Nathan looked at her expectantly, with a glint in his eye.

'Well, I thought you must have other plans by now so I'd—'

'Ah, Miss Lisa, you have boyfriend.'

Both Lisa and Nathan turned, eyes wide at Mr Chung as he beckoned his family from their stations in the kitchen. One by one they appeared at the door. Mr Chung pointed at Lisa and all eyes turned to her. 'Miss Lisa, she has boyfriend! We so happy for you.' He beamed and his family began to clap.

Lisa blushed. 'No, this ...' She motioned between herself and Nathan. '... this is not my boyfriend.'

Having stopped clapping, the now unsure smiles on the four people of varying ages, staring at Lisa from the kitchen door, faded. Lisa wasn't sure if they had understood what she said, but they must have got the gist as they each apologetically slipped back into the kitchen.

Mr Chung looked dumbfounded at Lisa. 'Oh yes, yes, you need boyfriend.' Before Lisa could protest again he raised a hand. 'Hold on, please.'

As he disappeared back into the kitchen, both Nathan and Lisa stared in his wake.

Lisa couldn't believe it. Why the man she had spent so long talking at had decided now was the time to reveal a greater command of the English language than she had ever given him credit for, she had no idea. But it was all getting very embarrassing. Not only did he seem to have the wrong end of the stick, thinking Nathan was her boyfriend, but he was also making her sound like a complete hopeless case, *in front of Nathan Baker for goodness' sake*. To add to her mortification, the other three customers, presumably still awaiting their orders, were now staring, waiting with anticipation for the next act in this strange pantomime to unfold before them. *He's your boyfriend! Oh, no, he isn't! Oh, yes, he is!* Lisa was sure she would never be able to return to the Chinese after this.

While the room remained silent, Nathan leaned round the counter to see what Mr Chung was doing, only to jump back as the old man appeared holding a bulging takeaway bag.

Mr Chung held out the bag to Lisa. 'Here, you take this. I put in extra for Miss Lisa boyfriend.'

Nathan looked bemused adding to Lisa's embarrassment and frustration.

'No, weeee … weeee wooon't be sharrrring this.' Lisa was

trying to make herself as clear as possible, and had started talking and gesticulating like a 1970s Englishman abroad.

'Oh yessssss, yessssss, Miss Lisa,' Mr Chung mimicked. 'Take this. You have this on house.' As he spoke Mr Chung lifted the hatch in the counter and stepped through. Stepping between Lisa and Nathan, he pressed the warm plastic takeaway bag into Lisa's hands and gestured for Nathan to come closer.

Lisa wanted to run. 'No, really, you have it all wrong.'

But Mr Chung was having none of it. 'Wrong? I not think so.' He beckoned Nathan in closer still and lowered his voice achieving a whisper that everybody could still hear. 'You want to be Miss Lisa boyfriend?'

It was all too awful; poor Nathan could not possibly be made to make a public declaration about Lisa again. Lisa pictured them standing in the middle of the dance floor at their prom and suddenly they were eighteen again, hearts pounding – his with anticipation and hers with panic. The whole situation was mortifying and it had to be bringing back too many hurtful memories for him. Lisa knew she had to do something.

The couple in the seats were staring, waiting; the man no longer even pretending to read the newspaper peered above his glasses. All sounds from the kitchen stopped. Lisa felt the weight of the expectant atmosphere in the room pressing down upon them.

She had to save him. She couldn't let the humiliation continue to unfold. 'Stop, please, we'll take it. I mean, yes, there you go, he's my boyfriend.' With that she leaned up and kissed Nathan firmly on the lips, the warm, soft, pink lips she had kissed so many times before. As she reluctantly pulled herself away she had to steady herself.

Mr Chung clapped his hands and the other customers

followed suit. Noticing the shock that swept across Nathan's face Lisa suddenly felt a fool. 'Oh, I'm sorry!' Desperate to be gone she turned and ran out of the door – Chinese still in hand. Thankfully, the Ford Fiesta had moved. She turned the key and cursed as her van spluttered before actually starting, and sped off.

Chapter Nineteen

Lisa went inside the house and threw the takeaway on the side. She didn't know what to do with herself. *What an idiot!* She kept picturing it in her head. She couldn't fathom what had possessed her. On reflection, she didn't even know why she had done it. Nathan could have just said, 'No, she's not my girlfriend.' What would it have mattered? Why had she presumed he needed saving from public humiliation, where there was truly none to be had? It was the thoughts of the prom that had done it. She felt so stupid. They were not eighteen any more and everything was completely different now. *What a fool!* She held her phone, pondering texting Felicity, but her hand was shaking too much and she had no idea what to say. How could you explain that level of humiliation in a text?

A ring at the door made her stop staring at the phone. *Oh God! Oh no!* Tentatively, she went to open it; *oh it can't be!* She really wanted to run and hide, but if she was right and it was Nathan, she knew she owed him an explanation – she just wasn't sure what that explanation was. Taking a steadying breath she opened the door.

With a bemused grin, Nathan smiled at her from the doorstep.

Lisa's stomach twisted into knots. It was hard enough seeing him before, but now she was staring at him with the memory of that kiss still on her lips. She offered him a weak smile, while she attempted to process what to say.

'I don't normally have women throwing themselves at me in the Chinese, but when they leave with free food for two, without so much as an invitation, well, then I draw the line.'

118

Lisa laughed despite the tension she could feel inside. 'Nathan, I'm so sorry. I shouldn't have ... They were just all staring and—'

'And you thought you'd kiss me!'

Her cheeks reddened. 'No, I ... I wasn't thinking.' If only that were true; really she had been thinking way too much of that moment – Nathan's declaration at their prom – and how this time she found she couldn't say no.

'Thinking's overrated, inhibitive. Sometimes you have to seize the moment, go with your gut ... and that's why I followed you.' Nathan revealed a bottle of wine he had been holding behind his back.

'Oh—'

'So are you going to invite me in?'

Lisa's mind scrambled as she tried to take in what he had said. *Oh God!* She didn't know what to do; part of her wanted to shut the door and hide. *What would Flick say?* Picturing Flick and Melissa's faces as she had told them about that hug in Wild, Wet and Windy, and their hopes of living vicariously, she realised she knew exactly what they would say and attempted to push the thoughts out of her mind.

'Or we could just eat here ... on the doorstep,' Nathan added.

'Eat ...' Lisa's mind finally registered what he was there for. 'The Chinese! Of course.' *Of course, that's what he's here for.* 'Sorry!' *It's the only reason he's here!* Lisa knew she really had to stop letting their past and feelings she thought she had buried long ago fill her head. He had wanted to 'catch up', that's what old 'friends' – as he insisted they were – did, and he wanted to eat 'free food'. None of his actions suggested anything other than that. *For goodness' sake, just let him in!*

119

As she held the door open and he stepped inside, Lisa couldn't help but notice how much more he filled the doorway than when he had entered her house as a teenager. He had always been tall, but his older, more muscular physique meant his shoulders were broader. Even through his jacket she could see the arc of his biceps, and remembered how it felt to be held in those arms from their encounter in Wild, Wet and Windy. But it was more than the physical changes; he seemed to have a greater presence, a confidence that showed in his demeanour. The boy who had been her first love had grown into a man.

'The food's in the kitchen,' she said, trying to keep the wobble in her voice on an even keel and hoping desperately that he couldn't hear how loudly her heart was beating.

Once in the kitchen he put the wine on the side and shrugged off his jacket. 'Corkscrew?' he asked.

'I'll sort it, you take a seat.' She needed him out of her proximity for a moment so she could refocus and gain control of her mind. Nathan Baker was in her house. After all the time that had passed, he was right there, in her kitchen, the way he had been so many times before. Her thoughts fizzed with the information, her past and her present colliding. *A catch up and free food, that's all it is!* She had a vision of them kissing by the kitchen counter, getting intimate in her bedroom, making out in the living room. Letting their teenage hormones get the better of them anywhere her parents could not see them. They had bribed her brother, Luke, to keep quiet about the things he had caught them doing so many times she wondered if they had actually funded his post university travels. *It's all in the past!* She blinked, trying to get the images out of her head as she fetched the plates and cutlery. *Oh no!* Her face flushed as it dawned on her that Nathan was almost certainly having the same flashbacks. A glance over her shoulder and the hint of a grin on his face suggested he was. Attempting not to show that her hands were trembling, Lisa carried the plates, cutlery and food to the table.

Time had altered them both. Taking in the sight of him, more properly now she was less caught off guard, it was clear he was carrying off the casual look a bit too finely, particularly as she still had her work clothes on and her long hair pulled into a messy ponytail. If she had known she would end up spending the evening with him anyway, she would have just stuck to their first arrangement. At least that way she would have showered, got dressed up and done her hair and make-up; she would have been generally more prepared.

'So how are you really, Lisa?' he asked, helping himself to chow mein and fried rice from the takeaway tubs she had placed in the middle of the table.

She couldn't help but look at his hands, distracted by the fine hairs and firm veins that had appeared on them since they had dated; masculine, grown up hands.

Nathan stopped and waited for her answer, forcing her to focus.

'Oh, umm ... good, thanks.' Lisa knew it was a bit of a lie but Mr Chung had made her look like enough of a hopeless case without her adding details. 'Well, this looks good.' She dished herself up some food, welcoming the opportunity for a distraction.

'I'd heard you were back. I thought you might be avoiding me.' Nathan smiled.

Lisa raised her eyebrows. So it seemed gossip wasn't entirely dead in her hometown, though clearly she was more the cause rather than the recipient of it.

'Then when I got your friend request—'

'Sorry about that—'

'Sorry about the friend request?' Nathan laughed.

'No, I mean, well, I'm not very good with Facebook.' Lisa couldn't tell him she had sent it after the shock of seeing Flick and then consuming too much cooking sherry, and decided to change the subject.

As the two of them chatted, Lisa's mind wandered, taking in the deeper sound of Nathan's voice. She noticed his deep-blue eyes that still had the same glint as when they were younger, but now there were creases around his eyes and a furrow on his brow she had never seen before.

She wondered if she would be attracted to him if it weren't for their past and the palpable chemistry – fuelled by the knowledge of the moments, feelings and emotions they had shared – she could feel reigniting between them. She didn't know if the fact his presence was making heat spread inside her was genuine or based on memories. Either way it didn't matter. She was home to attempt to continue healing over her loss and to get over all that had happened with Ben, adding getting involved with Nathan Baker into that mix wouldn't solve anything; not when he wanted to be friends and she wanted ... well, she couldn't allow herself to think about that. It would just complicate things further.

Listening to herself as she answered Nathan's questions, Lisa couldn't help but notice how good she had become at offering politician's answers about her life, skirting round anything she didn't want to discuss, deflecting questions and offering answers she thought the person she spoke to might want to hear; no wonder she felt so few people really knew her. She was an expert at not letting them in. She only truly felt herself and spoke her mind with Winnie, and even then she had held back, and omitted details about herself and her reasons for coming home. Talking to Felicity had been good, and easier than she had expected. She tried not to over analyse it, scared that picking it apart might make how right it had felt fall apart.

Nathan poured wine to fill the silence that fell between them. Having started with a flurry of idle chat, they were now each running out of 'safe' subjects to bring up. Lisa knew it was because neither of them wanted to accidentally allude to the stomping, great elephant in the room. Not broaching the subject of their past was adding an expectant weight to the atmosphere, smothering their conversation. It was making Lisa feel increasingly awkward. She wondered if she should be the one to bring it up. But what if Nathan didn't want to talk about it? He was the one who had said they were 'friends'. Perhaps he preferred to think of their former relationship that way. She didn't want to bring up hurtful memories. Not knowing what to say had been the main reason she had cancelled on him in the first place.

She looked at him across the table as he drank his wine, his Adam's apple sliding as he swallowed.

Realising she was watching him, Nathan paused and smiled. 'Who'd have thought you and I would be back here in your mum's kitchen.'

Oh no! The visions of the two of them together that she had attempted to push away earlier came flooding back into her mind. Lisa realised she had to say something, she just wasn't sure what. 'Look, Nathan—'

'Nate. Most people call me Nate now.'

'The thing is Nate …' Well, that felt completely weird. She didn't like it. He would always be Nathan to her. His name was etched in her memory as Nathan Baker, the way Flick would always be Felicity Forster, register names, the way you remembered everyone from school.

Nathan filled the silence. 'The thing is you're back!' He

smiled warmly. 'And you can call me Nathan, if you like. I'd forgotten how nice it was to hear you say it.'

Lisa attempted to ignore the little flip she could feel her tummy doing. She needed to gain control of this conversation and her reactions. 'The thing is, Nate ...' She was trying not to make him, or herself, reminisce. But calling him Nate just didn't feel right. She couldn't do it. 'The thing is, Nathan, it's been a really long time. Honestly, I looked you up to see how you were. I never meant for ... this.' She gestured to signify the Chinese takeaway, the two of them sitting in her mum's kitchen and the completely bizarre situation they found themselves in.

'I know, Lisa. The past is a long time ago. We're both different people now. I just thought it would be good to see you. You know we were friends once.'

Friends! Again he was calling them friends. They were definitely oh so much more than friends. Lisa attempted to quash the feeling of disappointment she could feel each time he said the word. 'I just don't know if it's a good idea.' *I'm not sure I can be just your friend.*

'Honestly, Lisa, you don't need to worry. Even though you kissed me, I'm not going to propose to you or anything!' He laughed.

Lisa wondered if her gasp was audible or in her head, as her cheeks blazed to beacon heat. 'Of course not.' He had raised it. The stomping, great elephant in the room was being invited to take a seat at the table! And Nathan was laughing about it. She wasn't so full of herself that she expected him to still be hurting from her public rejection of his unexpected proposal at their prom, but joking about it seemed a big leap when crying and saying their goodbyes was the last they had said of it.

'Oh, Nathan, I didn't think—'

'Honestly, it's fine. Hurt like hell for a while, but I know you had your reasons.'

Reasons. She knew she did have her reasons, that she had felt them with conviction at the time, she just wasn't sure what they were right now. Lisa swallowed in an attempt to encourage her mouth to work properly and to give herself a moment to know what to say. 'Nathan, I am sorry I hurt you.' She really was sorry for that. Trying to think clearly and to stop her heart racing she attempted to continue, 'I just wasn't—'

Nathan smiled. 'Lisa, honestly, I am over it. It's such a long time ago. Imagine, we'd be an old, married couple now, probably a couple of children in tow.'

'Yes, imagine.' Lisa's laugh was too light as she pictured herself with Nathan, a little boy and little girl mirroring each of them. The image seemed perfect in her mind. She swallowed and closed her eyes, as the thought of how much she wanted it was met with the realisation that a life and a family with Nathan was no longer hers to have.

'Anyway, I just thought it would be good to catch up,' he finished, touching her hand for a too-brief moment, making her want to reach out and hold on to him.

Chapter Twenty

Felicity took a breath. 'I'm sorry to do this to you at such short notice. Callum and Alice will sit through the whole performance, but I just can't trust that Fred will. Megan would be so embarrassed if he hollered in the middle of her dance and with the Halloween theme too, I'm just not sure he'll like it.'

'It's fine, really. I'm glad you called me.' It was a bit of an overstatement considering how nervous she felt about having Fred and the guilt she felt at postponing Jack's walk, but Lisa wanted Felicity to know she was there for her.

'Pete's mum is a pain. She saw the show last night, now she's too ...' Felicity paused to make air quotes round the next word as she said it. '... "poorly" to look after Fred for us so we can go today!' She rolled her eyes making her opinion on Pete's mum and her illness clear.

'Really, I don't mind. We'll be fine,' Lisa affirmed, trying to convince herself as much as Felicity.

'Melissa would have had him, but I know she's out on a spa day – never mess with a new mum on a spa day – and—'

'Flick!'

Felicity stopped and stared.

'Fred and I will be fine.' Lisa couldn't hear any more about all the people Felicity had considered before calling her; it was making her more nervous by the moment. 'We'll go to the park. It'll be fun and then we'll see you back at yours later. Are you sure you don't want me to have the others too?' Even as the question came out, Lisa was dreading Felicity saying yes; in all honesty she was terrified of looking after Fred. Having Callum and Alice as well would mean she would be outnumbered, and even further beyond her comfort zone.

'No, I am sure they'll be fine. Alice wants to go; she helped with the bandages and blood.'

Lisa looked confused.

'Megan's a zombie. And Callum's looking forward to it; he actually can't wait since Megan told him there's a skeleton dance in the second half,' Felicity explained.

'Oh, OK.' *Phew!* Noticing Felicity was loitering, reluctant to actually leave Fred in her care, Lisa attempted a reassuring smile. 'Well, wish Megan luck from me. And don't worry, Fred's in safe hands.' She swallowed.

'You're a star!' Felicity kissed Lisa on the cheek, hugged Fred goodbye and got in her car.

Lisa waved Felicity off, attempting to hold her smile in place until she drove out of sight, and turned to look at Fred standing in her mum's pristine hallway complete with change bag, lunch box, water bottle, car seat, raincoat and wellies. Pulling out a toy dinosaur and a chubby crayon from his pocket he gave Lisa a very mischievous grin. *Oh yikes!* Deciding getting out as soon as possible was perhaps the best course of action, Lisa picked Fred up and headed out to her van. Unsure how to co-ordinate putting Fred and all of his baggage in the van at the same time, Lisa wondered what to do. Leaving him to play unsupervised in her mum's house seemed as dangerous as letting him run loose on the driveway. Chewing her lip, she pondered the situation. Then she had an idea.

Popping Fred into the large dog crate she had in the back of the van, a game he luckily found funny, she grabbed the rest of his belongings and wrestled his car seat into place following the obscure set of pictorial instructions on the side. After some debate, in which Fred was reluctant to leave the crate, they set off. Lisa decided to head to the nearby town of Arundel. When she had walked dogs past the park there, it had seemed less busy than some of those she'd seen in Littlehampton, and more contained with only one entrance gate. In her mind, that meant there was less possibility of losing Fred.

Entering the park, Lisa felt Fred's dimpled hand in hers and grew a little taller; nobody knew he wasn't actually hers. With his blond hair – that bounced with each step – and blue eyes, he even looked a little like her. For a moment, she could simply pretend to be his mummy; *nobody will know*. She gave Fred a smile as she let the thought linger. The toothy grin he returned made a lump form in her throat and a fuzzy warm feeling spread inside her.

The ground was soft and spongy underfoot. It was a dry day, but recent showers meant the earth remained sodden – the autumn sun lacking the heat necessary to dry it out. Fred sploshed his Gruffalo wellies through every muddy puddle he could find. Despite the fact that Felicity had packed him enough clothes for a minibreak, Lisa congratulated herself on tucking his dungarees into his socks. *See, Flick, I've got this sorted!*

Being half term, the park was busy. Taking in the scene, Lisa could see parents gathered near benches, not quite committing to sitting on them now that they had taken on the damp they would keep until the spring. Two older boys were spinning on a 'witch's hat style' roundabout, a little too fast and without enough regard for the younger children in the park for Lisa's liking.

'Not that way, Fred!'

Another group of children, who had removed their coats

and fleeces and made them into capes, had taken over the wooden tower with the big slide and were shouting at each other in fake American accents. *Hmmm!* Lisa didn't want Fred picking that up before she returned him home, even if it meant he might describe their trip as 'awesome'.

Without pausing, Lisa led Fred towards the calmer-looking toddler end of the park, thinking he might like the bouncy horse thing – *or is it a dog?* – on a giant spring.

'Doggie. Yes!' Fred began to run towards it. The thick, tufty grass, streaked with yellow, and peppered with red, brown and orange leaves made a challenging terrain for somebody whose knees barely cleared the grass, turning his run into more of a stumble, step refrain.

Dog it is then! Lisa smiled and followed in pursuit. She loved how excited he looked. His cheeks were flushed and his eyes were bright from the fresh air. The low glow of the sun added to how perfect she found the moment. It was snapshot perfect. Getting out her phone she decided to take a picture and send it to Flick. But after getting Fred balanced and posing she realised her battery was dead. *How annoying!* She really wanted to save the moment and share it with Flick. Glancing back up at her lost photographic opportunity Lisa was shocked to see a boy, perhaps not more than three, weeing in the hedge behind Fred. 'Oh good God!' She couldn't believe it.

The boy's mum looked at her and smiled as if this was completely normal behaviour. 'He's been dry day and night for a couple of months now. How about yours, potty training yet?'

Trapped between being horrified that weeing in a bush counted as potty training, wanting to get Fred away from the boy and actually engaging in a moment of mumsy chat, Lisa scooped Fred up onto her hip – it was how they carried their little ones in *Neighbours* and felt the thing to do. 'No, not yet, he's only just had his second birthday.'

'Ah, yes, but when they're ready, they're ready. Don't miss the signs, I always say.'

'No, of course not.' Lisa attempted not to look puzzled. She had no idea what 'the signs' might be. Stooping or cocking a leg were standard signs in her dog walking world, or circling for other business. But she was pretty sure that wasn't what the woman meant.

Not knowing what on earth else to say, Lisa began to wriggle Fred. 'Oh look, he wants to get down and play.' In fact Fred didn't want to, he'd been happily chewing the strings on Lisa's hoody, but once Lisa started the wriggling game he found it funny and joined in. It was only as they both wiggled and began to laugh that Lisa realised she had mud from Fred's wellies all over the front of her. 'Bugger!' As soon as it was out of her mouth she realised her error. Thankfully, Fred didn't repeat her misdemeanour, but as Lisa's gaze met the other woman's glare, her son pulled up his pants and trousers, and ran off shouting his new word for all to hear. Lisa attempted to apologise. But it was no use, the woman was already marching off in the direction of a group of other mums, no doubt to tell them to avoid the sweary one with the muddy jeans. Lisa looked at Fred. 'Whoops!'

With the toddler area to themselves, Lisa and Fred played on. Fred had boundless energy, clambering up the small slide, crossing the bridge repeatedly for Lisa to do her who's-that-trip-trapping-over-my-bridge troll voice, and being guided down the firemen's pole over and over again. When Fred finally sat in the swing – the only place she could think to hold him still for a moment – eating a sandwich from his lunch box, Lisa paused realising how tired she felt. Enjoying the break she watched the other children in the park.

It was funny, she couldn't help but feel a pang of envy as they all played, giggled, and even cried with complete and utter commitment – no distractions to their purpose, none of the stresses that came from being an adult playing on their minds. They lived in and for the moment. She could remember her and Felicity playing in the same way in the playground, and on the field at school. So much had happened since then.

Feeling like she had exhausted herself more than Fred, Lisa decided she deserved a cup of tea and thought they should head off. Fred, on the other hand, had other plans. He was desperate to go on the big slide and was adamant he didn't want to leave until he had done it, stamping his Gruffalo welly to make his point clear. Not wanting to cause a scene now they had blended in once more, Lisa took Fred by the hand and led him over to the big slide; her plan was to show him that he was just too little for it. He wouldn't be able to get up to the top and as she had let him try it would not be her fault.

As Fred began to try to heave himself up the vertical ladder, with rungs too far apart for his legs, Lisa could see her plan was going to work. All she had to do was suggest they come back and try when he was a bit bigger, and she would be on her way to her cup of tea. What she hadn't accounted for was the group of children, still donning their superhero capes, seeing Fred's plight and deciding to make it their mission to lift, shove and haul him up to the very top of the ladder. Lisa could only watch in horror as the whole situation was taken out of her hands. *What would Flick think?*

'Please be careful!'

Once Fred reached the top and stepped over onto the summit of the wooden tower leading to the slide, the mini-superheroes cheered, their mission complete. Fred beamed with excitement and teetered around looking over the edge far too precariously for Lisa's liking.

'Sit down, Fred.'

But no amount of imploring on her part was working. Feeling torn between climbing up herself and judging when he might choose to come down the slide, Lisa asked the superheroes to help. Gladly accepting their new mission, they sprang into action. Thankfully, with them encouraging him, Fred sat ready for his descent.

Lisa positioned herself in readiness to catch him. There was about a foot drop at the end of the slide onto a rubbery surface and she didn't want him landing bottom first on that. The slide was steep, but she expected his wellies would slow him down and so wasn't too worried. But as he went to launch off, the experienced, older children shouted for him to lift his feet. Fred complied, the action resulting in him whizzing towards Lisa on his back, his feet in the air and his bottom facing her. *Oh God!* She prepared herself, but with the angle at which he was hurtling at her she didn't know what to catch. Grabbing at him as he reached her, she was pleased to gain a purchase, only to find that what she actually grabbed was his wellies. Fred flew past her and landed with a thump on the ground at the bottom of the slide and burst into tears.

Lisa panicked and picked him up. Sure that he would have a bruise to match the pattern of the rubber matting on his back, she stroked her hand up and down it. Poor Fred was in a state. The parents in the park were all looking in their direction, while the mini-superheroes promptly made themselves scarce. Lisa wanted the ground to swallow her up. To make matters worse as she rubbed her hand across Fred's back she could feel a lump, a large hard lump. *Oh no!* With no parents coming forward to offer help or advice and no phone to call Felicity, Lisa decided she had no other option. She would have to take him to a doctor and she would have to get him there fast before he ended up looking like the hunchback of Notre-Dame.

Chapter Twenty-One

Hoping desperately that Felicity was still registered at Dr Greene's surgery, Lisa carried Fred over to the reception desk. The woman, whom Lisa didn't recognise, continued to write without even the courtesy of a glance to acknowledge their presence. While Lisa was happy that Fred was now calmer than he had been on the journey, she couldn't help but think they might get more attention if he was still hollering as he had been in the van.

Waiting bought back memories of standing at the reception desk with Felicity when they were teenagers; back then they'd had to endure the disapproving look of her elderly neighbour, Mrs Bates – as if checking into the family planning clinic wasn't embarrassing enough when you were seventeen, without your neighbour judging you with the knowledge that planning a family was the antithesis of what was on your mind.

'Don't worry, Fred, the *nice* lady will soon take your name.' Lisa spoke loud enough to ensure the disdain in her voice was heard, while Fred took comfort in rediscovering and chewing the strings on her hoody.

Finally, the woman looked above the rim of her glasses. 'You can check in on the screen there.' She pointed at the wall to Lisa's left, offering a half smile that Lisa decided not to interpret as patronising.

Lisa looked at the large touchscreen asking her to check in. 'Oh, we don't have an appointment.'

'No appointment?' The tone and accompanying look removed any ambiguity as to whether the smile had been intended as patronising.

'But Fred here is hurt, he fell off the slide and—'

'We're not an Accident and Emergency service,' the woman scoffed.

'I'm aware of that, but you are roughly fifteen miles closer than the nearest Accident and Emergency, and this little boy is hurt.' Lisa looked at Fred, whose eyes were still red from crying, his face stained from tears.

'But—'

'Is there anybody who can just take a look at him?' Lisa tried not to sound exasperated, but it seemed that the medical assistance Fred might need was in grasping distance and the dragon of a receptionist, who obviously saw herself as the gatekeeper to that assistance, stood in her way.

'You should have called.'

'Yes, yes, I should have, or I should have called his mum or an ambulance or anybody who might be able to help me, but all of that, you see, all of that was not possible because my ...' Lisa paused, and held back the expletives she knew wouldn't help her cause. '... phone is dead!'

'So you're not the boy's mother?'

Lisa took a breath. 'No, no, I am not, but Fred here was entrusted to me, and he has fallen and hurt himself, and I would very much like to have him checked over, so if I could please see someone.' She felt tears welling in her eyes as her desperation increased.

'Peeeeees,' Fred added, with no idea what the general conversation was about, but recognising the word his mummy often asked him to repeat.

Finally the woman softened. 'Well, you could have a long wait as we don't have a doctor available, but we have a paramedic in clinic today who may see you—'

'YES! Yes, please.' Relief flooded through Lisa. Returning Fred with an injury was bad enough, but returning him with an unchecked injury might be unforgivable and she couldn't risk that. The repairs to her friendship with Flick were still too fragile to take any chances.

While Fred, who it seemed was quite the dragon slayer, charmed the receptionist with his smiles, Lisa answered her questions. Luckily, she now knew Fred's surname and date of birth – otherwise she would have been stuck. She held her breath anxiously as the woman searched for his details.

'Fred Willis, there you are. Take a seat, but, as I said, it could be some time.'

Relieved that she was right in her assumption that Fred was registered at the surgery, Lisa thanked the woman, whom she was increasingly warming to, and headed through the double doors to the waiting room. Scanning the rows of blue plastic, slightly-too-close-to-each-other chairs Lisa chose to sit within eyesight of the reception desk. That way she could monitor who came in and out, and ensure Fred's wait was not prolonged by queue jumpers.

Settling into her seat and ensuring Fred was comfortable on her lap, Lisa stroked her hand over his back, cringing as she felt the lump. While she was relieved it wasn't getting any bigger she really wished it would just disappear. How could she possibly explain it to Felicity? She had only had Fred in her charge for a short while and she had … *broken him!*

While Fred continued contentedly chewing the strings of her hoody, Lisa looked at the others in the waiting room. There were three elderly women – Lisa wondered if they were the same women who had resided in the waiting room when she was younger – curly grey hair, wide trousers, soft shoes, square handbags on their laps; the mainstay of all doctors' waiting rooms. There was a man with some kind of bite or sting on his leg, and a child of similar age to Fred cuddled up on what Lisa presumed to be her mummy's lap. Lisa thought how the poor, little love looked hot and sweaty, *feverish* she imagined her Granny Blake saying. *What if it's catching?* Offering a sympathetic smile Lisa turned Fred in the opposite direction. She couldn't have him getting germs as well as an injury on her watch; *whatever would Flick make of that?*

Slipping Fred's jacket off, Lisa wished she could remove her own too, but after hearing the power of Fred's lungs on the drive to the surgery she didn't want to disturb him while he was happily chewing, even if that did mean she felt herself sweating up in a similar fashion to the flush-faced girl. Wiping her forehead, Lisa wondered why the room needed to be so stiflingly hot. There wasn't a single open window and the small radiators running along the skirting boards were firing out an unnecessary amount of heat. She was sure she could feel the germs breeding around her. One of the elderly ladies coughed and Lisa sent her a glare before she could stop herself. She knew her panic was largely based on the paranoia about germs she had inherited from her mother. But, with Fred to look after, she couldn't help but fear that the dreaded lurgies were multiplying in anticipation of making him their next victim. The words '*a hive of germs*' rampaged through her mind as she realised the older she got the more she was turning into her mother! Before that thought could linger, a woman pacing up and down in the reception area walked too close to the sensors, causing the automatic doors to open. Lisa welcomed the hit of cool air.

Having chewed Lisa's hoody strings into a contorted shape from which she felt they might never recover, Fred began to fidget. Realising she had left all his things in the van, she looked round for something to occupy him. *Don't all doctors' surgeries have toys?* If only he were an adult, there would be plenty to keep him busy. It was a case of information overload. There was a large screen scrolling advice on head lice, diabetes and alcoholism, as well as displaying the BBC News' headlines in a constant stream across the bottom, in case the former wasn't depressing enough. Posters galore were housed in wipe-clean display boards all around the walls, and a table smothered in leaflets for all things medical and local stood in the corner. Spotting a shelf with second-hand books for sale, Lisa wondered if there might be something suitable for Fred. But as a closer look revealed that half the shelf was stocked with pre-loved copies of *Fifty Shades of Grey*, she decided to look elsewhere.

Rummaging in her bag, Lisa spotted a packet of chocolate animals Flick had given her as a mock 'thank you' after she had helped give out party bags with Fred. They'd be a good distraction she was sure – food always worked to take her mind off things. She offered them to him and Fred smiled; *success.* It was only as she opened them and saw his hand slip in the bag it dawned on her that she had no means to clean him up. Chocolate, a toddler and a warm room were not a good mix. Finding a tissue in her pocket, Lisa remembered how her mum used to spit on a tissue to wipe her clean as a child. *Hmmm!* There was no way she would be doing that. Lisa smiled, relieved that perhaps she wasn't turning into her mother after all.

As Fred slowly crunched and dribbled his way through the biscuits, the man with the bite or sting on his leg began tapping his foot on the shiny-plastic, fake wooden floor. Lisa tried to ignore it, but, coupled with Fred's eating, it was doing nothing for her nerves. For about the fiftieth time since leaving the park Lisa wished her phone was charged so she could call Felicity. She didn't want her to worry where they were, and, despite the fact she wanted to get Fred checked out before returning him, Lisa knew she would feel better if Felicity were there too. *Note to self, have a fully charged phone when taking out other people's children!* Not that she imagined that would be happening again any time soon.

Finally, Fred's name was called, stating that he needed to go to 'the treatment room'. As she did what she could to wipe his face with her tissue, Lisa hoped he wouldn't need any treatment and felt the weight of being there without Felicity even more keenly. What if he needed something done? She couldn't OK treatment without Flick's say so. She wondered why she hadn't just driven him home before going straight to the doctor's. And then she knew it was because she wanted to get it right. Overreact rather than not act at all and be the cause of something vital being missed. Some lessons were learnt the hard way.

Lisa knocked tentatively on the treatment room door.

'Come in.'

As Fred looked at her trustingly, Lisa attempted a reassuring smile and opened the door, but as she locked eyes with the paramedic, who was sitting behind the desk in full green-shirt-matching-trousers-and-steel-toe-capped-boots uniform, she did a double take.

He glanced up from his computer. 'Hello, I'm—'

'Dom!' Lisa finished, not quite believing her eyes. There was no trace of leather and the surroundings were much improved from their last meeting, but there was no doubting it; it was definitely him.

'Rose!' The surprise in his dark brown eyes was clear.

Lisa felt heat rise to her cheeks and hoped Dom didn't notice. She didn't know why, but she felt like she had blushed more lately than she ever did as a teenager. Back then she had been cool and collected, her emotions in check; a person who rarely gave thought to others' opinions of her.

'Lisa.' Fred laughed, jerking them both back into the moment.

'Lisa, yes,' Dom echoed, switching to a professional, formal mode, and directing both Lisa and Fred to take a seat. 'As you know, I'm Dom. I'm an advanced paramedic practitioner and I'm taking this clinic this afternoon.'

Lisa sat down as her mind continued to attempt to assimilate the information that Dom was sitting there before her, completely out of the context in which she expected to see him, and that he was a paramedic. Suddenly the words 'called away on an emergency' carried more weight.

'And you must be …' Dom glanced back at the computer he had been studying as Lisa opened the door. 'Fred,' he finished, with a smile.

Realising that Dom was now speaking directly to him, Fred hid his face in Lisa's arm.

Dom smiled. 'OK, Fred, I'll ask … Mummy.'

'Oh, I'm not his mummy.'

'I'm sorry. I assumed. Sorry. So you're Fred's?'

Oh Lord! It was like Jack all over again. 'Friend.'

'You're this little boy's friend?'

Realising how ridiculous that sounded Lisa grimaced. 'No, well, yes, but that's not what I meant. He's my friend's son.' Lisa inwardly cursed the fact she hadn't just said that in the first place.

'Ah, from pet sitter to baby sitter.' Dom laughed.

Lisa realised that explaining that Fred had fallen off the slide on her watch to the man who knew that Jack had run away also on her watch made her look like a terrible guardian of dogs and children alike.

Aware that Lisa was not laughing with him, Dom stopped smiling and returned to the matter in hand. 'So why don't you tell me what has happened to young Fred here?'

Lisa related the events of the park, minus the mini-superheroes and the fact that she was left holding Fred's Gruffalo wellies, ensuring she mentioned the lump on his back and the fact it had got no bigger while she had been monitoring it – saying that at least made her feel that she had demonstrated responsibility after the fact.

'OK, and did Fred bump his head at all on landing?'

'No, I'm pretty sure his back took the impact.'

'And has Fred been drowsy at all since, or felt sick?'

'No, he's been wide awake, he cried a lot in the car—'

'Cried in pain?'

'I don't know; it was loud.' Were there different types of crying? Lisa didn't know. 'He stopped when we got here and he's eaten some chocolate animal biscuits.' Lisa realised as she said it that she probably shouldn't have let him eat in case he had to have treatment.

'OK, and I can see from his notes he has no allergies and isn't on any prescribed medication at the moment.'

Lisa simply nodded and smiled, grateful that Fred's notes were able to answer questions she couldn't.

Dom asked for permission to examine Fred and pushed his chair back decisively. Lisa wished again that Flick was there, but knew she had to see the appointment through now. Leaving midway through an examination on a child probably looked worse than presenting with one who didn't actually belong to you. She nodded her head.

Fred was less willing to give his consent and began to squirm. Lisa didn't know what to do to get him to comply, but it seemed Dom had seen it all before.

'I have just the thing,' he announced, leaning over to a box of rubber gloves.

Lisa began to panic; she couldn't let him tranquillise him, that would be a step too far. 'Dom, wait—' But as she spoke she realised he was blowing one of the rubber gloves up.

Fred stopped to watch it get bigger and was delighted when Dom drew a face on it, which, in Lisa's opinion, rather expertly transformed it into a chicken. *Now that's a natural, Melissa*, Lisa thought, watching the way Dom was now able to use the balloon chicken to coax Fred to let him look at his eyes and listen to his chest. Having made a new best friend, Fred lapped up the attention, giggling and being compliant, with not a hint of the welly-stamping two-year-old to be seen.

As Dom checked each of Fred's vertebra, Lisa knew she had done the right thing bringing him. It made her feel some of the tension ease from her shoulders for the first time since the incident. She welcomed the smooth, calm voice Dom used as he spoke; she knew it was probably intended to calm Fred, but there was no doubt it was having a not-unwelcome effect on her too.

It was only due to the fact Dom stopped talking that she realised the examination was over and registered, for the first time, the grave expression on his face. Lisa looked at him, eyes wide, her breath suspended.

'Well—' he began.

'What? Is it bad?' Lisa wondered what the protocol would be if she should need Felicity there. She couldn't leave Fred to go and get her.

'What he has there, is a scapula, roughly triangular in shape, positioned on a posterolateral aspect of the thoracic cage.'

Lisa let out her breath and felt sick rise in her throat as

the colour drained from her cheeks. 'What does that mean? Oh my God, tell me. Is it bad?'

'It means he has ... a shoulder blade.' Dom delivered flatly before offering her a cheeky grin.

'What?'

'The lump you're feeling is his shoulder blade. It's meant to be there. In fact I'd be more worried if it wasn't. Here, feel; there's one on the other side too!'

Lisa cringed. 'Oh!' she wanted to cry and didn't know if it was from relief or embarrassment.

'Sorry, I shouldn't have joked about it. It's obvious you are concerned and it's always best to be on the safe side.' Dom reached out and touched Lisa's hand.

The gesture was reassuring and kind, and made her want to cry more. A noise in the corridor outside made them both jump. In a fluster Lisa pulled her hand away and decided she needed to be gone. 'I'm sorry.'

'Really, it's fine. He had a fall and you were right to get him checked. This kind of thing happens more often than you'd think,' Dom stated.

'Thanks, but I should go. You're busy.' Lisa thought about the little girl all hot and sweaty; there were people, children with genuine problems, who needed appointments.

'Not at all and, seriously, you should keep an eye on him in case he hit his head, but, honestly, he seems fine.'

Despite Dom's reassuring tone, Lisa felt too hot in her hoody and flustered as she attempted to exit. 'I'm sorry I've wasted your time.' Fred on her hip, she moved to go to the door but Dom stood in front of her.

'Look, if it makes you feel better, you owed me. I wasted your time before ... right?' Dom looked at her waiting for recognition.

Lisa looked at him puzzled.

'I heard you made it for our coffee; I'm sorry I—'

Now she was even more embarrassed as she remembered Celine Dion serenading her back to her van. 'Oh that, yes, very funny!' She attempted to move past him.

'I wasn't trying to be funny; please, if you'll give me another chance ...'

Lisa looked at his dark, chocolate eyes, tempting her to say yes, and then she thought about Nathan and the memory of looking into his eyes as they had said goodbye the night before. 'I can't, I'm ...' *Mortified at how stupid you must think I am, not sure what I'm doing, full of what ifs.* '... busy,' she finished.

Dom looked surprised and disappointed.

'But, thank you, really. Especially for this.'

Chapter Twenty-Two

'My God, Lisa, I was starting to get worried.' Flick stared at Lisa, only then realising that she had been crying.

Pete came to the door and took Fred. He began to say something, but Felicity placed her hand on his arm. He looked between her and Lisa. 'I'll take that as a cue to make myself scarce then, shall I?' Fred in his arms, he headed to the kitchen. 'I'll get him something to eat.'

Felicity mouthed, 'thank you' and led Lisa through the hall.

It had been years since Lisa had actually been inside Flick's mum's house, and it seemed, since inheriting it, Felicity and her family had made it their own. It was hard to take in how different it looked. The patterned carpet had been replaced by laminate flooring. There was an overflowing basket of shoes at the bottom of the stairs. The coat hooks were smothered in an array of coats in different sizes and colours. The once-bright-yellow walls were beige, and adorned with framed photographs of Flick and her family. It gave a sense of happy, homely chaos.

As they entered the lounge, Felicity pushed the door to, and attempted to keep her voice quiet and even. 'What on earth happened? Is everything OK? Was Fred OK?'

Lisa began to explain, her heart pounding. She knew Felicity would think she was a terrible friend. She had trusted her with her son for the first time ever and he had ended up falling off the slide. Albeit he had no actual injuries, but Lisa knew that was the result of luck rather than her babysitting abilities. Ben was right, how could she ever look after a child of her own? *Sometimes things really do happen for a reason*, she could see that now.

Felicity listened. Lisa told her about being in the park, the swearing incident and about Fred insisting on going on the big slide. Lisa repeated over and over that she knew she should never have let him. As Lisa got more and more animated in her explanation, Felicity watched bemused. When Lisa finally got to the part about being left holding Fred's wellies as he flew off the slide, silence fell between them. Felicity tried to offer a sympathetic smile, and to take it all seriously, but the image of Lisa holding Fred's Gruffalo wellies and him zooming off the slide made her begin to giggle.

'Oh, I'm sorry. But when I saw your face, I was just expecting something so much worse than that.' Felicity bit her lip in an attempt to stop herself from grinning.

Lisa stared in disbelief. 'It's not funny!'

'Oh, Lisa, it is a bit. I know what Fred's like. I bet he stamped his foot about the slide!'

'Yes, but I'm the adult. I could have ... should have ... stopped him.'

'OK, maybe you should, but he wouldn't have wanted to listen.' Flick put her arm round Lisa, feeling mean for laughing when she was clearly shaken by it all. 'He's baby number four, he's into everything and thinks he can do everything. He would probably have done the same if I were there. Lisa, really, don't beat yourself up about it.'

'But he landed on his back. I took him to see the doctor.'

'The doctor? What doctor?' Felicity realised she may not have taken the situation seriously enough.

'Your doctor, Dr Greene, but he saw the paramedic.' Lisa had no idea how to throw into the mix that it was Dom and decided to stick to the point in hand.

'Oh my God! Why did he need a paramedic?'

'He didn't, I just wanted him checked over. The paramedic was the only one free. I was worried he was hurt.'

'And was he? Is he OK? Why didn't you call?'

'My bloody phone was dead; I'm sorry. He is OK. I wanted to do the right thing. He had a lump—'

'A lump?' Felicity removed her arm. 'What do you mean he had a lump? Is Fred OK?' Her words came out more curtly than she intended, the thought of her son actually being injured sinking in.

'Well, I thought it was—'

'What?'

'Something broken, but I was wrong, he wasn't hurt. It was nothing.'

'Then what was the lump?'

'His ... well, his—'

'His what?'

'His ... shoulder blade.' Lisa felt stupid saying it. 'The lump I could feel was just Fred's shoulder blade.'

Felicity took a moment as she processed Lisa's reply before bursting into more laughter.

'I'm so stupid; how would I not know that?'

'Oh, Lisa, you are too funny!' Felicity managed.

With that Lisa began to cry. Not just a few tears, but big hearty sobs.

Felicity looked on stunned. She put her arm back round her in an attempt to get her to stop, but Lisa cried on – releasing all the tension of the afternoon, and the hurt and frustration that had built up over months. 'Lisa, it's OK. I'm sure they see that kind of thing all the time.'

'But you don't understand,' she managed between sobs.

'What? Tell me.'

'It's me. I'm so bad at this, so very bad.'

'Lisa, I'm sure that's not true.'

'But it is ... I ... I'm a bad pet sitter. Dogs run away from me. I was terrified when you asked me to have Fred. I swore in front of a toddler, I let Fred on the big slide, I thought I'd broken him, I didn't even realise the lump on his back was his shoulder blade and ... and ... I couldn't even take care of my own baby.'

The final part of the sentence coming as a complete shock, Felicity was taken aback; she didn't know what Lisa meant. She had no idea she'd even had a baby. 'What baby? Lisa, what baby?'

'My baby,' Lisa cried, the words coming out in long sobs that she had held on to for too long.

'What do you mean? Do you have a baby?' Felicity rubbed Lisa's back, trying to understand what she meant and realising how little they knew of each other's lives over recent years. 'Tell me, Lisa, what do you mean?'

Lisa could barely compose her voice; her head hurt and her nose ran as she began to speak, unsure where she was finding the words. 'My baby, the baby I lost; I was eight weeks pregnant.'

Felicity bit her lip, wanting to question everything, but knowing that she had to let Lisa speak.

'Barely pregnant at all really, I suppose, but I could feel it – my baby. It was there ... its heart beat inside me.'

Felicity watched as big tears slipped down Lisa's cheeks as she attempted to compose herself to speak.

'I couldn't talk to Ben about it. But it was part of me.' Lisa paused and wiped her hands across her sodden face, and ventured a small smile. 'When I showered or lay in the bath, when I was alone, I'd talk to my little Pip. That's what I called it; silly, isn't it?'

'It's not silly,' Felicity whispered, tears rolling down her face as she listened to Lisa speak. She thought about her own babies; they had all had bump names – names she and Pete had chosen together. After he had been born with a mop of red hair Callum had even remained her pumpkin.

'I'd felt some pains, strong, stabbing pains.' Lisa held her stomach, remembering how they felt. 'But I ignored them; I didn't want to think about what they might mean. I didn't tell anyone.' It was the first time Lisa had confessed it out loud. With the words spoken she couldn't hold back her tears.

Felicity reached over to a box of tissues on the coffee table and passed one to Lisa. Without acknowledging the gesture Lisa took the tissue and wiped her face before taking in a shaky breath and continuing.

'Then one morning I couldn't pretend any more. I went to the loo and the tissue was bright red, screaming at me. I called Ben, left a message and went to the hospital. I had to wait for a scan.'

Felicity passed another tissue.

'They sat me with the heavily pregnant women – their babies strong and thriving inside them while I could feel the blood seeping out of me. When they called me in, I already knew.'

'Was ... Ben with you then?'

Lisa took a breath, attempting to prepare herself to share the next memory.

Flick held her hand.

Megan burst through the door, complaining that Alice was wearing her ballet costume. She looked between Flick and Lisa, not sure whether to continue as she took in the scene.

Lisa hid her face, while Flick urged Megan to go and see her daddy in the kitchen.

Megan paused for a moment.

'Go on, Daddy will get Alice to take it off,' Felicity urged.

Megan stared. 'Why are you sad?'

'We're fine; go on, go see Daddy. Later you can tell Lisa about your ballet.' Felicity knew it was inappropriate, she didn't even know if being around her children would be too much for Lisa, but Megan didn't like to see people upset and needed the reassurance.

Megan left the room backwards, not taking her eyes off her mum until she had to.

'Oh God, Flick, sorry, how was the ballet?' Lisa realised she hadn't even asked.

'Don't you change the subject on me, Lisa Blake. Please, tell me. Did Ben go with you?'

Lisa swallowed. 'No. I went alone. I was so scared, Flick.' Her tears began again.

Flick hugged her a little tighter.

'At first I couldn't look at the screen, but the man was so bloody quiet, just clicking a button, staring at the monitor. He wasn't saying anything. So I looked. There was nothing. Dark emptiness. No heartbeat, no flicker of life. Empty. A dark void where my baby should have been.'

'Oh, Lisa.'

'They took blood, saying about checking hormones. But I knew. It was mad. I knew. They must have known. But they carried on talking like it might not be true. Like we needed confirmation of what we'd all seen with our own eyes. My baby was gone!'

'I'm so, so sorry for your loss, Lisa.' Flick had to say it, the words felt so inadequate, but she didn't know any others to convey how desperately sad she felt for her.

'I should have gone ... should have said when the pains started. Maybe it would have been different then.'

'Oh, Lisa, I'm sure that's not true. You can't blame yourself.'

In the days that had followed, as she sat alone in the flat she shared with Ben, Lisa had done nothing but blame herself with the if onlys, the maybes and all the things she thought she should have done differently.

Felicity took a breath and attempted to make her voice steady. 'At that time there's so much you have no control over; your little one was probably just not strong enough to make it.'

Little one. Lisa held on to the words. 'My little one. The doctor said the "embryo" had gone, the midwife said the "foetus" hadn't been "viable", and all the while I was screaming and shouting inside. It was my little one, Flick; it was my baby. I lost my baby, not an embryo, not a foetus, but my baby!'

Felicity could see the pent up anger in Lisa's face as she spat the words.

'Of course you did, Lisa. Your baby had been inside you the way each of mine grew inside of me. Why should yours be treated differently to mine? They all started out the same.'

Lisa looked at her, fresh tears welling in her eyes. 'But I will never know what it is to hug my baby, what the future would have been, all the days we should have shared. I never got to see my little Pip's face, to watch her grow.'

As Lisa sobbed Felicity continued, 'No, you didn't, and that isn't fair and it is so horribly sad ... but, Lisa, you must know, while your baby's heart beat inside you it felt your love; Pip knew your love. You never got to hold your baby in your arms, but Pip felt your love.' As the words came out Felicity hoped they weren't the wrong things to say; she didn't want to make Lisa more upset.

Unable to contain herself Lisa cried, letting her tears flow freely and her sobs come long and hard. The recognition that she had lost her baby and that somebody understood her, condoning the grief she felt and the tears she shed, overwhelmed her. When she lost her baby it had felt like the world had kept turning without even noticing that her world had shattered. Ben had said lots of things to try to pull her out of the deep, dark sadness she had felt, but she knew he didn't understand the depth of her feelings – how could he, when for him the loss was a release from a future he didn't want?

'And Ben?' Felicity ventured.

Lisa took a shaky breath. 'We should have split up before. Life in London, it was different to when we were travelling. Ben was different. He changed. I just didn't see how much, until I was pregnant. And then, when I lost Pip, he was relieved. He hadn't wanted the baby in the first place. He thought I was a "selfish bitch" for getting pregnant, that we were better off it being just the two of us. He wanted me to talk to the doctor about ways to "get rid of it". Our baby, Flick, how could he say that? Of course, I refused. And that made him angry.'

Felicity's gaze met Lisa's – the pain of the memory was reflected in her face.

'Did he hit you?'

Lisa bit a little too hard on her lip. *Never a hit, arms held too tightly, a grab, a shove – always the threat.* 'No. Ben's a manipulator and a shouter, and when that doesn't work, he's a sulker.' Lisa shrugged. 'And look, he got his way. Just like he always does. Even my own body agreed that I was kidding myself, I wasn't fit to be a mother. Ben was right, I'm not "mummy material"!'

That was the small part she had shared with Winnie. Lisa had never got as far as reiterating the exact anger-fuelled sentence that was branded on her mind; where Ben had spat every word, as he pinned her to the wall – punctuating the sentence with expletives – his hands too tight on her forearms, his breath too hot on her face. She had never shared the details of the loss of the baby with Winnie, or discussed her emotions – the way she had with Felicity – but telling Winnie she and Ben had disagreed about having a baby and that Ben said she wasn't 'mummy material' had set dear, sweet Winnie against him.

Felicity felt anger well inside. 'Lisa, you know that's not true, don't you? You know it wasn't your fault.' She didn't know Ben, but he sounded like a horrible bully. The things he said were inexcusable and cruel.

As Felicity went to speak, Pete knocked on the lounge door and opened it just a bit. 'Look, I don't know what's up, but Megan said ... well, anyway, I thought you might like these.'

Felicity's heart swelled at the sight of Pete with two glasses of wine in his hands. It was one of those moments she could feel how much she loved and appreciated him. She wanted to hug him as she watched him place the glasses on the coffee table.

'Dinner's nearly done, it'll be about five minutes. Why don't you both join us? Fred wants you to.' Pete offered a small smile.

Flick looked at Lisa, unsure if she was up to sitting down amid their family and eating. How did you follow a conversation like that? There seemed no right way to proceed.

Lisa thought for a moment. She didn't want to be alone. Being at Flick's with the noise of Pete and the children in the kitchen, she felt less lonely than she had for a long time. 'That would be ... lovely ... thanks.' She sniffed and wiped her blotchy face.

Felicity leaned over and passed her a glass of wine. 'Here, get some of this inside you, and then why don't you pop upstairs and help yourself to whatever you need to get sorted.'

'Thanks, I'll try to make myself look human again.' Lisa's voice was still shaky and she realised her nose was running and wiped it.

'Bloody hell, don't push it; there's only five minutes before dinner.'

Lisa hit out at Flick.

With red eyes and tear-stained faces, they hugged.

As she went upstairs, avoiding the toys stacked to the side of the first three steps, Lisa looked at the pictures on the wall. Each showed a snapshot of Flick's life since she had not been a part of it. There were photographs of days out, holidays, the children all so much younger, and Flick and Pete getting married – the two of them looking so young. Flick looked stunning on her wedding day and Pete looked thoroughly besotted with her.

Almost at the top of the stairs, Lisa paused, the pictures that had been too far up the wall for her to notice on her way in stopping her in her tracks. Photographs of Felicity with her mum took her back. *I can't believe you've gone, Mrs F!* Felicity's mum had always been kind to Lisa, despite the fact that some of the antics she and Flick got up to must have tested her patience. Lisa remembered how she made the best chips – real ones, made in a deep-fat fryer – while her own mum had insisted oven chips were healthier and less smelly. *Real chips and a runny egg, please Mrs F!* Lisa could almost taste them.

Spotting a picture of herself with Flick brought a lump to her throat and caused tears to well in her already-stinging eyes. They must have been about sixteen; dressed to impress, arms linked round each other, pulling faces. Lisa remembered Flick's mum standing behind the camera, trying to take a sensible shot while they were being too silly to comply. The fact that Felicity had kept the picture, had it hanging on her wall along with her family photographs, made a sob escape her. Feeling how grateful she was for Felicity's friendship she wiped away a tear. *Only a true friend can turn sad tears to happy tears.*

Chapter Twenty-Three

Feeling refreshed from the warm flannel she had held on her face, but not really looking any less blotchy, Lisa took a seat at the kitchen table. Looking around, she took comfort in the fact that little had changed in the kitchen since they were younger. There were definitely more things around them, comics and colouring pens pushed to the back of the table, a highchair, toys and baby wipes, as well as all-new, green kitchen accessories – as opposed to Mrs F's choice of red – but the foundations were the same. The lino, the fridge, the cupboards – they were all exactly as Lisa remembered them. Despite the fact Megan was eyeing her suspiciously and everybody had to squash up at the table to make room for her, Lisa felt like she belonged.

Pete got out plates and cutlery before taking chicken and wedges out of the oven. At the same time Felicity microwaved a pot of mashed potato, explaining that Fred didn't like wedges, and strained the peas and carrots from a saucepan that had been bubbling away on the hob. Lisa watched Pete and Felicity moving together in a well-practised routine. She noticed how Pete brushed past Felicity, touching her at the small of her back, moving her away from the open oven and hot baking trays. She wondered if Flick noticed the contact or the simple gestures that showed he cared.

Looking at him properly for the first time, it was clear Pete spent time outside; his face and arms were tanned and slightly freckled. His auburn hair was dark, but exposure to the sun had streaked it with redder highlights. His hands and arms revealed someone used to manual labour, showing strength in the manner his muscles flexed and his pumped veins traced the contours of his forearms. Lisa thought of Nathan's arms and how it felt when he had hugged her goodbye on the doorstep, with a warmth that filled her mind with reminiscences and her body with longing.

When, finally, the tomato sauce had been fetched and cups of water filled, Flick, Pete and all the children joined Lisa at the table. Lisa realised it was the first meal she had shared as part of a family for a long time and enjoyed the moment. Her head still ached from the tears she had shed with Felicity and she wasn't sure the wine was helping, but somehow she felt lighter for having shared all that had happened.

While she had once feared she might find it hard to see Felicity with her *four* children, seeing her so at ease amid her family, Lisa felt genuinely happy for her. She knew harbouring jealousy would not make things different. Her little Pip would not be brought back by resenting others any more than she would by wishing. God knows she had tried that.

As they began to eat, Felicity noticed that Megan was still eyeing Lisa suspiciously. She was so much like Pete in the way she always wanted to protect her; it was sweet, but sometimes stifling. Lisa must have noticed it too, as she began to ask Megan about her ballet. Flick was pleased that Lisa appeared genuinely interested and Megan relaxed as she lapped up the attention.

Feeling more at ease now Megan was looking happier, Felicity sipped her wine. But, as she leaned back, she noticed that Alice was not eating. Sighing, she turned her attention to her. 'What's up?'

'I can't eat while Callum's doing that!' Alice pointed an accusing finger at her brother.

'What? Pumpkin, what are you doing?'

Callum shrugged his shoulders, looking innocently around the table.

'Eat up,' Pete interjected.

'But I can't. I can't eat while he's doing that!' Alice repeated, more insistent this time.

Felicity sighed. 'What is it, Callum? What are you doing?'

'Nothing,' he insisted, offering a smile that revealed a mouthful of dinner.

'There, see, he's not doing anything,' Felicity said, lifting her glass.

'But he's holding his penis!' Alice blurted out.

Felicity sprayed a mouthful of wine across the table and grabbed the baby wipes. Lisa slapped her hand across her mouth to stifle a giggle, Pete's cheeks turned red and all eyes turned to Callum.

He looked confused. 'My peanuts?'

'No, your penis, you don't see me holding my vagina, do you?' Alice continued.

'Oh my goodness, that's enough,' Felicity demanded. Turning to Lisa she continued, 'I'm so sorry; she's been learning sex ed. at school and now she's like an anatomical dictionary.'

'Well, you don't, do you?' Alice added, ignoring Felicity.

'You're so embarrassing. I was trying to talk about my ballet,' Megan complained.

'Sorry.' Still trying not to laugh as she bit into a piece of chicken, Lisa encouraged Megan to go on. 'Tell me more.'

'Well, I—'

'Well, at your ballet, I could see that boy's p—'

'Alice, you could not. Now, please, stop saying these things at the table and in front of our guest,' Felicity interrupted.

'I could too, in his tights.'

Lisa attempted to chew her chicken and not to let her amusement show.

'Alice, you are being rude!' Felicity glared, eyes wide.

Alice shook her head and spoke on an indignant sigh. 'Oh, Mummy, if I end up being a doctor, I'll need to use those words you find so rude!'

'Well, when you are a doctor you may use them, right now we're eating,' Pete said, sounding like the final authority on the matter.

But clearly Callum wasn't ready to let the subject go. 'At nursery, I told Lily she has a van ... van-gi-nar ... but she said it's a noo noo.'

Felicity put down her knife and fork. 'Not now, Callum!' Realising she had lost all control of the conversation and reminding herself to have a word with Alice about what she was teaching her brother, she had to bite her lip. She dreaded what Lisa was making of the madness that was dinner with her family. It was hardly the impression she wanted to give.

'She said I've got a winkle,' Callum said, biting on a potato wedge.

'Mum, make them stop!' Megan demanded.

'Winkle, winkle little star,' Fred sang.

Callum began to giggle wildly while the girls looked suitably horrified.

'Oh my God, I'm so sorry about this!' Felicity said to Lisa.

Lisa let out the laugh she had been desperately attempting to hold in, as Pete fetched the bottle of wine from the fridge.

Chapter Twenty-Four

Wishing he would let her help, Lisa watched Pete as he cleared up and loaded the dishwasher. She tried to think of something to say to fill the awkward silence, but Pete was a stranger to her, though she suspected he knew more about her than most other people she knew. Listening to the footsteps and mayhem upstairs, Lisa wished Flick had not insisted that she must have had enough of her 'nutty tribe' for one day and that she should stay downstairs, while she sorted the children for bed. It was a well-meaning gesture, but being amongst the children would have made her feel less out of place than sitting alone in the kitchen with Pete. She took a long drink of her wine.

'Thanks so much for letting me stay for dinner.'

Pete cursed as a spoon in the sink sent a spout of water over his T-shirt. He wiped it, before turning to face Lisa. 'You're welcome. Flick's happy to have you around, so ...'

'It's so kind of her—'

'She's like that, you know, kind. Sometimes she's too ... forgiving.'

The not so subtle hint hit home. Lisa took another drink of wine and swallowed hard. It was clear Pete was not impressed by how Felicity was letting her back into her life. A small part of her felt indignant. *What do you know? She was mine before she was yours, Pete Willis!* 'We've shared a great deal, Flick and I—'

'I know she used to talk about you a lot when we were first together, get excited over your calls, or the odd letter, get low when she didn't hear from you, and then even when all that had stopped, there were times when I think she needed you. Like when her mum died.'

Ouch!

'But we got through it, the two of us.' The judgement in his eyes was clear.

'I never knew about Mrs F or I would have come. Honestly, Pete, she meant a lot to me too. And so does Flick.'

Pete scoffed.

'Really, she does. I've let too much go, too much slip by. My life, with Ben, it didn't leave room for anything else.'

Pete paused midway between the sink and dishwasher, and raised his eyebrows at Lisa.

'I'm not trying to justify the past and I am not making excuses.'

'Look, Lisa, Flick is really happy you are back and that's great. I want her to be happy. Just don't … don't hurt her again. After her mum, she's more fragile than she lets on. Losing someone else, it could knock her back again.'

Lisa nodded silently. Pete was all muscle and manual labour on the outside, but on the inside he clearly cared a great deal for Felicity. And Lisa knew that words and reassurances could not prove she was here to stay – only actions could do that.

Hearing Felicity's footsteps on the stairs, Pete carried on loading the dishwasher and changed the subject. 'So have you got in touch with anyone else from the past since you've been home?'

'Didn't I tell you? Lisa is um … rediscovering Nathan Baker.' Felicity laughed as she entered the room.

Lisa choked. 'Hardly rediscovering; we've had a chat. We were friends once.' Again Lisa thought about saying goodbye to Nathan on her doorstep and pushed the feeling of that kiss away. 'We can be friends again.'

'Friends, yes, that's what you were.' Felicity sniggered and picked up her wine.

'OK, so maybe we were more than friends back then, but now, now we can only be friends; we are both grown-ups, so I'm sure we can manage that.' *So long as we avoid doorstep goodbyes, and knee-weakening reminiscences – I can manage that.*

'Nathan Baker, is that who you said? Is that who it was ... from the prom?'

'Yes, you remember, Pete. I told you that years ago.' Felicity rolled her eyes at Lisa.

Pete shrugged.

'He was Lisa's teenage crush, her first—'

'Flick!' Lisa interrupted.

Pete closed the dishwasher and leaned on the kitchen counter looking thoughtful. 'There's a Nate Baker that comes in the bar.'

'Bar?' Lisa looked at Flick.

'Pete's a landscape gardener by day, but at night he works for a mate of his at Cin Cin.'

Lisa still looked puzzled.

'A bar, in Arundel. I don't think you'd know it. I'll take you there sometime. Pete says the cash is handy, but with all these nights out I think he is up to something!' Felicity joked.

Pete ignored the comment. 'Nate Baker comes in sometimes, him and the rest of his crew.'

'Nate, yes, that's what he prefers now.' Lisa pulled a face at Felicity. 'He's a fireman.'

'That's him. I didn't make the connection; I didn't realise—'

'You didn't say he was a fireman – wait until I tell Melissa!' Felicity put her wine down, grabbed her phone and started a text.

Pete shook his head. 'I'll go and check they're settled upstairs.'

As Felicity's phone buzzed, she read the almost instant reply. 'Melissa says, "You know what they say about firemen." What do they say?' Felicity looked up puzzled.

'Mess with them, and they, or you, might get burned?' Lisa offered.

Felicity's phone buzzed again; she looked down and read the message before bursting into laughter. 'I prefer Melissa's answer: "They're hot stuff and they've got big hoses!"'

Lisa looked at Felicity who was still laughing. 'That's not even funny.'

Having decided that too much wine had been consumed and it had got too late for Lisa to go home, Felicity prepared her a bed on the sofa and told Pete he might as well head up himself. She didn't want to leave Lisa until she knew she would sleep. It had been a long day for her and, while Flick hoped the alcohol might take the edge off her raw emotions, she knew from experience, after her mum's death, that it wasn't always enough.

'He's lovely, your Pete. You're lucky to have him,' Lisa slurred.

'Thanks a lot. I'm not so bad myself you know!' Felicity laughed.

'That's not what I meant. He really cares about you. It's really obv ... obv ... clear.'

'I know! He is lovely, I just wish ...'

'What? What do you wish?' Lisa wanted to be a good listener, and she wanted to be the friend Flick had been to her and listen to what was on her mind. She just wished the room would stop spinning long enough for her to focus and do that.

'That we got a break sometimes, that we could find our ... I don't know, mojo, I guess.'

Lisa could only picture the chewy sweets she and Felicity used to get from the post office.

Felicity continued, 'I'd love that! We used to blow each other's minds back before life got so full of children and stuff.'

'And a mojo will fix that?' Lisa's mind wasn't keeping up.

'Yes, I often imagine just us on a hot beach, lying in a hammock, making slow, mind-blowing love.'

Finally, Lisa realised what she was talking about. 'So don't you now? Not the beach thing, but don't you make mind-blowing love?'

Holding the baby monitor, Pete stopped in his tracks outside the door.

'Hmmm, well ... it's all about the conservation.'

'Talking is important.'

'Not conversation, you bloody drunk, con-ser-vation. These days we mostly have ... conservation sex.'

'You do?' Lisa had no idea what that was. 'Is it en ... en ... environmentally friendly?'

'No, it's relationship friendly. I often feel too tired; my head isn't with it. I can't switch from Mummy on call to sex goddess. But I don't want to say no or appear like a miserable cow. I used to be bloody hot, you know. So instead I settle – conservation sex. I do it anyway, or something that will keep him happy. It keeps things ticking over.'

Lisa thought for a moment. 'Well, it sounds a bit shit!'

'Says the woman with a hot fireman, with a big hose at the ready. You lucky cow!'

Pete walked away. He had heard enough. He had his suspicions that Felicity wasn't completely happy, but hearing her describe their love life in that way, he knew he was right not to call things off at the bar. It was just a matter of picking the right time and then he would tell her.

'Pete's every bit as hot as any fireman. I bloody love that man! I want him. I just wish I had the time to breathe and to give him all of me. For him to just take all of me and for my mind to be where my body is.'

'I see.' Lisa really didn't see; in fact she could barely see anything with her eyelids getting so heavy.

'Not drifting off, thinking of shopping or washing, or what time the children are going to get me up in the morning.'

'I see.' Now Lisa was pretty sure all she was looking at was the inside of her eyelids.

'But it's not just that. I spend half my day with children clambering over me. Callum and Fred love their mummy cuddles and I love them hugging me, Megan and Alice too, but by the time they are all finally in bed I want my body back; a moment to be me. Sometimes it feels like I've given so much in the day I've got nothing left. And I miss enjoying sex. I feel sorry for myself, if I'm honest. Pete and I, we were great together. We couldn't keep our hands off each other once. I'd love to get that back!'

Lisa shifted on the sofa and Flick realised how tactless she had been; how could she complain about all those Mummy cuddles and having the children clamber over her after all that Lisa had said earlier? Guilt washed over her. 'Oh, Lisa, I'm so sorry. I—'

Lisa snored, finally succumbing to her desperate need to sleep.

Chapter Twenty-Five

'Well, it's good to see you smiling and looking happy, my lovely.' Winnie opened the biscuit barrel and poured the tea, while Jack settled into the prime spot for crumbs under the table.

'Thank you, I feel happy.' Since her talk with Felicity, Lisa was feeling happier than she had ever imagined she could when she had returned to her mum's house. She knew nothing had actually changed, she had still lost her little Pip and nothing could change that, but sharing her grief and having someone tell her it was OK to feel the depth of the loss she had been struggling with made her mind feel lighter. She felt more able to cope knowing she could talk to Felicity.

'So have you been getting out and about? Been anywhere or met anybody new?'

Lisa smiled. 'Well, nobody new, exactly.'

'If you're going to tell me that you're taking that dog swimming again, there'll be no custard creams for you, Lisa Blake.' Winnie placed her hand over the top of the biscuit barrel.

'A bit harsh, Winnie!' Lisa protested, pulling a mock shocked face. 'And I took Toby swimming just the other day. He was a very good boy; I went in with him. It was fun.' *Almost!* Lisa had to admit playing with Toby had been fun; she could have done without Babs insisting on joining them in the water with her pair of 'Newfs', but up until that point – when the water had turned into dog-hair soup – she had enjoyed it.

'I don't want to know about that daft dog. Tell me what or who has put that smile on your face.'

'Well, the truth is there's nobody new, but things with Felicity are going well. We feel like friends again. I'm not sure her husband is too keen on me, but I'll show him I can be a friend to Felicity. He's just worried about her, I'm sure.'

'Maybe he feels threatened by you.' Winnie bit her ginger nut biscuit.

'Me? Why would he? That makes no sense.'

'From what you've told me you two were close once. He must know that. With you around he has to share his time with Felicity.'

'Maybe.' Lisa wondered if what Winnie said was true, she was normally right after all, but, other than that one evening, she had not taken up any of Pete's time with Felicity. Besides, he didn't seem the type to be possessive over Felicity's time. Lisa knew all too well what that looked like. 'No, he can't be threatened by me.'

'And you left to travel, didn't you, my lovely? Getting married and having a family weren't for you. Maybe he's scared that you'll remind Felicity of the things she didn't do – of what she missed.'

Could that be it? 'But I don't think she's missed anything. She has her life left to travel and see things.' *There's no time limit on that; no clock ticking!* 'Her children will get older. If she wants those things, I'm sure she wants them with Pete. They love each other – I can see that.'

'That may be true, but sometimes people can't see the wood for the trees.'

Lisa sipped her tea, convinced that Winnie was talking in riddles again.

'So that explains the smile; now how about the twinkle in your eye?'

Lisa laughed. 'Honestly, Winnie, I'm just happy to have

friends like you. Work is going well – *no lost dogs recently* – and I'm really pleased to be reviving old friendships.'

'So it's not just Felicity.'

Damn. Lisa realised she had implied too much. Miss Marple clearly had nothing on Winifred Adams when it came to sniffing out a clue. Should she tell her about Nathan? She could do without Winnie making more of that situation than there was, or should be; she had Felicity and Melissa for that. If only she had lined up another drink with Dom; now she knew he was not a contender for *Crimewatch*, she could have mentioned that.

'Um ...'

Winnie sat forward in her seat.

Jack raised his ears.

Lisa inwardly berated herself; hesitating was building her news into something more than it actually was. 'There is ... someone.'

Winnie clapped her hands and swung her slippered feet in the air, causing Jack to scuttle out from under the table.

Oh no! Both Winnie and Jack had their eyes on Lisa in anticipation of an exciting morsel, and all she really had to offer was a once-rejected boyfriend who she was attempting to remain strictly friends with for fear of releasing all of those feelings she had attempted to quash over the years only to have to get over him all over again.

'Not that sort of someone.'

Winnie harrumphed back into her seat. Jack took his cue from her body language and slumped back under the table.

'It's ... it's another old *friend* ... like me and Flick.' *Really not like me and Flick!* Lisa knew her cheeks were turning red and hoped Winnie would not read too much into it. The fact she and Nathan had been more than friends in the past didn't mean they couldn't be just friends now. All she had to do was set some mental – if only she could control her wayward thoughts – and physical boundaries; boundaries that didn't involve moonlit goodbyes, and the feel of Nathan's muscular arms wrapped around her. 'Nathan Baker and I went to school together. I saw him the other evening.'

Winnie smiled and sipped her tea, her silence encouraging Lisa to continue when she hoped to leave the conversation there.

'We chatted; it was … nice.' *Perfect, like old times, once we both relaxed.*

'Uh-huh.' Winnie smiled.

'Nathan and I …' *Nathan and I?* That sounded way too couply. 'Nathan thought it would be nice if we saw each other again …' Lisa was about to add 'as friends', but realised that would imply they had once been more than friends.

'Well, I'm pleased for you, my lovely.'

Phew, well navigated, Lisa.

'And when are you seeing him again?'

Or not! 'Oh, I don't know.'

'Why not? Lisa, my lovely, when I saw you that first day, putting up your advert in the post office, you looked like a lost soul. Look at you now – there's a glow to your cheeks and a twinkle in your eye. Don't let the offer of friendship slide when it comes your way.'

Lisa felt a pang in the pit of her stomach; letting friendships slide was what she had done too much of in the past and she was not going to do it again. She had promised herself that. 'Well, he texted yesterday.' Lisa had ignored the text until now, but with Winnie's words fresh in her mind she took out her phone. 'He asked if I wanted to go to the fireworks on Saturday night, for old times' sake.' Finding

Nathan's message and deciding not to think on it any more, Lisa hurried off a text saying it would be fun and pressed send.

'Ooh, we all deserve some fireworks in our lives,' Winnie chortled.

Oh Lord! Lisa needed to change the subject before Winnie got too carried away. 'And how about you – spoken to your son?' *Ah ha, Winifred Adams, if I have to sort my life out then so do you!*

Winnie's eyes welled up. 'I wrote him a letter.'

'Oh.' Lisa put her cup down and held Winnie's hand – papery, cool skin over knotted bones.

Chapter Twenty-Six

You absolutely will not come with us!

Lisa read the text she had received from Felicity, smiled and sent her reply: I thought it would be fun, you know, seeing the fireworks with you, Pete and the children.

Felicity's response arrived moments after: Pete has to work tonight, now. I'm taking my lot for a quick look at the parade and back. And that's not the kind of fun you should be thinking about tonight.

Lisa rolled her eyes before sending Felicity a text telling her to behave, but Felicity's reply, I will if you don't ;-) made Lisa giggle. She had butterflies in her stomach and told herself they were caused by the excitement of a Saturday night out, as opposed to an evening in with Simon Cowell et al.

It had been years since she had been to see the bonfire procession and fireworks in town. In fact, the last time she had gone was almost certainly with Nathan. Prior to that teenage stand of independence, she had gone annually with her dad and brother, Luke, while their mum stayed at home with warmed pyjamas and hot chocolate ready for their return. Smiling at the happy memory, Lisa decided to give her parents a quick call.

'Hello, darling, what's wrong?'

'Nothing.' Lisa frowned; why an unexpected call made her mum assume something was wrong she had no idea. 'I was just thinking about you. It's the bonfire parade in town tonight and—'

'Oh, how awful.'

'Mum!'

'Well you remember what it's like, all those people you spend most of the year avoiding, dressed up and waving at you as if you haven't hated each other for years; pretend soldiers – cheeks bursting as they try to belt out a tune on a trumpet – with some wannabe sergeant major up front waving a baton; and those grumpy pom-pom girls – too fat for their miniskirts – followed by some beaten-up, old van driven by someone looking like a 1970s *Top of the Pops* presenter—'

'Mum, that is a terrible account of a lovely community event.' *And I suppose the French do it so much better!* 'Why would you say that? It's not like you even came with us!'

'I did when you were little. Why do you think I offered to stay at home and make sure the hot chocolate was ready for when you got back for all those years?'

Lisa couldn't believe it. As the memory, briefly warm and beautiful, fizzled into insignificance, extinguished by her mum's words, she decided not to mention that she was going, or whom she was going with. 'Well, I loved going with Dad and Luke.'

'I know you did, darling. Talking of Luke, have you thought any more about Christmas? You'll need to book soon if you're flying out. He's really looking forward to seeing you. We all are. Your Dad and I were just saying how lovely it would be to share our Christmas here with you both. It really has been too long since we've had a real family Christmas.'

A real family Christmas. Lisa bit her lip; why did family have that special knack of winding you up completely, making you feel guilty and reminding you how much you love and miss them all at once? 'I haven't forgotten—'

A ring at the doorbell made Lisa jump and her tummy flip.

'I've got to go, but I will sort Christmas soon, I promise. Love you, Mum.'

'Love you.'

Checking her appearance in the mirror, Lisa went to the door. *Just friends, just friends catching up!* The memory of the last time she had stood on the doorstep with Nathan made her cheeks turn pink and she blew out a steadying breath; *strictly no moonlit hugs.* Lisa knew she could do without such complications, her mind was getting too carried away. But Winnie was right, she did need friends and friendships were important. The fact she and Nathan had once dated did not have to complicate the issue, did it?

As Lisa opened the door, Nathan smiled. She liked his smile, she always had. He had a couple of days' worth of stubble across his chin, which she was beginning to realise must be a permanent fixture, and pre-ruffled hair. Both added to the rugged look of his outfit, which Lisa decided was Timberland does Canadian lumberjack.

'It's going to get bloody freezing later. Are you going to be warm enough?'

Lisa looked down at her jeans and jacket. 'Oh, hold on,' she said, and went back inside to grab her new scarf and hat. She picked up her gloves and hesitated, before putting them back on the side, telling herself it was too mild for gloves and that leaving them had nothing to do with hand holding opportunities that might arise during the evening.

The fact she had not yet worn any of her new knits dog walking meant they still looked a bit too new. The thought that Nathan might think she had bought them especially for the evening amused her. In London, accessories had been jewellery, expensive bags and shoes chosen by Ben. Now she was wrapped in woollies, in a way her Granny Blake would have approved of, and she felt more excited about going out than she could remember for a long time.

Stepping out into the cool evening air, Lisa was determined not to let her mum's words affect her judgement. She had always loved bonfire night and the expectant atmosphere it induced. She was almost thirty and she could still feel it. As excitement grew inside her she thought of the procession; the bonfire; the greasy, over-priced hot dogs – as her dad called them, while buying them despite his protestations – and, the climax of the evening, the grand firework display holding their attention until the final flash of colour lit the sky – a sign saying 'goodnight'.

Walking along the streets and seeing families leaving their homes and setting off in the same direction brought back happy childhood memories. Lisa remembered how excited she and Luke used to get if they glimpsed any fireworks in the dark evening sky en route to the procession. She always envied those families who had fireworks in their own gardens, while her mum would never allow it; she was always too worried about the scorch marks and the scattering of empty firework shells destroying her lawn. Lisa remembered how it had taken her mum weeks to recover from the horror of their neighbour, Mr Bates, almost setting fire to her weeping willow – a tree that Lisa felt made far more mess than any firework display would – with a rocket that went astray.

'Where do you want to stand?'

'Oh, anywhere really, I'm just happy to be out, away from my *X Factor* and *Strictly* friends.' Lisa cringed, realising that what was meant to be a joke made her sound rather sad. 'I mean, you know, it's Saturday night. It's been a while since I've had any excitement on a Saturday night.' *Shut up, shut up now!* 'I mean, in London I was out all the time.' *Oh yes, a party animal, that's me.* Lisa closed her mouth to stop herself rambling on further.

'Well, we could stand on the corner by Doc Green's surgery; that way we can get a drink en route, watch the procession and get down to the beach before everything else kicks off.'

'Sure.' Lisa wasn't sure she wanted to stand by the doctors' surgery, but she could hardly explain that she had made a fool of herself there, *taking Fred in for having a shoulder blade, for goodness' sake*, and that, for some reason she couldn't explain to herself, she felt awkward at the thought of bumping into Dom while out with Nathan. How could she possibly begin those introductions?

As they made their way towards the pub, their feet scrunching through fallen leaves, Lisa decided to let Nathan do the talking. She listened as he told her about the places he had travelled in search of the best wave, the most technical ski run, and the best climb. He was completely animated as he spoke, full of passion for his action-packed life. Lisa thought back to the Nathan she had known and the things he had wanted. She wondered if he ever considered how his life might have been different if she had said yes to his proposal, back when he thought the biggest thrill in his life would be saving enough for them to put a deposit down on a house. When she refused his proposal, she had set both of their lives on a different path.

Ironically, it seemed now, both of them had gone on to experience new adventures. OK, so it had been some years now since Lisa had done any thrill seeking, but in the early days, when she first went on her travels, she had embraced opportunities as they arose. She had learnt to snowboard, she had ridden jet skis and she had been brave enough to parapente off mountains in Chamonix. She had left her hometown to experience the world and she had – well, India and parts of Europe anyway. As Lisa continued to listen to Nathan talk about his love of travelling and extreme sports a thought slipped into her mind, one she had never considered before: *Would he have come with me? Could we have done it all together, if I had stopped to ask?* She decided to push the thought away. *Bloody what ifs!* Lisa knew they could eat you up if you let them.

Brushing past a man carrying an enormous bunch of helium-filled, Disney-character-adorned, glow-in-the-dark balloons, Lisa spotted Felicity and Melissa in the gathering crowd on the opposite side of the road. Bella was presumably somewhere hidden within the huge hood and warm cosy-toes of her pushchair, while Flick's children sat in a line along the edge of the kerb. Spotting Lisa they gave her a wave, flashing a variety of neon glow sticks, lightsabers and twirling, light-up butterflies in her direction. Touched that they looked so genuinely happy to see her, Lisa waved back, and laughed as Alice picked up a no-parking cone and plonked it on Callum's head. About to berate her daughter, Flick noticed Lisa and beckoned her over.

Lisa smiled. 'Look, it's Flick; let's say a quick hello.' The words slipped out naturally before she considered the fact that she, Flick and Nathan had not all been together since the night of the prom. And as if that didn't make the situation awkward enough, Lisa began to recall all of the silly comments Flick and Melissa had made about firemen.

Nathan seemed reluctant, but followed Lisa as she made her way across the road, dodging cars attempting to find their way out of town – avoiding roads already closed for the parade.

As Lisa neared Felicity and Melissa she mouthed 'Behave,' and gave them a 'don't you dare' glare, resulting in them doing shocked faces, portraying false innocence and giggling by the time they actually reached them.

'Nathan, look at you.' Felicity placed her hands on Nathan's biceps and turned to wink at Lisa.

Oh no! Lisa wished they'd just waved from afar.

'It's been a really long time.' Flick leaned in and gave Nathan a kiss on the cheek before letting him go. 'Though I think my hubby said he's seen you at Cin Cin. He works there some nights, you might know him, Pete—'

'No, sorry, I mean, I don't go there often,' Nathan interjected.

'Oh, OK.' Flick shook her head. 'I was sure Pete said—'

But before she could quiz Nathan further Melissa was introducing herself to him, and they were making small talk about the weather being perfect for the parade and fireworks, while the children started doing a light show for the benefit of their new audience.

'So how about you, Lisa, looking forward to the fireworks later?' Flick lifted her eyebrows suggestively.

'Yes, I'm sure they'll be good,' Lisa hissed, trying to remove any innuendo from Flick's comment, 'the display always used to be great,' and failing miserably.

Felicity sniggered and Lisa blushed.

'Anyway,' Lisa continued, 'we better go if we are going to get a drink before watching the parade.' To move Nathan away Lisa took hold of his arm, a move not missed by Felicity and Melissa who smiled as they said their goodbyes.

'Is Nathan Lisa's boyfriend?' Alice chirped after them.

'No, darling, he's her friend.'

Lisa smiled in relief, embarrassing moment avoided.

'Where's his big hose? You and Melissa said you might see Nathan's big hose!'

Lisa's eyes went wide and she picked up her pace, practically dragging Nathan along behind her as he barely bothered to stifle his laughter.

The pub was warm and busy. Lisa found it almost overwhelming. It had been a long time since she had been amongst so many people in a similar atmosphere. While she loved having her own business, working for herself and by herself, looking after pets whose owners were often out at work or away meant she could go whole days without speaking to other human beings. And while she always chatted to her furry clients they weren't exactly great conversationalists. Lisa knew isolating herself from the world around her had become an unhealthy habit. She needed a life. She was almost thirty and, despite how sad she had been recently, she knew she was not yet ready to give up on life and what it had to offer.

Nathan returned from the bar holding a wine for Lisa and a Peroni for himself.

'Here's to us,' he announced cheerily, passing her the wine and clinking glasses.

Lisa swallowed.

'Friends.'

'Friends.' Lisa took a big drink of her wine.

Leaving the warm pub made the evening air feel chillier in contrast to when they had gone in. Lisa wrapped her scarf back round her neck and pulled her hat down over her ears. She felt the cold seeping into her jeans.

As they took their place at the edge of the pavement outside the doctors' surgery, Lisa welcomed Nathan standing behind her, shielding her from the chilly breeze. They could hear the parade in the distance and see the grey haze wafting into the air caused by the torches of fire being carried. Children around them were becoming increasingly excited as their parents fuelled their anticipation – their own enthusiasm stoked by their proximity to the pub and the swift one they had allowed themselves while waiting.

'Here it isn't,' one dad repeatedly teased as his son groaned at him.

Nathan leaned down to Lisa. 'I wish here he wasn't,' he whispered, sending a shiver down her spine as his breath brushed her cheek.

Lisa nudged back into him in an attempt to get him to be quiet, but bumping into his firm torso did nothing for the goosebumps she could feel on her arms as she fought the urge to stay pressed against him.

Finally, the parade drew near. Lisa watched with a big smile on her face, just as she had for many years as a child. OK, so she could see a bit of what her mum meant, not all the pom-pom girls wore their skimpy outfit or a smile that well – but then who could blame them given the temperature – and she did get the occasional wave from people she could vaguely remember from school but hadn't seen for years. But it was clear that most people had made quite an effort.

The costumes worn by those brave enough to be carrying torches, with huge orange flames lashing up into the night sky, were amazing; not a hint of a last-minute dash to the fancy dress shop about them. Lisa had always loved the spectacular, feathered headdresses, though she hadn't noticed the small bells that chimed on the Native American Indian costumes before. As each of the torch-carrying walking groups went by, there was an awed hush from the crowd, punctuating the noise and mayhem from the rest of the parade. The Tudor lords and ladies that followed were every bit as impressive too.

Less impressive were the too-tight-fitting Spiderman costumes worn by a marching band of elderly gentlemen, who were showing off more than their musical skills with the cut of their tights. Sure that Alice would have had something to say about that, Lisa was pleased not to be standing with Felicity.

Despite the too-tight tights, Lisa had to admit the band was entertaining, carrying out a little sketch right in front of them in which one of them got shot by a man dressed as the Green Goblin who appeared from within a spacecraft – aka a shopping trolley – but nevertheless Lisa admired the effort. She glanced up at Nathan as they both laughed; she couldn't help but think how attractive he looked, with his features illuminated by the flashes of colour from the parade and glow-stick carrying spectators, and, how, despite how she had promised herself she would resolutely quash it, she liked the feeling stirring inside her reminding her of the connection they shared. *Oh Lord!* She let her stare linger a little too long as she looked from his lips to his blue eyes. He smiled inquisitively as his gaze met hers. She felt the beat of the bass drum thud through her as the band started on their way again, and smiled back as the noise and mayhem around them slipped into insignificance.

'Nathan—'

'Oi, give it back!'

Lisa spun around and watched as her bobble beanie, warm and cosy on her head one minute and whipped off her head by a passing pirate the next, was being thrown from person to person on a float bedecked in a Peter Pan theme. Nathan ran the few paces after it and impressively leaped up onto the side in one swift movement. He seemed to know the perpetrators, who laughed and launched the hat in the air towards a crows' nest where Captain Hook caught it. Lisa watched open mouthed at the whole episode, her mind racing from the intimate moment they had just shared to the fact Nathan was now several feet away on a float in the middle of the bonfire procession.

The sign on the back of the float, which had come to a halt while the elderly Spidermen, now further up the road, re-performed their sketch, indicated a link to the local fire brigade. The words 'Supporting those who run in when others are running to safety' made her breath hitch. She had never really thought about it like that before. Looking at Nathan as he started to climb the rigging in an effort to retrieve her hat it was as if she was seeing him anew. He was not the boy she had dated all those years ago, he was a grown up, responsible man – someone who runs towards danger as others are running away. *He's a real life hero!*

Shaking herself back to the moment and issue in hand, Lisa looked up to see the crow's nest swaying precariously as Peter Pan and a way-too-large Tinkerbell urged Nathan down. The crowd were enthralled and the cadet band following, spotting the spectacle, started to play the theme to *Mission Impossible* without missing a beat. Realising his predicament in the swaying crows' nest Captain Hook motioned defeat – much to the excitement of the crowd who whooped loudly. But as he threw the hat to the ground it was swept up by a waiting crocodile – or at least a man in a crocodile suit who seized his opportunity to take a starring role in the unfolding farce and revelled in the boos from the crowd. Walking along the line of onlookers in an attempt to keep up with the now steadily moving float, Lisa watched as Nathan leapt from the riggings and started to pretend to wrestle the crocodile. She couldn't help but laugh. *OK, so not entirely grown up!*

When, at last, he retrieved the hat, Nathan took a bow and began to beckon Lisa. She shook her head. There was no way she would manage to climb on board a moving float with anything like the ease Nathan had. She was pretty sure she was more likely to be crushed as she slipped from the edge under one of the huge truck wheels than arrive on board with a hint of decorum.

'Come on, I'll catch you!' Nathan put out his arms.

The crowd started to join in, calling for her to jump, and the band were hovering on the ending of the *Mission Impossible* theme, drawing out committing to the final note.

Oh bloody hell! Lisa wished she could just slip away amongst the crowd, but too many people had their eyes on her. She was pretty sure that leaping onto a truck – albeit a very slow moving one – broke many health and safety rules, and, really, anyone connected to the fire brigade should have known that. Taking a breath and doing a backward swing as if she were about to embark on the high jump, Lisa launched herself forward with the crowd cheering her on. It was only as she got nearer to the truck that she realised she was never going to make it. It was way too high, the angle was completely wrong. She didn't know whether to throw herself at it or run on by.

Just as it came to the crucial do-or-die or do-*and*-die moment, as she thought it might be, Lisa was swept up under the arms. She had a pirate either side of her, lifting her aloft and giving her enough elevation for Nathan to haul her up from them. While he smiled as he did so, Lisa was pretty sure the gritting of his teeth and the quake of his arms suggested she could have done with fewer Chinese meals and custard creams over recent weeks. Nevertheless, she had a huge grin on her face. The crowd were cheering, the cadet band released the final note of the *Mission Impossible* theme tune, the variety of steam engines following the band gave timely peeps and whistles, and Nathan pulled her into his arms and kissed her. It was unexpected, tender, fuelled by memories of their youth, and yet made more spectacularly knee-weakening by their increased experience. *Flipping heck*, it felt good!

Chapter Twenty-Seven

As they got off the float before it pulled into the final road, where it would park up, Lisa and Nathan started to head across the green, towards the beach and bonfire.

Nathan took her hand. 'So we don't lose each other.' He smiled, moving them through the crowd.

Part of her, somewhere now buried deep inside, knew she should let go. That the dizzy feeling she was experiencing from his touch was induced by the wine, the magic of the darkened sky, the bonfire beginning to take hold as more and more torches were thrown onto it, and the anticipation of the fireworks to come. She was no longer a teenager, but in that moment she felt like one and she wanted to hang on to that carefree feeling, her wanton emotions inside overriding all other sensible thoughts. She knew she was letting herself be swept along with it, but decided, just for tonight, not to overthink it.

She had spent a long time overthinking her behaviour, worrying what Ben's reaction might be to the things she said or did. Constantly modifying her interaction with others for fear of upsetting him. His overprotective manner had been sexy at first; she liked the fact he wanted her all to himself. Friends had told her how lucky she was – that it was all very *Fifty Shades* – and they wished their partners could be half as bothered as Ben was to be jealous of others.

But it's not sexy when you're living on a tightrope, never knowing when you might inadvertently slip. Or when the hand on your arm in a club, at first protective, squeezes a bit too tightly to let you know you've somehow overstepped a mark when your thank you to the bartender inspires a wink.

And it's not sexy when that jealousy becomes an obsession. When it becomes easier to comply and not spend time with work colleagues, old friends and family than it does to risk the unpredictable response on your return.

Now she had some distance from it, Lisa knew Ben's insecurities had pressed on her for too long; she had allowed him to make decisions about her time, her relationships with others and what was right for her. Complying made him happy and when Ben was happy they got along better. She believed him when he said it was because he knew best – until she lost Pip. Only losing her baby had made her see how warped their relationship had become. It wasn't 'for the best' if it stayed just the two of them, not when that came at the price of losing their little Pip. She couldn't and wouldn't accept Ben's take on that as her own. That realisation had sliced through his nasty, bullshit façade for her once and for all.

Lisa knew she deserved some fun. It had been so long since she had let herself go. And maybe, because of the feelings she still had for him, Nathan was the wrong person to do that with. But the thought of just going with it, seeing where it might lead, was so very tempting. And she was very much liking the feeling of Nathan Baker pressed up behind her, his arms wrapped around her waist for warmth, as the two of them took their place near the bonfire.

Together they watched as the flames from the torches, which had been thrown on to start the bonfire, grew in strength, devouring the offerings left over the passing weeks with an intense greed. The heat spread into the crowd, causing them to edge further back. Lisa looked up at Nathan's flushed cheeks and knew they mirrored her own. Her toes felt the cold ground biting at them while the rest of her felt warm, her senses enlivened from the heat and

Nathan's proximity. The crowd spread across the green and the seafront just beyond, lost to darkness. Some children in pushchairs had succumbed to sleep despite the spectacle and noise, while others, still fuelled by enthusiasm, sat on their parents' shoulders still keenly waving glow sticks. Families further back, taking better positions to see the fireworks, huddled together against the cold, not feeling the benefit of the bonfire. Everyone seemed to move in shadows, silhouetted by the flames. Lisa saw young lovers holding hands and kissing, reminding her of herself and Nathan in the past. What decisions lay ahead for them? What would shape their futures? The figures moved before them like the ghosts of their past.

Returning her attention to the fire, Lisa watched mesmerised as the bright orange flames leapt and danced triumphantly from the top of the pyre, roaring in the wake of their victory. She remembered again the words on the back of the float, 'Supporting those who run in when others are running to safety', and drew Nathan's arms a little closer around her, a move that made him lean down and ask if she was OK. Lisa felt the brush of his stubble against her cheek and felt goosebumps ripple down her side, despite the increasing heat.

The first firework sent a plume of bright lights into the night sky and a bang ricocheting off the nearby buildings. It made Lisa jump and laugh in equal measure. She listened for the thud of the next rocket being launched and looked skyward when it came, watching the smoke trail as the rocket wound its way ever higher before bursting into an array of bright sparks cascading earthward. She was surprised that there were no 'oohs' and 'ahs' of appreciation, as there had been when she was younger. Instead, people had their mobile phones held high videoing and taking pictures

– their enjoyment to be shared virtually via social media as opposed to in the moment with those around them. Traffic light fireworks popped and twirled into the sky – green, red and yellow – before a fizz of white lights burst into the air dissipating into smoke. Another thud signalled a rocket being launched moments before it burst spectacularly into a plume of gold stars.

Unable to help herself, or contain her enjoyment of the fireworks, Lisa made 'ooh' and 'ah' noises, just like her dad had done when she was younger. Making Nathan smile she continued, aware he was watching her more than the display. When she could ignore his gaze no longer, she turned to him, allowing her eyes to meet his. She bit her lip, unsure of her next move, but as her eyes moved to his lips she couldn't hold back and leaned up to kiss him; her hand slipped into the back of his hair and his arms drew her in closer, until she was pressed against him.

Warm and tender at first, they eased into rediscovering each other's mouths. Lisa welcomed the need she could feel in Nathan's touch and the longing that spread through her as she responded to his every move. Everything around them became insignificant. Lisa was lost in the kiss and the moment.

When they finally paused for breath, Lisa felt herself wanting more. Nathan leaned down and whispered into her ear, but as the fireworks were building into an ever-increasing crescendo she couldn't hear him properly. So when he repeated the words, 'I should get you home,' even louder for her, she had to fight the disappointment that gripped her. The sudden feeling of being so utterly stupid to have let her emotions get the better of her made her want to run away.

Without even bothering to point out that she hadn't yet

seen the 'goodnight' sign, the bit she would have resolutely made her dad wait for, Lisa followed Nathan solemnly through the crowd. The fireworks still lit up the night sky in flashes of colour, but, for her, they had lost some of their sparkle. She was a fool. She wasn't a teenager any more. She and Nathan had history, a history that could not be overcome by a kiss – even a very good kiss, or two – and he had seen sense and realised that, even if she hadn't.

As they emerged from the crowd and cut across the dark tennis courts opposite the beach, they reached the terrace of tall, Edwardian houses that lined the seafront. Lisa ran the evening back through her mind. It had all seemed to be going so well. She had felt so happy. It sounded silly, but feeling genuinely happy hadn't been her natural state for some time. The noise of the fireworks continued to echo off the faces of the buildings, but now, for Lisa, the sound seemed hollow. She sighed, wishing she'd stuck to her trusty friends, Simon Cowell and *The X Factor* and *Strictly* gang.

Nathan paused and Lisa looked at him.

'So, this is it,' Nathan said, his breath rising like ethereal plumes into the cold night air.

She could see the hint of nerves reflected in his expression as she watched him. She held her breath, preparing herself for Nathan's words. Would he remind her they were just friends? Was this to be their last goodbye?

'Mine's at the top.'

'What?' Well, that was not what she was expecting. Lisa looked at him, puzzled.

'My place. We can have a drink and watch the end of the fireworks from there.' Nathan looked up to the furthest windows at the top of the building.

Lisa swallowed. *Oh!* She bit her lip and held back the giggle that wanted to burst free and betray how relieved and suddenly nervous she felt. She had not wanted the evening to end so abruptly and, if she were honest, being in Nathan's company and back in his arms had felt so right. But this, this was something else, wasn't it? Was it genuinely an offer of a drink and watching the fireworks, or was it more? *Isn't it always more? But how much does Nathan want? What if it is just one night? Can I handle that?* With her mind about to overthink everything, Lisa reminded herself that tonight was about having some fun. She needed to have some fun. It had been a very long time.

'OK.'

With her mind trying to keep up with the fact that she would soon be in Nathan's flat, Lisa followed him up the stone front steps of the building. He unlocked the door and a light came on to reveal a communal hallway. It was tidy and clean. Lisa thought her mum would approve, then squirmed and attempted to push all thoughts of her mum out of her mind. She did not want to be thinking of her right now. The intricately patterned tiles on the floor looked original, as did the slightly wonky staircase and wooden banister. Glancing at herself in the large mirror to their left, Lisa took off her hat and put her fingers through her hair; her nose and cheeks were glowing from the cold. The evening air had brought a sparkle to her blue eyes; she barely recognised herself.

Nathan gestured for Lisa to lead the way up the stairs. As they made their way further upward, she wished she had worn a longer jacket to cover her bottom. She knew it wasn't overly big, but nevertheless it was hardly something you wanted someone staring at for four flights of stairs.

'The top, really?' Lisa breathed heavily, hoping Nathan wouldn't notice how unfit she sounded.

'The penthouse!' Nathan declared.

Lisa laughed, but decided to save her breath for fear she may pass out before she got to the top. Walking she could do, even at the frenetic pace of some of her more enthusiastic clients, but climbing several flights of stairs with her heart pounding inextricably fast felt a challenge.

When they finally reached Nathan's door, Lisa took a breath and realised how nervous she felt. This really would be entering the adult world of Nathan Baker. She wasn't quite sure what to expect; not the basketball hoop on the back of the door, the high bed with sofa underneath, the blue duvet cover with red zigzags on it or the picture of the tennis player showing her bottom, which had annoyed her when they were younger, when Nathan lived in his parents' house. This was his home.

What she discovered was polished, wooden floorboards; tasteful decoration; and black-and-white pictures of Nathan and friends on their various expeditions and exploits, similar to those she had snooped at on Facebook. A quick glance confirmed there was no significant female presence, a fact that made her more relieved than it probably should have. Nathan took Lisa's hat, scarf and jacket from her. She slipped off her boots, revealing fluffy woollen socks, and took off her jumper. Adjusting to the warmth, she hoped her nose wasn't running.

In the lounge there were the gently glowing embers of a real fire in the original fireplace and an old, school-style radiator adding to the warmth of the room. A polished, wooden surfboard hung on the far wall. A lamp, made of what looked like driftwood, was dimly lit in the corner. The soft lighting and fire made Lisa wonder if finishing their evening here had been premeditated. Not that she could judge Nathan for that; she knew she had put a bottle of wine in her mum's fridge, just in case she had wanted to invite him in at the end of the evening. *Friends can share a drink*, she had told herself almost convincingly. The wooden floors continued throughout. There was a large rug and a brown, leather sofa making Nathan's flat reminiscent of Wild, Wet and Windy with a bit more personality thrown in and slightly fewer displays of sports equipment. A cat appeared from behind the sofa, arched his back and elongated his front legs into a long stretch as if woken from a deep sleep.

'That's Uno. Uno meet Lisa, Lisa Uno.'

'He's gorgeous.' Lisa walked towards the large cat she recognised as a domestic shorthair, or moggy as they were often called. His striped, tabby coat and green eyes were stunning. 'I never imagined you having a cat.'

Nathan laughed. 'OK, I'm not sure how to interpret that.'

'I just meant, you're all extreme sports, travelling,' she said, gesturing to the pictures around the room, 'and um, muscles.' Lisa bit her lip to stop herself from rambling further.

Nathan grinned, walked over and picked Uno up. The cat purred and rubbed his face into Nathan's chest. 'Well, Uno here was my first rescue when I joined the brigade.'

'Ahh. Stuck in a tree?'

Nathan laughed. 'No. That's not as much of a thing as you might think. Uno was in a house fire. I spotted him in the beam of my head torch, lifeless on the kitchen floor. When I picked him up, he wasn't much bigger than my glove. The smoke had got to him, so I carried him out and used the oxygen mask we have for babies to bring him round. I wasn't sure he was going to make it. When he moved ... '

Lisa could hear the emotion in Nathan's voice.

'Anyway, he was a bit woozy for a while.'

'And his owners?'

'Turned out the place was abandoned and Uno was the only kitten we could find. His mum must have made it out with any others. There was a cat flap, signs they'd been there. So with no mother around, that left Uno – with his big green eyes, paws and ears he needed to grow into – all alone. I took him to get him checked at the vets'. Once he got the all clear I brought him back here to look after him for the night.'

Lisa stroked Uno's soft fur, pushing away an image of him lifeless from smoke inhalation. 'When was that?'

'About three years ago. I wanted to be sure he was OK.' Nathan grinned.

Lisa looked at Uno, purring in Nathan's arms. 'Well, I guess it's best to be sure.' She laughed.

The thud of a firework drew their attention back to the display.

Lisa padded over to the window seat in front of a large sash window. Nathan placed Uno down and followed Lisa as the cat made his way to his food bowl in the kitchen.

'See, the perfect view.'

Lisa looked out at the fireworks from her fresh vantage point. The atmosphere of being part of the crowd was lost, but she quite liked the new atmosphere made for two. The contrast to how busy it was outside, just a couple of hundred metres away, made Nathan's warm, welcoming flat feel even more intimate. 'We could have watched from here all along!' she mused, her voice sounding a little too light, betraying the butterflies she could feel inside.

'Hmm, I'm not sure you'd have said yes if I'd suggested it earlier.' Nathan laughed, as he walked over to the small kitchen, which was adjacent to the living room.

Lisa smiled, knowing he was right. Earlier in the evening she would have worked harder to convince herself that being in Nathan's flat was a bad idea. 'But now?'

Nathan appeared with a bottle of wine and two glasses. 'Let's just say the fact you didn't punch me when I kissed you on the float made me think you'd say yes.'

Lisa blushed, accepting her glass, remembering that there had been a time when he had thought she would say yes before.

Nathan turned off the lamp, to improve the view out into the darkness, and joined Lisa by the window. Her body responded to his. She could smell his aftershave – tones of amber and sandalwood – mixed with the scent of the bonfire and evening air that hung upon them both. She felt him trace a line down her side with the lightest touch, sending shivers down her spine. She didn't move; she didn't attempt to stop him.

His hands moved to her sides, only the cotton of her T-shirt separating their skin, and his arms, more muscular than Ben's, slipped round her. She could see their reflections in the window looking back at her, with the two of them framed in a perfect moment – an image of what might have been. She looked beyond to the fireworks as she felt Nathan shift position. His right thigh rested against hers as he mirrored her stance. His thumbs stroked across her ribs, his hands tantalisingly close to her breasts.

Lisa attempted to maintain steady breathing while they watched the last of the fireworks burst into the sky – their sound made more dramatic by the ricochet from the glass. Heat spread through her body, while her mind whirred with anticipation. When it was clear the display was over and the crowd began to disperse, Lisa turned to Nathan. 'There was no goodnight ...' Looking into the heat of his eyes, she faltered.

He leaned in and kissed her. His hand slipped round her waist and her skin tingled at his touch, with the sensation spreading through her, enlivening every nerve. In response she moved her hands round his torso, and even through the cotton of his T-shirt she could feel the outline and movement of each of his honed muscles. She heard a change in his breathing and enjoyed the fact that her touch was affecting him; his response urging her on. Her mind could barely keep up, unwanted thoughts of Ben got pushed aside, but, as she thought of Nathan, her Nathan, it was hard to assimilate her memories with the firm, fit-bodied man caressing her now. This was oh-so grown up, no fumbling, no misdirections and, *bloody hell*, this Nathan knew exactly what he was doing.

Chapter Twenty-Eight

Daylight flooded the room. Lisa blinked. It was bright, too bright. With her mum's penchant for lined curtains, waking to the harsh light of morning wasn't something Lisa was used to. She squinted, attempting to take in her unfamiliar and overly illuminated surroundings. *Oh God!* She was not in her own room. Her eyes flashed open as realisation dawned. She was not in her own bed and she was not alone. Wincing as much from the realisation as the light, Lisa attempted to gather her thoughts. She was in Nathan's room, in Nathan's bed. *Nathan Baker's bed!*

Lisa felt the weight of his arm across her back, warm and muscular, skin to skin. She listened to his breathing. He was sleeping. Thoughts of the night before drifted into her head. It was all so unguarded, so unlike her; letting herself go had seemed like a good idea. It certainly felt like a bloody good idea at the time. But now ... now she was naked in Nathan's bed without a clue what it all meant or what to do next.

Lying still, listening to the rhythmic sound of Nathan's breathing, Lisa began to question her actions. The night had been ... well, it had been amazing, but what did it mean for her ... for Nathan? Was it a one off? *'For old times' sake,'* Nathan had said when he had asked her out. Was that true of the whole evening? *Let's see the parade for old times' sake, let's watch the fireworks for old times' sake* and *let's just do it once more for old times' sake?*

Hours ago, a night of fun was exactly what she wanted ... but with Nathan? For her the night had been perfect; they had relaxed, laughed, and trusted in each other as they had in the four years they'd dated as teenagers. But what if he didn't feel the same? She tried to stop her mind racing, closed her eyes and took a steadying breath before slowly turning round. Nathan's arm slipped to her waist.

Lisa looked at Nathan sleeping. It occurred to her that she had never spent the whole night with him before; her parents would never have allowed that when she was a teenager – such was their conviction that they'd only get up to 'no good' if they spent the night together. *Little did they know*. But, now, here she was in Nathan's flat, all grown up, spending the night and feeling more confused than she ever had back then.

Nathan was a good-looking sleeper. Lisa studied his face, looking at the angle of his jaw, the stubble she had felt rub against her body, his closed eyes revealing long dark lashes, his lips … Lisa swallowed as she recalled the feel of those lips on her body. His hair was ruffled; she dreaded to think what her own hair looked like, but she was sure he was pulling off the bed-hair look better than she was. Her eyes ran to his broad shoulders and chest. She had run her hands all over the contours of that chest as they had moved and flexed together. She had to stop herself touching it again. She wondered about looking under the sheet and cream marl throw that covered them from the waist down, but didn't dare for fear of waking him up and being caught. A vision of him, all of him, in front of the glowing fire drifted into her mind; *bloody hell!*

Knowing she needed clarity, to clear her mind and gain some perspective on the situation she was now in, she decided to get up, go to the bathroom, freshen up and get a glass of water; anything to give her a moment to get her head together.

Slipping from under Nathan's arm and out of his bed Lisa suddenly felt extremely exposed. Being naked in front of someone seemed very different in the cold light of day than it did in the throes of passion in front of a glowing fire in a dimly lit room. And she really didn't want to start any awkward morning-after conversation while still in the buff. She glanced round the room. Unable to locate her clothes, she hoped to find a top of Nathan's to slip on. Unfortunately, there was not a single item of discarded clothing to be seen, and she could hardly rummage in his closet or drawers; being caught doing that would be worse than being caught naked – *well, almost!*

As Lisa pondered her predicament, Nathan turned and stretched. Without thinking she dived to the floor and held her breath, her ears pinned as she listened for his breathing to steady again as he stopped moving. Her eyes met Uno's as he peered curiously out from under the bed and she automatically placed her finger to her lips. *What the hell am I doing?* She saw herself, as if having an out of body experience – bottom up, face to the floor, urging the cat to be quiet – and hoped desperately that Nathan wouldn't wake up. Eventually, daring to peek above the line of the bed, she saw he was still sleeping and let out a breath. Spotting the duvet on the floor – they'd abandoned in the heat of the night – she pulled it over herself. Not wanting to stand and risk waking Nathan, she set about crawling out of the room; with the duvet draped over her she felt like an oversized witchetty grub. Once clear of the bedroom, she stood up, wrapped the duvet round herself and shuffled into the living room. She saw their wine glasses on the hearth; the memory of Nathan's cool mouth, from the chilled wine, on her body did nothing to help her focus.

Spotting her clothes, she gathered them up. Still huddled in the duvet, Lisa looked out of the window. The reality of the morning after was a stark contrast to the magic of the night before. Council workers were picking up the litter left by those who had watched the bonfire and fireworks. The fire, now largely a pile of ash and charred embers, was smouldering on the green. The hot dog and other stands were packed up ready for the off.

Lisa sighed and headed for the bathroom. Deciding to get a drink of water en route, she wandered into the kitchen. Leaning across the counter for a glass, she couldn't help but see Nathan's phone flash with a message. It was plugged in, discarded on the side. She didn't mean to look; it was an automatic reaction. But seeing the message was from Pete, the word 'Flick' calling to her from the screen, she couldn't help but look. She picked the phone up. Her heart pounding, she stared in disbelief, trying to take the words in before the message disappeared from the screen:

Thanks for keeping quiet, mate. I'll tell Flick soon. It'll be easier for us all then.

What? She didn't know exactly what the message meant, but she knew she didn't like it. It was Pete and he was talking about Flick; her Flick, it had to be. It was hardly a common name. *'Tell Flick soon', tell Flick what soon?* Lisa remembered Flick saying that Pete had been working extra hours at Cin Cin; *why?* And Nathan, Nathan had dismissed Flick when she asked him if he knew Pete. *Why would he lie? What are they hiding?* Lisa chewed at her lip as she remembered that Pete had changed his plans about going to the fireworks with Flick, *suddenly having to work ...* She didn't like it. She didn't like lies and she didn't like the fact that these lies seemed to be pointing to something that might hurt Flick.

She thought about watching Pete and Flick together the night she had stayed over, they seemed so happy, *but could it all have been fake?* To the outside world, she and Ben had looked like a happy couple, but nobody knew the reality of their relationship; she barely knew it herself at the time! But Pete had made a point of saying how fragile Flick was since her mum's death. It didn't make sense. He had made a point of saying how important it was for her not to lose someone else. Lisa thought it over, she couldn't remember exactly how he had phrased it, *but maybe he meant as well as him.* Lisa didn't want to believe he was hiding anything bad; Pete and Flick seemed so right together. Lisa tried to think what it was Flick had said about their sex life, but couldn't remember. If only she hadn't been drunk when they'd had that conversation, maybe Flick had been trying to tell her something important and she hadn't paid full attention. *God, I am a shit friend!*

Feeling cold, despite the fact she had drawn the duvet closer around herself, Lisa headed straight for the bathroom. Desperate to be gone before Nathan woke up, she moved quickly. She needed to be out of his flat. She needed to think this all through. Something was going on and she didn't know what, but she didn't like it. Her mind churned it all over repeatedly; her relationship with Flick was still too fragile for her to wade in with unfounded suspicions, but she also didn't want to let her friend down if there was something going on she needed to know, or in fact should know.

By the time she reached the flat door, Lisa's heart was pounding; with every moment she lingered she risked Nathan waking up. Uno appeared from the living room, meowing he rubbed himself against her legs, lifting his front paws in an effort to get her attention. She stroked his head. 'I'm sorry. I've got to go,' she whispered. Lisa found her jacket, boots, hat and gloves. Not stopping to put them on, she slipped outside and slowly – trying not to make too much noise – closed the door behind her. Realising, with all of the stairs to go, she was still very much in Nathan's building, Lisa started on the too-long trek down to the ground floor. By the second flight of stairs she had wriggled into her boots and by the final flight she was also in her jacket. Once her feet hit the ornately tiled floor of the hallway she stuffed her hat into her pocket and got outside as quickly as she could.

Lisa shut the door and paused, taking a breath. Like her, the world seemed to have a severe case of 'the morning after' about it. The sky was grey and the breeze was cold. Wrapping her scarf around herself, she set off for home.

Chapter Twenty-Nine

A steaming shower, some clean clothes, a coffee and two slices of toast later, Lisa knew she couldn't keep avoiding her phone. Before turning it on silent and discarding it to shower she had heard it ring and beep with messages. Pouring herself another coffee, she picked it up and curled herself into her mum's wicker chair in the conservatory. There was something about looking out into the garden that made it easier to think, and sometimes easier to breathe. Nathan had phoned and left a message. Lisa pressed play:

'Wow, you've run out on me ... again!'

He seemed to be laughing, but the words stung. She hadn't stopped to think about how it would look to him when she decided to leave the flat.

'I thought last night was fun ... good,' he corrected. 'Lisa, I ... I would have made you breakfast. Call me.'

Lisa felt bad; *breakfast, that would have been nice*. It had been a long time since anyone had made her breakfast, *breakfast and ...* Lisa reminded herself to focus. Looking out towards her mum's weeping willow she growled in frustration. The evening before she had enjoyed herself, felt more like her old self than she had for a long time and, as much as not knowing what it all meant scared her, hanging around to find out might have been preferable to an early morning flit. For about the fiftieth time since leaving Nathan's flat she wished she had never seen the stupid message on his phone. In the shower, trying to focus beyond the smell of Nathan's aftershave on her skin, she had pondered her options and realised they were limited. Each scenario she thought of carried an unfavourable outcome.

She knew the easiest thing to do would be to simply ask Nathan what it meant and why he had lied about knowing Pete; however, in order to do that she would have to confess to nosing at his phone. It had been an 'accident', but still, nobody ever took kindly to having their private messages read, *did they?* She didn't like the fact Nathan was hiding something, but she also didn't want him to think badly of her; at least no more than he probably already did after she had spent the night in his bed and then left without explanation. *Oh Lord!*

Of course she could confront Pete, but Lisa knew she was on precarious ground with him and didn't want to make it sound like she was accusing him of something, like *keeping secrets* and *lying to his wife*. It could all be innocent – *hmmm, as husbands lying to their wives often is* – and then she would never be able to repair any damage done by making erroneous accusations.

And, finally, she could tell Flick. She could just slip it into conversation. '*You'll never guess what, after the most amazing night with Nathan Baker, I saw a message from your Pete on his phone implying they were both hiding something from you.*' Lisa cringed. It wouldn't have been an easy conversation if they'd remained solid friends over the years, let alone the fact they had not long rekindled their broken friendship. *She'll shoot the messenger,* Lisa thought, realising that was exactly the kind of thing Winnie would say. If only she could ask Winnie what to do. But it would most certainly be overstepping the client-customer boundary that was, after all, the foundation of their relationship.

Expecting her texts to be from Nathan too, Lisa was surprised to see they were from Flick. Then it dawned on her that she would be after the gossip. She would want to know all about the evening before, and the details; *oh, the details!* An image of herself and Nathan entwined in front of the fire, so fresh she could still feel the effect on her body, flooded her thoughts. Lisa forced herself to refocus.

Pressing to read the first of Flick's texts she did a double take.

If you are not tied up ;-0 come and save us. Melissa and I are on safari!

Lisa didn't know what the cryptic message meant. Confused, she scrolled to the next:

Sainsbury's road. Turn in at the elephant. You can't miss us. We neeeeeeed you!

Lisa knew she should go. She couldn't let Felicity down if she needed her, but she also wasn't sure what to do or say about the message. Deciding to tackle one issue at a time she sent Nathan a message:

Sorry, I didn't want to wake you – *and talk about seeing what was on your phone*. I wasn't running out on you. Last night was – *mind blowing, pretty damn amazing ... confusing* – fun. We must catch up again.

Lisa wondered if that made her sound too casual, which really she wasn't. She had never been good at one-night stands, let alone mind-blowing one-night stands with a history! When she had first left home, Lisa had thought one-night stands might be the way to forget Nathan Baker, but she quickly learned they weren't. They just reminded her of how much she missed him.

Lisa glanced down at her text. Hoping to make it sound less casual she added, Soon x. She pressed send and then panicked that the 'Soon x' might make her seem clingy or needy. While she pondered it, her phone buzzed with a response:

Cool

Cool! Who says cool? And what the hell does cool mean?

Cool was the antithesis of how she felt; the distinct opposite of how she would sum things up after their intensely hot, thoroughly erotic night in front of the glowing embers of the fire. Feeling completely discombobulated, Lisa decided talking things through with Felicity and Melissa might be just what she needed. And while she didn't know what to say to Felicity about Pete's obscure text, she knew seeing her would give her an opportunity to sound things out, and see if she opened up to her again like she had the night she fell asleep on her. She fired off a text telling Flick she was on her way and headed out to her van.

Chapter Thirty

Lisa turned in adjacent to the life-sized elephant marking the entrance to the safari adventure golf course and wondered how she had not registered it before. She spotted Felicity, her children and Melissa almost immediately amidst a host of jungle animals and scenes – each presenting a new adventure golf challenge with a variety of hurdles, twists and turns to the flag. *It's crazy golf; I'm at crazy golf … on a Sunday morning!*

As she got out of the van and felt the chill air of the dank Sunday morning – a stark contrast to the warmth inside – Lisa could not help but think that lying in bed with Nathan, just hours ago, seemed like a dream. She clenched her thighs together; *a bloody amazing, knee-trembling dream.* As thoughts of Nathan led her to recall Pete's text, Lisa reminded herself to keep a clear head. She needed to sound things out. She needed Felicity to confirm that all was well at home and that Pete wasn't hiding something that would hurt her. How she would elicit that information while negotiating an adventure golf course with four children, Melissa and a baby in tow she wasn't sure. But she knew she wanted to try and, while she was at it, she might also be able to gain some advice on how to proceed with Nathan. *Cool indeed!*

The sight of Felicity and her children being pleased to see her made her feel fortunate. *Please don't let that bloody text be anything bad!*

As Lisa neared the group, Melissa smiled, and held out a golf club and blue ball. 'Great timing; you can take my turn. Bella needs changing. I won't be long.' With Bella in a sling

Melissa marched off, stopping only to call back, 'Don't spill the gossip without me.'

Lisa opened and closed her mouth. Looking at the club and ball in her hand she turned to Felicity. 'Crazy golf? Really?'

'Adventure golf actually.' Felicity pulled a face and gestured to a large sign with a cheery gorilla welcoming all to adventure golf.

'OK, adventure golf. What's the difference?'

'I have no idea.'

Lisa laughed. 'And you need me because ...'

'Because we are at adventure golf on a Sunday morning.' Felicity swung her golf club and sent her ball down a mini waterfall that carried it almost to the flag.

Lisa looked confused.

Felicity gestured for her to take a turn and continued, 'We need you to tell us the gossip about Nathan; we need to hear about your date so we can fantasise about nights out with hot firemen, as opposed to facing our reality, which is currently adventure golf on a cold Sunday morning.'

Lisa laughed and took her swing, her ball nudging Felicity's as it emerged from the waterfall run. 'Why come if it's that bad? Why crazy, I mean adventure, golf?'

Felicity took a breath. 'It's not something I normally do, believe me. But Callum has sodding Weekend Bear so—'

'Weekend what?'

'Weekend Bear; look at him with his smug little smile.' Felicity pointed over at her children who were two holes ahead.

Megan was taking pictures on a phone, Alice was lining her golf ball up ready to make her swing, while Callum and Fred were holding a teddy bear, dressed in khaki shorts, aloft as they ran through the water sprayed by a rumbling volcano. Their shouts of, 'It's going to blow!' were interspersed with screams and fits of laughter.

Lisa looked at their happy faces. 'Who? Callum?'

'No, not Callum. The bear.' Felicity pointed. 'That is sodding Weekend Bear – the secret assassin of weekend fun.'

'That little bear? The one in khaki shorts? He's the secret assassin of weekend fun?'

'Yes, him. He comes with a suitcase of clothes for all adventures and a diary you have to write in. Oscar took him to Egypt in half term. Egypt, for God's sake!'

Lisa didn't know who Oscar was, but decided not to interrupt Felicity in full flow.

'I could hardly let Callum say he took him to play on the trampoline in the back garden or to Tesco, could I?'

'So instead you're at adven—'

'We're on safari.' Felicity opened her arms as if the surroundings made that entirely obvious. 'The golf is irrelevant really, but they wouldn't let us in without saying we wanted to play. It's the pictures we really want.'

Lisa laughed. 'That's mad.'

'I know! But honestly – and don't tell Melissa I said this, she's a teacher – Weekend Bear is sent home as this "nice" link from school, but it's just extra homework in disguise and his diary is one massive exercise in one-upmanship.'

'Wow!' Lisa could tell Felicity was quite passionate in her contempt for Weekend Bear and all that he stood for, and decided not to point out that Felicity's safari expedition suggested she was more than a little gripped by one-upmanship fever herself. 'That's crazy!'

'That's school politics for you, my friend.'

'What is?'

Both Lisa and Felicity turned as one to face Melissa. 'Nothing,' they chimed innocently and pressed on towards the next hole. As they caught each other's eyes they smiled, each recognising that their knack of quick collusion when needed remained true to form.

Not wanting to share her Weekend Bear wisdom with Melissa, Felicity changed the subject. 'Lisa is about to tell us about her night with Nathan.'

'Night?' Lisa echoed, her cheeks turning a darker shade of pink as she wondered how Flick knew.

'Yes, your night out. Hold on—'

'Yes, my night out. The parade was good, didn't you think?' Lisa deflected.

Felicity and Melissa looked at each other and raised their eyebrows.

'Hmmm, well I liked it, didn't you, Melissa?' Felicity mocked, feigning interest in the subject before moving swiftly on. 'Of course, we don't mean the parade, you fool. We saw the parade. How was Nathan?'

Lovely, great, bloody amazing. 'Good, he seems to be really enjoying life, quite the adventurer.'

Felicity pulled a face. 'Melissa, is it just me or do you think Lisa seems a bit cool about her evening?'

Cool. No, she wasn't cool. Apparently Nathan was 'cool'. 'I—'

'Mummy! Weekend Bear fell in the crocodile pit!' Callum bellowed, holding Weekend Bear up to show just how covered in swamp grass and soggy sand he was.

Megan held the phone aloft. 'I got a great photo of it.'

'Let's take him home. I'll operate.' Alice leapt with glee.

Lisa breathed a sigh of relief; *saved by the bear!*

As the three of them sat in Felicity's lounge drinking coffee, while the children played upstairs and Weekend Bear dripped soddenly on the radiator – not needing an operation after all – Lisa decided not to reveal too much about her evening to Felicity and Melissa. It felt very personal to her, and already it didn't seem casual. She told them she'd had a good time and about the bobble-beanie palaver. Felicity and Melissa loved the part where Lisa got swept up by the pirates and hoisted onto the float. And while they swooned over that moment Lisa could only think about the kiss that followed. It felt like a claiming moment – in front of all those people. But not in the over-bearing way Ben would treat her in front of others. Nathan had made it feel like nobody else was there, that nobody else mattered. It was very much about the two of them and not the onlookers. She could not bring herself to relate it all and then tell them Nathan had dismissed her with the word 'cool'. They might ask her what else she expected and she really didn't have an answer for that. Lisa checked her phone, there were no messages from Nathan, but looking at the screen reminded her of the message she had seen earlier. The message she wished she had never seen.

'So Pete had to miss the fireworks then?'

'A last minute drama at Cin Cin or something. He really didn't want to go. He didn't want to disappoint the children.'

Lisa smiled and pondered Felicity's response while Melissa told them how her Adam was sorry to have missed it too. *Pete didn't want to go, he didn't want to disappoint the children!* Lisa felt relieved. *Of course he didn't. Pete loves his wife. He loves his children. See, it's nothing.* She really wanted all to be right in Felicity's world. If Flick and Pete, who had been together forever and presented the picture of familial harmony despite their children's best efforts to lead them into conversational minefields, weren't happy, what hope was there for anyone else? If they couldn't make it work, then who could?

'That's three times this week he's been called in!' Felicity added.

'Bloody hell, really?' Lisa bit her lip as she realised her response was too much.

Felicity and Melissa looked at her quizzically.

'I mean, you ... umm, you have to stand up to these bosses. They can't just call people in at the drop of a hat! Is there no respect these days?' *Drop of a hat ... no respect these days!* Wondering why the pressure of Melissa and Felicity staring at her had made Winnie's voice come out of her mouth, Lisa paused.

Felicity looked at her. 'Are you OK? You seem—'

'Sorry, I ... it's just that it used to happen all the time in London.' *Phew!* Pleased that something plausible had come out of her mouth Lisa decided to change tack. 'Any more coffee in the pot?'

With Felicity heading for the kitchen to sort the coffee, Lisa turned her attention to Melissa. As much as she hated the idea, she knew that Melissa was more likely to be Felicity's confidant if she needed someone to talk to than she was. They clearly spent a good deal of time together.

'So Flick and Pete, they're happy, right?'

Melissa lifted a snoozing Bella on to her shoulder. 'I think so, why do you ask?'

'I don't know, it's just ...' She didn't have anything to finish the sentence with, other than mentioning the text. Lisa knew it would hardly make sense to say Felicity and Pete seemed really happy together when she had spent the evening with them. Then she remembered there was whatever Flick had tried to tell her, whatever she had tried to reveal to her as she had drifted off to sleep the night of shoulder-blade-gate. She wondered if Melissa might know what it was. 'It's just Flick mentioned their issues.' The words, not being entirely true, felt disloyal as they came out of her mouth, but the look on Melissa's face seemed to suggest recognition of something.

'It's tough. I mean, we have trouble finding time with Bella, let alone having four of them to run around after.'

'I'm sure.' Lisa nodded, not sure at all what Melissa was on about.

'But they'll sort it. From what I've heard, Flick's got a few tricks up her sleeve.'

Lisa was baffled, but tried hard not to show it. She decided not to speak but simply to nod in the hope that Melissa would clarify what she was on about.

'Avocado starter, salmon for the main, strawberries and chocolate for desert, red wine—'

'Mmm, yummy!' Lisa had no idea why Melissa was off on a tangent and reciting a menu.

'I know she's missed the classic oysters, but she says five of the top ten aphrodisiacs ought to do it.'

Aphrodisiacs; oh no, so there is an issue!

Chapter Thirty-One

As she got out of her van, the air felt cold. Lisa preferred crisp autumn days, with blue skies providing the perfect backdrop to the changing leaves. They were the type that inspired woodland walks and wrapped-up outings. But this wasn't one of them. The air was damp and the sun was nowhere to be seen, adding to how cold it felt. Winter was underway, but today she didn't care. The thought of a walk in Houghton Forest with Jack, followed by a cup of tea with Winnie was enough to brighten any grey day.

Lisa reminded herself to let Winnie know she would be heading off to France soon. After sharing just a few too-casual-for-her-liking texts with Nathan, Lisa decided that letting herself go, living life again and having fun should not be dependent on others. If being back had taught her anything, it was that she used to be driven, she used to know what she wanted and she never used to let others dictate how she should live her life. Reconnecting with her past had reminded her of that.

Lisa knew the next step in that reconnection was to go and spend time with her parents. They had supported, even encouraged, her in her younger decisions, they had not tried to hold her back, and she had repaid that kindness with slipping further and further away from them. Now they were the ones building a new life and she had barely paid attention to it. Dismissing their life in France had become a habit and yet it accounted for over half of their year. And Lisa was sure it was only a matter of time before they made their move more permanent. She wanted to share her new-found realisations with Winnie. She hoped she might even inspire Winnie to keep at her effort to reconnect with her son, despite the fact he had ignored her heartfelt letter.

Knocking on the door, Lisa was surprised not to hear Jack's welcoming bark. All was silent. She checked her phone, but there were no messages from Winnie. She wandered round the windows attempting to peer in, but Winnie's net curtains weren't giving anything away. Lisa went to her van and rummaged for her key in the glove box. Winnie had given it to her early on, in case she was ever out when Lisa arrived – not that Lisa had ever had call to use it until now. It felt strange letting herself into Winnie's house. Of course, she did it all the time at other clients' houses – the fact they were out was generally the reason they needed a pet sitter or their dog walked – but Winnie's was different. Going to Winnie's was more than a job.

As she stepped inside, the place felt strangely still without Winnie's warm welcome and Jack bounding up to say hello. It felt colder than usual, like the heating hadn't been on for a while. Lisa didn't like it. She called, 'Winnie,' and then, 'Jack,' into the empty hallway, but there was no answer. She wondered if she should just leave a note, go and call Winnie later. Turning to look at Winnie's telephone on the table below the coat hooks in the hall, Lisa saw an envelope with her name on it. She picked it up and opened it:

Lisa, my lovely, if you are reading this then I have gone. It's been a long time coming. Please don't be cross with me for not saying. I know I should have told you, especially after all we've shared, but I could barely take the news in myself. And you know I don't like a fuss and nonsense, it just seemed easier to slip away—

'Oh God!' Lisa sobbed on a shaky breath. Tears welled in her eyes, preventing her from reading on. She couldn't take it in, her heart was racing and everything around her seemed to be moving. She held the wall in an attempt to steady herself. Realising she needed to sit down Lisa moved down the hallway. She looked at the kitchen door, but couldn't face going in. Not without Winnie – her biscuit barrel at the ready and her smile as warm as the teapot. Instead, Lisa made her way to the living room, the ice-cold chill of shock spreading through her.

Lisa pushed open the door and it dawned on her that she had never actually been in there before. The hallway and the kitchen had been the only places she had been in, and always in the presence of Winnie and Jack. It felt a little like intruding, but Lisa knew if she didn't sit down she might fall. Her pulse was racing and she was shaking; she felt engulfed by an overwhelming sense of loss.

As she succumbed to the tears that wanted to flow, Lisa knew she couldn't read on; even looking at the letter scrawled in Winnie's cursive script made her want to cry harder. Through her tears, she attempted to take in her surroundings. Winnie's home – empty and soulless without her and Jack to bring it to life. She touched the arm cover on the high-backed chair she sat on, imagining Winnie doing that hundreds, possibly thousands, of times before her.

The teak coffee table had a well-thumbed copy of the *Parish News* magazine on top. The gas fire looked functional, as opposed to inviting, but the patterned rug at the hearth looked well worn. Lisa imagined Jack curling up there. *Oh Jack*. She wondered where he was and who had him now. A flashback to him lying on Stan's grave caused her lip to tremble. *What will he do without Winnie too?* Lisa stood up, unable to sit still any longer.

She knew she ought to go. There was no reason to stay. Winnie was gone and Jack, well, she didn't know where Jack was, but later, when she could bring herself to read

Winnie's letter, she was sure she would discover that he was being well looked after. She stood and attempted to fluff up the cushion, long since devoid of stuffing, that she had sat on.

About to leave the room, Lisa noticed a picture of Winnie and Stan on their wedding day hanging on the wall. Both looked young and vital. Winnie's figure was shown off to perfection by her no fuss, no frills, empire-line dress. She looked a woman in her prime, while Stan looked every bit the young gentleman in his dapper suit – pride beaming from his face. *Reunited at last*, Lisa thought, attempting to find some comfort in Winnie's loss. She moved along the mantelpiece, and a picture of a young man at the far end made her do a double take. He looked familiar. She lifted it for a better look. Presumably it was Winnie's son; he looked a little like Stan, but there was something more, around the eyes maybe.

Taking a final glance around in readiness to leave, Lisa was struck by how much the living room reminded her of her Granny Blake's. The furnishings made it look like a home frozen in time. Lisa brushed her hand over the patterned upholstery of the chair she had sat on. She thought about Winnie buying that chair. *Was it with Stan? Had they known that furniture shop would be their last?* Lisa wondered if there was a time in their lives when people thought that the choices they made would be the ones that would see them through to the end; *choose wisely, this will be with you until the day you die!* Lisa shook her head, upset at the thought.

Preparing herself to go, Lisa jumped at the sound of the back door opening. Her heart in her throat, she edged to the living room door attempting to see who was there. Fear spread through her on two counts: firstly, she didn't want anyone to think she was snooping round Winnie's house with her gone; and, secondly, she feared that it could be someone breaking in. After all, whoever was coming in that way must have bypassed the option of the front door. Winnie's house backed on to fields.

Through the slit in the door she could see the back of a tall man, dressed in black, riffling through the largest kitchen cupboard. *Oh hell!* Panicking, Lisa wondered what to do. If only Jack were there he would see the intruder off. She thought about calling the police, but if she spoke she was sure to be heard – and then what? Alerting the intruder to her presence would make her lose her advantage. Her mind racing, Lisa looked around for a heavy object. She had no intention of using it as a weapon, but hoped she might be able to startle the intruder if she ran at him looking like she might. Spotting a large book on the lower shelf of the coffee table she decided that would have to do. Sure that the sound of her own heart was going to give her away, she crept back to the crack in the door, weapon of choice held aloft. The man had moved. She couldn't see him. Lowering the book Lisa squinted and attempted to change her angle.

'Rose!'

Hearing a voice behind her, Lisa swung round, swiping out with the book as she went. The thud of the contact she made jolted down her arms. She watched in horror as Dom – Dom from the forest, Dom the paramedic, Dom who clearly did belong on *Crimewatch* after all – toppled sideways.

'What the hell are you doing here?' Lisa screeched as the thought that he had followed her hit home.

With the sound of Lisa's voice ringing out, Jack burst through the back door and bounded towards her. He was caked in mud and leaving dirty paw prints all over the floor, Lisa's jeans and top. Lisa tried to take it in while Jack's long wet tongue slobbered her face. Tears sprang to her eyes as she found herself hugely relieved to see him. The momentary distraction diverted her attention and Dom staggered back to his feet. Jack instantly turned his attention to him. But instead of the barking and growling Lisa had hoped for, he gave him the same warm greeting of muddy feet and slobbery kisses he had given her. He certainly was not reacting as if Dom was a trespasser on his territory. While the scene reminded Lisa that Jack had met Dom before, she doubted that his over familiarity was the cause of one meeting and a shared bacon butty.

'What the hell is going on here?' she managed.

Dom smiled. 'I'm sorry, I should have told you when I first met you, or when I met you the second time or the third ... but—'

'What?' Lisa recoiled at the mention of their third meeting; shoulder-blade-gate was something she would rather forget.

'I'm Dom—'

'I know that.'

'Dom Adams.'

Lisa stared, no flicker of recognition.

'Winnie's grandson,' Dom clarified.

'What?' Lisa couldn't take it in. *Winnie's grandson? Her little ... little ... what's his name? Winnie's grandson isn't Dom ... he's ... he's ...* 'Nicky!'

'That's me,' Dom said, rubbing the side of his head.

'But you're Dom.'

'Dom-i-nic. Nicky to my gran only – who gets away with it because she wanted me named after Granddad.'

'Stan?'

'Stanley Nicholas Adams – Gran usually finds a way of getting what she wants.'

216

Lisa remembered her trip to the cemetery, Stan's full name etched in the white marble and the blank page left for Winnie. She gasped against the tightness in her chest. With the shock of the loss of Winnie, Jack still jumping around between them and the dawning realisation that she had just hit Dom – Dom who was Winnie's grandson, no less – around the head with a book, Lisa staggered.

Dom caught her. 'Maybe we should both sit down before we fall down,' he said, putting his arm round Lisa's back.

Lisa felt too dumbfounded to resist as they made their way to the kitchen. As she sat at the table watching Dom put the kettle on, she knew it should be her doing it and checking he was OK.

'I'm so sorry. I don't normally hit people around the head with books, or anything really. I mean I don't normally hit people. It's just—'

Dom smiled. 'It's OK. I knew you were coming. I should have checked to see if you were here. It's just Jack was so muddy – my fault for taking him over the brook out the back – I was looking for an old towel and—'

'And I hit you!'

'Yes, you did. But don't worry,' Dom said, feeling down the side of his face, 'not everyone can say they got sucker punched by Leonardo DiCaprio.'

Lisa gave him a quizzical look. Surely, as Rose, she'd be Kate Winslet? Dom slid the offending book across the table and Lisa realised it was a book of the film *Titanic*. Leonardo DiCaprio, standing in his finest at the bottom of the grand staircase, was on the front cover.

Lisa began to laugh. It was completely inappropriate. Winnie was gone and she could have killed Dom with the blow to his head. But the thought that she had hit the man who had repeatedly called her Rose since they met and embarrassed her with the theme tune to *Titanic* on a tannoy with a book of the film, simply made her hysterical. Jack tilted his head at her quizzically while her emotions ran free: tears, laughter and sobs escaped simultaneously.

Lisa realised Dom wasn't laughing. But despite the fact she knew her reaction was inappropriate – Dom had recently lost his gran and would be quite within his rights to charge her for assault – she couldn't stop.

'I'm sorry!' she uttered between gasps of air.

Jack became more animated and Dom sent him to his bed before moving closer to Lisa. He fixed his gaze on hers and spoke calmly, the way she had seen him speak to Fred. He told her to breathe with him, deep and slow. As much as she could she mirrored him. The two of them sat holding hands, looking into each other's eyes for several minutes while Lisa managed to regain her equilibrium.

'I'm sorry, Dom, I—'

'I shouldn't have made you jump like that; it must have all been a bit of a shock.'

'Really, I'm fine. I should be the one checking you are OK!' Seeing a bruise forming on the side of Dom's face Lisa reached up, but realised touching it wouldn't help. 'Does your Gran have any parsley?'

'Parsley?' Dom looked at her, brows furrowed.

Aware Dom seemed to think she was talking gibberish Lisa continued, 'Seriously, I'm fine. We need parsley to help your bruise.'

Dom scoffed. 'Parsley, really?'

'It is a tried and tested remedy in the Blake household—'

Dom pulled back from Lisa and laughed. 'Well, in this house most things get solved with a cup of tea.' He met her eyes. 'Trust me, I'm fine.'

Lisa watched as Dom made the tea. She offered to wipe

off what little remaining mud there was on Jack's paws; she needed to feel that she was doing something to help. Jack welcomed being allowed back out of his basket and rubbed himself against Lisa's legs. When he was finally clean and suitably fussed over, Lisa turned to the table. The sight of the teapot and biscuit barrel was sobering. The fact Dom had brought both to the table showed it was a ritual he and Winnie had also shared many times. Lisa swallowed hard.

Dom got an ice pack from the freezer, wrapped it in a clean tea towel and held it to the side of his face. Before Lisa could point out that parsley was an equally good option he motioned to the book. 'It's Gran's favourite, you know, *Titanic*. I've watched the thing so many times with her.'

Lisa bit her lip to prevent it from quivering, the realisation that Winnie had gone once again washing over her.

'Have you seen it?' Dom continued.

'Yes.'

'It's the end. Gran loves the end. Jack and Rose back together again. It gets her every time.'

With her emotions already too raw, Lisa couldn't stop her lip from quivering any longer. 'Like her and Stan, reunited at last,' she spluttered.

'Stan?'

'Yes, Stan and Winnie together at last.'

'But my dad's Robert.'

'What?'

'Gran, she's reunited with my dad. They're together now, as we speak. Granddad's name was Stan. He passed away a few years back.' Dom looked at Lisa confused.

'I know, I went to his grave, after the service for Saint Ass ... Ass something. But, wait, what are you saying?'

'Gran wrote to Dad. They haven't seen each other for too

long, not since Granddad's funeral I don't think, and after he got her letter he came down here. Well, not straight away, as he can be a stubborn bugger, but Gran's letter, and a push from me and Mum was all it took in the end. I'll admit she nearly died from the shock, but it will be some time before my gran's ready to meet her maker, as she'd say ...' Dom took a breath.

'There's plenty of life in the old girl yet!' Both Lisa and Dom spoke in unison and then laughed.

'Oh my God, I thought ... well, I thought ... I'm sorry, Dom, I thought she'd died.' Lisa breathed, feeling guilty that she had ever had the thought.

'Died! Why?'

'She wrote me a letter—'

'I know, about the fact she's gone to stay with Dad and I'll be looking after Jack for a bit.'

'Oh!' Lisa did a few steadying breaths as her mind caught up with the fact she had been jumping to erroneous conclusions and Winnie was still alive.

'Dad came and collected her. It was like one of those Holly Willoughby programmes you see at Christmas, all shock and tears. With a shed load of things left to talk about, but, you know, at least being together means that might happen.'

Lisa raised an eyebrow.

'Hey, that's more TV I watch with Gran; obviously, I watch *The World's Strongest Man* and other things that make you go grrrrr when it's my choice!'

Lisa laughed. As she watched Dom smiling she realised she must look a mess. In the time since she had arrived at Winnie's she had cried, been completely slobbered by Jack, almost passed out and had an inappropriate fit of hysterical laughter. But she didn't care, Winnie was OK. Hopefully better than OK, as she was finally catching up with her son. It was the best news.

'Gran will be so sorry to have worried you—'

'Don't you dare tell her! I can't possibly have Winnie thinking I thought she'd … she'd gone.'

'Good point. I won't tell if you don't. And I'm pretty sure Jack's not going to confess to leaving mud everywhere – so our secret is safe!'

Lisa smiled.

'So how about, to put all this behind us, you agree to come out for a drink with me? And I don't mean from a tea kiosk!'

Chapter Thirty-Two

Felicity leaned over and pushed the car door open. 'Road trip! Whoop whoop, I've got supplies!'

Lisa offered a smile and slid into Felicity's car. She wished she could share her friend's enthusiasm for the journey ahead, but she felt sick at the prospect of returning to the flat she had shared with Ben. She didn't want to face it, but she knew it had to be done. She needed to collect her things, and to walk away from their life together once and for all.

'Rosy Nose?' Felicity slid a bag of Rosy Noses towards Lisa.

Her stomach flipped at the sight of the fruity marshmallow and gum snouts. 'I'm too nervous, but thanks anyway.'

'I've got Globetrotting Percies if you'd rather.'

'Honestly, I'm fine. I just want this to be over with.' Lisa organised her rucksack at her feet and put her seat belt on. True to her word, Felicity had removed the back seats from her car in preparation for Lisa's belongings. She knew she could have driven herself, but her van needed a service, and if she was honest, she wanted to keep her new and old lives separate. Pulling up in her 'purrfect pet sitter' emblazoned van would no doubt evoke comments from Ben. If he was there, she didn't want to hear his thoughts on her new career or life. Besides, Flick's seven-seater had easily enough space for the things she wanted to take, and the added bonus of her friend along for company and fortification for her already-waning courage.

Felicity turned from the wheel. 'I know, sorry. It's just ... well, I knew you'd be feeling like shit so I thought we'd make it about us, instead of ... instead of what it is. We never did a road trip together; remember, we used to speak about travelling together?'

Lisa looked at Flick. 'It would have been great, you know, if you could have come with me ... when I left.'

'I know, but I couldn't just go and live in another country. You know my mum expected me to get a job, have a career. And, well, I didn't ... but it turned out for the best in the end ... If I hadn't have got pregnant when I did ... well, Mum and I had so little time together.'

Lisa touched Felicity's arm.

'Anyway,' Felicity said with a sniff, 'when you asked if I'd drive you I thought, so—'

'So why not now?' Lisa smiled. She knew Felicity was right. This trip didn't have to be about Ben and the past. It was about moving on, her future and a new beginning. Sharing that with Felicity made it even more significant. She popped a Rosy Nose into her mouth and winced, it really was very sweet for quarter past nine in the morning.

'That's more like it: you, me, the open road and Robbie Williams ...' With that Felicity pressed play on Robbie's greatest hits, waved to Harold Martin, who was on a march down the road, and drove off.

As 'Let Me Entertain You' burst from the speakers, Lisa felt her spirits lift. Her mum had hated her listening to Robbie Williams when she was growing up. That disapproval coupled with her teenage-inspired insistence on liking any music her mother didn't ensured she had become an avid fan; she and Flick knew all the words.

Having karaoked and filled their faces with the entire bag of Rosy Noses and a few of Percy's globetrotting friends for a large part of the journey, both Lisa and Felicity welcomed the sight of the service station. They were in much need of a cup of tea, the toilet and savouries to see them the rest of the way. It was their first opportunity to talk since they had set out and Lisa decided to tell Flick about all that had happened with Dom.

'So it turns out him being at Houghton wasn't a coincidence at all. He was checking me out.'

'It all sounds a bit dodgy!'

'No, his gran hired me to walk her dog. He didn't want anyone taking advantage of her so he kind of followed me.'

'As I said, dodgy!'

'No, caring.'

'So you must have made a good impression.'

'No, terrible as it happens. I lost Jack, that's the dog, and he found him, or rather Jack found Dom!'

Felicity laughed.

'It's bad, isn't it! I asked him why he didn't get me sacked. He said that my concern for Jack made it clear I cared. That and the fact he couldn't resist calling me Rose were good signs.'

Felicity looked at her confused and Lisa decided explaining the whole *Titanic* link would be a step too far. She gave a shrug as if that had been a completely normal thing to do under the circumstances.

'OK, I won't ask. But you must have died when you found out he was your client's grandson.'

'It was a bit of a shock. He apologised for not saying before. To be honest, I'm not sure how much of a chance I ever gave him, and you know what it's like when you've gone too far with something.'

'Well, he hid it from you, and that's not good.'

Lisa swallowed. She still hadn't discovered what Pete's

secret was and thought about the fact he was hiding something from Flick. What would she make of that? Having got no further with uncovering the reason for Pete's text, Lisa changed the subject. 'Anyway, despite the fact Dom knows I lost Jack and that I took Fred to the doctor's for having a shoulder blade—'

'How—'

'He was the paramedic who saw him.'

'Wait, so Dom the grandson is also the paramedic who saw Fred?'

'Yes and yes.'

'And Nathan's a fireman?'

Lisa felt a pang at hearing Nathan's name. 'Yes.' She sipped her tea.

'Are you trying to work your way through the cast of "YMCA"?'

Lisa swallowed her tea in a lump. 'Cheeky bugger, and, as I am sure you know, there was neither a fireman nor a paramedic in the "YMCA" line-up. In fact, I'm pretty sure none of them were my type.'

Felicity laughed as they made their way across the car park back to her car. 'Seriously though, what about Nathan? What happened there? I kind of always felt you two belonged together.'

Lisa got in the car. 'I don't know. It was lovely – really lovely to spend the evening with him. But I think our timing is all wrong, again. We want different things.' *And I can't just be his friend.*

'Oh, Lisa, I'm sorry I encouraged you to go there.'

'It's fine, I had a great night.' She turned and grinned. 'A really great night. My God he still does it for me!'

Felicity looked shocked.

Lisa burst out laughing and turned the music back on.

'Road trip!' she chanted, clearly not about to give anything else away.

Lisa had convinced herself that Ben would be there. She had spent most of the night wondering what she would say to him, or rather what he might say to her. The fact he wasn't made the whole thing easier. It really would be just a matter of collecting the boxes he had already parcelled up for her and closing the door on that part of her life.

Walking into the flat that had been her home, Lisa was surprised to feel disconnected from it. Of course, Ben had moved things and removed all the things relating to their relationship, and that made it feel different. But still, she realised, as she came to terms with her lack of emotion, she hadn't missed it. Not even in those early, lonely months at her mum's house.

Her boxes were piled at the side of the living room. The flat was furnished when they took it on, so there were only clothes and personal effects to collect. She didn't want to take anything else: the stereo, pictures, kitchen utensils – the things they had amassed along the way – she didn't need and had told Ben to keep.

With Lisa and Felicity working together to take things to the car, it didn't take long until just two boxes remained. Lisa glanced round the room. She looked at the couch. A vision of her and Ben snuggled up together and laughing there came to mind. There had been happy times, she knew there had. She just hadn't noticed when they started to fade. A glance at the bathroom made her think of the morning she had lost Pip. The pain, the loneliness and the emptiness she felt. She turned to face Felicity. Without saying anything Felicity gave her a hug. It was exactly what Lisa needed.

'Do you want to leave a note or anything?'

'No, I'll just check that I've got everything, and then we'll take these two boxes and get going, shall we?'

'Sure, whatever you want.'

Lisa began checking around, and went into the bedroom. Opening what used to be her wardrobe she found a box marked 'Tip' and looked inside. It contained the collection of artefacts she and Ben had gathered on their travels. Never anything big, back then they didn't have the money or space in their luggage to keep unnecessary ornaments, but pebbles, shells, postcards, leather and string friendship bracelets they had made each other, beer-bottle tops from drinks they'd shared on special occasions, and coasters from various bars. They were small but significant things, each marking different moments of their life together. Lisa sighed; they were happy then. When it really was just the two of them. It was only as they had returned to England and embarked on settling down that the little things had become less significant to them and Ben had changed. She decided to leave the box where it was. Its placing was probably intended to ensure she saw it and maybe even to hurt her. But, really, it just made her realise how much their relationship had changed since those days.

Felicity called out that she was going to use the bathroom and Lisa took one more look around. As she entered the living room, the sound of the front door opening startled her and, before she could panic, she came face to face with Ben. Lisa felt her colour drain.

'Ben! I'm sorry. I hoped ... I mean, I thought I'd missed you.'

Ben slid his tie down. 'I was going to stay away. I wanted to stay away. But, as much as I tried, I couldn't. Being here is against my better judgement, but I knew I had to see you. You see, the more I thought about it the more I thought ...

well, I thought if I came back, spoke to you face to face, maybe—'

'I'm not sure we have anything left to say.'

Ben moved closer to her. 'I know you think that. And I did too, but we were good together, you and I.'

Lisa thought about the box in her wardrobe and the happy times they had shared, when life was an adventure. 'Yes, we were, once.'

'And we could be again.'

'Ben, too much has happened. You've changed; I've changed. We're both so different now compared to—'

'I know, but we can be like that again.'

'Oh, Ben.' Lisa sighed.

'Everything just got a bit messed up there for a bit, with the ... you know ... the baby. It all got a bit mad.'

'Mad,' Lisa echoed thinking how inadequate a word that was for the hardest and saddest time of her life.

'Yeah, crazy.' His eyes softened and he tilted his head.

It was a look Lisa had seen many times before. The look that used to win her over – that always came complete with the you-know-I-am-right-and-this-makes-sense smile. She wondered if this time it was sincere. If this might actually be it; was he trying to apologise for his behaviour over Pip? *Say it, Ben, say you're sorry; say losing our baby mattered to you too.* She didn't really need him to say it for her, not now, it was too late for that, but she wanted him to say it for Pip. To show the little life they had made and lost mattered to him too.

'Yes, you went a bit mental there for a while.'

Lisa physically recoiled from his words.

Felicity opened the door.

Ben turned in surprise. 'Who are you?'

'Felicity,' she responded flatly, 'and there's no doubt who you are, so, Ben, why don't you make yourself useful and hold that door open while we take the last of those boxes down to the car.'

Ben looked at the force of nature that was Felicity in full flow and back to Lisa. 'We were just talking. Lisa might not be ready to leave. Isn't that right, Lisa?'

His words were calm, but Lisa noticed the twitch at the edge of his jaw.

Felicity blustered on. 'Oh, she's definitely ready to leave.'

Clearly taken aback, Ben continued, 'Who did you say you were?'

Lisa recognised the tone and the 'I'm pulling rank' attitude. He was going into belittling mode. 'Flick, don't, it's not worth it.'

Flick continued regardless. 'I am Felicity and, as Lisa's friend, I can tell you there is absolutely no way I am leaving here without her.' She picked up a box and looked at Lisa. 'Ready?'

Lisa picked up a box, but Ben blocked their exit.

Felicity's cheeks blazed. 'I think you'd better move.'

'Flick, it's OK.'

'Lisa—'

'It's OK, I just need to say something.'

Felicity stepped aside. But she wasn't putting the box down and she wasn't leaving without Lisa. Whatever Lisa wanted to say she would have to say it in front of her.

'Ben, when we travelled together we had fun, life was fun and for that I am really grateful to you. And when we got back it was exciting for a while. We got our jobs. We got this place. We had good times.'

'And we could again—'

'Don't interrupt me!'

Felicity had to stifle a giggle at the unexpected force with which Lisa spoke and the shocked look on Ben's face.

229

'But, increasingly, over time, you have become selfish, manipulative and, as much as I hate to say it, an all round nasty bastard. You don't love me, Ben, I'm not sure you even know who I am any more. And the way you treated me when I told you I was pregnant with our baby, our baby, Ben,' she reiterated for extra emphasis, 'was cruel. I can never forgive you for that and I don't even want to try.'

Ben was taken aback. He stared at Lisa.

'I don't love you and I am not staying here with you, Ben. This is it. This is the part where you agree we had good times, but we are certainly over. You open the door, and my friend Felicity and I walk out.'

'Yes.' Ben stared dumbfounded.

'Goodbye, Ben. Come on, Flick.'

Lisa led the way out of the flat.

Neither Lisa nor Felicity breathed until they reached the car and put the boxes down. Felicity wrapped her arms around Lisa.

'Bloody hell, I'm proud of you!'

'I'm shaking!'

'I know, but you did it.'

'I did, didn't I?'

'Yep! And watching was even more satisfying than my thought of kneeing him where it hurts!'

Chapter Thirty-Three

Having reassured her on the phone that it would not be on his motorbike, Dom picked Lisa up. Not that she had an aversion to going on the back of a motorbike, but it altered her outfit choices. After a day spent swimming with Toby, battling with Dexter the parrot, and cleaning out chickens called Princess Layer, Hen Solo and Jabba the Cluck, Lisa welcomed the opportunity to get showered, do her hair and make-up, and to get dressed up to go out.

Having all of her own clothes back meant she was more spoilt for choice than she had been in a while. Unsure where she was going, she put on her classically lined, black midi dress and opaque tights. When she saw Dom she was pleased she had made the effort but had remained understated. He looked good in mid-wash jeans, a white shirt and a fitted jumper, with an unbuttoned, charcoal reefer coat. He was doing smart-casual very well. Lisa slipped on her jacket and decided it wasn't an occasion for her hat, scarf and gloves.

As they headed off, they chatted about the news from Winnie. Lisa was pleased to hear that she and her son were spending some quality time together and that they had talked over some of the issues of the past. Dom said he and Jack were going to join them for Christmas. Lisa didn't know what was going on with her emotions, but she felt tears well in her eyes. She hurriedly wiped them away. After her performance the other day she could hardly descend into tears in Dom's presence; he would think she was an emotional time bomb. She really was very pleased for Winnie though, and she was proud to have played a small part in encouraging the reunion. She asked Dom if he would mind taking her gift for Winnie when he went and made a mental note to add Winnie to her Christmas shopping list. She had been a bit lax about writing cards and buying presents, but with her trip to France looming she knew she had to get on top of it.

'So I thought we'd go to Cin Cin; that OK with you?'

'Umm, sure.' Lisa didn't really want to bump into Nathan. They had been texting each other, but the casual, friendly, sometimes teasing nature of the texts after the time they had shared made her heart ache. He had asked her out for a drink, but she had said she was busy. She couldn't do it. She couldn't share moments like they had and then be 'cool'. Not with him. And he was colluding with Pete to hide something from Flick, and Lisa knew that couldn't be good. But at least going to Cin Cin would give her the opportunity to see Pete at work, and maybe that would give her some clue as to what he was up to.

The place was buzzing. Most seats were taken along the copper-topped communal tables and there was a small crowd at the bar. The volume reflected how busy it was. It looked like one group of people were on a Christmas do. They had made an appropriately Christmassy effort in their attire. The sparkles were out.

Lisa attempted to lead the way to the bar and spotted Pete. He looked smarter than she had ever seen him before in his bartender uniform of black trousers and shirt, a waistcoat and purple tie. Even his usually scruffy auburn hair was gelled. As they approached him all Lisa could think about in the back of her mind was *have the aphrodisiacs worked? Have you and Felicity solved your ... problem?* A female waitress came up behind him. She put her arm round his shoulder, said something and laughed. *Hmmm!* Lisa decided she didn't like her. She was too flirtatious and being too familiar. Lisa moved closer to the bar and said hello.

Pete smiled, seemingly unfazed by the fact that Lisa had witnessed the exchange with the waitress. 'Lisa, you finally found Cin Cin, and you're looking good this evening too.'

It wasn't what Lisa expected. 'Thank you.' She assumed he was on bartender-charm-assault mode. What was it about bars that led even the most normal of people to go up a notch in their general level of flirtatiousness?

'Much happier than when I last saw you.'

Oh! Lisa remembered the last time Pete saw her was the night she had told Felicity about Pip followed by her groaning at him from his own sofa, too hung over to move the following morning. She had not been a pretty sight.

'I am. Thanks, Pete.' Although the recollection was grim, she felt genuinely pleased he noticed and cared enough to say it.

Dom put his hand on her shoulder reminding her of his presence.

'Oh, sorry. Pete this is Dom, Dom this is Pete, my friend's husband – gardener by day and bartender by night,' she added.

'Dom?' Pete enquired. 'The paramedic?'

Lisa smiled and nodded hoping that he wasn't going to make a quip like Felicity's about 'YMCA'.

'That's me.' Dom shook Pete's hand.

'It's always good to meet someone in the emergency services.'

Oh God!

'And I have to thank you. I believe it was you who confirmed my son has a shoulder blade.' He laughed.

Dom looked torn between wanting to laugh and sparing Lisa's feelings.

Lisa's cheeks blazed. 'Thanks for that, Pete!' she cringed. She might have known Felicity would tell him about Dom! They were a no-secrets kind of couple; at least as far as Felicity was concerned. Upon reflection it was better than the Lisa-is-working-her-way-through-the-emergency-services-type joke she feared Pete might have been going to say.

Drinks in hand, they made their way to the nearest available seats. With the mirrors along the back wall Lisa could see the bar and watch the waitress and Pete without looking suspicious. Settling into conversation with Dom, she realised how much more at ease she felt than when she and Nathan had gone into the pub, on the night of the bonfire parade. She knew it had nothing to do with the company. Rather, she felt more comfortable in herself. She felt more like she could face the world again.

As he told her about his job, Lisa looked at Dom's eyes. That was what she had found familiar about Winnie's son's picture. He had strikingly dark eyes and Dom had inherited them. He was attractive, there was no doubt about that, but she wasn't sure that she was attracted to him. She thought about the first time she had seen him and the time she had thrown herself into his chest in the rain. Perhaps it was the leathers, she was definitely more attracted to him then. It was Nathan's fault, she was sure. She couldn't get the night she had spent with him out of her mind. He was in too many of her thoughts, both awake and asleep; the way he had been when they were teenagers.

'Don't you agree?'

Oh bugger! Lisa had stopped paying attention. She was miles away. She hadn't listened to Dom, and she had forgotten to watch Pete and the waitress. 'Sorry?' she offered pathetically, pretending she couldn't hear and hoping he would repeat the gist of the question.

'I thought you'd drifted off there.' Dom laughed. 'I was going on a bit. Sorry, tell me more about the life of Lisa Blake, "the purrfect pet sitter".'

'No, honestly, what you do is much more interesting. I was just …' *Thinking about Nathan.* '… reminding myself I have cats to visit in the morning, that's all.' She wished she had thought of something more sensible to say.

'Hmm, I'm not much of a cat person; it's the claws. More of a dog person really, but I guess you have to get on with all animals in your line of work. What's the weirdest animal you've come across?'

Lisa took a breath and glanced up at the mirror. 'Nathan!' She couldn't believe she said it aloud and shrunk down in her seat. Luckily the table of Christmas revellers chose the same moment to do a rapturous laugh, drowning her out.

'Pardon?' Dom leaned closer to her.

But the sight of Nathan standing at the bar made her forget what she was supposed to say. The waitress was smiling at him in a much-too-familiar way for her liking, and the rush of blood and the thump of her heart was the only sound Lisa could hear. 'I … um … just have to go to the toilet.' She needed a moment. A moment to get herself together. She picked up her bag, stood up and slipped away. Once in the sanctuary of the toilet she decided to text Felicity.

Oh help! Dom and I are at Cin Cin. Nathan is here too and I don't want him to think I said no to going out with him so I could go out with Dom.

Felicity texted back. It's bedtime here, which means baths, teeth to clean, stories and general pandemonium.

Lisa felt bad. Of course Felicity had more than enough to do without throwing her problems at her too. She was about to text back saying sorry when another message came in.

Great, I love a distraction! This is much more fun.

Lisa replied with the word fun in capitals, three exclamation marks and a winking, tongue-out emoji. Hiding in the toilets while she contemplated what to do didn't feel like fun.

So you are out with Dom instead of Nathan, but you don't want Nathan to think you are out with Dom instead of him???

Yes.

Why?

Because I said no to Nathan for a different reason.

I'm going to need more.

Because I like him Flick. I really like him! And he doesn't want the sort of commitment I want.

Bloody hell! OK. I thought it was just fun ... that he still 'did it for you'! I was thinking friends with benefits. Not heartfelt reunion.

He does still do it for me, but in more ways than one. Seeing him again. It made me realise I never really got over him.

Lisa couldn't believe she was confessing to her feelings via text, in a toilet cubicle, while Dom waited for her at the table.

Right. Pete is working tonight. I'll get him on the case – I'm sure he can help.

Lisa's eyes boggled as she read. *Oh God, no!* She hurriedly fired off another message. Don't worry. I'll sort it. She had no idea how, but she was sure anything she came up with would be better than Pete's approach. She didn't know him well, but she did know subtlety was not his forte. Lisa let out a breath to compose herself and flushed the toilet she hadn't used.

Read that too late, but don't worry, he's on it.

Oh no! As she left the toilet Lisa could see Pete talking to Nathan at the bar and realised she may not have given him enough credit. *Distraction, thanks Pete.* She breathed

236

a sigh of relief and felt bad for thinking he might make a bad situation worse. She smiled at Dom and returned to her seat.

'An iguana,' she announced.

Dom looked confused.

'I looked after an iguana for a day, but I'm never doing it again. I'd read they are vegetarian, but the owner insisted I feed it worms. It was an experience not to be repeated.'

'I'm sure.' Dom laughed.

Lisa's eyes flicked back to Pete and Nathan. 'So, talking of food ...' It was a tenuous link but she was thinking on her feet. '... I think there's a nice Italian up the road, are you hungry?' Leaving Cin Cin and moving on somewhere else was the only plan she could come up with.

'I think the Italian closed a couple of years back.'

'Oh!'

'It's a gourmet burger place now.'

'Great, let's give it a go.' Lisa smiled, attempting to hide the fact that she wasn't hungry, hated burgers and knew they were a tad overdressed even for a gourmet burger bar.

'OK, but you know they do food here.'

'Yes, but it's noisy here. Let's go somewhere it's easier to talk.'

As Lisa stood up she was relieved to see that Pete and Nathan had moved. All she had to do was get Dom out of the door before they appeared again, continue with her evening and at some point have a sensible, grown-up conversation with Nathan telling him ... well, telling him what exactly she didn't know.

'Lisa!'

Lisa stopped at the sound of Pete's voice and turned to thank him for distracting Nathan, but as she did so she saw him standing at Pete's side.

'You know Nathan, don't you?' Pete smiled and nodded as if urging her on.

Lisa swallowed hard. She didn't know what Pete was doing, but she wanted the ground to open up and swallow her.

Nathan gave her a warm, welcoming smile. 'Lisa, you look stunning.' He leaned in and gave her a kiss on the cheek.

She smelt his aftershave, and remembered the smell of it on her body. Her hand rested on his bicep as he kissed her.

As Nathan pulled back, Dom stepped forward and Lisa faltered. Lisa gave a weak smile and began her introductions, feeling as if the whole thing was unfolding in slow motion. Nathan shook Dom's hand, going from friendly to formal in a matter of moments. He told them to have a good evening, offered Lisa a smile and then left. Lisa looked at Pete, incredulous. *Why, why would you do that?*

Chapter Thirty-Four

Lisa rested her head on the table and groaned. Even the smell of the gingerbread latte and the sound of Michael Bublé attempting to spread some Christmas cheer to the coffee shop crowd wasn't doing it for her. Christmas shopping usually meant ordering a hamper from the nearest department store to be delivered to her parents and sending a voucher to her brother. This year she wanted to try harder. She wanted to hand pick them something special. But, when she arranged the day, she hadn't imagined it following a night of her lying awake overthinking every minute of seeing Nathan in the bar, and then getting up early to feed Kitty-Kat, Sheldon and Mr Mistoffelees before being picked up by Felicity and Melissa.

'I'm so sorry, Lisa. I really thought Pete would help.'

Lisa lifted her head and peered at Felicity with one eye open. 'It's not your fault Flick, or Pete's, you were trying to ...' She lifted her head fully off the table, revealing dark rings under her eyes. '... well, to be honest, I don't know what Pete was doing, but you were trying to help.'

'He said he thought he'd force the situation. See how Nathan would react to you with Dom. He thought then you'd know if he liked you back.'

'Oh God, did you tell Pete I like Nathan?'

'Yes, but—'

'He didn't tell him, did he?'

'No, definitely not. I checked and swore him to secrecy.'

Secrecy; the word stung, reminding Lisa that Pete and Nathan were conspiring with secrets of their own.

'Wait, you like Nathan, as in "like" like?' Melissa swung

her head between Lisa and Felicity. 'When did that happen? At golf you seemed—'

'I don't think I ever stopped liking him.' Lisa was surprised by the ease with which she spoke the words. It seemed since confessing her buried feelings to Felicity she was willing to share them with anyone except Nathan himself. 'Pete won't tell him, will he?'

'No. I don't think they even see each other much. Didn't Nathan say at the bonfire parade he hardly ever goes to Cin Cin? It was just unlucky for you he was there, I guess.'

'Hmmm.' With the familiarity of the waitress and seeing Nathan and Pete together Lisa was pretty sure Nathan was a regular.

Melissa stirred her coffee. 'So how did he react to seeing you with …'

'Dom,' Lisa and Felicity finished together.

Picturing the situation again, Lisa cringed. 'He left.' She banged her head back against the table.

Melissa wasn't ready to let it go. 'But, hold on, how did he leave?'

'Does it matter? He left.'

'Well, did he seem casual, did he seem hurt, did he give you a longing look, did he clench his jaw or his fists, did he push past him banging shoulders and giving him a hard stare?' She took a breath. 'Ooh, did he challenge Dom to a duel?'

Flick burst out a giggle and then coughed. 'Sorry, Lisa. If Melissa appeared on *Mastermind* her specialist subject would be films of the last decade. Since having Bella her cinematic cravings and lack of sleep mean she's clearly overdosing on Netflix. I didn't mean to laugh.' Turning to Melissa she added, still trying to control her desire to laugh, 'This is real life and that's not helpful.' *Though it is bloody funny!*

'OK, not the duel thing,' Melissa conceded, 'but how he reacted must have told you something.'

Lisa pondered. 'He seemed ... he seemed ...'

Flick and Melissa leaned forward, tilting their heads in anticipation.

'He seemed *cool* about it.' Lisa sighed.

Both Felicity and Melissa resisted the urge to slink back into their seats.

'He was polite, he shook Dom's hand and left like a normal, *cool*, unfazed person who bumped into someone they knew in a bar. No jaw clenching; no pistols at dawn. No duel.'

'It is a reaction,' Melissa offered weakly.

'Not the one she wanted,' said Flick.

'It's OK, I knew it. We went out for old times' sake. Maybe for him that put to bed ...' She blushed at the reference. '... I mean, maybe that gave him closure over the past, over what happened at the prom.' *For me it made me see what I let go.* 'I knew he was cool about *us*, me,' she corrected. 'He told me.'

'Oh, Lisa.' Flick went round to Lisa's side of the table and rubbed her back. 'I suppose when people break up it's because something is broken, like the clue is in the title.'

But nothing was broken, it was just ... I wasn't ready ... back then.

'I am sorry I encouraged you,' Flick continued.

'Me too,' Melissa added.

'Honestly, it's fine,' Lisa lied. 'Let's just enjoy Christmas shopping, it's been years since I have done it properly.'

'Are you sure you're up to it?' Flick asked.

Lisa took a swig of her latte. 'Definitely.'

'OK.' Felicity scooted back round to her own side of the table, rummaged in her bag and produced an A4 print out of a spreadsheet listing Christmas presents for each of her children.

About to comment, Lisa noticed that Felicity was extricating another neatly folded piece of paper from the depths of her bag. This one had the names of family members down the first column, followed by their gifts and what they would be getting for her children in the next two. 'Wow. That's organised.'

'Believe me, four children and Christmas means being organised or going insane.'

'It's impressive.' Melissa smiled, revealing her own handwritten list. 'I've found it harder this year; exciting too, of course – it being Bella's first – but what do you suggest when everyone wants to know what to get a baby who wants for nothing?'

'I know, and I have four to sort; sometimes it feels more like a military operation than Christmas.'

Lisa picked up the spreadsheets. 'We'll need more than a day to do this lot.'

Felicity sat up, a knowing smile on her face. 'See those in red, they're coming from Amazon; those in blue, they're pre-ordered from Argos – and are ready for collection now. That leaves a few stocking bits, biscuits and vouchers for Pete's side, and chocolates for the teachers to get. I figured if we get that done this morning we could fit in a leisurely lunch and maybe even the cinema. How about it, ladies?'

'I'm in! Most of what I need to get is on order from ELC, Next and Mothercare.' Melissa smiled.

'I thought you were actually Christmas shopping today.' Lisa wished she had been more organised, Christmas was too close and she had too much work on to fit in another shopping day.

'We are!' Melissa and Felicity chimed together.

'Well, at least as far as Adam and Pete know. This way they get some quality time with the children, and we get to sit down and eat lunch in a fancy restaurant with the only dinner we have to cut up being our own.'

'Bliss.' Melissa sighed.

Lisa smiled; *oh bugger, is it too late to order a hamper?*

Chapter Thirty-Five

Lisa checked again that she had her passport and tickets. She looked at her packed case. She had decided on one medium case with wheels and a pull-along handle, hoping it would be manageable at the airport. She could hardly believe she used to fit her belongings in a backpack. As it was, she had to force a few extra clothes into her hand luggage to make everything fit. Her dad had told her there had been a fresh dump of snow in Samoëns, so she had bought some thermals and new boots. She didn't own any ski clothes, as she and Ben had cleared theirs out a few years back, but her mum had assured her she had enough for her to borrow if she fancied hitting the slopes.

The house was quiet, it always was, but it seemed the nearer to Christmas it got, and the more it contrasted with the bright lights in the street and the bustle of the shops, the emptier it felt. The holidays were supposed to be enjoyed with the ones you loved; Lisa was pleased she had said yes to visiting her parents in France. She was looking forward to seeing them and her brother. Luke had arrived from Australia and had, as her mum put it, 'grumped about the weather and sat on top of the fire' since he got there. But Lisa didn't care; she hadn't seen him in too long, and couldn't wait to catch up and meet his girlfriend. She was also looking forward to finally seeing her mum and dad's chalet. It was a trip she and Ben were supposed to take, but each time the opportunity arose Ben had a big deal on at work or other commitments came along. This visit was, Lisa knew, long overdue.

The trains had been unreliable lately. As a result, all

of the taxi companies Lisa called had laughed at her and the week's notice she tried to give them in preparation for her trip to the airport. None could spare someone with pre-booked work and school runs making their schedules 'chocka' as one man unhelpfully guffawed at her. Driving herself and leaving her van at the airport was her only option. As she wheeled her case onto the gravel driveway she cringed at the noise. It was five o'clock in the morning and she didn't want to wake the neighbourhood.

'Need a hand?'

'Bloody hell, you scared me!' Lisa couldn't believe she had just sworn at Harold Martin, but the fact he was snooping around in the street at such an early hour made her think he deserved it.

'I was out for my morning constitutional. Saw your lights on. It's an early one for you, isn't it?'

'Yes,' Lisa confirmed, purposely not giving anything else away.

'Well, you need to be careful, a young girl like you.'

Lisa was flattered; she was almost thirty, but compared to Harold she guessed that made her a young girl. She softened. 'Thank you, Harold, I'm sure I'll be fine.'

'Well, there was that man, the other day—'

'Man?' Lisa didn't know who or what Harold was talking about.

'Parked on the drive.'

'My drive?'

'Said he was doing routine checks—'

'Harold, what man and what checks?' Lisa didn't know what Harold was talking about, but with her about to leave her parents' house unattended she didn't like the sound of a strange man being parked on the driveway. It sounded too much like a scene from *Home Alone*. 'Did he have a van?'

'A van? No.'

Of course not, fool, this is real life! Her mind echoed the response Felicity had given Melissa when she had jumped to film inspired conclusions.

'A Range Rover, I'd say.'

'What?'

'A Range Rover.'

'A Range Rover, here?' Lisa gestured at the gravel to make herself completely clear.

'Yes. One of those rapid response vehicles.'

'A what?' Normally getting information out of Harold Martin about the goings on in the street was as easy as saying good morning. She didn't know if the early hour was making him seem vague or the fact she was in a hurry was making her impatient, either way she wished he would get on and explain exactly what he had seen. 'Harold, what are you talking about?'

'One of those rapid response vehicles used by the fire brigade.'

'The fire brigade?' Lisa felt her stomach twist.

'Yes, generally used for road traffic accidents, four-wheel-drive capability, they carry only light weight equipment—'

Lisa couldn't believe the tangent. 'Harold, when?'

'Oh, right, yes. It was last weekend, I believe.' Harold flipped open a pocket notebook.

Lisa did a double take. *A notebook, really?*

'Yes … Last Saturday morning, zero eight hundred hours.'

Lisa's mind flicked back to that Saturday morning. She had left the house early to feed the cats before going Christmas shopping. 'Did the driver give you his name?'

'No.' Harold appeared embarrassed not to have the detail. 'What did he look like?'

Harold smiled, now these were facts he could supply.

'Tall, around six foot two, muscular, blue eyes, blond hair and brigade uniform.'

Lisa didn't need the photo-fit picture, which she feared Harold might be able to supply, to know he was referring to Nathan. At her house. In her driveway. *In his uniform.* Lisa reprimanded herself for the tangent now. That was the morning after Nathan had seen her at Cin Cin with Dom. 'And did he say anything?'

'He said you can't be too careful, as fire safety is an issue this time of year.'

Lisa didn't want to talk fire safety. She wanted to know why Nathan was really there and what he had wanted. And he had found her ... out. *What would he have made of that?* After the night Lisa had spent with Nathan, she could only guess at the conclusion he may have jumped to having seen her out with Dom the night before.

'Christmas lights, candles, all potential hazards—' Harold continued.

Trying to take it all in, Lisa snapped, 'No lights, no candles—'

'Away for Christmas then?' Harold jumped on the point and gestured at Lisa's case.

'Visiting my parents.'

'Ah well ... Passez le bonjour à vos parents de ma part et dites leur que je jetterai un coup d'oeil sur leur maison pendant votre absence.'

Nosy bugger. Lisa smiled. 'Thank you, Harold, I'll pass on your good wishes and I am sure they appreciate your vigilance with the house.' It seemed keeping an eye on her parents' home was Harold's hobby. 'Now, I really must go or I will miss my flight.'

Lisa checked her watch and realised she really did need to go. She thought the journey to the airport would take less than an hour, but she hoped to have time to get a drink before her flight, and maybe even something to eat.

After finally convincing Harold to leave the driveway, Lisa closed up the house and got in her van. When she turned the key nothing happened. She couldn't believe it. Her chat with Harold had already delayed her and now her van wouldn't start. She tried the key again a few more times. Still nothing happened; she cursed the fact she never got round to booking it in for a service and looked at her phone wondering whom to call.

Scrolling through her contacts she realised that the limited number of people she had to call on in a crisis was testament to how small her circle of friends had become. She knew Felicity would drive her, but it hardly seemed fair to call her when Pete had been working late and she had all of her children to organise. She thought about Melissa. With Bella's poor sleeping habits she was probably already awake. But despite having her number she hadn't yet used it; calling on her in a crisis seemed a bit cheeky.

Looking back at her phone Lisa hovered her thumb over Mr Chung's number. She had never had her Chinese delivered, but she did know Mr Chung's son had a delivery van. She dismissed the idea almost instantly. Not only was it too big an ask, she had been avoiding the Chinese since the incident with Nathan. Her cheeks burned at the memory and she scrolled to Nathan's number. Even his too-cool-for-her-liking text messages had dried up since he had seen her and Dom at the bar. And yet he had been to her house. *Why?* She couldn't deal with that right now; calling Nathan was not an option. Dom on the other hand might be a different matter.

Lisa knew he and Jack were travelling to his parents' to see Winnie later in the day. If Dom was willing to make a slightly earlier start than he had anticipated and a small detour to Gatwick, she still might make her flight. Pondering for a moment as she tried to decide if it was too much to ask of someone she had shared an odd – in more than one sense of the word – evening with, she jumped at the sight of Harold Martin peering in her van window.

'It's not turning over.'

Cheers for that, Sherlock! Lisa sighed.

'Engine trouble?' Harold spoke, forming his words as if she might be lip reading through the window despite the fact she could hear him clearly.

Lisa took a breath and wound her window down. 'It was due a service.'

'Ah, neglect today and regret tomorrow. Servicing an engine is essential to maintaining performance. The trouble with the youth of today—'

'It's booked in the day I return,' Lisa lied.

'Terrible timing with your trip.'

'Yes.' Lisa bit her lip; there was only so much of Harold's stating the obvious she could take. 'Look, if I don't get on I am going to miss my flight.'

'Need a lift then?'

The kind offer took Lisa by surprise. She was almost tempted to accept, but she had seen Harold drive. Whatever his role in the army had been she was sure it had more to do with stealth than speed. Dom, on the other hand, was a paramedic. Lisa felt that his job must involve driving at speed. 'That's very kind of you, but I've already sent a text to a friend,' she lied. 'I'm about to call to check he's on his way.' *Decision made.* She pressed her finger to her lips, put up her window and made the call.

'Thanks so much for this,' Lisa thanked Dom, who had said

he was leaving at seven anyway and so was up and almost ready to go when she had called.

Dom put Lisa's case across the back seat. Jack gave an excited whine from his place in the boot at the sound of Lisa's voice and Dom let him out briefly so he could say a proper hello.

Lisa greeted Jack with a cuddle, a good rub along his sides and a tickle behind the ears. 'You say hello to your mummy for me. Tell her I miss her.'

Jack's tail wagged wildly as he leaned into her.

'We'll pass the message on, won't we, Jack?' Dom confirmed. 'And we have your present. I'm sure she'll love it.'

Lisa smiled. She really hoped so. With her Christmas shopping trip turning into lunch, too much wine and a trip to the cinema, she had resorted to ordering what she could from the internet, still trying to focus on making a more personal effort in her present buying than usual. Pic Me Today had inspired her enough to purchase presents for all of her friends and family, while her furry clients had a range of toys from Tesco. She really hoped Winnie would like her new and positively plump cushion with a picture of Jack's face imprinted on it. After Jack had slipped his collar and Dom had challenged her taking him back – albeit for his own amusement, it seemed – she had decided to keep photographs of all her charges on her phone, just in case. A small fact Winnie need never know.

Chapter Thirty-Six

Once they were on their way, Lisa thanked Dom again for picking her up. The roads were busier than she had anticipated for so early in the morning and she was grateful not to be the one weaving through the traffic, especially with commuters, general Christmas chaos and train cancellations causing 'Carmageddon' as Dom muttered more than once.

Taking advantage of his kindness, Lisa couldn't help but feel awkward about the way she had behaved on their night out. To say she had been distracted by seeing Nathan was an understatement. She had barely touched her gourmet, chargrilled, no-bun chicken burger or super-boost quinoa salad. And, when Dom dropped her home, she had almost leapt out of the car for fear he might want to kiss her goodbye. Since then she had seen him only briefly when she dropped Winnie's Christmas present off to him.

She wanted to apologise, or at least give him an explanation, for the way she had behaved. Lisa knew Dom deserved that, even before he had come to her aid. She just wasn't sure what to say. She could hardly go into detail about the Nathan situation when she barely understood it herself. But if she didn't say something, she felt it would be one of those things she would regret. Dom was kind and sweet; she didn't want to take things further with him, but he was Winnie's grandson and she hoped they could be friends.

Lisa realised she could just say she felt rough the night they went out; that she had a stomach ache. She didn't need to add that seeing Nathan was the cause of the knots that twisted inside her, making her unable to concentrate or eat her meal. Dom's eyes were on the road; the fact he couldn't easily see her face would make it easier to seem breezy about it all.

As they hit the A23, Lisa decided to seize the moment. 'About the other night.'

Dom laughed. 'I don't know who that guy was in Cin Cin, but it was pretty obvious you two had something going.'

Oh God! Lisa's cheeks turned so red she realised it didn't matter that Dom wasn't looking directly at her; she was sure he could feel the heat from them. *Was I that obvious? Did Nathan feel it too, and is that why he left so quickly?* She swallowed in an attempt to encourage her mouth to work. 'Dom, I'm sorry. I know ... I mean ... I ... it wasn't fair.'

'Really, it's fine.'

'But you're right ... Not that there is something going on. I mean, not now. But I was distracted ... by him, he's ... well, it's complicated. I wasn't trying to lead you on and—'

'Lisa, really, it's OK. Look, I didn't want to tell you before because I didn't want you to think I'd only asked you out because of Gran—'

'Winnie?'

'Yeah. It wasn't a conspiracy or anything.'

'What wasn't?' Lisa wasn't sure how the conversation had moved so quickly from Nathan to Winnie, her mind was trying to catch up.

'I used to take Jack out when I could, and then Gran said she wouldn't need me to walk him any more.'

Lisa remembered the day she had met Winnie; she recalled her saying her dog had the energy of a 'whippersnapper', but was never walked. *Why lie?*

'She said she met you putting up your advert, and that you needed to walk Jack.'

Lisa remembered how grateful she had felt when Winnie

asked her to walk her dog. Standing in the post office she had attempted to look professional while holding back tears, as Winnie suggested she visit her for a cup of tea so she could meet Jack.

Dom continued, 'I didn't understand it, but I learnt a long time ago arguing with Gran is futile. I did tell her you could be a headcase or something; a candidate for *Crimewatch*.' Dom laughed shyly at his confession.

Lisa bit her lip, deciding not to say anything.

'She said you were just a bit ...'

'Go on.'

'Lost ... that you needed someone to have faith in you. That you seemed lonely.'

Tears welled in Lisa's eyes. 'Oh!'

'Look, I didn't want to tell you before ... in case you thought I had only asked you out because of that.'

A pity date. That was exactly what it sounded like.

'I didn't even tell her I'd met you. She thinks you're great. She would definitely have tried to matchmake us.'

Despite her thoughts of pity dates, Lisa laughed and felt flattered that Dom felt Winnie would even consider her good enough for her grandson, especially as she knew how scathing she'd been about his previous girlfriend.

'And, after I saw you for the first time, I wanted to get to know you for myself.'

Lisa conceded that was actually quite sweet. 'Hmm, I'm not sure I've given you a very good impression.'

'Don't put yourself down. You're funny and caring, and you've got a mean left hook.'

Lisa cringed. 'Oh God, I'd forgotten about that.'

Dom flicked his head towards her. 'Look, the thing is, I'm not a fool. Even without Gran telling me, I can see you've got things you're working through and so have I.'

Things?

'And I'd be lying if I didn't say I'd like to get to know you better.'

'Dom, that's—'

'But I mean as a friend. Look, to be honest,' Dom said, swallowing, 'even if you didn't have something going with the hot Chris Hemsworth type from Cin Cin, you're just not my type.' His cheeks flushed.

'Seriously it's fine, I hadn't presumed—'

'No. What I mean is … you're lovely, it's just … well, my interest in the film *Titanic* is more Leonardo DiCaprio than Kate Winslet.'

'Oh.' Lisa took a moment to absorb what he was saying. 'But Winnie said—'

'I have terrible taste in girlfriends?'

'Well, not exactly that, but yes.'

Dom laughed. 'On purpose. Can you imagine how excited she'd be if I brought a keeper like you back to meet her? She'd bypass the formality of a cup of tea to march us to the church before we'd even got in the door.'

Lisa laughed. 'But why not just be honest?'

'Because Gran's from a different generation and I don't want to hurt her – to let her down. There's been enough heartache in our family.'

'But Dom, that's … do your parents know?'

'They've known for a while and they're sworn to secrecy during Gran's visit.'

Lisa thought for a moment. 'Look, Dom, I know Winnie's from a different generation but I think you should give her more credit. No wonder she hasn't liked your girlfriends if they don't make you happy. Winnie wants you to be happy. And I think she's more open minded than you might think.' Lisa considered mentioning Winnie's days of going alfresco with Stan and reminded herself it probably wasn't something a grandson needed to hear about his grandparents, no matter how open minded it made them seem.

Dom fell quiet.

'Really, she might surprise you.'

'But—'

'Wouldn't you be happier if she just knew?'

Dom sighed. 'Well, yes … but … I mean, I don't know. Look, I'll consider it—'

'I really think you should—'

'I'll consider it only if you'll agree to let me get to know you better. God knows, if I tell Gran, I might need a friend!'

'I'd like that, but, Dom, please don't feel—'

'Hey, it's got nothing to do with what Gran said about you. It's just you spread a certain amount of chaos in your wake. I like that.'

'Chaos?' Lisa didn't particularly consider herself the type of person who spread chaos.

'OK, not chaos – mayhem, is that the word? Anyway, you make me laugh, in a good way, and I could do with a friend who makes me laugh.'

'Really?'

'Yes.'

'In that case, I'd like to get to know you better too. I haven't amassed many friends over recent years.'

'OK, so now I'm gonna sound like Gran, but hey, you know I watch *Titanic* and soppy Holly Willoughby stuff, so here goes: it's not about the number of friends you can count, but the number you can count on!'

Lisa laughed. 'You do sound like Winnie.'

'I know, and now I am going to have to swear at some motorists and drive like a bit of an arse to recover some masculinity!'

Chapter Thirty-Seven

Lisa was no stranger to travel, but she realised this was the first flight she had taken without Ben since they had met. She missed having him along to share the experience. She always found airports so full of anticipation, excitement, and hustle and bustle – a unique, highly charged atmosphere. As it had been some time since her last flight, she realised she felt a little anxious about being in the right place at the right time for each of the steps she needed to take before she reached the aeroplane. She took a breath in an attempt to quash any nerves she could feel simmering at the surface and reminded herself of the confident young woman who had taken it all in her stride when she was eighteen. That person was still inside, somewhere; albeit that she was a little buried by time and life.

Following the guidance of the young people wearing 'ready to help' fluorescent jackets, Lisa checked her suitcase in and cursed the fact it was slightly over the weight limit –resulting in an excess baggage charge. Looking around, she could see other people had had the sense to wear their big coats and winter boots, rather than pack them. *Oops!* She really was out of practice.

Once through customs, Lisa wondered about getting a cup of tea and some breakfast, but, with her late start and the fact the food places all looked rammed, she decided to forgo the toast she could almost taste. She got herself some Percy Pigs instead and smiled as she recalled her road trip with Felicity. She took a picture of them and sent it to Felicity, with a message saying breakfast was sorted.

Seeing that her flight was being called, Lisa looked for her gate. Typically, the signs were all pointing in the opposite direction to the way she had walked in search of sustenance. She hurried along corridors and down escalators, and past signs advertising exotic destinations and lands filled with adventures. She felt a flicker of excitement inside. She had forgotten how good it felt to be going somewhere, how easy it was for the travelling bug to get under your skin. Checking her watch and hoping the gate wouldn't be too much further, Lisa manoeuvred past the people on the travellator, who were standing still – making it slower than if they just walked next to it. Relieved to finally see her gate, she joined the small queue that had formed.

Looking at her phone Lisa saw a message from Felicity:

Ah fab! Bon voyage, mon amie.

Lisa smiled and started to reply, but as she got as far as typing 'merci' another message appeared. It was a picture of the Village People with the comment:

Stay away from the gendarmes!

Lisa laughed out loud, causing the people in front of her to turn around. She blushed and looked back down at her phone, replying to Felicity that she would do her best to resist, with a winking, tongue-out emoji. She then sent a text to her mum to let her know she was boarding, and another to Dom thanking him for the lift, the offer of friendship, and for being a nice person. Dom's reply saying she was welcome and he was now doing press ups made her smile.

As she was called forward to have her boarding pass and passport checked, Lisa's phone began to ring. She ignored it and realised she should have called her mum. She would want to tell her to have a safe flight, as she always used to, *bless her!*

Once on board the aeroplane Lisa located her window seat and began to settle in. She slipped her jacket under the seat in front and put her seatbelt on. As she was travelling alone she wanted to be sorted before anybody sat down next to her. She didn't want to have to get them to budge if they had a big bottom or engage in conversation throughout the flight if they were really boring. It sounded harsh, even in her own head, but back in the day she had done enough travelling to know you should keep yourself to yourself until you knew who you were befriending. Sitting with people who travelled regularly for work normally resulted in knowing too much about how many miles they had travelled and how they rated the in-flight refreshments.

While Lisa looked out of the window, the seats around her began to fill up. She was in luck; a young girl, probably similar in age to Flick's Alice, sat in the centre seat – meaning Lisa had plenty of room – while the girl's mum sat next to her. Judging by the way they were working together to get their hand luggage and coats sorted, Lisa assumed the man and young boy on the opposite side of the aisle made them a family of four. The whir of the engine began; everybody settled into their seats and the plane filled with hushed voices, muttering in anticipation of the flight.

Prompted by the announcement, Lisa leaned down and took out her phone, ready to switch it to aeroplane mode. She did a double take as notification of a missed call from Nathan flashed up on her screen. He hadn't left a message. Lisa looked around. There was no time to call him back and she had no idea what to text him. He hadn't contacted her for a while and she wondered what he could possibly want now. And if Harold Martin's information was correct – and the fact the man kept a notebook suggested it was – Nathan had been to her house the morning after seeing her at Cin Cin with Dom. If he had something to say to her, Lisa wondered why he didn't just get on and say it. She switched her phone off in frustration and put it away.

The cabin crew began to go through their safety talk, reminding passengers of the escape procedures. Lisa thought about how – much more these days than when she had travelled in the past – taking a flight meant you felt like you were putting your safety in the hands of the other passengers as well as the aeroplane, crew and pilot.

The young girl sitting next to her picked up the safety card as directed by the air steward. 'Look, Mummy, a slide! Can we go on it?'

'Let's hope not.' The girl's mum laughed, smiling at Lisa.

The sight of her mum, dad and brother standing at the airport holding a sign saying 'Lisa Blake – it's about time too' made Lisa laugh and cry all at the same time. She rushed into their awaiting arms, realising with that embrace how much she had missed them all. She clung on to them, crying at how good it felt to be within the comfort of their arms. It was the feeling of home and security she had sought when she had returned to her parents' home. Of course, she knew now it wasn't the place but the people she had craved when she felt so low. Sometimes, no matter how old you are, only a hug from your family will do, Lisa conceded. Most of the people from her flight had left the airport by the time she was ready to relinquish her grip on them.

As they went to the car, Lisa clung on to her brother. Luke's hair carried highlights from the sun and contrasted with his tanned skin. He seemed taller and broader since she had last seen him, though some of that could have been down to the many layers he was wearing.

'You look like the Stay Puft Marshmallow Man,' Lisa teased as they took their seats in the back of her dad's car.

'It's bloody freezing here,' Luke scoffed.

'Ah, are you missing the sun?'

'Too right,' Luke groaned. 'Sun, surf, Se—'

'Luke!'

Lisa burst out giggling, it felt so good to be enjoying familiar family banter. Less than half an hour since they were all reunited and her mum was already telling them off. It felt so normal.

'I was going to say Selina.' Luke crossed his eyes at Lisa behind his mum's back.

'Selina? Your girlfriend? Isn't she here yet?' Lisa hadn't given her a thought at the airport. But the mention of Luke's girlfriend reminded her that she should have arrived before her.

'She's staying with her folks in Ireland; turns out now they've got her they don't want to let her go.' Luke sighed. 'I'm heading there for New Year instead.'

'Meeting the parents?' Lisa scoffed.

'I've already met them actually. In Oz.'

'What?' Lisa wondered how she had missed this piece of information. Her brother had never been serious enough about anyone before to meet their parents.

'See, if you ever checked in with your brother, you'd know these things.'

Lisa felt a pang of guilt. Not only because Luke was right, she hadn't checked in with him in any meaningful way for a long time, but also because she was pleased Selina wasn't joining them in France. It gave her time to have her family to herself.

Once off the main road from Geneva, the journey to Samoëns was picturesque, winding increasingly upwards through mountains. It was breathtaking. The sky was clear blue and the sun glistened off the snow. It had been years since Lisa had been to the area. As children, they had often visited, staying in small rental properties. She remembered the area as pretty and fun. She had liked playing at the lake in the summer and skiing in the winter. As an adult, she could see exactly why her parents chose to spend half their year in France. The space and open landscape made it somehow easier to relax and breathe. It was hard to imagine that, just hours before, she had been travelling, pushing through the traffic in London with Dom, and even harder to imagine that she used to live in the heart of London.

Lisa had seen pictures of her mum and dad's place, she had even had the FaceTime tour, but none of it had done justice to the beautiful, three-storey chalet they pulled their car up in front of. Set in its own land with a view of the surrounding mountains, the once-farmhouse-cum-food-store had been transformed into an impressive residence encompassing the right mix of traditional and modern in its design.

'Wow! If I had known it was quite like this, I would have come sooner.' Lisa's eyes swept the area. The air felt cold to her cheeks and began seeping through her too-thin jacket but, after the confines of the plane, it felt refreshing. Sitting above the main village of Samoëns, the view from the chalet was stunning in every direction.

'You'll never get rid of her now, Mum!' Luke joked.

'You know your sister is always welcome.'

Lisa hugged her mum as she got out of the car; perhaps it was the cold, but she wondered if she saw a tear in her eye. Her mum rarely showed emotion.

'I've missed you, my darling girl.'

The words and the kiss on her head made tears well in Lisa's eyes too.

'Come on now, let's get out of the cold.' Lisa's dad lifted her case from the car.

'Bloody good idea.' Luke shivered.

'Your mum's got Milka hot chocolate and some of that marble cake in for you.'

'Oh my God! Did you Mum?' The excitement Lisa felt made her feel like a little girl again. It was what they'd had as a treat whenever they had visited France when they were young: chocolate milk, cold in the summer and hot in the winter, and marble cake no matter what the occasion.

After enjoying too much hot chocolate and a large slice of marble cake, Lisa unpacked and lay on her bed. It was warm and cosy in the room she decided to designate as her own from now on. The seasoned-pine walls perfectly framed the view of the snow-covered mountain from her window. The whole place was Christmas card perfect. As soon as she had walked into the chalet, seen the elegantly strung holly garlands on the banisters, and smelt the heady mix of oranges, cinnamon and cloves, Lisa understood why her mum had scoffed at the thought of Bing. He would never have fitted into this Christmas ideal. Lisa's mum had hung a painting of a stag on the wall next to her bed; Lisa felt him watching her, but liked his friendly face. His slightly wonky eyes reminded her of Jack.

Lisa rolled over to the side of the bed and glanced at her phone. Nathan hadn't called back. She decided not to call him. Pete had put his feelings to the test at Cin Cin and he had made it clear how he felt when he walked away. She couldn't answer casual calls and casual texts, and he deserved to know why. She wanted to tell him how she felt, but would need to do that face to face. Lisa realised how wrong she had been when she had agreed to them just being friends. With Dom the thought of friendship felt exciting, fun, right; with Nathan it made her heart and body ache for more.

There was a knock at her door. Lisa sat up.

Her dad put his head round the door. 'Dinner's almost ready.' Taking in the sight of Lisa he faltered. 'You OK, love?'

'Yes, thanks. It's really good to be here. To see you all.'

Lisa's dad sat on the edge of her bed placing his hand on her leg. 'I'm sorry we haven't been around for you. You look … well, I can see you've had a difficult time.'

Lisa was grateful her dad hadn't gone for a full on 'you look terrible', especially after she felt she was looking so much better lately. 'Gee, thanks, Dad!'

'You look pale and skinny. You know what I mean.'

'I'll take skinny as a compliment.' Lisa laughed.

'You need to get some of your mum's cooking inside you and a bit of time on the piste will get the colour back in your cheeks.'

'Thanks, Dad.' Lisa smiled. She hadn't told her parents why she had split up with Ben, but the fact she had moved home meant they knew it had knocked her.

Her dad stood up and jumped at the sight of the stag. 'Bloody Nora, I thought I'd seen the last of him!'

'I quite like it. Why don't you?'

'He's been staring at me for months, your mum painted it in her art class and hung it in our room.'

'Art class? Mum?'

'Yes, she's quite the joiner here, you know; any excuse to test out her French.'

'Well, I like it.'

'Tell her that and you'll be in her good books forever.'

Chapter Thirty-Eight

Being down first in the morning meant all was quiet. Lisa padded across the stone floor, welcoming the warmth from the under floor heating. She opened the curtains and inhaled at the sight of the mountains silhouetted against the pink-streaked sky. Small patches of grey cloud were interspersed with smaller cotton-wool tufts illuminated by the sun as it began its climb above the mountain to cast warmth into the valley below. Lisa recalled her mum telling her it was a view you could never tire of – and she could see why; it was constantly changing and yet always stunning. The village at the foot of the mountains looked sleepy, covered in its blanket of snow. Lisa watched as lights were gradually turned on in the houses, their distance from her vantage point making them look like fairy lights. Across the valley, Lisa could see snowploughs grooming the pistes ready for the day ahead. She opened the door onto the balcony and welcomed the cold, crisp air as she stepped outside. It was enlivening. Only the sound of the birds broke the snow-muffled silence.

'Quite a view, isn't it?'

Lisa jumped at the sound of Luke's voice behind her. 'It's—'

'But if you don't come in and shut that bloody door, I'm locking you out there.'

'You know you could put some more clothes on.' Lisa glared at her brother in his low-slung lounge pants. She walked back inside, sliding the door behind her, causing a final burst of cold air to surge into the room.

Luke threw a cushion at her. 'I will before Mum gets up.'

Lisa threw the cushion back. 'What?' As Luke turned to pick up the cushion Lisa gasped. 'You got a tattoo?'

'Keep it down!'

Lisa squealed. 'Oh my God, Mum doesn't know, does she? You wait until she sees that!' The silhouette of a surfer riding a wave across Luke's right shoulder blade, the words 'surf's up' below it, was actually quite good. The colours in the wave were sharp and the image well drawn. He had obviously paid for a quality job. But there was no way Lisa was going to say that before she had finished having fun. 'You know surf is spelt 'ur' not 'ir', right?'

Luke swung his head as if trying to see his back.

'Got ya!'

'I know it's spelt right!' Luke protested, attempting to recover from his automatic reaction as he slumped off, leaving Lisa giggling.

By the time Luke returned wearing a sweatshirt, he was carrying a mug of coffee for each of them. The sun had risen higher into the sky, almost breaking over the tallest mountain peak and changing the tapestry of the view once more.

Lisa leaned forward, taking her coffee and thanking Luke. 'Mum and Dad seem really happy here, don't they?'

'Yeah, they do. Mum's much more relaxed.'

'Not enough for you to tell her you've got a tattoo though,' Lisa scoffed.

'Sod off.'

Lisa giggled. 'It is really lovely though, isn't it?'

'My tat?'

'No, you fool, here.' Lisa gestured out the window. 'This place.'

'Yeah, it's odd seeing so much snow after months of sun, but it's all good.'

Lisa sat up and stared out of the window.

Luke paused with his coffee to his lips, watching her, intrigued.

'Do you know what though ... it's funny ... there's all this snow and yet—'

'What?'

'Well, at home, if it snowed, what's the first thing we'd do?'

'I don't know ... Facebook it ... put a picture on Instagram?'

'After that.'

'Phone in sick?'

'After that.' Lisa glared at Luke, urging him to think, as if the answer was obvious.

He looked at her blankly.

'Build a snowman!'

'When we were twelve!' Luke mocked, sitting back and drinking his coffee.

'OK, point taken.' Lisa poked her tongue out at him. 'But, on the way here and looking out now, I've not seen a single snowman. That's weird, isn't it? There must be plenty of children round here. Do you think it's a French thing?'

'I don't know, maybe it's more of an in-town rather than on-a-mountain thing, or a "why build a snowman when you can ski, sledge and snowshoe?" kind of thing,' Luke joked, looking out across the village below, registering the lack of snowmen for the first time.

'Well, I think it's a shame; it's Christmas, there's snow and not a single snowman in sight,' Lisa harrumphed back and sipped her coffee.

'Well, let's do it. Let's show them how it's done.'

Lisa raised her eyebrows. 'I think Mum would kill us if we messed up her picture perfect garden.'

'Oh, there'll be more snow to cover it. Come on, let's do it.'

'Luke, it was just a silly observation.'

'Come on, where's your sense of adventure? Christ, if I'm willing to wrap up and go for it so you can have your bloody snowman, the least you can do is join in. Come on … it's Christmas and all that,' he mocked.

Lisa had stopped listening after the 'Where's your sense of adventure?' He was trying to reel her in, she knew it, but he was using bait she found hard to resist. 'I do have a sense of adventure.'

'I know. I remember.'

'Remember?' Lisa's eyes went wide.

'Yeah, when you used to be fun.'

'*Used to be?*' Lisa leapt off the sofa, putting her coffee mug down more forcefully than she intended. 'I'll build a bloody snowman with you,' she huffed.

Luke laughed.

Lisa marched to her room to find warm clothes suitable for snowman building. *Tell me I've lost my sense of adventure!*

After the two of them had built the biggest snowman they could out of the slightly-too-powdery snow – that perhaps explained the lack of snowmen – created snow angels – or at least Lisa had while Luke threw snow at her – and were midway through a full-on snowball fight, their mum appeared carrying two mugs of hot chocolate. She raised her eyebrows at them, as they each dropped the fistfuls of snow they were holding. They were both nearer thirty than thirteen, but a reproachful look from their mum could reduce them to teenagers.

'Well, you can take the children out of England …' was all she said as she deposited the mugs of hot chocolate into their hands, turned and went back inside.

Luke and Lisa looked at each other and burst into peals of laughter.

'I think it might be warmer out here than inside for a bit,' Luke shuddered.

Christmas Eve started with an early ski and a soak in the hot tub. Even though she had stuck to the more picturesque green runs, instead of joining Luke on the blue and black runs, Lisa's muscles felt sore; she really needed to exercise more regularly. Within five minutes of winding down in the stiff-muscle-relieving water, Lisa felt that lazing in a hot tub surrounded by mountains, snow and clear blue skies took relaxation to a whole new level. Sitting in the steaming water, with snow all around her and being stared at by a snowman, was a wonderful and yet surreal experience – the view contrasted with the heat on her skin to create an exhilarating assault on her senses. A fresh dump of snow had hidden the 'mess', as her mum called it, that she and Luke had made of the garden, though even her mum had to admit, now that the snowman was surrounded by fresh snow he added a touch of magic to the perfect Christmas scene. Lisa teased Luke for keeping his black T-shirt on, while he did his best to convince everyone he was warmer that way. It made no sense, but their mum seemed to buy it.

While her mum started work on the magret de canard aux cranberries she had chosen for their evening meal, Lisa decided to phone Felicity. She was missing her and thought how lovely it must be to have four children on Christmas Eve; in a house so full, the excitement must be palpable.

'Don't eat raw pastry!'

Lisa looked at her phone. 'I'm not!'

'Not you; we are making mince pies for Santa and Fred seems to think it's OK to eat everything in sight. I told you

Santa won't want them after you've nibbled them and then he might not leave any presents. Fred, I can see you putting that pastry in your pocket!'

Lisa laughed. 'Shall I call back later?'

'No, now's fine; hold on.'

Lisa heard Felicity bellow for Pete, followed by her hastily instructing him on the finishing touches to be done to the mince pies before they went in the oven.

'Right, I'm in the lounge, and the door is shut. I'm here.'

'Really, I was just saying hello.'

'No, your timing is great; we were about to egg wash and "stab" the pastry as Alice is insisting on calling it, and that won't be pretty.'

'Oh, poor Pete!'

'Oh, he'll be fine. Now how's France?'

Having been on an emotional trip to the crematorium with Felicity – the two of them laying flowers for Flick's mum and Lisa's Granny Blake – before she came away, Lisa felt aware that Christmas must be a difficult time of year for Felicity. So while she was honest about how good it was to see her mum, dad and Luke, she quickly moved on to telling Felicity about Luke's tattoo and her parents' fantastic place. She added, as the realisation dawned on her, that it would be ideal for them all to go together for a weekend, perhaps to celebrate their thirtieth birthdays in the coming year, as a bit of that travelling they had spoken about before.

'That would be bloody marvellous!' Flick wowed. 'If I survive Christmas, that is.'

'A bit full on, is it?'

'It has been, but I'm just about done now I think; pressies wrapped, mince pies in the oven – hopefully. Pete has to go in to work later, which is a shame, but I'll get the kids to bed early ready for tomorrow.'

'You and Pete are sorted though, right?' Lisa bit her lip as soon as she said it; Felicity didn't know about the secret Pete was keeping, whatever that was, or that Lisa knew they had been testing out aphrodisiacs.

'Hold on, Lisa, Pete's yelling something.'

Lisa could only hear muffled sounds as Felicity covered the phone.

'Sorry, he was only asking if Fred could eat the leftovers; honestly, it's raw bloody pastry!'

Lisa had no idea if raw pastry was bad for you, but assumed from Felicity's tone it wasn't something you should let your children eat.

'Right, sorry. Yes. Me and Pete. We haven't got each other presents.'

Lisa didn't know whether to be relieved that Felicity had misunderstood her or concerned that she and Pete hadn't got each other presents. 'Oh, really?'

'Yes, we're putting the money towards something for the house in the sales instead.'

'Oh!' Lisa thought how unromantic that sounded.

'But, der der derrrrrrr ... Pete's been hiding something.'

Lisa felt her stomach twist.

'I've been nagging him to tell me what it is, but he says he has an announcement to make on Boxing Day, when his mother is here! God knows why it's got to be while she's here, but, hey, he's not giving anything else away.'

'Oh, OK.' Lisa didn't know what to say.

'I'm hoping for fewer hours at the bar – that would make my Christmas. Oh, you don't think it's more hours, do you?'

Lisa really hoped, for Flick's sake, that Pete's announcement would be something so innocent.

With her phone call on her mind, Lisa went to find a glass of wine. She found her mum in the kitchen, poured them both a glass of Sauvignon Blanc and made herself comfortable on a stool at the breakfast bar. Watching her mum cook reminded her of being young. She thought about Felicity cooking with her children and about her own little Pip. This would have been her baby's first Christmas. It was hard to assimilate her feelings about the loss of her baby with the realisation she now had about the reality of her relationship with Ben. She rubbed her forehead.

Lisa's mum picked up her wine and took a breath. 'So, when is it you are going to tell me why you're here?'

Lisa looked at her mum. 'To see you, Dad and Luke. It's Christmas.'

'And that's lovely, Lord knows it's been too long, but—'

'I'm sorry I left it so long, Mum, I really am.' Lisa took a drink of her wine. 'Life in London ... I don't know where to start really; it all seems so far removed now. I wasn't myself for a bit.'

'Yes, Ben said—'

'Ben?'

'I'm sorry, Lisa, but I knew you were holding something back, so I called him a few times to check you were OK.'

'He never said.'

'He said you ... well, he said you had been seeing someone else and that you two were trying to work things out. That's why we didn't come to see you at Easter; we thought you needed time. Then when you called to say you wanted to come home, I assumed working things out hadn't gone so well.'

Lisa was shocked. 'Mum, I never ... that's not what it was.' Lisa broke down. It was all too much. She told her mum about her relationship with Ben and losing Pip. Her mum listened and cried with her. When Luke blustered into the kitchen in search of food she shooed him away.

'Lisa, I can't believe how much you've been through. Why didn't you say? You and Luke, you can tell me anything, you know. I am here for you. Things are important. God knows I love this place and the life we have now, but, Lisa, none of it matters without family. Having you both here with us, it makes it all perfect. You, your dad and Luke have always been my world.'

Lisa almost ventured a joke about a tidy house being her mum's world, but realised it wasn't the time. Instead she hugged her mum. 'I love you, Mum.'

'I love you too, darling. Now,' she said, wiping her eyes on her apron and taking a deep breath, 'is there anything else you want to tell me?'

Lisa sighed. 'No, I think that is everything. Unless you mean about Luke?'

'No.' Lisa's mum rubbed her back. 'He'll tell me about his tattoo when he's ready.'

Lisa burst out giggling and turned to face her. 'You know?'

'Of course I do. He's always been terrible at hiding things … Unlike his big sister.'

'I'm not hiding anything, no more secrets here,' Lisa affirmed.

'So, no blast from the past, as they say, that I might need to know about?'

'I told you Felicity and I are friends again.'

'And there's nobody else you want to mention?' Lisa's mum looked directly at her.

Lisa's cheeks coloured. *Oh!*

'Only now you're back, I wondered … I mean, I know I influenced you, telling you not to get too involved too young.'

Lisa recalled her mum and Mrs F frequently telling

her and Flick that they shouldn't settle down too soon. 'There's a whole world waiting for you Lisa', her mum had frequently said; they were even her parting words on the night of her prom.

'But I've often wondered, if I hadn't pushed you—'

'Ah, Mum. When Nathan proposed, it was me who said no.'

'Yes, but—'

Lisa touched her mum's hand. 'I was eighteen. I made my own choices. I'm not sure they were all the right choices, but look at the things I have seen and done. And if I hadn't gone away I would probably have "what ifs" of a different sort.'

'And do you have "what ifs" now? I mean about Nathan?'

Lisa looked into her mum's eyes. 'Honestly?'

Her mum nodded.

'All the bloody time.'

'Oh Lisa love ...' Her mum pulled her into her arms.

When they broke their hug Lisa blew her nose and wiped her blotchy face.

Her mum poured them both more wine and looked at her tentatively. 'I didn't know if I should say, but ... Harold Martin called—'

'Is there any chance of food this side of Christmas?' Luke appeared round the door.

'Flippin' heck, I forgot to put the duck in!' Lisa's mum leapt into action.

By the time they sat down to a late roast they had all consumed too much wine.

'When in France ...' Lisa's mum announced as she presented her platter of delicious-smelling roast duck and cranberry sauce.

'And there I was thinking eating late had more to do with you getting plastered than French tradition.'

'Luke, darling, unless you don't want to eat I suggest you are quiet.'

Lisa's head was spinning. She felt like she needed her bed more than she needed a hearty roast, even one that had filled the chalet with delicious smells all evening, but knew she didn't dare say that to her mum.

They all filled their plates and glasses before making a toast to their Granny Blake, their first Christmas in France and Christmases yet to come. Ones Lisa promised herself would always involve appreciating time with her family.

Chapter Thirty-Nine

Lisa woke to the sound of her phone buzzing with messages. She rolled over, and her head thumped with the movement, but she smiled at the sight of Felicity and her children opening their presents. Stage-by-stage photographs of the wrapping being undone on the array of toys she had bought for Flick's children – once she had managed to convince her that she absolutely was buying them presents no matter how many times she told her there was no need – some weird tool for Pete that apparently she would appreciate if she were into gardening, and a framed picture of herself and Felicity that she took on their road trip. Lisa had included a card saying how much she loved the one Felicity had hanging in her hallway and how happy she was that they were making new memories together – how grateful she was for that opportunity. Felicity sent her a text saying great minds think alike and that she hoped she liked her present.

As she went to put her phone back on the side and slide back under her covers, it rang. The noise made her jump and hold her head all at the same time. As she focused on the screen she saw that it was Dom, and felt a flash of disappointment that it wasn't Nathan.

'Hello, my lovely. Happy Christmas.'

'Winnie!' Lisa sat up at the surprise of hearing Winnie's voice.

She thanked Lisa for her cushion, making her laugh when she said that Jack 'the blighter' was after it for himself. She told Lisa that she and her son were making progress, and welcomed the news that Lisa was enjoying the festivities with her family. They ended their chat with the promise of a cup of tea and a biscuit in the New Year. Dom wished Lisa a happy Christmas and confirmed that things were going well, despite the fact Jack had christened his dad's Christmas tree. He also stated he hadn't forgotten their chat and that Lisa would be the first to know if the opportunity arose to talk to Winnie.

Christmas had barely started and Lisa already felt blessed. The year had been tough, tougher than any other she had experienced and yet, now it was drawing to a close, she was with her family, and had friends who cared enough to send her messages and call her on Christmas Day. She thought about the previous year, when Ben had got up and gone for a jog, they had gone to his friends' apartment for drinks and wandered through Hyde Park, past Winter Wonderland, which looked soulless due to being closed for the day. She questioned why she had ever thought she would miss it before realising she had been concentrating on the ghost of Christmases long past, as opposed to the reality of what her life had become. Not that it mattered now. This year she was waking up in a real winter wonderland and felt more full of Christmas spirit than she had for a very long time.

Excitement built as she thought about the presents they'd all placed under the tree the previous evening. She was pleased her mum had decided to forgo the French tradition of opening them after the Christmas Eve meal, with the words 'oh sod it, we're English', when they decided they were all too full of wine and roast dinner to enjoy it.

There was a knock at her door. Lisa sat up as her dad carried in a mug of coffee for her.

'Merry Christmas! We are all starting the day with one of these, your mother especially.' He winked.

'Sorry, I encouraged her.' Lisa smiled.

Her dad put the coffee down and sat on the edge of her bed. 'I'm not sure she needed much encouraging. She ... I mean, we ... love having you here.' With that he gave her a hug.

'Thanks, Dad. Merry Christmas.'

He stood up to leave, but as he got to the door he hesitated. 'And, Lisa ... I'm sorry to hear about ... about everything really... but especially about the ... about the baby. You know I never would have pushed so hard about starting your business if I'd known.'

Lisa swallowed back tears. She knew her mum would tell her dad; that was the way they worked. Telling one of her parents anything always meant she was indirectly telling both, but she hadn't expected that. 'Thank you,' was all she could manage. At some point she would thank her dad properly, as she knew there had been days when having her business and clients depending on her had been the only thing that had kept her going, her only reason for getting out of bed and going through the motions of the day.

Her dad wiped his eye and offered a small smile, before leaving the room.

Once they had finished the selection of pastries their mum had got in for breakfast, they gathered round the tree that Lisa and Luke had helped choose just days before. It was tastefully decorated and hadn't dared to shed a needle since being put in place adjacent to the fireplace and log-burning stove. It wasn't Bing, but Lisa had to admit it was pretty. As they opened their gifts, Lisa smiled at the framed photograph Felicity had given her, another image taken on their road trip, only hers came complete with a bag of Percy Pig and Pals and the message, 'Let's stick together'. It was perfect.

Lisa was pleased her parents liked their present – a photobook of highlights from her and Luke's childhood, with holidays they had been on, birthdays, special moments and special people. Her mum and dad had both welled up flicking through it. Lisa's mum said how lovely it was to have such precious memories with them in France – an added bonus Lisa hadn't thought of. It all made the hours of sorting the box of photographs, scanning them in, attempting to get the pictures and captions in the right places, losing it when almost finished and starting over, worth it. After Luke had given them tickets for the Aiguille du Midi cable car and a meal at the 3842 restaurant, named after its altitude, she was worried her present would look a bit homemade, but they loved it.

Luke's faux leather passport case printed with a picture of Bondi Beach, which she hastily pretended was to go with a helicopter ride over the Alps she wanted to get him, did look rubbish though, especially after he had clubbed together with her mum and dad to get Lisa a cookery weekend in Italy. It was extravagant and amazing. She was almost speechless; it was such a lovely gift.

'Well, you used to love Italy and when Harold said you'd been eating a lot of Chinese takeaway—'

'What?' Lisa nearly dropped her gift.

'Well, haven't you?'

'Yes, but—'

'So there you go.'

Lisa didn't know whether to be horrified that Harold had been keeping an eye on her or grateful now that she had such a lovely present as a result. Either way, she would be more careful regarding her privacy once she was back in England.

As they cleared up the wrapping paper, there was a

knock at the door. Nobody had called since Lisa had been at her parents', but she knew they had friends among their neighbours.

'I'll go!' she bellowed as she ran down the stairs preparing to say 'joyeux noël' in her best French accent.

She swung the door open. 'Joy—' Lisa's eyes went wide as the words she had rehearsed were taken away by the hit of cold air and the sight of the person standing in front of her.

'Merry Christmas, Lisa.' Nathan smiled, looking almost hesitant, as he awaited her response.

It took her a moment to find the words. 'M- merry Christmas ... Nathan, you're here!' Her cheeks burned hot despite the cold air and her heart thudded against her chest.

'May I come in?' Nathan's blue eyes sparkled more brightly with the contrast of the snow. He was there, larger than life, hair ruffled and stubble at least a day old, looking thoroughly lovely in the doorway.

Lisa realised she should step back, open the door wider and welcome him in, all things that would be appropriate if only she could move. 'It's you ... you're here ... at my parents'—'

'Your mum knows I'm coming.'

'She does?'

'I'd like to explain, but it's freezing out here.'

Snapping out of her stunned paralysis, Lisa moved back from the door. 'Of course, come in.' She looked up towards the first floor as she heard her mum, dad and Luke scuttle back from the banister.

Still taken aback, Lisa took Nathan's coat, the smell of his aftershave and the feel of his hand brushing against hers proving to her senses that he was actually there, that this was actually happening. He slipped off his boots, revealing thick socks. He was wearing jeans and a jumper that touched in all the right places to show his muscles. Lisa wished she had made more of an effort instead of hurrying out of the shower, excited to open her Christmas presents. She didn't know why he was there, but the fact it was Christmas Day and her mum knew he was coming had to be good signs, didn't they?

Lisa directed Nathan up the stairs and followed behind him, noticing the quiver in her legs with each step.

'Nathan, it has been a very long time.' Lisa's mum kissed Nathan on both cheeks. 'I'm so pleased you found us OK.'

Lisa looked at her dumbfounded.

While Nathan moved on to shaking hands with her dad and Luke, exchanging Christmas greetings, and talking about the condition of the roads and the snow, Lisa took her mum by the elbow. 'Come and help me fetch Nathan a drink,' she insisted, throwing the words 'excuse us,' as casually as she could behind them as they went.

Once in the kitchen, Lisa took several deep breaths and raised her eyebrows expectantly at her mum.

'I hope I've done the right thing,' her mum whispered.

'Mum, Nathan is here.' Lisa attempted to maintain a hushed tone, while hoping to elicit more of an explanation.

'I know! He's come all the way to France to speak to you. He's been travelling for hours.'

Lisa couldn't help but think that, for somebody who was whispering, her mum seemed desperately animated and excited.

'Harold said—'

'*Harold?* Mum, what is it with you encouraging Harold Martin to snoop into my life?'

'I haven't encouraged him to snoop, darling, just to keep an eye on you.'

'An eye! Honestly, I'm beginning to think he's been living in the loft or something. Oh God, Mum, he hasn't been living in the loft, has he?'

'Lisa, darling, you're not still watching those silly crime programmes that scare you, are you? Of course he hasn't been living in the loft. Now, calm down.'

'I'm sorry, it's just, Harold is … and this is … well, it's all …' Lisa poured herself a drink of water from the cooler on the fridge and drank it straight down. 'Nathan is here, in France, in your chalet and I don't know why or how.'

Lisa's mum walked over and stroked Lisa's arm, in an attempt to calm her down. 'Why, I'll leave to him. How … well, let's just say he's been paying a lot of interest in our house back home, and eventually Harold told him he needed to know who he was and why he was there, or he would be forced to make a citizen's arrest. Not wanting to do anything to overstep the mark if Nathan was telling the truth about knowing us, Harold phoned me a few days ago to see if I could corroborate his story.'

Corroborate his story? Lisa couldn't help but think that Harold had danced, skipped and leapt over the mark some time ago, but decided to stick to the matter in hand. 'But he is here, Mum. How has Nathan ended up here, on Christmas Day? It's Christmas Day, for goodness' sake!'

'I know, isn't it perfect? I can't believe he got a crossing at such short notice.'

Needing something stronger than water Lisa turned the coffee machine on.

'After our chat yesterday, when you said about the year you'd had and about the "what ifs" … I just thought … well, no matter what you say, I know I encouraged you not to get too serious too young. I know I influenced you with all the things I told you I'd missed out on. But, Lisa, you're all grown up now. And Nathan, well, even though I know you were up to all sorts behind my back – never trust your brother to keep a secret, darling – Nathan always made you happy. He was crushed when you left and word is he never got serious over anyone else. So when Harold said he had been hanging round the house and you said ... well ... I wanted to make you happy. To see you smile on Christmas Day.'

Lisa looked at her mum, tears welling in her eyes. She put down her empty glass and gave her a hug, not knowing what to say to her kind words.

'So I, um, well, what is it Luke called it? I drunk dialled him last night. I told him if he was that desperate to see you he should stop skulking around and come here, and find you.'

'Mum!'

'Harold had got his number, as a security measure or something. I hope I did the right thing. I hope I haven't ruined your Christmas. He's been travelling for over eleven hours!' The words came out in a rush.

'Any chance of those drinks?' Lisa's dad appeared in the doorway, gesturing towards the living room with his head, giving a look that said they were running out of small talk.

On her mum's instruction, Lisa went to rescue the situation. She invited Nathan to join her at the table. From there the view was an easy talking point. She had so many other things she wanted to say, but with Luke in earshot, and her mum and dad fetching drinks she couldn't bring herself to ask the questions leaping and fizzing round her mind. It reminded her of being a teenager – the two of them waiting for Luke and her parents to go to bed so they could be alone. With hours to go until bedtime, Lisa wondered if she should suggest going for a drive, but as Nathan had been driving for hours she thought better of it.

When Lisa's parents appeared from the kitchen her mum was carrying a bottle of wine, two glasses and some festive nibbles on a tray. 'There now, I thought something stronger than coffee might be in order.' She placed the tray down on the table. 'You two have a drink; the rest of us are going snowshoeing.'

Lisa mouthed thank you and gave a grateful smile.

'What?' Luke looked horrified at the thought.

'You remember, your mum said she wanted to show us that route through the woods out the back,' her dad added, picking up his jumper and slipping it on.

'Really?' Luke remained unconvinced.

'Just because it's not as cool as surfing, riding the wave when the surf's up, doesn't mean you won't enjoy it.' Lisa grinned and raised her eyebrows suggestively ensuring he registered the link to his tattoo. He didn't know their mum already knew and Lisa decided her need to be alone with Nathan was greater than the moral implications of an implied threat.

Luke glared at her.

'You should tell Mum—'

'Right, well, it's been good to see you, Nathan; I'm sure we'll catch up when we get back.' Luke stood up. 'If we haven't frozen, or got lost in the woods or attacked by wild boar on Christmas Day.' He continued to mutter as he made his way down the stairs to the boot room.

Chapter Forty

Once her family had finally bustled out of the door, the chalet fell silent and Lisa felt the effects of being alone with Nathan, the fire, the Christmas tree and the perfect backdrop of the mountains. Her mind wandered to the last time they had been alone in front of a log burning fire. She blinked the images away.

'Nathan, I—'

'Lisa, before you say anything, can I kiss you?'

'Kiss me?' she asked coyly, while warmth spread through her body at the thought.

'Yes, kiss you.' Nathan stood and pulled her up next to him. She felt him pressed against her and welcomed the sensation of his lips on hers. He slipped his hands down her back, round her bottom and under her thighs, lifting her on to his hips while never breaking from her mouth. With her legs wrapped round him, Lisa kissed him back with all the emotion she had been holding in since they had spent the night together. She needed him, to feel him close to her. Nathan moved, resting her bottom on the table, freeing his hands to move up and around her back and into her hair. With her balance steadied, she moved her hands inside his jumper, feeling his taut muscles flexing. Lisa's mind attempted to tell her she needed to speak to him, to ask him why he was there, while her body throbbed all over with wanting him.

Eventually, it was Nathan who breathlessly broke their kiss.

'I have wanted to do that since I woke to find you had left my bed,' he whispered, pressing his forehead against hers.

She breathed heavily, missing the contact of his lips. 'Me too.'

He stepped back. 'We need to talk.'

Lisa could hear the effect of their kiss in his voice. It made her want him more.

Before they could talk, she insisted on pouring them both a drink. Realising her mum hadn't opened the wine, she went in search of a corkscrew. Welcoming the opportunity to gather her thoughts, she paced the kitchen, took a few deep breaths and pondered texting Felicity with the words 'Oh my God, Nathan is here!' – the only words she could seem to muster, despite the pacing – before finally concluding that attempting to think wasn't helping and returning to the lounge.

Nathan was standing, looking out of the window. She allowed her eyes to take in the scene. Outside, the clouds hung low on the mountains. She knew they would be casting shadows into the valley. The tallest pines and some craggy rocks, exposed by wind during the night, contrasted against the snow. Inside, Nathan's silhouette revealed strength and vitality; from his broad shoulders to his muscular legs, he looked entirely at home against the backdrop of the rugged terrain. The fire glowed, while the tree lights sparkled. If she had asked Santa to deliver her up a winter wonderland fantasy for Christmas, this would have been it, but, with the uncertainty in her mind about what Nathan wanted to say, she knew it might all turn out to be an illusion. She coughed, making her presence known.

As they sat at the table, the scent of the Christmas tree and heady spices filled the air. Nathan reached over and held her hand. The contact sent tingles through her body. He took a long drink of his wine and looked at her; his eyes looked darker, more serious now.

'Lisa, I've come here to tell you I can't let you go. Not again.'

She felt a warm flush spread across her neck and suppressed the urge to leap up and hug him, aware that he hadn't finished.

'Not without telling you how I feel.'

Wait, what does that mean? She forced herself to breathe and to stay focused.

'I've tried to play it cool. "Cool", God I hate that word. As if I could ever be cool where you are concerned. I've tried to be casual, so I didn't scare you away, but when I saw you in Cin Cin I knew I couldn't carry on.'

Oh God, Pete's plan; his bloody stupid plan!

'The pretence is killing me, Lisa. I can't stop thinking about you; you are in my thoughts day and night. I don't know who he is, the man you were with—'

'Nathan, it's not what—'

'And if that's what you want, to see other people, I'll just have to accept that and leave you alone because I can't keep pretending to be cool where you are concerned. I can't do casual. I can't do just friends. I was struggling to keep the act up before I saw you with him. After, I knew I couldn't—'

'But—'

'And I know you don't want commitment, and that a family and settling down isn't for you.'

But I do want that. She swallowed past a lump in her throat, unable to form the words she wanted to say.

'That's why I needed … need to speak to you. I didn't want to do it by phone or text, and it turns out you're a difficult person to track down.'

Lisa thought about the times Harold had seen Nathan at her house; the times she had missed him since they had spent the night together. 'It's a busy time of year for a pet sitter,' she responded on autopilot, the words not seeming to belong to the conversation.

Nathan laughed, before returning his gaze to meet hers. 'Lisa, the thing is, I've had adventures, I've taken risks and I've travelled. All things I know are important to you.'

In the past. It was too sad to bear. *They were all important in the past.*

'And, while these days my life is more ... settled – my travels, more holidays really – I'd do it all again, if that's what you want. Because Lisa, and I can't tell you how many times I've regretted not saying this to you when we were eighteen, above all – above all those things I said I wanted – I want a life with you.'

Lisa stared at him, unable to speak, wondering if her mind had drifted back to her fantasy and she was imagining his words.

'I love you, Lisa. I always have.'

Holding back a sob, Lisa responded instinctively, 'I love you too,' her words coming out as a whisper. Now she said them aloud the honesty of owning those long put down feelings felt entirely right.

Nathan stood, pulling Lisa in close to him.

She looked into his eyes and said from her heart, 'And I want a life with you, but, Nathan ...'

She felt his body still.

'I do want all those things you once said you wanted. Commitment, a life together and a family – I want it all, and, if you'll still have me, I want them with you.'

Nathan looked into her eyes. 'Really? You do?'

'I do.' She laughed and sobbed all at the same time, at the words and how right they felt.

She felt Nathan's arms around her, and placed her head against his chest as he took a deep steadying breath. Happy tears slid down her cheeks, with the knowledge that it was finally their time. She thought about the family she had sat next to on the aeroplane. The children were mini-adventurers full of tales of skiing, climbing and mountain biking; they were a family embracing life together. The thought that one day she may have a family of her own, that she and Nathan could have that together was almost overwhelming. Lisa looked up into Nathan's deep blue eyes. Sensation spread to every nerve, as she slid her hand round the back of his neck and drew him closer. Their lips met and she closed her eyes welcoming the depth of his passion-fuelled kiss.

When Lisa eventually leaned back she looked at Nathan, a grin tugging at her lips. 'You've always loved me?'

'Yes, I always have.'

She smiled.

'Of course I've had girlfriends; it's been a long time.' He smiled cheekily.

She giggled. 'I'm not sure I need to know about those.'

'But I never loved them, and I never wanted them the way I want you.'

Lisa pulled him closer, stopping him talking with a kiss.

Chapter Forty-One

Felicity gathered all the chairs she could muster from around the house. Having Pete's mum, sister and family for Boxing Day dinner meant setting three extra seats and an extra highchair around the table. The variety of seats meant there would be a mismatch of heights, but it was the best she could do. Her plates were odd too, some from her mum's collection that she couldn't bring herself to get rid of, and some she and Pete had bought to add to them. Ordinarily she didn't notice such things, but with Pete's mum coming too she was on high alert to imperfections, of which she felt there were many as she turned her attention to finding glasses.

'Pete, please tell me we have at least enough glasses for the adults. How have we only got three wine glasses?'

'I think we've got plastic cups left from Fred's party.'

'*Fred's party?* Pete, we can't give your mother wine in a plastic cup with jungle animals on it.'

'We won't, you and I will have them to match the kids; problem solved.'

'I knew I married you for a reason.' Felicity smiled.

Pete scoffed. 'After all these years, that's the best reason you can think of?'

Felicity didn't answer, she still had crackers to get off the tree and matching cutlery to find – which didn't involve plastic handles, princesses or Mr Tumble. The day had barely started and already she was looking forward to the evening when she and Pete might get a moment to themselves; a moment to breathe.

She thought about Lisa and her call the previous night

when she had excitedly told her the news about Nathan's arrival in France. It was so romantic, *lucky moo!* They were only in France and yet when she thought about the two of them, in a chalet in the snow, it seemed a million miles away from her own existence. OK, so sun was more her thing than snow, and Lisa and Nathan weren't alone, but, nevertheless, it sounded bloody bliss compared to the day she had planned. Checking her watch she sent Lisa a text:

I hope you managed to get some sleep ;-) And, ooh, it's big secret day!

Trying not to admit to Pete that she was desperate to know what it was he was hiding was driving her crazy; that and the thought that his mum might already know.

Lisa sat up. She looked at Flick's message and realised, with the excitement of Nathan turning up, the shock of his declaration and the added shock of her mum not minding them sharing a room together – cosmopolitan living was obviously agreeing with her – she had forgotten to ask Nathan about Pete's secret. She wanted to get to the bottom of it. She needed to know that Felicity was OK, and she didn't want the fact she had seen the message hanging unsaid between her and Nathan. She just needed to pick the right time to broach the subject.

She slipped out of bed.

Nathan yawned and stretched his arms above his head, causing the sheet to slip lower on his firm stomach, revealing the top of his black hipsters. 'You know, we have missed out on a lot of time together.'

Lisa pretended not to be fazed and turned to open the curtains. She looked at the mountain, the snow glinting in the early morning light, and the sight of her parents and Luke driving off on their daily trip to the boulangerie. 'We'll have to think of ways to make up for all that lost time.' She grinned, placing her hands on her hips, slightly lifting her T-shirt as she did so.

'Oh, I've got ways.' Nathan leapt out of bed, and Lisa screamed and ran.

He chased her. Lisa's heart thudded as she laughed, squealed and ran all at the same time. When Nathan caught her she was heading for the stairs. He grabbed her and put her over his shoulder. Lisa squealed in mock protest. As he threw her back down on her bed, he leaned over her.

'Don't run away from me again, will you?' His breathing was heavy, he was being playful, but Lisa could see the vulnerability in his eyes and hear the sincerity in the question.

'I won't run,' Lisa replied, pulling him down closer to her so she could feel the weight of him pressing against her.

Nathan leaned down to kiss her, but paused. 'The morning after the bonfire, you ran; why?'

'Nathan, I didn't run ... well, I did, but not because of us ... I mean, what happened between us. That was ... amazing.' Lisa coughed. 'Unexpected, but amazing!'

'Unexpected?' Nathan scoffed. 'So based on previous knowledge you weren't expecting amazing?' He raised his eyebrows in anticipation of her answer.

'Pah!' Lisa burst out a giggle.

'I'm hurt.'

'And there I was meaning it as a compliment for your new skills.'

'OK, that I'll take.' He kissed her.

Lisa started to lose herself in the kiss as her hands traced down his spine.

Nathan pulled back. 'So why did you run? If it wasn't because you were afraid of ... us?'

Lisa shifted, moving Nathan as she sat up. 'Look ...' She took a breath. '... I didn't tell you before because I didn't want you to think I was snooping.'

'Snooping?' Nathan laughed at the word. 'Why would I think that? Uh oh, you didn't find Napoleon, did you?'

'What? No. Who?' The bizarre question threw Lisa when she was all set to confess to reading the message on his phone.

'Napoleon Boneypart, the skeleton in my closet!'

Lisa looked at Nathan's straight face. 'You aren't joking, are you?'

'Would it be better to say I am?'

'Nathan! This is serious.'

'So is Napoleon, he takes things very gravely.'

Lisa took a breath, deciding to ignore the joke. 'That morning, when I left, it was because ... because I saw your phone, in your kitchen. I mean I saw a message on your phone ... from Pete.'

Nathan looked at her blankly as he tried to process what she was saying.

'Flick's Pete. I saw a message on your phone from Felicity's husband Pete.'

'Oh.' Nathan sighed, the flicker of recognition on his face causing the playful atmosphere in the room to disappear.

Lisa started to panic. 'I wasn't going through your phone or anything. I was getting some water. Your phone was charging and Flick's name appeared on the screen. Looking was automatic, not really intended.' Lisa's cheeks flushed at the confession.

Nathan frowned. 'You could have asked me about it.'

'I'm asking now.' Lisa hoped it wasn't too little too late.

'But if you'd stayed to ask me then, I wouldn't have thought you had run away. You'd have been there when I woke up and we wouldn't have wasted more time.' He kissed her, first on the lips and then in a trail around her neck.

Lisa tried not to succumb to the distraction. 'So what would you have told me, if I'd asked you then? What is Pete hiding from Felicity?'

Nathan stopped kissing Lisa and looked at her directly. 'I would have said I couldn't tell you, because I gave Pete my word.'

Lisa bit her lip. She didn't want secrets between her and Nathan, and she didn't want Pete having a secret from Flick; one that he had to wait until after Christmas and to be in the presence of his mum to share. 'But you lied to Felicity.'

'When?' Nathan looked taken aback.

'At the bonfire, you told her you didn't know Pete; you said you hardly ever go to Cin Cin.'

'I didn't lie. I don't know Pete that well and I do hardly ever go to Cin Cin. He got my number from a mate because he knew I'd seen ... well, I'd seen something at the bar. So we shared a couple of texts.'

Lisa thought about the barmaid. She'd seen her and Pete being touchy-feely at the bar; they barely bothered to hide their friendship, relationship or whatever it was. Her stomach turned at the memory.

Nathan continued, 'Pete only contacted me because of you. In case I told you what I'd seen.'

Lisa looked puzzled.

'It's not that complicated. I saw something, he learned I was seeing you, and you and Felicity are friends. I guess he was just taking care of the trail.'

'The what?'

'The trail.'

'What does that mean?' She thought she had heard the phrase before, but couldn't think where.

'Pete was taking care of the trail that would lead back to Felicity. He wants to tell her himself. It's fair enough. It's nobody else's business to let it slip.'

'*Really?*' Lisa felt it was her business if her friend was in anyway going to get hurt. She glanced over at her phone. Whatever it was Pete was hiding, Felicity would soon know. Lisa realised that even if she did know what it was and it was something bad, she was too far away to be anything other than a distant comfort. She decided to wait it out. The heat she had initially felt as Nathan had thrown her on the bed was dissipating as her concern for Felicity grew.

Nathan pulled Lisa closer and kissed her. She tried to protest, but her body started to respond, goosebumps pricking at her skin while heat spread inside. She forced herself to stay focused.

'Can you at least tell me it's nothing that will hurt her?'

Nathan looked into her eyes. The longing she saw in his gaze was distracting.

'Lisa, I gave my word.'

'So is it? Is it something that will hurt her?'

Nathan sighed. 'Look, I'm not supposed to say anything, but if I tell you Pete wants Flick to be happy, can we leave it? You know she's going to call you later and then you'll know everything. OK?'

'Wait, was that "and then I'll know everything's OK", or "and then I'll know everything. OK"?'

Nathan sat up. He pressed a kiss to Lisa's mouth before lifting her T-shirt off over her head. She attempted to focus on continuing her line of questioning, but with the feel of Nathan's mouth on her body the words escaped her.

Chapter Forty-Two

Cross-country skiing was harder work than Lisa imagined. When Nathan had suggested it, she thought it sounded more romantic than joining everybody else queuing up at the local ski station and hitting the busy pistes. As they had breakfasted with her parents and Luke, she had thought a touch of *ski de fond*, on the undulating, groomed trails across the local parks and into the woods, sounded dreamy. As she face planted into the snow for what felt like the tenth time as she attempted to negotiate a small hill, she decided it was turning into something more akin to a nightmare. Under normal circumstances she was a competent skier, but switching her skis for ones that seemed twice as long and half as wide made the task of staying upright more difficult than she imagined possible.

A group out for what looked like a fun family outing passed by, all gliding without difficulty and saying 'Bonjour', as they floated by on their skis, waving and smiling at her predicament. Lisa tried to respond and maintain some decorum despite the fact she had rolled over and was sitting on her bottom in the snow. Inside, she was desperate for them to pass and sure the heat in her cheeks, from the exertion and the embarrassment, might actually start melting the snow if they didn't hurry along. When the last, a boy of about nine making *ski de fond* look like a casual walk in the park, had passed by, Nathan swung round in front of her. He offered his hand.

'Come on, we'll go across the park; it's flatter there.'

'I can ski,' Lisa protested. 'I just seem to be terrible at this.'

'Next time we'll get you classics instead of skate skis.'

Lisa smiled at the thought of there being a next time, as Nathan helped her stand and find her balance.

'How come you make it look so easy?'

'Hmm, well, I've had lessons; this is one of those sports that's harder than people think. You have to learn the technique.'

'And now you decide to mention that!'

Nathan laughed. 'Come on, you're doing well.'

Lisa swiped her gloved hand over her head in an attempt to keep her hair out of her face while she got going again. She had started off wearing her woolly hat and a buff; she really wanted to take off her gloves and jacket, but knew Nathan would insist on carrying them for her and she didn't want to add to his load. Not when he was already carrying a backpack that contained both of their water bottles, her woolly hat and buff, as well as a map, torch and whistle she had mocked him for. About to push off, Lisa heard her phone buzz. 'Ah ha, saved!' She took out her phone, and saw three missed calls from Felicity and a message. She felt the colour drain from her cheeks. *Oh, please let everything be OK.*

'Lisa, what is it?'

'Hold on, I don't know yet. Flick has tried to call me.'

'The signal dips in and out here; she'll be wanting to share her news.' Nathan smiled.

Pulling off her gloves Lisa pressed to read Flick's message: I've tried calling, but it's going straight to voicemail. What should be such a happy day has gone so horribly wrong. I can't believe it. Call me.

'Oh no.' Lisa felt the breath leave her. 'It's not good. Something bad. I need to call her.'

'What?'

'This bloody phone has lost its signal again. Nathan, I need to call her.'

'But she can't be upset. She should be happy, really happy!'

Lisa felt her feet slip from under her again and landed in the snow. 'Please help me get out of these bloody skis and tell me what is going on. Felicity is clearly upset.' With that she read Felicity's text out loud.

'Well, it must be the submarine trip. I told him it might be a step too far, but still, I think she's overreacting.'

Lisa glared, incredulous. 'Nathan, please don't make stupid jokes now. I'm really worried. Can we just go so I can call Flick?'

'Of course, but it wasn't a joke.'

'Not a joke? Oh my God, Pete hasn't joined the navy or something, has he?'

'The navy? No.'

'Then what?'

As they started striding back to the car, skis in hand, Lisa was grateful for the fact Nathan had decided if Felicity now knew what it was Pete was hiding, then he wouldn't be breaking his word by letting her in on the secret too. Lisa attempted to summarise the situation, still trying to process what she had heard.

'So, Pete has worked all those hours at the bar to save up to take Felicity to Barbados.'

'Yes, a long overdue honeymoon, I think he said.'

'And that was his only reason for working at the bar and all that overtime?'

'I guess ... I don't know him that well.'

'And the waitress?'

'What waitress?'

'The one there the night I saw you, she seemed a bit ... a

297

bit over friendly with him … and you too, now I come to think of it.'

'Katie? She's the owner's wife. I think she and Pete go back years, and, as for me, we put out a fire in the kitchen last year. She's grateful, that's all.'

'Oh!'

Nathan stopped walking. 'I do believe you were jealous there for a minute.'

Lisa trudged on, sticking to the edge of the piste, the rough snow helping her keep her balance. 'No. Just curious.' She felt her cheeks flush.

'Jealous.' Nathan laughed, running to catch her up.

'No more than you seeing me with Dom,' she retorted. She had explained that she and Dom were just friends, and, while at no point Nathan's interest in their relationship felt like the kind of jealousy she had experienced with Ben, the fact that seeing them together had inspired his trip to France meant he could hardly argue.

'Ha, touché!'

Having won the point, she returned to establishing what Pete had planned for Felicity. 'And they're leaving the day before New Year's Eve, for a week?'

'Apparently.'

'And, along with wildlife and beach excursions, he has booked an Atlantis submarine excursion?'

'Yes, that's the brochure I saw. I said I'd travelled a bit so we had a chat about it, before he knew that I knew you, obviously.'

'OK.'

'And I said to him that maybe a two-hour submarine trip, going over forty metres below the sea, might not be for everyone. I guess he didn't listen.'

'I don't think that can be it. Can it?'

'Whatever it is, if Flick needs you, if you need to get back, I can drive you, OK?'

Lisa looked at Nathan, warmth spreading through her, and wondered why she had ever let him go.

Not wanting to risk a dodgy signal, Lisa waited until they were back in the chalet before calling Felicity, and her heart sank at the sound of her friend sobbing at the other end of the phone. Lisa told her to take a breath and to start at the beginning. She listened, while Felicity told her how wonderful Pete was and about their trip to Barbados. Despite the fact she already knew, Lisa found she didn't need to force a reaction, she felt genuinely happy for them. Barbados would be Felicity's idea of heaven and Lisa knew the two of them loved their children to bits, but needed some time for themselves. As Felicity continued Lisa could hear the strain of holding back tears in her voice.

'And Pete's mum was going to have the children. That's why he wanted to tell me while she was here. She wanted to help. He said she had offered when he mentioned it. I couldn't believe it, I'm not sure Pete could either. But then … then …'

'What? What happened?'

'She fell down our bloody stairs. Trod on some Lego and lost her balance.'

'Oh no! Is she all right?'

'No, that's the thing.' Felicity sniffed.

'Oh, Flick, what's happened?'

'Pete's at the hospital with her now; she's broken her ankle. Just like that, on our stairs. How bloody unlucky is that?'

'That's terrible.'

'I know, so now we are going to have to cancel.'

Lisa didn't like to say she meant it was terrible for Pete's mum, not when Felicity had had the holiday of a lifetime whipped out from under her before she had even felt the sand on her feet. 'But isn't there anyone else?'

'No. Pete's sister will have to look after his mum and Melissa's away with friends until just after New Year. She said once she's home it's no problem to have them until we're back. It's the worst timing ever. We can't change the flights and we can't leave the children home alone for three days until Melissa returns. We're buggered. What a bloody disaster.'

'Oh, Flick.' Lisa took a deep breath in as a sudden realisation hit her. 'What about me? I could do it.' Her words sounded more confident than she felt, but it made sense. *It's just covering until Melissa gets back. You can do it!* Lisa was supposed to be away and so knew she had no clients booked in, and while she would be sad to leave her parents earlier than expected it would be with the knowledge that they were all due to meet up again at Easter, when her parents would be flying home for a few months. It seemed a logical – if not entirely sensible given her childcare credentials – solution.

The line went silent. Lisa stared at the phone, wondering if the signal had gone. Finally she heard Felicity breathe. 'Flick? Are you OK?'

'That's ... I mean, really? Are you sure? Aren't you in France until next week?'

'Nathan said he could drive me. If you need me, Flick, I'll be there.' The words felt good to say. She had absolutely no idea how to look after four children, but her friend needed her and she was determined to do her best not to let her down.

Felicity burst into new tears, her sobs loud in Lisa's ear.

'Flick, it will be OK. I can do it.' *Perhaps if I say it enough ...*

'It's not that, I know you can.'

Lisa couldn't help but think Flick's confidence was perhaps misplaced, but she didn't want to quash her optimism if it meant she would get on the plane and have her holiday. 'Then what?'

'I'm so pleased you're back. I've missed you, Lisa. I forgot what it felt like to have you covering my back in a crisis.'

Lisa felt a tear run down her face.

Chapter Forty-Three

Lisa rushed around the living room picking up toys and attempting to make it look tidy. While they had all enjoyed an exclusive guided tour of the fire station that morning, the afternoon had been spent with Callum and Fred moving round the house like stealth toy bombers, scattering plastic debris in their wake, followed by Megan and Alice emptying out the entire contents of the art cupboard in order to make cards for Pete's mum, who promised to have them for a long weekend as soon as she had recovered. Lisa was in much need of a cup of coffee and a five minute sit down, but, with Nathan due to join her to see the New Year in, she wanted to make the lounge cosy, order their Chinese and have a quick shower before he arrived.

Once she had found homes for as many toys as she could, Lisa decided to turn the main light off and the Christmas tree lights on; it gave the illusion of a tidy room. Flick's tree was a fabulous reflection of her home and life, full of colour and chaos. Decorations made by the children hung heavily on the branches, which were strewn with random pieces of tinsel in a variety of sizes and colours. Compared to her mum's colour co-ordinated tree it looked like the inside of a Quality Street tub. Lisa loved it. She touched a gold star and swallowed at Megan's writing, wishing her Nana a happy Christmas in heaven. Lisa looked up to the wonky angel at the top of the tree. 'Merry Christmas, Mrs F, your grandchildren are lovely, but I think you already know that,' she whispered.

About to head upstairs, Lisa was delighted to get a call from Dom to say that so far talks with Winnie had gone well, albeit that he needed to work on her knowledge of politically correct words when discussing people's life choices. He said after the initial shock and the disappointment that great-grandchildren might be an issue, she had hugged him and told him that his happiness was all that mattered. Having prompted Dom to tell her, Lisa breathed a sigh of relief. When they ended the call it was with the promise to catch up soon.

Looking in on each of the children en route to the shower, Lisa was pleased to see they were finally settled. Bedtime seemed to take hours and involved the words, 'that's not how Mummy does it' more times than she cared to count. Looking at the children now, cuddled up in their beds all clean, fresh pyjamas, still and silent, they looked so peaceful. She felt a swell of pride at her achievement in getting them through the day and into bed without incident, and her heart melted a little at the sight of them. She smiled, until the thought that they were recharging their batteries slipped into her mind.

The shower was refreshing. Felicity had so many lotions and potions, Lisa felt like she was in a hotel as she selected which to use. Taking a moment to relax, she thought about Felicity and Pete, who had arrived safely and settled into their luxury hotel. They had spoken to each of the children earlier in the evening. Megan confirmed Lisa was taking good care of them, Alice rejoiced in telling them Nathan had a skeleton he was going to bring round for her to examine with her medical kit, while Callum and Fred were full of their trip to the fire station and wanting to know when their mummy and daddy were going under the sea like the Octonauts.

Lisa hoped Felicity and Pete's belated honeymoon would be a dream come true for them. After her day with the children, she realised how much they must need the break. Their children were lovely and funny, but their ability to get into mischief and their energy levels were relentless. Lisa determined to offer to babysit more often once they were back. After all, as Pete pointed out, she owed him after his master plan with Nathan clearly worked out. And, who knew, in the future maybe Flick and Pete would be returning the favour for her.

Just forty minutes later, Lisa got the plates and cutlery ready, and poured herself and Nathan a glass of wine while he went to answer the door. Hearing a commotion Lisa went to investigate. Seeing Mr Chung, takeaway bag in hand and a broad smile on his face, was an unexpected pleasure.

'Ah, Miss Lisa, they say it was you on phone.'

'Mr Chung, I thought your son did the deliveries. It's so lovely to see you.'

'I make special journey for you, Miss Lisa. Check you OK. We miss you.'

'I've missed you too.'

'But now I know where you been.'

'You do?' Lisa wondered if Harold Martin made everyone aware of the details of her life.

'You busy with boyfriend.' Mr Chung looked happily between Lisa and Nathan, his eyes sparkling.

Nathan laughed and put his arm round Lisa. 'She certainly has been, and I plan to keep her that way.'

Mr Chung clapped his hands. 'I knew you two make happy couple.'

Lisa blushed, thanked Mr Chung, and surprised him with a hug and a kiss on the cheek. She promised to see him in the New Year, albeit that she would have to remind herself to disguise her takeaway bag from Harold Martin's prying eyes.

Once she had eaten and had a few glasses of wine, lying her head on Nathan's chest, the hum of the television and the lights of the tree felt perfect. She felt content and cosy; too cosy. Despite her best efforts to stay awake, Lisa succumbed to the fatigue of the day.

When she heard Nathan's voice, she jumped. 'Oh no, I'm so sorry. I didn't mean to fall asleep.'

'It's OK, but it's almost midnight. I thought you'd want to be awake for twelve.' Nathan kissed her on the forehead, slid out from under her and topped up their glasses.

They watched as the television switched to Big Ben and the countdown to midnight began. On the first strike of twelve, the London fireworks burst into life on television and Lisa's phone began to buzz with messages from family, and friends old and new – all special people she had no intention of ever losing contact with.

Lisa looked at Nathan and smiled as they clinked glasses.

'Happy New Year, Nathan.'

'Happy New Year, to us.' He smiled.

Us, Lisa liked the sound of that. She pulled Nathan closer to her, welcoming his arms around her as their bodies met and she felt his soft lips on hers. Nathan Baker was back, in her life and in her arms and this time she knew without doubt she intended to keep it that way. She felt tears well in her eyes and a swell of happiness inside. She wasn't just starting the new year with the man who had been her first love, but the one she knew she wanted to be her last – together forever and always.

Thank You

Dear Reader,

Thank you so much for reading my book. If you enjoyed *The Purrfect Pet Sitter* please tell your friends, and take a moment to leave a review on the site where you purchased it. Reviews, no matter what their length, help authors and their work get noticed. They really are hugely appreciated.

If you would like to find out more about my writing shenanigans you can find my details at the end of my author profile. I enjoy getting my followers involved, occasionally asking for research help, so why not give me a follow, say hello, and join in? I'd love to hear from you.

Carol

x

About the Author

Carol Thomas lives on the south coast of England with her husband, four children and lively young Labrador. She has been a playgroup supervisor and was a primary school teacher for over fifteen years, before dedicating more of her time to writing. Carol is a regular volunteer at her local Cancer Research UK shop. She has a passion for reading, writing and people watching and can often be found loitering in local cafes drinking too much tea and working on her next book.

Find out more about Carol Thomas here:
www.carol-thomas.co.uk
www.facebook.com/carolthomasauthor
www.twitter.com/carol_thomas2

More Ruby Fiction

From Carol Thomas

Maybe Baby

Just when you thought you had it all worked out …

Best friends Lisa and Felicity think – maybe, just maybe – they finally have everything sorted out in their lives.

Lisa is in a happy relationship with her old flame, and busy mum Felicity has managed to reignite the passion with her husband, Pete, after a romantic getaway.

But when Lisa walks in on a half-naked woman in her boyfriend's flat and Felicity is left reeling from a shocking discovery, it becomes clear that life is nothing but full of surprises …

Visit www.rubyfiction.com for details.

More from Ruby Fiction

Why not try something else from our selection:

The Best Boomerville Hotel
Caroline James

Let the shenanigans begin at the Best Boomerville Hotel …

Jo Docherty and Hattie Contaldo have a vision – a holiday retreat in the heart of the Lake District exclusively for guests of 'a certain age' wishing to stimulate both mind and body with new creative experiences. One hotel refurbishment later and the Best Boomerville Hotel is open for business!

Perhaps not surprisingly Boomerville attracts more than its fair share of eccentric clientele: there's fun-loving Sir Henry Mulberry and his brother Hugo; Lucinda Brown, an impoverished artist with more ego than talent; Andy Mack, a charming Porsche-driving James Bond lookalike, as well as Kate Simmons, a woman who made her fortune from an internet dating agency but still hasn't found 'the One' herself.

With such an array of colourful individuals there's bound to be laughs aplenty, but could there be tears and heartbreak too and will the residents get more than they bargained for at Boomerville?

Visit www.rubyfiction.com for details.

Arlette's Story
Angela Barton

**One woman's struggle
to fight back against the
enemy in order to protect
the ones she loves.**

When Arlette Blaise sees a
German plane fly over the
family farm in 1940, she's
comforted by the fact that the
occupying forces are far away
in the north of the country.
Surely the war will not reach
her family in the idyllic French countryside near to the small
town of Oradour-sur-Glane?

But then Saul Epstein, a young Jewish man driven from his
home by the Nazis, arrives at the farm and Arlette begins to
realise that her peaceful existence might be gone for good ...

Visit www.rubyfiction.com for details.

Evie's Little Black Book
Hannah Pearl

Is hunting down every man you've kissed the answer to finding Mr Right?

When Evie is invited to the wedding of the guy she'd fancied throughout her teens, it's the final straw. What's wrong with her and why can't *she* keep a man?

In between consoling herself with ice cream and chocolate, and sobbing her heart out to her cousin Charmaine, Evie has a brainwave – and it all centres around her 'little black book' (well, more floral patterned notebook really) – which contains the details of every man she's ever kissed or dated. Perhaps the cure for her disastrous love life has been nestled within its pages all along …

Does Evie's little black book really hold the answers, or will learn she learn that exes are exes for a reason?

Visit www.rubyfiction.com for details.

Introducing Ruby Fiction

Ruby Fiction is an imprint of Choc Lit Publishing.
We're an independent publisher creating
a delicious selection of fiction.

See our selection here:
www.rubyfiction.com

Ruby Fiction brings you stories that inspire emotions.

We'd love to hear how you enjoyed *The Purrfect Pet Sitter*.
Please visit www.rubyfiction.com and give your feedback
or leave a review where you purchased this novel.

Ruby novels are selected by genuine readers like yourself.
We only publish stories our Tasting Panel want to see in
print. Our reviews and awards speak for themselves.

Could you be a Star Selector and join our Tasting Panel?
Would you like to play a role in choosing which novels
we decide to publish? Do you enjoy reading women's
fiction? Then you could be perfect for our Tasting Panel.

Visit here for more details …
www.choc-lit.com/join-the-choc-lit-tasting-panel

Keep in touch:
Sign up for our monthly newsletter Spread for all the latest
news and offers: www.spread.choc-lit.com. Follow us on
Twitter: @RubyFiction and Facebook: RubyFiction.

Stories that inspire emotions!